A NOVEL BY
Robert Greenfield

HAYMON'S CROWD

7334

Cop.a

Summit Books · New York

A portion of this book
originally appeared
in *Esquire* magazine
Designed by Irving Perkins
Manufactured in the United States of America

1 2 3 4 5 6 7 8 9 10

Library of Congress Cataloging in Publication Data

Greenfield, Robert.
  Haymon's Crowd.

  I. Title.
PZ4.G8137Bo [PS3557.R3943]   813'.5'4   78-3743
ISBN   0-671-40012-6

for my mother and father, a mighty love

"... for in the bank of life is not good that investment which pays the highest and most cherished dividends?"

JOHN COLTRANE, liner notes, *A Love Supreme*

PROLOGUE · A Saturday in March, 1959 · Almost the First Day of Spring

ON A Saturday afternoon so bright and shiny with the promise of spring that even the store windows along Brighton Beach Avenue gleam friendly, the soft scent of new grass and warm earth mingles with the hard odor of dog shit that has lain cold and frozen on the sidewalk for months. Shoppers pound down the avenue past a gauntlet of discount emporiums and cut-rate bazaars where bargains cry out to be bought. The sun, slashing through the crossties of the great trestle that supports the BMT, both local and express, casts bands of ice-dark shade on the pavement. Few have the time to notice.

Which storekeeper is so addled from a long day of defending his merchandise against the handlers and squeezers, so giddy and light-headed from battle that he will let something go at below cost? Is it damaged, irregular, one of a kind? So much the better. Lugged home without the benefit of wrapping, it will be displayed proudly as a trophy of the hunt, its new owner eager to point out the small irregularity that caused its price to be reduced to an irresistible level.

In the front window of the corner delicatessen in Brighton on

Saturday afternoon, the hot dogs turn in greasy contentment. Across the street, by the red-brick savings bank in the sun, the old women turn in their beach chairs, seeking more warmth and a little *luft*, a breath of fresh salt air among the bus fumes.

The old women remember everything. They recognize everyone. Their memories are unwrinkled. To walk past them, en route to Hirsch's for the paper and a cup of coffee, is to bear the weight of their impossible scrutiny.

The old women remember Abe Reles. Kid Twist, the mad Jewish punk who provided the muscle for Murder, Incorporated, getting himself arrested forty-two times in the process. Abe's worst mistake, and his only crime, so far as the old women can recall, was to make a deal with the Kings County DA to tell all he knew. The DA gave Abe a room of his own in which to do this in the then palatial Half-Moon Hotel by the boardwalk in neighboring Coney Island, with five cops and an assistant DA assigned to watch over him day and night.

The next morning, they found Abe's crumpled body forty-odd feet below an open window, a fall from grace that transformed Abe the *momzer* into Abe the martyr. Saint Abe, whose blood still sanctifies these sidewalks, bathing the old women who sit along them with a cynicism so profound that they trust only one another, and then only occasionally.

But let the sun come out, as it has today, and the women assemble, as though summoned by some trumpet only they can hear, to talk of children who have moved away and the incredible bitterness of being old. Although their gallbladders are painfully inflamed, their intestines choked with tumors as big around as grapefruits (none smaller, ever), not so much has really changed in nearly twenty years. In Brighton, the ghost of Abe Reles still whistles around the hard edges of the buildings.

When Liddel Gross passes by, bouncing a basketball on his way to the schoolyard, the old women whisper of his tramp of a mother and his bookmaker father, noting with pleasure the pack of cigarettes jammed into the back pocket of his torn pants. Definitely. Another Abe in the making.

Slowly then, they turn their chairs into the sun, moving with it, first around the corner and then down the block. The old women of the tribe. Even during the years spent wandering the desert in search of the Promised Land, the hot sun felt good on the arthritis. The old bones have not forgotten.

Three blocks away, their husbands, aging warriors with calf muscles knotted like gnarled and stunted oaks, chase the hard black rubber handball. They pull at leather gloves that cover their calloused palms. They spit copiously, and often, as though to affirm that they have indeed made it through another winter alive. Honey Kreiger smashes a game-winning killer to the base of the wall and laughs out loud, showing a set of perfect teeth. Beads of sweat roll down his lined forehead and strong hooked nose. What a day. The air warm and sweet yet spiced with the tang of salt from the sea. Although the hair on Honey Kreiger's barrel chest is tangled and gray, today he feels like a spring chicken. He knows he will live to see a hundred more days like this one come to Brooklyn. Who would dare stop him?

At the other end of the schoolyard the younger men congregate, the sons and nephews, who have come either to sit and watch or to play and argue about the only game that has any meaning at all for them—basketball. On the stone steps that lead up to a set of double doors that are nearly always locked, the experts recline, a copy of the *Daily News* folded beneath them to sit on, a copy of the *Post* open to the line for the evening's games. The odor of their cheap cigars mixes with the smell of sweat as the game goes on, always the game, on and on, an endless round of half-court, seven-basket, three-man contests.

Reed Kreiger sits by the polished metal banister that divides the steps. Its surface has been worn smooth by the thousands of tiny hands that grasp it on the way in and out of school each day. By all rights, Reed Kreiger should be splayed out on the concrete along the fence where the ballplayers arrogantly sprawl. But he is too thin. Unlike his muscled father, his arms and legs are thin. His ankles too. His thinness embarrasses him. It keeps him from ever wearing shorts to the yard or playing on Saturdays, though he spends hours shooting around by himself when no one else is present.

On a day like this, Reed Kreiger is content just to be where he is, at the very epicenter of the universe, the place where news begins and history is made, the schoolyard. Closing his eyes, he lets the throbbing buzz of the conversation and the warm sun transport him. He has no problems.

When he opens his eyes, Reed Kreiger finds himself staring at the largest white man ever to enter the yard. Stooping so as not to ram his head into the iron bar that forms the top of the side gate is a giant, with large, spatulate hands shoved deep into the pockets of a pair of khaki chino pants that are ripped at the knee and a good four inches too short at the ankle. An expanse of hairy calf flashes from above cheap cotton socks. Arms jut out from his sides at odd angles. His head looks as though it was put on with a pipe wrench.

The look on the giant's face gives him away, completely. Reed Kreiger has seen the look before, in the junior high school cafeteria during lunch hour, where the weak quietly give up their nickels and dimes to avoid being beaten to a pulp by those who earn their weekly allowances by preying on others. The big man is terrified.

· 15

From his position along the fence, Liddel Gross casts a cold eye over the newcomer. "No way," he says in a hard, flat voice. "No way he can touch the rim. I got a dollar says he can't."

"Bet," Buttsy Klein says quickly, hungry for some action. Then he catches sight of the giant's feet. "Fuckit," he says disgustedly. "He ain't even wearin' Converse."

Converse, the sneaker of the pros, perpetually marked down and for sale on Kings Highway, are the mark of a true ballplayer. Only *shvartzers* can play without the athletic shoe that bears Chuck Taylor's actual signature on the round white disc that hugs the bulge of the anklebone. *Shvartzers,* it is well known in the schoolyard, can play in anything, open-toed sandals, penny loafers, highly polished black alligator shoes. They are exempt. White men *need* Converse.

"We're on next, right?" Liddel asks, already knowing the answer. "I'm gonna take him on. For a goof.

"*Hey!*" he shouts in the giant's direction. "You wanna play?"

The big man looks around to see whom Liddel is talking to. He paws at the ground, blinking furiously. "S-sure," he says.

"Great." Liddel beams. "You got it."

Then he turns and squints into the sun, his small ferret face gleaming with delight. "This," he mutters so that only those sitting around him can hear, "is gonna be a *pisser!*"

Hooking his fingers into the repetitive octagons of the wire-mesh fence, Liddel Gross turns and stares out into the street. By the fire hydrant, double-parked, sits a familiar fire-engine red convertible. Behind the wheel is an older man. His face is angular, all bone. What can be seen of his body is equally stark, lean, stripped, and sinewy. All morning he has been driving from schoolyard to schoolyard, looking for a game. His sneakers and basketball are in the trunk. Before he can be bothered to take them out, he must be sure that he will be able to find some true competition, a real run.

Liddel Gross waves a tentative hand in greeting but the older man does not respond. His attention has been captured by the big kid near the steps. A player that size in Brighton that Max Trapp does not know? Impossible.

On the first court, the team that has been winning all afternoon casually vanquishes another opponent. They are three-fifths of the squad that dominates the night center year after year, the blue and white braided laces in their Converse attesting to this fact, each lace threaded so that it begins *atop* the bottom eyelet rather than below. Their woolen sweat socks cost a dollar a pair. They are that perfect shade of Clorox yellow that comes only from repeated washings with strong bleach.

Everything about them is perfect. Despite that, when Liddel Gross leads the giant and Buttsy Klein on court to oppose them, he does so with an arrogance that is unmistakable, as though eighteen thousand fans have jammed Madison Square Garden just to see this happen. Liddel begins guarding Mikey DiAngelo by thrusting an outstretched hand into his stomach, signifying that he is prepared to play Mikey head-to-head all over the court. With somewhat less of a flourish, Buttsy picks up Tommy Falcone, called the Falcon, leaving the big man with no choice but to try to contain Sammy Stein, known to all as Sponge. Sponge always wears as many different colored pairs of sweat socks as he can cram into his size twelve sneakers. He can leap like a black man. In the schoolyard, they like to say that he can take a quarter off the backboard and give you change. It is only an expression. Sammy Stein, called Sponge, never gives anyone anything, much less correct change.

Mikey Dee inbounds to the Falcon, who dribbles to the key, waiting for Sponge to make a move. Playing to the spectators on the steps, Sponge head fakes toward the foul line, then bursts toward the basket like a fullback making for the goal line. The Falcon hits him with a high, spinning pass that Sponge catches on his way up. A soft, creamy look takes possession of his face, a half-mad grin that in future years will come to grace police folders and prison files. Everyone on the steps leans forward, anticipating what will happen next.

Sponge is going to jam, smashing the ball downward from above the rim with so much power and authority that Liddel's team will collapse in awe and shock and slink back to the fence, grateful to have escaped with their lives.

As Sponge begins to rise, the giant rouses himself and tries to get back in the game. From the foul line, he takes one long step and then another, the distance between him and his man disappearing as he stumbles forward, an awkward avalanche looking for a city to engulf. At the very last moment, the giant manages to gain control of himself. He launches his body upward in a little pitty-pat leap that is no match for the graceful elevation Sponge gets when he leaves the ground. Still, it is enough.

Hand and ball come together in midair, one descending with force, the other rising with velocity. The ball vectors crazily against the backboard and caroms straight out into the waiting hands of Liddel Gross, who scoops it up and rams it home for an uncontested layup.

Slapping his palms together in celebration, Liddel bounces up and back on the balls of his feet, shouting, "Atta way, big man. Atta way, *keed*." Quickly, he inbounds to Buttsy, who goes up for a long jumper from the right side. Buttsy follows with another from the opposite corner, falling away. Liddel chips in with a long set shot and quickly they are away, four–nothing, the ball bouncing as though it had eyes and a distinct preference for being handled only by them.

Under the basket, another game is going on. Sponge is working over the big man with all the precision of a woodsman trimming a tree. A shot to the ribs. An elbow to the small of the back. A knee in the thigh. Mikey Dee yells at his teammate to play the game, but Sammy Stein is beyond hearing or caring. No one stuffs Sponge and walks away unscathed to talk about it.

The teams trade baskets. With Liddel's squad needing but one to win, Buttsy runs the Falcon into a pick at the foul line and rolls to the hoop. Sponge is forced to come out and pick him up, leaving the big man free under the basket. Liddel flings him the winning pass, the ball transcribing a series of backward pebbled circles in the sunlight. The big man jumps for it, his body turning awkwardly in midair.

From out of nowhere, Sponge comes flying down the lane. He shoves his shoulder in at a point somewhere below the giant's hip, bridging him so that when the big man falls, he comes down ass backward, his huge body striking the concrete with the hard, percussive *whomp!* of an anti-aircraft shell hitting home.

The big man lies on concrete in a pile of bone, elbows bloodied, chest heaving. A ribbon of spit pearls from one corner of his mouth. The whites of his eyes are very large and wild, like those of some thoroughbred waiting to be destroyed after cracking a forelock in the stretch.

"*FOUL!*" Liddel screams. "*FUCKIN' FOUL!*"

"Let *him* call it!" the Falcon says automatically.

"Call this, *PRICK!*" Liddel explodes, flinging the ball at Sponge's head. Sponge ducks and the ball slams into Mikey Dee, knocking him to the ground.

Falcon and Liddel leap on each other with the relish of old and practiced opponents. They roll on the ground, chopping punches to each other's heads. They fart and grunt, their clothes scraping horribly along the concrete. Reed Kreiger watches in fascination, unable to move, as a squadron of older men vaults off the steps around him to pull the two apart. Liddel comes off the ground steaming, blood and snot running from his nose. His T-shirt is torn in three places. A row of fresh tooth marks adorns his neck.

"*HE BIT ME!*" Liddel howls, fingering his wound, trying to push through the cordon of peacemakers to take yet another shot at the Falcon.

"*FUCKIN'* . . . *FAGGOT!*" he screams. "If you wanted to gimme a hickey, you shoulda asked."

Falcon balls his fist and takes a threatening step toward Liddel. Then he bursts out laughing. "Fuckin' Liddel," he says, shaking his head in wonder.

"Fuckin' Lid-*dell*," Mikey Dee echoes. "You crazy, man. You know? C'mon. Play the game."

Liddel pulls away from the circle and goes over to the steps, where the giant has resurrected himself into a half-sitting position. Reed sits just by his shoulder, watching.

"Hey?" Liddel asks. "You okay?"

The giant nods. His drooping head is bent, his eyes half-closed. Like some great sunflower, he is wilting in the warm spring sunshine. He tries to speak but is unable to force the words from his mouth. Grasping the smooth metal banister in his hand, he tries to stand. He sinks back down, gasping for air.

"Our ball," Liddel notes encouragingly. "One to go."

The giant shakes his head. "P-p-pick someone else," he stutters. "I'm through."

In a schoolyard where no one sits down unless he has suffered a compound fracture, with the jagged bone piercing the skin as proof, the big man is tired. Overheated. Suffering from fatigue. He is quitting. An unheard-of violation of the code.

Liddel looks at him for a moment in disbelief. Then he scans the steps for a replacement. For one heart-stopping moment, he considers Reed Kreiger. Then he keeps on looking, finally selecting a more suitable sub. When the game begins again, Buttsy Klein immediately hits a long and anti-climactic jump shot to end it. Liddel's team has won.

"*Awright!*" Liddel says out loud to himself. "All *fuckin'* right!"

Outside the fence, Max Trapp is already gone, in search of better competition. Three blocks away, the old women give up on the sun, fold their canvas weave beach chairs, and set out for home to begin cooking dinner. *Shabbos* is almost over. The sun disappears behind gray and puffy clouds with the dun color and abrasive consistency of steel wool. It is not yet spring. Not yet. The day grows cold.

BOOK ONE · **BOX AND ONE**

"When an opponent has an unbalanced offensive game, a box and one will occasionally stop the big scorer and throw the team off stride or into panic."
    DELMER HARRIS, *Multiple Defenses for Winning Basketball*

CHAPTER ONE

IN THE tight little enclave that is Brighton, geography is everything. The block on which you live determines whom you will know, whom your children will grow up knowing, perhaps even what they will become. As the side streets fan out one after another from Brighton Beach Avenue, they increase in desirability as they approach Oriental Boulevard and the spun sugar, fake white Gothic mansions of Manhattan Beach. Conversely, the blocks closest to Coney Island are not worth very much at all, unless the address happens to be on Ocean Parkway itself, the broad boulevard that divides the two neighborhoods like some great asphalt river.

The Kreigers, Honey, Rhoda, and Reed, live on a street in the middle of Brighton on the third floor of a not-so-new, not-so-old six-story building squeezed in between two more modern, larger apartment houses. A medium-sized apartment on the middle floor of a middling building on a so-so street. Just so. For on the local social ladder, the Kreigers occupy that very rung, high enough up to have someone beneath them yet so far from the top that they know better than even to try to better themselves. In Brighton, such stagnation passes for contentment.

The pecking order in Brighton of course takes no notice at all of similar orders that exist all around it, on every side, in Sea Gate and Manhattan Beach, where the Jews with real money live, or in the "projects," the new red brick complexes that are mini-cities unto themselves. It completely ignores the Italians and Irish, who preceded the Jews into this section of Brooklyn by the sea and still live in the small weathered clapboard houses that stand in clusters on the dead-end streets around Sheepshead Bay.

To extend the circle once more, the Brighton social order takes no account at all of the hundreds of other elaborate neighborhood groupings, formal and informal, that make up the borough of Brooklyn, said to be but one-fifth of the city of New York.

For those who live in Brighton, it is too much to consider. Manhattan is the "city," Brooklyn the county, Brighton the village. Honey and Rhoda Kreiger shop only with local merchants, all of whom are old friends or adversaries. They send their son to the public school four blocks away, knowing that he will hardly ever have to come in contact with the crazy *Italianers* and gypsy kids who sometimes seep into the neighborhood from the wastelands around Cropsey Avenue.

In the fifteen years since he came back from World War II with a duffel bag on his shoulder containing a machine gun and a thousand rounds of live ammunition stolen from a locker at Fort Hamilton, Honey Kreiger has done well for himself. He has moved his wife, Rhoda, and young son, Reed, from a cold-water flat in Coney Island to Brighton, his wife taking advantage of the confusion of moving day to dump his precious "war souvenirs" into Gravesend Bay. He has bought himself a car, a secondhand green 1955 Chevy that he keeps in perfect repair with his own hands.

Honey Kreiger is a happy man. He has the beach in summer, the boardwalk all year round, and the salt air from the ocean to cleanse his nostrils when he gets off the train after a long day spent managing a hardware store on the fringes of Harlem.

In his work, as in the neighborhood, there is no reason for Honey Kreiger to push himself. He will not be moving up. The black man who owns the hardware store is not about to sell to anyone. Honey will manage the store until one of them dies.

A short, square man with a hooked nose and heavy hands that more than once have twisted the fingers off some young punk who thought he could steal something from under his nose, Honey Kreiger regularly cuts himself in for a share of the store's profits, bringing home with him the fruits of his labor, which he calls "fringe benefits."

Ball peen hammers, sets of metric wrenches, Black and Decker drill bits, four way sockets, tubes of pipe dope, and rolls of adhesive tape lay stockpiled in the locker in the basement of the apartment building where the Kreigers live, a safeguard against some future hardware shortage. Piece by piece, Honey has toted it all into the basement from his car under the cover of darkness lest some neighbor be watching. Why, he never explains. Why not? It never hurts to have something on hand when you need it.

Honey Kreiger works. He saves his money. He expects his meals on the table every night at six. Not a quarter after. Not five-forty-five. Six. Should the food be cold or overcooked or not plentiful enough, the neighbors will hear about it. Honey Kreiger has a *shtimma,* an authentic foghorn of a voice that would win him immediate respect in the din of the Fulton Fish Market at six in the morning. He can make the thin walls of the apartment rattle when he is displeased. After work comes food. This is what his father taught him. This is the philosophy he has instilled in his wife. You work, you eat. All else is secondary.

The ritual of supper, *brust* with cabbage, chicken thighs and neckbones, vegetable soup thick with barley and heavy bones filled with sweet marrow, this is Honey Kreiger's daily reward. The resounding belches he gives out with after a meal are the only sign that he is satisfied.

The effect is not lost on his son. From infancy on, Reed Kreiger is a "picky" eater who toys with food until he is shouted at to eat it or throw it away. Physically, he resembles his father not at all, being slight, pale, almost neurasthenic. "He eats like a bird, my son," Honey often grunts as he sits sopping up the last bit of gravy from a beef goulash heavy with paprika, a chunk of dark corn-bread in his hand. "Like a *fagela.* In that respect, he don't take after me."

Honey Kreiger is a *galizianer* and proud of it, a drinker of ice-cold Schaefers and Rheingolds, an indefatigable polisher of his car, a slammer of handballs, an enthusiastic street corner advocate willing to argue about anything, with his voice always the loudest. Within the confines of his tiny apartment, though, Honey is curiously docile, able to sit for hours staring at the small television set in the living room as though it will soon tell him something he doesn't already know.

As he sits before the TV, bitching about the Knicks in winter and the dear, departed Dodgers in summer, Honey comforts himself by spooning out great rippled slabs of butter brickle and vanilla fudge ice cream directly from the carton. He buys the ice cream himself, in half gallons, on Saturday mornings, when he goes to the appetizing store to pick out the best lox, the freshest bagels. Rhoda he simply can't trust to do this kind of shopping. She lets the guy behind the counter intimidate her.

Rhoda can be relied on only in the kitchen and, by extension, the tiny dinette where the ancient red and gray Formica table with tubular chrome legs stands. She sits here while the food cooks, day after day, flipping through the *Post,* humming constantly to herself in time with the music from WQXR. The shelves that separate the dinette from the living room are filled with jade elephants, alabaster swans, glass flowers blooming inside cut crystal balls, wicker dolls and straw baskets stamped "Made in Mexico" on the bottom. Rhoda collects *tchochkes*, assigning each piece a place on her shelves, where she will keep it dust-free, spotless.

When the dishes are done for the night, Honey having once again implanted himself before the television set, Rhoda Kreiger sits herself down in the dinette to read. She is not particular. As soon as a title makes its way to the top of the best-seller list posted in the local library, she must have it, the book's status as part of the pay collection assuring her that it is worth paying a nickel a day to read it. "Read faster," Honey will often shout to her from the living room, making a joke. "You're costing me money."

The subject of money is a passion with Honey Kreiger. To hear him tell it he is penniless, and has always been, and even now supports his family by sleight of hand. Honey takes extra pleasure in destroying men who are younger and more successful than he on the handball court, particularly doctors or lawyers. Even those twenty years his junior cannot hope to handle the bullet-like returns he rifles to the base of the wall with either hand. To be beaten into the ground by the man is to understand him instantly, in a way neither his wife nor his only son ever does.

It is not until his sixth birthday that Reed Kreiger conclusively proves himself to his father. With things going none too well at the store and money generally tight, every kid in Brighton Reed's age is first demanding and then receiving a wooden hobbyhorse for his birthday. The fad sweeps quickly through the small community, a herd of steeds mounted on polished runners coming to rest in cramped bedrooms all over the neighborhood. Reed decides he must have one of his own.

Each night before he falls asleep, he visualizes how his horse will look, its color, size, and shape more special than anyone else's. As often as possible, he leaves crude crayon drawings of horses on the dinette table. Every Sunday, as his father sits with the various sections of the *News* strewn around him, Reed manages to point out the hobbyhorse ad in the classifieds, grinning and laughing and saying, "Horsie, horsie," until his father growls, "Okay, kid, I got the picture. You wanna grow up to be a jockey."

If such a gift is to be bought, only Honey can do the buying. He alone has read all the ads and compared the prices. He alone knows where he can get it at discount. On the Saturday morning before his son's sixth birthday, Honey takes Reed to downtown Brooklyn. To be taken shopping by his father is a special occasion, one Reed knows will end with the hobbyhorse he so desperately wants being unloaded in front of the apartment building in full sunlight, so that everyone on the block can see how much his parents love him.

In the basement of a store crowded by women handling dresses heaped on tables, to the sound of parrots squawking madly from their cages in the pet department, as escalators chime with a maddening mechanical rhythm of their own, Reed lets his father lead him down the aisle to the toy counter. The glorious wooden horses stand everywhere, awaiting riders. A dollar at a time, Honey Kreiger counts out the thirty-five dollars necessary to purchase a hobbyhorse. The girl behind the cash register stares at him in wonder.

"A hobbyhorse costs this much," Honey says, showing his son the pile of money. "Reed, you're listening? This much. You still want one? Take a look around, see if you see something else."

Wanting only to be a good son, Reed walks away from the wonderful herd of wooden hobbyhorses. He finds his way to a glass-topped counter where a flotilla of rubber dump trucks sits. At a dollar sixty-nine each, they are good value. He picks one up and looks at his father. "Truck?" he says.

Honey sweeps his son off the ground, hugging the child so fiercely that the smell of his after-shave and the feel of his grizzled cheeks stay with the boy well into manhood.

"*Boychik!*" Honey cries. "Already you're a *mensch!* Come. I'll buy you the truck, we'll have a frozen custard, then we'll go home. Come."

For years afterward, Honey Kreiger tells and retells this story. How his boy, Reed, aged six, already knew the value of a dollar. A dollar sixty-nine to be exact. Cheap enough for a toy the child never plays with, preferring to lie on his bed and dream about being a rider on a magic wooden horse he knows for sure his father could never afford.

THREE-QUARTERS of a mile away, on a corner of Cropsey Avenue, sits the small gray house where Haymon Jacobs, the oversized giant who could not last out a game in the schoolyard, lives. Never does he dream of toys his father cannot afford. The children of Cropsey Avenue fashion their own toys from what they find in deserted lots where the corpses of long dead automobiles lie rotting alongside ancient white refrigerators that gleam among the weeds like the discarded teeth of some primeval monster. Although Haymon has been forbidden by his mother ever to venture into those dangerous weeds, he does so on occasion, always first making sure he will be able to find his way out again.

In front of his house, which is sided all over with gray stucco shingles and roofed with tar paper, there is a tiny rock-filled garden where once a pink and blue plaster reproduction of the Virgin Mary and Babe beckoned to motorists making the long, sweeping approach to the Belt Parkway. Nothing grows in the garden now, save for the hole left by the missing statue. It gets larger each year, as though mourning the departed Saviour.

In this neighborhood, it is Christ the King who saves and the Jew bastards who nailed Him to His cross. Each Christmas Cropsey Avenue comes alive with light, glowing red and green bulbs strung festively over fence post and doorway, winking in the night. Gypsies live here, great family tribes supported by what the men can make by working in the local body and fender shops and the watermelon stands that blossom along the avenue in summer. Most of the time, the gypsies cruise the streets, six to a car, looking for free-lance work. For ten dollars, they will fix any kind of auto body damage, on the spot, while you wait.

More than one prospective customer has turned down their grinning, gat-toothed offer only to return to find a formerly slightly damaged vehicle transformed into a pancake on wheels, the gypsies having gone at it with sledgehammer and tongs in his absence. Soon enough, another car will come by filled with second cousins and brothers-in-law of the first detachment kindly offering to repair the damage. For thirty dollars.

The schoolyard nearest Haymon's house does not even have any rims left on the backboards. For all Haymon knows, the gypsies have torn them down and melted them into armbands. Gypsies eat live chickens and fornicate with their daughters. This is well known. Never does Haymon Jacobs walk home alone after sundown without fearing that a band of them will come howling at him from out of the weeds, gleaming razors in hand.

For their part, the gypsies could care less. Even as a boy, Haymon Jacobs is so outsized and obviously pathetic that they cannot be bothered to do any more than laugh when he passes. To actually go after him would be like stirring up a pool of sewer water to get at the lone and pitiful carp living off the shit on the bottom. More of an outcast than they are, he is no threat at all to their manly, grinning self-assurance. They leave him be.

Haymon Jacobs' father, Shmuel, called Samuel in America, no longer works. Having suffered a series of heart attacks in his fifty-sixth year, he has left behind him his job as a night watchman in a furrier's loft. Retired, he now sits by the front window of the little gray house, watching, as though he hopes to catch someone in the act of trying to return the statue of the Virgin he tore from the ground with his own hands ten years ago. Day in, day out, winter and summer, Samuel Jacobs keeps watch. What little money he makes comes in from a thin stream of disability checks and an occasional reparations payment from some European government trying to buy back its conscience with pennies. Sam Jacobs' only distractions are the *Daily News* and the *Daily Forward*, which he calls the "Forvetz." Both of these he reads daily from cover to cover, turning the pages with a gnarled forefinger that he licks until it gleams bright with spittle.

Within the confines of the little house, hours are marked by ticking of the little Big Ben clock in the kitchen and the rustle of pages as Sam turns them one by one by the front window. Only when Naomi, the mother, arrives home after a day of sewing hooks and eyes in the foundation garment outlet on Nostrand Avenue does the house come alive.

Then the rolling smell of chicken breasts, peas, lentils, and parsley tied in bunches with a piece of white cotton thread boiling in the old pot on the stove fills the little house, making it expand with a rich, thick, reverberating odor.

Although it is a *shanda,* an out-and-out disgrace, for a respectable Jewish family to live in a neighborhood filled with gypsies, in a house built by a drunken housepainter who slapped on a bathroom only as an afterthought to a memorable binge that caused him to forget to wait for the cement to settle before closing in the foundation, Naomi's two sons eat well and wear clean clothes to school. With a husband who does not work, it is an accomplishment.

Still, as a child, Haymon Jacobs learns to hold it in, always, until he gets to school. There, real steam heat provided by the city clanks in the pipes. There is plenty of toilet paper. It is infinitely preferable to squatting in the freezing little outhouse at home.

Haymon and his brother, Mase, who is younger, brighter, and thank God shorter, share a single bedroom, the beds squeezed so tightly together there is no way to get between them. Mase is the hope of the family. Haymon . . . well, Haymon is Haymon. There is nothing to be done.

A giant from the time he begins elementary school, Haymon soon learns that he is special, one among the many. To be tall is one thing. To be taller by a head and a half than anyone else in the entire school is something more, an embarrassment of the first order, like a crippled arm or a cleft palate.

Haymon's classmates at P.S. 80 in Coney Island single him out for unremitting abuse. "Tramp, tramp, tramp," they sing in assembly each Friday, changing the words of the song they have been taught to fit the occasion, "Hear the feet of Haymon Jacobs/Ten thousand pounds or more. . . ." Over and over they sing this refrain, their teachers seemingly never able to hear the alterations they have made in it. Haymon comes to dread the moment when his class must exit up the center aisle of the auditorium. All along the rows on either side of him as he passes, taunting voices serenade him. Girls and boys alike singing out in lusty unison, laughing as he stumbles up the aisle, struggling to lose himself among classmates who come up no farther on him than his belt.

Haymon is too big. He can be found in any crowd. Once school lets out for the day and there are no teachers to protect him, he is the most obvious target. Tormentors veer toward him across the open, empty schoolyard. They seize his books, his hat, his bus pass. Like birds of prey picking a scarecrow clean, they swoop in, wreak their havoc, and then soar away, leaving destruction in their wake. Books he has spent hours carefully covering with brown paper cut from shopping bags are jerked free from his grasp to tumble into the gutter. There, they are quickly soaked by falling rain and swelling streams of water rushing toward the sewer.

When it snows, Haymon knows he will have to run the gauntlet to get home, packs of smaller, swifter kids waiting to ram iceballs down his neck and wash his face in slush. When Halloween comes, only Haymon arrives home with his clothes chalked all over, an easy victim for those he has done nothing to offend.

It becomes a game to chase Haymon Jacobs home each day. A beat behind, a step behind, louder even than the alarming sound of his heart pounding in his chest, he can hear them. They are coming. They are closing in. There, just over his shoulder, he can see them. The sound of their pounding footfalls beats a faster rhythm than his own. Their shouted promises of what they will do when they catch him ring in his ears. The fear is the worst part. The fear of what they will do when they get him. The fear turns his legs to rubber and makes him sick to his stomach. The fear is there every day.

One day his pursuers go too far, rounding the very corner on which he lives, chasing him to his house. Sam Jacobs, who has seen them coming, is ready. As Haymon comes stumbling up the pathway through the empty garden, mouth hanging open, eyes filled with tears, face smeared with sweat and spit, his father is already going the other way with a broom handle in his hands.

Haymon watches, fascinated, having never before seen his father act this way. The blue veins in Sam Jacobs' skinny arms pulse. Although it is a freezing, midwinter day, Sam Jacobs wears only a T-shirt. He does not feel the cold. His anger burns brightly enough to warm a mansion.

Screaming curses as he runs, Sam Jacobs' eyes are wild, his features contorted with fury. Wielding the broom handle like a bat, he wades into the horde of children gathered outside his garden gate, shouting, "HITLER JUGEND! SS BASTARDS! *BASTIA! TCHA CREFF!*"

Flailing away with the broom, he chases the frightened children down the block and into the gutter, sending them home to tell their own fathers about this madman who came at them for no good reason. After they are gone, Sam Jacobs deals with his own son.

"Haymon, *der bist ein grosse shtik drek!*" he hollers, his thin lips quivering. "Why you don't fight back? In Europe also, they didn't fight back. This is how it begins. With children in the streets."

"I . . . I was scared," Haymon stutters.

"Scared?" Sam Jacobs says, his narrow chest palpitating. "I ever see this again," he says, wheezing for breath, "you'll have this waiting for you." Looking up in disgust at his son, who is already a head taller than him, he slaps Haymon across the face with so much force that the boy is too stunned even to cry. *"You'll have this waiting for you!"* Sam Jacobs screams. "You understand?"

Haymon comes to understand that he is caught between two opposing armies. There is no telling which side is worse, those with whom he must go to class each day pretending that nothing at all happened to him the day before or the terror of a father who awaits him at home, ready to slap him senseless if he does not fight back.

He soon learns to hide his real emotions always, leading his tormentors away from the house when they chase him, running them until they are out of breath and bored with their game. Only then does he walk home slowly so that his father will think he has solved his problems on his own. Never does he let anyone see what he is really feeling. Not anyone. It is a lesson imprinted for life.

When Haymon comes home after having played basketball in the schoolyard for the very first time, he finds his father by the window like always. The long dead smell of old soup, furniture polish, stuffed cabbage, and the shirt his father insists on wearing for six days at a time hangs heavy in the house. Sam Jacobs grunts when the door closes, acknowledging the arrival of his firstborn. He removes the wire-rim spectacles the union bought him years ago from the bridge of his nose.

"*Nu*," he says, "you're home?"

Haymon grunts in response.

"Where you were today?"

"Brighton."

"So far?" the old man says, annoyed that he has to twist his chicken-scrawny neck backward in order to look up at his son. The boy is too big. "How come?"

"To play ball," Haymon says.

"Oh? You're a ballplayer now, too?"

Haymon says nothing, unwilling to give his father satisfaction. The old man tries again. "They play ball in Brighton on *Shabbos*?" he says.

So far as Haymon knows, his father has never kept any of the commandments of the Hebrew religion, going so far as to eat three full meals on Yom Kippur because fasting might hurt his heart. He says he lost his faith in the camps.

"Why not?" Haymon says.

"Why not?" his father echoes. "In America they do everything." Already he has lost interest in the subject.

"I was wondering," he says. "You think you could go get me a *News*? By the time I got to the candy store this morning the *Italianer* bastard was all sold out. He knows I take one every day . . . you think he would offer to keep one for me? Never."

Haymon wants to ask his father why he never orders one kept for him but he remains silent. It is the only way to deal with the old man. Wait him out. Make him come to the point.

"You think you could go to Hirsch's for me?" Sam asks.

"*Hirsch's?*" Haymon says. "I just come that way. It's back in Brighton."

"This time on a Saturday afternoon you won't find one anywhere else."

"Wait till tonight," Haymon advises. "The Sunday *News*'ll be out."

"I KNOW WHEN THE SUNDAY *NEWS* COMES OUT, *MOMZER!*" Sam Jacobs shouts, the cords in his neck tightening until it seems certain they will explode, the blood purpling his face. "What I'm asking is that you walk over to Hirsch's *now* and buy me today's. If you're so tired from a day's ballplaying, never mind I asked. Never mind. I'll wait for your brother to come home. I waited before you were born, I waited by Hitler, I can wait now."

"Okay," Haymon says, "I'll go."

What is so important that his father must read the paper every day, Haymon can never figure out. It's not as though he's interested in anything, like sports or what's playing in the movies. He hardly ever leaves the house. Still, there is no winning an argument with him. Not ever. He is an old, stubborn man, more like a grandfather than a father really. If he wants the precious paper, Haymon will *shlep* all the way back to Brighton and get it for him, a nickel clutched tightly in his palm, his steps hurried by the knowledge that if he comes back in darkness, the gypsies will be lurking in every shadowy recess and doorway, waiting for him.

As Haymon Jacobs plods toward Hirsch's, Liddel Gross is already there, sitting at a back table just in front of the twin telephone booths where men holding dead cigars can often be seen frantically trying to get a bet down before the last race goes off at Belmont.

Before him, on a thick white china plate edged in restaurant green, sits a shrimp salad sandwich on rye toast with extra mayo oozing obscenely through tiny holes in the stiff brown bread. A mound of golden brown french fries, done just so and doused with ketchup, spills out around it. A large Coke filled to the brim with chipped ice in which half a lemon floats completes what will be both Liddel's lunch and supper.

With no mother at home to *shtip* him with food, and his father too busy to ever get off the phone for long, Liddel Gross takes nearly all his meals at Hirsch's. So far as he can tell, his father's credit there is never ending.

As a matter of actual fact, Abe Hirsch has taken nearly a life-time to pay Cookie Gross back for the loan that enabled him to buy the store twenty years ago. As a matter of good business and personal courtesy, Hirsch has fed and kept careful tabs on Liddel ever since he was a kid.

It is the least Hirsch can do for a man who has his hands full just getting from place to place, much less trying to raise a son. Born a cripple to a mother who never wanted him, it is a miracle that Cookie Gross is still alive, not to mention a well-respected local businessman who has become a fixture in the neighbor-hood.

Although few in Brighton besides Abe Hirsch know the entire story, it is a fact that Cookie Gross' mother liked nothing more than to drink herself blind in the Irish bars of Coney Island and then go home with whoever bought the last round. One night no one did, and they found her the next morning lying frozen to death on the sidewalk beneath the station where the BMT dead-ends on Stillwell Avenue. They buried her in Potter's Field.

Only fourteen years old, Cookie Gross took to the streets, ped-dling papers and pencils on the corners by day, sleeping in corru-gated boxes and old refrigerators in empty lots at night. By the time he was eighteen, Cookie Gross had found a calling.

Twice a day, like clockwork, he could be seen lurching down Mermaid Avenue to Louie's Barber Shop and then back again. As he struggled past like some drunken sailor trying to make his way on dry land, the young mothers of Coney Island would clutch their offspring tighter by the wrist and point him out. "See?" they'd whisper in their children's ears as he passed. "See what happens when you don't listen to your mother? He didn't listen either . . . now look at him."

Although he had a fair idea of what the young mothers were saying about him, all Cookie Gross could do was grunt and con-tinue on his way. Suspended between cane and crutch, at ten in the morning and again at seven at night, he would slowly make his torturous way along the avenue. His broad wrestler's chest and truckdriver's shoulders kept him aloft, like some king being borne past his subjects. His toothpick thin legs, as dead white and withered as wilted stalks of old celery, dragged noisily on the pavement behind him.

For although his body was twisted and had been since birth, even back then Cookie Gross' brain was hand-tooled, a precision instrument not to be equaled until the advent of the computer. Then, as now, Cookie could add long columns of figures and belch forth the results with lightning accuracy. He could figure percentages without pencil and paper and work out the odds on any kind of payoff, no matter how complicated.

How it was that he could do these things without having attended any school that people in Coney Island knew about, no one could say. Louie the Barber himself never asked. Even he had the good sense not to question the prodigy who had fallen into his lap.

For seven long years, Cookie Gross worked the back room of Louie's three-chair shop where the cops made very sure never to ticket anyone who had to double-park outside in order to take care of a little business. Every Saturday, after paying off Cookie for a week spent juggling difficult odds to come up with a line that no one could beat, Louie himself would take home twenty times as much, stuffing it into the ancient mattress where he had maintained a savings account ever since coming from the old country. On Sundays, thanks to Cookie Gross, Louie could sit out under the trellis in his backyard drinking his own sour wine, pretending that he was back in Palermo, a much loved and well respected man.

On the day two punks came to blow Louie's brains out with a sawed-off shotgun, the remains of his charred and gutted mattress of a savings bank smoldered in the street for hours, the stink getting into everyone's nostrils. Twenty-five years old, Cookie Gross made a decision. Like some pioneer setting out for the frontier, he moved one neighborhood over to Brighton Beach, where the details of his life were not common knowledge.

Working from a little three room apartment overlooking Brighton Beach Avenue, Cookie did well from the start, piling up enough money to attract the interest of a woman named Blanche. In many ways not so very different from Cookie's own mother, Blanche moved into Cookie's apartment with her infant son, conveniently forgetting the child when she moved out again three months later. The neighbors took sad note of the arrangement. Blanche had come and gone, leaving no forwarding address. Liddel stayed behind. Soon enough, only the old women on the corner remembered that Liddel had in fact not been born Cookie Gross' son.

For although he had neither the time nor the patience to raise his child the way the Kreigers and the Jacobs tended to their firstborn, Cookie Gross tried. Despite the fact that as a boy Liddel Gross could almost always be found roaming the streets of Brighton long after most of the other kids had to be at home, sitting around the dinner table, he could always eventually be found in Hirsch's. Using the profits from the well-balanced handbook from which he made his living, Cookie Gross found a way to provide his son with what he himself did not have to give him—a place in which to grow up.

For Liddel, Hirsch's is home. He alone is allowed to look through the magazines without buying them. He alone has the run of the back counter where beneath a thick slab of glass, boxes of pink rubber Spaldings, rolls of black friction tape for binding up stickball bats, wooden airplanes encased in clear plastic, balls of kite string, and the precious Duncan yo-yos are kept. Liddel even gets his school supplies from Hirsch each September.

Any kind of cigar, any kind of magazine or piece of candy you want, Hirsch has got, rack on rack and box on box, stretching along the walls all the way back to the single green leatherette booth in front of the twin telephones. The long Formica counter is all the time filled with people smoking one cigarette after another, Chesterfields and Old Golds, as they blow on their coffee to cool it down. The women from the beauty parlor down the street drift in as a matter of habit, their hair still in curlers, to sit *shmoozing* away the afternoon.

In Hirsch's, the air is always blue with smoke, crinkle-cut potatoes deep-frying in oil, hamburgers splattering and flattening on the grill as the sandwich man slices up another BLT down, to go. The pleated metal walls are dotted with grease, the racks and rungs of the stove coated with it. The warm and seductive odor of grease gets people sliding on to one of the old red stools by the counter, ordering everything advertised on signs that hang from the ceiling, swinging in the faint breeze from the exhaust fan. Coke with a hamburger. Coke with tuna on rye. Coke with an order of french fries.

Whenever Haymon Jacobs comes into Hirsch's, he does so cautiously, for fear that he will knock down one of those signs and be forced to pay for what is portrayed on it. The smell, the incredible smell! Food that his mother has absolutely forbidden him to eat, as though he might ever have enough money on him to afford it. Were it not for bus passes, he would be walking to school each day.

This day, Haymon grabs a *News* from the pile by the door, throws his nickel onto the red rubber change mat on the front counter and turns to leave, anxious to be away from all this temptation. *"Hey!"* someone shouts out. *"Big guy!* Over here!"

Haymon peers down the length of the candy store and sees the little guy who picked him in the schoolyard sitting comfortably in a back booth. Unaccustomed to being recognized anywhere by anyone, for a moment Haymon stands frozen, not knowing whether to wave and leave or go over and sit down, or what.

"C'mon back," Liddel commands, motioning toward the table he is sitting at. Trying to keep his eyes off the racks of magazines on which half-naked women are getting undressed, Haymon sidles the length of the store, stooping.

"Siddown," Liddel says. "I thought it was you. You don't come here regular, do ya?" Swallowing some of the food crammed in his mouth, he says, "I know you don't. Guy your size. I woulda remembered."

"I come to get a paper for my father," Haymon says, trying not to stare at the food.

"Checkin' on his stocks, huh?" Liddel says.

Haymon nods, distracted. "Hey," Liddel says, seeing what he is looking at, "you hungry? Gowan. Go-*wan*. I'm full up." Haymon looks at him to make sure it is all right. Then he sits down, picks up half a sandwich, and begins to eat.

"So where did you say you live?" Liddel asks.

"Cropsey Avenue," Haymon admits, around a mouthful of creamy shrimp salad.

"Jamoke land, huh?" Liddel says. "They got a night center there?" Haymon shakes his head. "You play CYO, industrial league, anything?" Haymon shakes his head.

"Jesus," Liddel says, "you oughta. Ain't too many guys ever stuffed the Sponge. *Ever*. You oughta come down on Saturdays. That's when we play."

Haymon nods, the food so rich and delicious in his mouth he wants to close his eyes and go on eating forever, then take home some of the magazines on the racks and lock himself in the bathroom.

"Come down," Liddel urges, "now that you know where it is. Can't hurt to play some. Can it?"

Haymon does not answer. When the week ends and it is Saturday once again, he is up early and out of the house before his father can send him on any errands. He makes the long walk to the schoolyard by himself. No one there pays much attention to him, save for Liddel. In a schoolyard where athletic ability means everything, Haymon is beneath contempt. Although he towers over everyone, he can be pushed around by the smallest opponent. He is always the last man picked in any game, a distinct liability to whatever team is saddled with him. Still, it pleases him to have somewhere to go. After the games are over, he walks home by himself, taking care to stop off at Hirsch's to buy a paper for his father. Sometimes, Liddel will walk with him that far and sit them both down in the back booth. It becomes a routine. Saturdays, Haymon Jacobs goes to the schoolyard. It is better than being at home.

One Saturday at the end of June, with junior high school just about to end, Haymon and Liddel sit at the back table, a pair of froth-flecked malted glasses empty before them. A magazine Liddel has pulled off the rack lies open on the table. Liddel pokes Haymon in the shoulder with his fist, that being his way of getting complete attention before making any statement he deems important.

"Goin' out for the team next year?" Liddel asks.

"The night center team?" Haymon says. "Nah. They still got Sponge." He turns his attention toward the magazine. On page thirty-seven, a girl named Dolores seems to be taking a shower.

"Not the night center, *shmuck*," Liddel says impatiently, "the team. Miller."

"Me?" Haymon says, trying to get a better look at Dolores.

"No," Liddel says, a disgusted expression curling his thin lips. "Her." He jabs a fist at Dolores' creased brown stomach and flips the magazine shut. "Your mother. Yeah, you. You even thinkin' about it?"

"Am I not," Haymon says, using the current schoolyard slang for "no."

"I'm gonna be jayvee manager," Liddel brags. "It's fixed. Away games, comps, the whole *shmeer*. You oughta think about it."

"Managin'?"

"*Playin'*, asshole."

"You think I got a chance?" Haymon asks, the notion that he, Haymon Jacobs, could actually wear a Miller High School jacket a prospect he has never before considered.

"What do I know?" Liddel says. "I look like the coach to you? You're big. You play all summer . . . shit, you ain't even full grown yet . . . you play all summer, who knows?"

"I doan know. . . ."

"You work on dribblin' and shootin'," Liddel says, "it could happen. Tell you what. When I come home from camp in August, we'll go one-on-one. You ain't any better, I tell you straight out and that's it. Whatta you got to lose?"

"Nothin' . . ." Haymon says. "Only how am I gonna practice by myself? I ain't got a ball."

"You need a ball?" Liddel says, slamming his hand against the cover of the magazine on which Dolores is proudly showing her natural assets. "There's ways to get a ball. *If* you got balls."

One week later, Liddel presents Haymon with a brand new outdoor ball, replete with pin for easy inflation. Along with it comes a pair of Converse, size eleven, irregulars. Three days earlier, both items vanished mysteriously from the large sporting goods store on Flatbush Avenue where Buttsy Klein has gone to work for the summer.

That day, Buttsy distinguished himself by seizing the arm of a very young and frightened black girl who had just pocketed two pairs of sixty-nine-cent sweat socks. Despite her squirming, tearful pleas, Buttsy held on until every security cop in the store, as well as the manager, came running.

In the ensuing confusion, no one could blame the disappearance of a ball and a pair of sneakers on anyone, much less eagle-eyed Buttsy or his good friend Liddel, who just happened to be browsing in the store at the time. It is with an act of larceny that Haymon Jacobs' basketball career officially begins.

CHAPTER TWO

By THE end of June, everyone with enough money and any sense is gone from Brighton. Honey Kreiger and his family are installed in a bungalow colony on a lake no more than ten miles from the sleepaway camp where Liddel Gross spends his summers courtesy of Charlie Oceans, who by June always owes Cookie Gross a year's worth of gambling debts.

Both the camp and the bungalow colony, but a hundred and ten miles from the city itself, are displaced persons centers, temporary harbors for urban refugees fleeing the heat and humidity that cloak New York in summer. The horror stories told about exotic snakes lying in wait in the lake to attach themselves to a child's leg and drain all the blood from its body are the fevered product of urban imaginations more used to the soothing whine of traffic on asphalt than the singing of birds in pine trees.

Pavement is what these people are accustomed to, hard concrete sidewalks and storm sewers. When the rains of August turn the Catskills into a muddy brown bowl of soup, many families abandon their summer shanties and head for home long before Labor Day, terrified that they themselves will be washed away. Until that happens, the husbands must drive up for the weekend each Friday night. Exhausted after a long week of work in the city, they spend six to seven hours battling traffic as it winds along Route Seventeen through Goshen, Tuxedo, Sloatsburg, and Wurtsboro. More than one old and trusted family car gives up the ghost after making it over the Wurtsboro hills, its smoking radiator coughing steam as its battered transmission emits the final death rattle. On Sunday night, they all go the other way, back to work. It is still better than spending summer in the city.

For on July Fourth, God draws the curtain down on all of New York. Temperatures rise to above the ninety-degree mark and stay there, day after day. The gutters melt. Nightly, jagged bolts of heat lightning streak the sky, promising cooling nuclear thunderstorms that never come.

The beach in Brighton disappears under the onslaught of bodies. Crying, sun sick children wander the sand, seeking their mothers. City firemen enjoying themselves on their day off are pulled from the murky brine like sea bass, blue around the mouth and twitching, heart attack victims. Old women cling to the third barrel of the ropes, so many arthritic sea lions rocking with the waves. Everyone pisses in the ocean without thinking twice about it.

Beneath the boardwalk at night, blacks from New Jersey, Italians from Bay Parkway, and the Cropsey Avenue gypsies fornicate with vigor. Where they have lain, the sand is dotted with "Coney Island whitefish," used condoms. The city is an inferno in which Haymon Jacobs alone has been left to burn.

Each day, Haymon sets out from the little gray house, basketball in hand, an old and ragged towel looped around his neck. He carries his new sneakers with him under one arm so they will not be smeared by the simmering black tar pools along the street. By the time he reaches the schoolyard, droplets of sweat have already begun to roll down his neck.

In summer, the schoolyard is open and empty, a great desert of scorched and shimmering concrete left for those mad enough to attempt to cross it. Haymon lays his towel down by the steps and forces his feet into his still new sneakers. Then he begins to shoot. Ten jump shots from a foot out on the right side of the basket. Ten from a foot out on the left side. Ten from two feet out, on either side. Ten from three feet out, working his way back until he is shooting from the absolute corners, where the end lines meet to form a right angle.

As he shoots, the heat builds. The redbrick walls of the old public school bounce it back at him in undulating waves so that the handball courts seem to tremble where they stand. Broken bits of glass and scraps of mica embedded in the concrete break the light into glittering shards that pierce Haymon's eye every time he turns his head too quickly.

After half an hour, the sweat begins to run in earnest, coursing down his face in twisting streams and rivulets. Sweat traces the outlines of the bones of his forehead and jaw, dripping from his chin and sliding into a saline pool at the base of his neck where a pulse he never before knew existed throbs with a rhythm of its own. His heart beats counterpoint, a deeper lob-lob-lob, bumping ribs and sternum. Salt cakes his lips. His breath comes to him in hot, desperate gasps, stinging like a gritty desert wind.

After a while, there is nothing but ball and hoop. The hoop is dead and the ball has a life of its own. Spinning in circles as it comes up off the concrete, it must be coaxed in order to enter the basket in the proper manner. The only noise is the steady thump of ball against concrete, the *brrring* of the hoop when a shot hits home, the scuffing of Haymon's sneakers as he drags his foot on yet another layup.

Repetition is the key. Everything must be done over and over so that it becomes automatic. By noon, it is close to a hundred degrees in the yard. Haymon permits himself to sit for a moment in the shade of the building, sweat spooling off him like drops of rain, dotting the sun bleached concrete around him. When he stands again, his legs feel as though they have been pounded with a rubber mallet. He then shoots fifty foul shots, to sharpen his concentration.

If he hits more than sixty percent of his shots, Haymon permits himself to walk slowly to the beach, past the massive private beach club where only those with money can afford to take lockers for the season and lounge in comfort beside a huge saltwater pool. At the beach, Haymon never swims. Rather, he allows himself only to sink slowly into the murky, cooling ocean. The swells rock him. Ten minutes after he leaves the sea, the hot sun has dried his shorts and he is ready to return to the schoolyard for more. Then he goes home to sleep.

By six-thirty, he is back in the yard once again. By now, the sun has lost most of its firepower. Heat pours off buildings that have been soaking up sunlight all day long. Those few who have also been left behind in the city straggle in and take up places on the steps, to watch those with enough energy play.

With the sun fading behind the houses and the streetlights just coming on, Haymon tries to do the things he has practiced during the day. Shots that fell cleanly for him when he was alone more often than not bounce away wildly in real games. He finds that he is easily spooked, upset by the shouts of both teammates and opponents. His body is a cumbersome burden, holding him back. He must struggle for every point.

Night after night, players who do not practice one-tenth as much as he does fly over and around Haymon. Like great horn players taking their cue from the music itself, they improvise, faking and double-pumping in ways they have never planned, letting the flow of the game lead them to the basket with an instinct and intuition Haymon knows he will never have. Haymon keeps on practicing.

July ends with a series of thunderstorms that soak the scorched streets. Rising steam and falling rain commingle to form a primitive urban mist. When the mist lifts, it is August. The humidity rolls in, covering everything with a thick, gritty blanket of discomfort. Haymon plays on, tunneling deeper into the endless conduit his summer has become.

The soles of Haymon's sneakers are mute testimony to the wear and tear he is inflicting on himself. Properly cared for, a pair of Converse will last for nearly a year. After a month, his are no longer white. Rather, they have turned a permanent sweat-soaked yellow. Beneath the ball of his left foot, where he pivots, a hole the size of a dime has been worn through three layers of rubber. In order to protect his socks, Haymon must insert a piece of cardboard inside his sneakers before he plays.

By the end of August, the breeze blowing through the schoolyard at night has lost its fire. The games are more fiercely contested, the steps crowded. People have begun returning to the city. Liddel reappears looking a good ten pounds heavier, tanned, nearly healthy. The first thing he says to Haymon is, "Guess what I got this summer, buddy."

"*Bar mitzvahed*," Haymon says.

"Your ass. Guess again."

"Diarrhea."

"Funny guy," Liddel says. "Are you wrong! Cherry-o-ed."

"What?"

"Nookie," Liddel clarifies. "A piece."

"Talk English," Haymon says.

"*Laid.* I got laid, you dumb prick!"

Haymon's eyes widen. "No shit," he says. "You wanna play one-on-one right now?"

Liddel rolls his eyes and grabs his crotch. "I GOT *FUCKED*," he hollers, leaping off the steps and careening onto the first court, where there is a game in progress. Bouncing up and down like some maddened Easter bunny, he yo-yos across the court yelling, "I . . . GOT . . . *FUCKED!*"

"You're gonna get fucked good you don't get off this court," Mikey Dee hollers.

"Up yours." Liddel laughs defiantly, giving him the finger. "You wouldn't know what to do with it if it bit you, meatball. A *bah fungoo!*"

The next night, Haymon and Liddel play one-on-one, Haymon beating the little man three in a row, accepting a punch to the gut in the final game that would have laid him low two months earlier, then going in to lay up the winning basket.

"Awright," Liddel says when it's over.

"Yeah?" Haymon asks.

"*Yeah,*" Liddel says flatly. "Fuckin' coach don't take you on, he needs glasses. I guarantee it." He slams his fist onto his palm, then lays it out like a black man for Haymon to slap. "We," he says modestly, "have got it made."

TWO WEEKS later, high school begins. Miller, the ancient red-brick building where the children of Brighton and Coney Island have gone to school for generations, is not good enough for Honey Kreiger's son. Honey convinces Reed that he has a "natural" aptitude for science. He owes it to himself to take a special exam and enroll at Brooklyn Tech, an all-boys school downtown where the future engineers and scientists of New York get a head start on their careers. Leaving the neighborhood to attend school each day effectively ends Reed's chances of ever getting really to know anyone in the schoolyard. Brooklyn Tech is another universe entirely. He might as well be going to school on the face of the moon.

Sentenced to ride the BMT two hours a day, imprisoned by schoolwork, it is not until Thanksgiving that Reed discovers what the rest of the neighborhood already knows—Haymon Jacobs is going to lead Miller to a city title. Soon.

In the annual schoolyard calendar, Thanksgiving is a signal event, the weekend when every schoolyard boy who managed to wangle his way into an out-of-town college comes home for the first time. One by one they stroll into the yard, looking cool and casual in their new school jackets and cashmere sweaters adorned by pledge pins. They talk of women and drinking and life in the dorm. Many are now so sophisticated they can no longer be bothered to bring their sneakers with them. At seventeen, they are elder statesmen, too suave even to consider getting sweated up in a meaningless three-on-three game. Reed regards them all with wonder. So this is what going to an out-of-town school does for you. Incredible.

On Thanksgiving Day in the schoolyard in Brighton, a gray wind blows the ice-cream wrappers and fallen leaves in whirling circles. All across America, families are getting ready to sit down to turkey dinners. On television, the Macy's Parade is about to come to an end in a flurry of toy commercials designed to drive children mad with greed a full month before Christmas. In the schoolyard, no one cares. Charlie Oceans is holding court.

Settling his great bulk in against the bricks and turning the collar of his nylon windbreaker up against the cold, Charlie Oceans pushes his heavy black eyeglasses farther up the bridge of his flattened football lineman's nose. "He is a dumb fuck," Osh says, "and a very very sick sonofabitch to boot. I know he never taught you how to play defense. That's why you lose last night. You remember the second half? Stand up, Haymon . . . I'm gonna show you."

Osh rises and all around him the bodies part respectfully to let him through. Haymon follows obediently. Although Osh is a good twelve inches shorter than Haymon and fifteen years older, he is a full forty pounds heavier. When he talks, everyone listens. Osh has been known to bite the ear off those whose attention wanders while he is talking basketball. Or so the story goes.

Wearing high black handball sneakers and an ancient gray Athletic Department sweat shirt under his windbreaker, Osh stares up at Haymon. "That *shvug*," he says, "he comes outta the corner at you, right? So whatta you do, Haymon? You back away from him. *Haymon*," Osh shouts. "You fuckin' *back* away from him and *wave*, like some fuckin' matador or something.

"F'Chrissakes," Osh says. "Never give baseline." Everyone on the steps nods in agreement. In the schoolyard, this tenet is as basic and binding as any of the Ten Commandments. "*Never*," Osh repeats, "give baseline. Step *up*, force your man to the middle, and let your guards bother the shit out of him. Your fuckin' coach ever tell you that? Nah. He's too busy worryin' about sportsmanship and losin' like a gentleman, right? Those fuckin' practices of his. Right outta the book. One day he loses that book, they'll have to disband the fuckin' team. Ah," he concludes, "he makes me puke."

Osh waddles back up the steps and sits down again. "Lid," Haymon says, turning to Liddel for help, "make him gimme a break, huh?"

"*Break?*" Liddel says incredulously. "Are you fuckin' me? The way you played last night, you stiff? He oughta fuckin' break your head is what he oughta do."

"*Heey!*" Haymon protests. "I got . . . what, twelve?"

"Ten," Liddel says flatly. "You got ten. I kept the book. You shoulda had thirty. You got called six times for walkin' and turned it over another seven on bad passes. You missed foul shots, layups . . . you name it. Were you *bad!*"

"Was I *not!*" Haymon protests. "A little nervous maybe."

"Lousy," Liddel says.

"Uncoached," Osh states categorically. "Not his fault."

"Ah," Haymon tells Liddel, "you just jealous, man. That booster, the one you like, she always cheers when I come back to the bench."

"*YOU PRICK!*" Liddel shouts. "I'll have my rod up her ass before you get to hold her hand. You remember you heard it here."

"Better get her a tweezer to hold it," Haymon says, "and a magnifying glass to find it. . . ."

The boys on the steps crack up and begin slapping five. Liddel vaults over two of them and swings a flurry of mock punches at Haymon, who catches them all on his elbows, laughing.

Haymon looks good. His body, hardened by a summer spent on the concrete, has begun to fill out. His pants, which his mother has finally let out, nearly fit, jutting over the top of the team-issue Converse he always wears so everyone will know he is a ball-player. No longer does he flinch when he talks, as though expecting someone to smack him across the face just for being alive.

Having made the jayvee team on height alone, without ever bouncing a ball, he has acquired real status in the yard. He is somebody. He has a future. At home even his father takes note. "You know, *boychik*," Sam tells him, "between you and me, on high school sports, the *News* got nothin'. You're gonna play, maybe I'll start takin' the *Post* or the *World-Telegram*."

It is a sign of Haymon's newfound worth that Charlie Oceans, a man whose life is devoted to making high school boys into college athletes, is even bothering to talk to him. Osh is a legend at Miller, where he works as an assistant football coach. Standing five-eight, weighing two hundred and thirty pounds, Osh has hands like slabs of meat. Driven by a kind of determination that takes no notice of what others call facts, Osh is a well-known miracle worker. Each summer, he takes awkward, gangly kids to the sleepaway camp in the mountains where he runs the waiter program and brings back ballplayers.

Osh and the basketball coach at Miller have hated each other for years. It is a standing rule that any player seen talking to Charlie Oceans on school grounds will be suspended from the team. Osh is never allowed in the Miller gym during practice. Even during games, when no one can keep him out, a close watch is always maintained on him. There is no telling what Osh will do to inspire a team to victory, pull the plug on the scoreboard, punch out some incompetent referee, yank his boys from a game if he dislikes the way things are going.

But no one can stop Osh from running a clinic on the school-yard steps. There he is a never-ending fund of advice. "Keep it in your pants," he will tell anyone willing to listen. "You can't be a ballplayer and a C-man too. How many guys have I seen with a real future wind up married to some pig, livin' in the basement of her mother's house on Avenue Z? Huh? Too many! *TOO FUCKIN' MANY*. You wanna play ball for me, take my advice, keep it *zipped*."

Although no such temptations have yet come his way, Haymon listens intently to everything Osh has to say. Osh is an adult, a teacher. He *knows*. And Haymon is eager to learn.

Around the league, news of "Miller's Killer" precedes the team. Crowds come out early for the jayvee games to see this giant who will be the cornerstone of a dynasty. Whenever a rival gym filled to the rafters with fans gets its first look at Haymon Jacobs, there is a collective gasp, as though they have all been punched in the gut somewhere below the solar plexus. He is that big.

It is only when Haymon starts to take layups that their astonishment turns to derision. For Haymon is a giant who cannot dunk. Twice the ballplayer he was six months ago, he is still awkward and ungainly, a loose collection of limbs trying to arrive at the same place all at one time. It is much like finding out that the deadly Dr. Fu Manchu is in reality a waiter in the Chinese restaurant around the corner. Miller's monster can hardly dribble without stumbling over his own two feet.

At more than one enemy court, with the final seconds ticking away in some meaningless jayvee game, the crowd rises as one to pay Haymon the ultimate tribute. "ONE/TWO/THREE/ FOUR," they chant, "JACOBS EATS IT OFF THE FLOOR." Like some great locomotive picking up speed as it chugs downhill, the sound grows in size and dimension, swelling to fill the gym. "ONE/TWO/THREE/FOUR/JACOBS EATS IT OFF THE FLOOR."

Haymon cannot help hearing the taunts as he puffs up and down the court in wild slapdash contests that no one cares about, mad chaotic affairs that are textbook primers on how not to play the game. Only he is singled out for abuse. Only he is pointed at and called names. *"Hey, big guy!"* they scream. "Hey, piece of shit! *Phone it in."*

When the season ends, Haymon knows one thing for sure. Either he becomes so proficient at the game that the crowd will be forced to cheer him or he'll give it up entirely. It's just too painful to consider another season like the one just past. Without informing the Miller coach of his decision, Haymon goes to Charlie Oceans and begs to be allowed to spend the summer working for him as a waiter.

Liddel applauds the decision. He himself will be up at camp to help. And although Haymon is authentically frightened by some of the horror stories he has heard about the damage Charlie Oceans has inflicted on his boys once he gets them where no one can help them, he resolves to stick it out, come what may. No sacrifice is too great, so long as it takes him farther down the holy road that leads to becoming a ballplayer.

CHAPTER THREE

THE CHARLIE OCEANS who sits pontificating from the schoolyard steps vanishes once the city has been left behind. In camp, Osh becomes a squat, toad-like monster seemingly driven mad by the abundant fresh air and constant sunshine. When he is not screaming at his waiters to clean off their tables in the dining room and then mop the floor underneath, he has them out on the basketball court playing one-on-one in the blazing sun.

Some nights, he returns to the tumbledown bunk they all share so drunk that he throws on all the lights, howls out, "PECKER CHECK," and charges up and down the aisle with a ruler in hand to measure which waiter is approaching manhood the quickest. On Friday evenings, as innocent campers sit in the rec hall attending services, Osh has his boys parade across camp draped in white bed sheets, carrying homemade wooden crosses, chanting, "MOC-KEE FUCK, MOC-KEE FUCK." There is no method to his madness, no reason at the root of his insanity. The waiters need understand only one thing. Osh is king. He will be obeyed.

For days on end, Osh says nothing but "*ARE YOU TOUGH?*," bellowing the question into waiters' ears when they least expect it. Applying a variety of submission holds he learned in the Marines, Osh brings waiters to their knees in pain if they ignore him. He prowls the bunk and the dining room like a vengeful drill sergeant preparing his charges for the battlefield. As Osh's "special project" for the summer, Haymon takes more than his fair share of abuse.

In the dining room, Haymon waits on three tables, one more than anyone else. Osh forbids him ever to appear in public without his weight spats, ten pounds of lead ingots slung into leather belts that tie around the ankles. Haymon even sleeps with them on, tossing restlessly in the lower half of a double-decker bed he shares with Liddel, whose feathery weight barely makes a dent in the springs above his head.

The waiters, who are overworked and paid nothing at all, soon find ways to get even with their captors. When Barry Berman, whom Osh has decreed must be called the "Buzzard," works the staff table where the camp's hated ruling family eats, he first places upon his bare and sweating feet the two red water pitchers the head counselor loves to drink from during the meal. Only after clomping back and forth in them across the wooden dining room floor does the Buzzard fill them. During lunch, the head counselor is seen replenishing his glass many times. The waiters watch with interest, waiting for the HC to drop from some exotic tropical disease.

When Marvin Mones, whom Osh has decreed must be called "Mongoose," takes over the station, he clams into the kosher spaghetti sauce. Liddel circulates the word that for a fee, he is prepared to jack off on top of the head counselor's oatmeal. No one dares take up a collection to see him do it.

Haymon does not participate in any such activities. He is too homesick. For what, he does not know. Each night, the waiters' bunk comes to smell like a brothel, the thick sweet odor of Canoe and Brut and Mennen Speed Stick wafting up to the bare rafters as the waiters daub and spray themselves for another night of grind and grunt along the stone fence known as Makeout Row. Haymon can only sit helplessly on his bed and watch.

For he is *shy,* a condition as defined as being tubercular. In camp, the only member of the opposite sex to whom he can speak without growing red in the face and stammering is a blond ceramics counselor from the University of Vermont whom he serves three times a day in the dining room.

For some reason, she believes him to be "sensitive." She gives him a book by her favorite author, Nathanael West, which he tries valiantly to read. He returns it to her, lying that he liked it. Wanting only her approval, he gets instead paperback copies of *Miss Lonelyhearts* and *The Dream Life of Balso Snell.*

So he eats. Haymon is possessed by a raging hunger that he

cannot satisfy, no matter how many cartons of milk, both white and chocolate, he consumes. No matter how many clandestine sandwiches Liddel slips him from the kitchen, where he has the entire staff paid off with pints of Ten High and Fleischmann's, Haymon's hunger still rages.

Haymon eats himself a new pair of shoulders and thighs. Still, he cannot put on any weight around his ribs. They stick through his skin like the skeleton beams of a building peeping through a primer coat of paint. He takes care never to be seen with his shirt off.

As the summer wears on, the waiters whisper about Osh's annual tournament, the feared Blood Games. No one seems to know the precise rules or regulations, or even when the tournament will occur, but all are aware that it is something special, the emotional high point of the season.

One morning in August, the bunk comes awake to find that the appointed day has arrived. By the door, Osh has posted four lists, dividing the twenty waiters into four five-man teams. Below the lists is an old Number Six pineapple can into which each waiter puts five dollars, with the winning team to take it all.

That afternoon, during rest hour, as campers sit penning letters home on their slatted beds, the waiters assemble in secret on the old basketball court half-hidden in the woods. Under a blazing sun, they nervously shift from foot to foot on a court covered with gravel and bits of broken concrete.

Osh makes his way slowly across the court, holding in his hand a large white bedsheet that has been cut square and sewn to a branch. He climbs slowly up into the rickety wooden bleachers and pushes his thick black frame glasses up his nose. In a loud voice, he intones, "YOU WHO ARE ABOUT TO PLAY, I SALUTE YOU. THE ANNUAL BLOOD GAMES ARE ABOUT TO BEGIN. THERE WILL BE NO TIME-OUTS, NO STOPPING FOR INJURIES, NO FOUL CALLS. ONE HUNDRED DOLLARS TO THE WINNERS. REPEAT AFTER ME."

The waiters stiffen to attention. Osh bellows, "YEA, THOUGH I WALK THROUGH THE VALLEY OF THE SHADOW OF DEATH, I WILL FEAR NO EVIL. . . ."

The waiters repeat the words after him, as though hypnotized.

"FOR OSH IS MY SHEPHERD. . . ."

"Osh is my shepherd. . . ."

"HE MAKETH ME TO LAY IN JUMP SHOTS FROM FAR CORNERS. . . ."

". . . lay in jump shots. . . ."

"HE ANOINTEST MY HEAD. . . ."

". . . my head. . . ."

"WITH THE BLOOD FLAG OF 1960."

Leaping straight up in the air, Osh waves the white banner

back and forth over his head until it catches the breeze and begins to billow in the wind. "LET THE GAMES BEGIN," he cries, blowing a long blast on the whistle he wears around his neck. On two separate courts, the waiters start to run. What Osh is waiting for is not long coming. Billy Berman, the Buzzard, throws up a long jump shot and is fouled from behind. He stumbles and falls, one knee scraping the rough ground. Only then does Osh blow his whistle to stop play.

Tenderly, with all the care a lover takes to ensure the well-being of his beloved, Osh waddles on court, bends over Billy Berman, and dips the bedsheet to his lacerated knee. When he lifts it again, there is a small red spot in one corner. The blood flag has been marked.

Osh blows his whistle and play starts up again. As though spurred by the realization of what these games are all about, the waiters begin to battle in earnest. Clubbed players fall regularly to the ground where they lie gasping for breath, their team forced to play shorthanded until they can rouse themselves and stumble back into action. The area under the hoop becomes a dangerous no-man's land where only those with a suicidal gleam in their eyes and a profound disregard for their own safety dare go. Backcourtmen try to beat the men guarding them downcourt again and again, running flat out as the sweat pours down their bare and shining backs.

Osh's whistle sounds continually as bodies slam onto the hard concrete. Soon, there is little white left on the flag, one irregular red island finding its way into another and combining to form continents. The blood flag becomes a blood map, running red.

After an hour, only two teams remain, the squad led by Barry Berman and the one on which both Haymon and Liddel play. It is hotter now and quieter, the buzz of mosquitoes from the lake the only sound. The shouts of one waiter to another have died with the breeze, just as the game itself has resolved itself into something more grim and basic than basketball. In the blazing sun of early afternoon, there is only the steady wheeze of bodies battling for breath as players push themselves to make one more pass, gather in one more rebound, launch one more pealing run downcourt.

In the final game, Barry Berman's team spurts to an early lead, thanks to the Buzzard's unselfish passes to his basket-hanging teammates. To make the tournament even, Haymon and Liddel have been saddled with the three worst players in the bunk. As a further handicap, Haymon is playing with his weight spats on.

Mouths hanging open, sweat-stained chests heaving, both teams lumber up and down the court like a pack of spavined horses seeking the finish line. Players mumble incoherently, push teammates toward missed defensive assignments, and clutch at their sides where the pain sticks at them like a sharp knife slid deftly between the ribs.

"ONE MINUTE," Osh bellows from the stands. "ONE MINUTE LEFT."

Barry Berman shouts to his teammates, imploring them to hold on. They do not hear. They are dead men, their eyes glazed, so many puppets held upright by an unseen length of string. Their hands are numb, their brains like melted butter, their mouths open, slack, gasping for air. Haymon's team begins to narrow the gap. With less than thirty seconds to go, an errant pass bounces crazily toward midcourt. Both Liddel and Barry Berman take off for it with all they have left. Whoever gets to the ball first will have the game, the tournament, the twenty dollars a man that goes to the winning team.

As though yoked together, the two of them run down the center of the court, the Buzzard muscling his way toward the ball like a rampaging jammer bursting through the pack in roller derby. Liddel is buffeted by a series of elbows and forearms. For a long moment, the two run in perfect time. Then Berman draws ahead, elbows and knees pumping, the blood rushing to his face.

He leans and reaches out, straining for the ball. Something gives in his leg. A look of pain and surprise crosses his face as he loses his balance and begins to stumble. What an hour earlier would have been a routine fall becomes something else entirely. The Buzzard's body betrays him and he pitches face forward to the ground, his head striking the concrete first, the report like that of a rifle being fired in a small room.

Haymon, who has been following the play all the way, chases the still-bouncing ball to the end line. Not knowing if there is enough time left in the game for him to dribble, he gathers it in with a single motion and goes up from where he is, launching a high, spinning jump shot from in back of his head that seems to fade as it rises, gaining just enough momentum to barely clear the front rim and fall cleanly through the hoop as the sharp sound of Osh's whistle cuts through the humid haze. The Blood Games are over.

A winner, Haymon walks to the edge of the court and throws up. Liddel sinks to his knees where he is and stays that way, stunned, unable to believe he has come through alive. Only the Buzzard does not move. In the hot afternoon sun he lies with eyes closed. They carry him to Osh's car and Osh drives him to the hospital.

That night, they operate on the Buzzard to relieve the pressure on his brain. He remains unconscious throughout the operation. Osh spends the entire night and the whole next day at his bedside, neglecting everything, not sleeping. The Buzzard's parents are notified. There is talk of a lawsuit. The camp's ruling family hushes up the incident by promising the waiters that if anyone so much as breathes a word about the tournament, Charlie Oceans will surely go to jail. The blood flag is burned.

When the Buzzard finally comes to, he is much the same grinning, cheerful Barry Berman as ever, willing to put pitchers on his feet and clomp-clomp-clomp across the dining-room floor once again. He blames no one. His first question upon regaining consciousness is, "Did it go in?"

But the camp's ruling family is up in arms. What if the boy had died? Think of the group insurance rates. Consider the camp's good name, the possible effect all this will have on enrollment for next season. Osh has become an embarrassment.

The head counselor gives Osh two hundred dollars and sends him packing, making Osh promise he will leave camp without making a scene or it will be the police for sure. In the dead of night, Osh silently loads his ancient car, with only a pint bottle of Carstairs for company. When the Carstairs is gone and both Charlie Oceans and the car well loaded, he pushes open the screen door of the waiter bunk for a last look at his sleeping charges.

The waiters are up and standing at the end of their beds for him. They have stolen a basketball from the camp equipment shack and Liddel has spent the entire afternoon hitching to the hospital and back. There, by the seam, is Barry Berman's signature. Below it, the names of all the rest, Haymon, the Mongoose, all of them.

Something snaps inside Osh when they give him the ball. He sinks down onto his newly stripped bed and begins to cry. Two waiters, having forgotten that only a week ago they hated Osh so much they would have killed him if given the chance, break into tears and begin to sob along with him.

As a farewell gesture on his way out of camp, Osh splinters a thirty-three ounce Richie Ashburn model Louisville Slugger bat against the head counselor's shack, waking up half the boys' campus. The children fall back asleep to the dying thrall of Osh's old car as it chugs over the hill out of camp.

On the last day of summer, the blond ceramics counselor, beside herself with auld lang syne, allows her tongue to wander into Haymon Jacobs' mouth down by the boathouse. Camp is over. Whatever else happens now, one thing is sure. Haymon Jacobs has survived the Blood Games. He will be a ballplayer.

WHEN LIDDEL and Haymon return to Brighton, it is as though they have been gone for twenty years. Neither can stand to spend more than half an hour at home dropping off their stuff. With their tip money burning a hole in their pockets, they rendezvous at the schoolyard and take a bus to Coney Island. A celebration is in order.

For two months, Haymon has fallen asleep each night dreaming of how he will stuff himself at Nathan's when they get back. He begins slowly with a large order of french fries coated with a layer of grease so persistent it wears translucent spots through the cardboard container. Three roast beef sandwiches follow, thirty-five cents apiece, the meat sliced thinner than tissue paper, then passed through a mysterious vat of brown salt gravy. Haymon then moves down the counter, ordering two hamburgers with onions and a chow mein sandwich.

Then he joins Liddel at the seafood counter for three shrimp sandwiches, the fried shrimp rubbery brown, covered with thick mayonnaise and tartar sauce starred with bits of green piccalilli. Two lobster rolls follow. Then Haymon moves off to the delicatessen counter for a corned beef sandwich on a roll with a sour pickle and a side order of cole slaw. By the time Liddel catches up with him, Haymon is already around in back working on a hot corn dipped in melted butter. He follows this with a slice of pizza and three large orange drinks and is talking about going down the block for some cotton candy, caramel corn, or a jelly apple for dessert when Liddel says, "*Hey!* Either you quit . . . or I puke."

Haymon concedes. They board the Surf Avenue bus, get off near Sheepshead Bay, and walk down quiet tree lined streets to Manhattan Beach. The first court here is the proving grounds, the open-air asphalt courtroom where the old men sit in judgment, hitching their beach chairs closer to the end lines when the games get good. Many a famous ballplayer has come before them and been found wanting, to be dismissed with a wave of the hand and the comment "So he's got a name? What else has he got?"

Others, like the almighty Connie Hawkins from Boys, Roger Brown from Wingate, and Tony Jackson from Jefferson have been judged truly immortal, to be respected for as long as they live.

When Haymon comes through the gate by the first court at Manhattan Beach with Liddel leading the way, the crowd stirs. Old men look up from their reflectors, young girls in ripped dungaree shorts and white-and-black saddle shoes poke one another and giggle. Fellow ballplayers come to greet him with hands proffered in tribute.

"*Haymon!*," they grin. "How you *been*, man! You grown, *Jack!* I swear. No shit. You bigger, man. You guys do good up there with Osh? Huh? You playin' or what? So what you just ate. You got your stuff, right? Come on, *play!* Yeah. I got first. I swear on my mother's head. I only need one. Just one. Come *on*. You gonna? You will? *All right*, Haymon!"

When he finally gets on court, clad in an amalgam of all the athletic gear he has been given during the summer, the change in Haymon is apparent. Even Reed Kreiger, standing by the fence with those who come only to watch, can see it.

The big man is no longer afraid. Rather, he plays with an elbow-swinging confidence that causes other players always to look out for him before shooting. This is Osh's legacy, the lesson imprinted day after day in the mountains. To leave no doubt in anyone's mind about his ability, the first time Haymon touches the ball on offense, he fakes once, losing his man at the foul line, then goes straight for the hoop, soaring up, up, up, over the rim for a crashing slam dunk that leaves the backboard trembling in its wake. The big man is home. He has announced his arrival for all to see.

Standing half-hidden in the crowd, looking more than a little uneasy, is Charlie Oceans. The beach is way out of his territory. Something about the place bothers him, all the young girls busily rubbing Bain de Soleil into their fine brown stomachs. He comes only for the action and he cannot help noticing that Haymon has found his way down here without him. The kid has changed for sure.

"He's nice," the man standing behind Osh says. "Last time I seen him," he says, in a thin and nasal voice, "he had trouble walkin' . . . looked like a stiff . . . and now here he is, lookin' . . . *nice*."

Osh turns quickly, as though he has been struck from behind. "Only a junior, Max," he says too quickly. "Only sixteen."

"So?" the man says, running his hand down the fabric of his suit jacket, bought in an exclusive men's store on Kings Highway. "A junior can't be nice?"

It is still a little early in the season for a jacket but the man is wearing one, looped over his shoulders in the manner of an Italian film director. "Not gettin' a little nervous in your old age, are you, Charlie?" he asks, rubbing a long and crooked finger along the incline of his nose. "Spendin' as much time as you do with these kids could drive anyone crazy. Me, I'm just a fan." He laughs, as though nothing could be funnier. "A concerned fan."

"This is a good kid," Osh says.

"So who said he wasn't?" Max replies easily. "They're all good kids, right? Until they don't need you anymore. No?"

"This one's different," Osh insists.

"Different how?"

"I don't see as how I could explain it."

"Try."

"Watch him," Osh says. "For once in your life, Max, be just a fan. Just watch him."

Max shrugs, his eyebrows and shoulders rising together to elegantly accent the gesture. "What else is there for me to do anymore, Charlie, but watch?" he says. "He even reminds me a little of myself at a similar age. Without the hook shot, of course."

Suddenly Max smiles, his teeth blazing brightly in an angular

face dominated by high, peaked cheekbones. The effect is that of
a candle being lit inside a jack-o'-lantern. Osh lets his breath out
in a whoosh and moves away, eager to lose himself in the crowd.

Behind him, Max Trapp grins. He runs a skeletal hand through
his thinning hair, the tips of his fingers moving automatically to
the bald spot in back where once the hair fanned out in a dark
and curly corona. He stands there like that for a long time, just
watching, lost in thought. Max the Lawyer. A schoolyard legend.
Then he catches Liddel's eye.

The boy comes over to him immediately. "Uncle Max," he says,
using the title to which the man is not entitled, "how is it?"

"How should it be, Liddel? Like always. Yourself?"

"Good," Liddel says enthusiastically, "good. We just got back
from camp. Me and the big guy."

"So Charlie Osh wasn't telling me." Max grins. "What a character he is. Ten years I know him and he ain't changed a hair."

Liddel laughs and starts to tell Max of the night Osh left camp
with a splintered bat in his hand as a souvenir. As Liddel talks,
the older man stares past him at the big kid standing on court.
Haymon has his hands on his hips. He is laughing at something
someone has said, his thick lips drawn back over his large, un-
even teeth. The skin on his face is stretched so tightly over his
cheekbones that his face has become an eerie Chinese mask.
Definitely a face only a mother could love.

Max grimaces and gathers his coat around him. The breeze has
picked up, whipping the sand along the beach into little wind-
storms, turning the ocean the color of chipped lapis. "Big guy
looks good," Max says casually. "Last time I seen him I thought
he was gonna die on court. And now here he is, a ballplayer.
Remarkable improvement."

"Osh," Liddel says succinctly, "kicked his ass all over the
mountains this summer. Lemme bring him over."

"Sure," Max smiles. "You do that."

Liddel goes over to Haymon and grabs him by the elbow.
"*Hey*," he hisses, "I want you to meet an old friend of my father's.
Max the Lawyer. Be nice."

Max Trapp. Although Haymon's a little hazy about the details,
for sure he knows the name. Everyone in every schoolyard in the
Bronx, Manhattan, and Brooklyn does. If you're a ballplayer, if
you've ever put on two pairs of sweat socks and a pair of ragged
shorts and gotten out on an asphalt court and shown some ability
with a basketball in the greater metropolitan area, sooner or later
you find yourself being introduced to this tall, stooped man who
is getting a little bald in back but still has this classic, sweeping
windmill hook shot.

Black, white, Irish, Italian, Jewish, it doesn't matter as far as
Max Trapp is concerned. Can you shoot? Can you hit the open

man on the fast break every time? If so, Max will stand you to a meal, lend you his car, get you laid, and become your best friend, asking only that you befriend him in turn.

Max Trapp. As Haymon comes walking toward the fence, the name turns cartwheels in his brain. An All-American at Columbia or NYU back in the fifties, Max Trapp had actually made it into the pros for a season with Rochester or Fort Worth or some other team that had long since changed both its name and home city. Thrown out of the NBA for betting or something but not so that anyone could prove it. Shit, Max Trapp was ancient. Old bones. Older even than Osh. He had to be thirty-five, if he was a day.

So what? As Haymon lets himself be led toward the fence, he knows only one thing for sure. A man who once made his living playing *pro ball* wants to meet him. It is all he can do to keep from breaking out in a smile.

When Max Trapp straightens up and offers Haymon his hand, he is nearly as tall, his grip so powerful Haymon knows for sure that this man can still palm a basketball and ram it through the hoop any time he wants. They begin talking about Miller's chances for a division title this year. Like Osh, Max Trapp doesn't seem to have too high an opinion of the Miller coach. All in the buzz of the moment, Haymon doesn't bother to defend him.

After a while, Max asks, "You need a ride anywhere? I'm goin' home myself." Haymon looks at Liddel for the answer. Liddel nods. Together, they follow Max out to a fire-engine red convertible with custom leather upholstery that sits parked right out in front of the beach by a hydrant, with its top down.

Max keeps the top just that way as they cruise through Brighton, bursts of brilliant sunlight exploding through the gaps in the tracks overhead like star shells blossoming over a battlefield at night. Haymon lies sprawled across the entire length of the back seat, staring up dreamily through the old wooden ties and crossbeams of the el at the clear blue sky above. He cannot remember a day when things have been this good. Camp is over, school still a week away. His junior year is going to be something special. Already it has begun. More people like Max Trapp will want to know his name. Never before has he ridden in a convertible with the top down. It feels good, very good, as good as he imagined it would be. In fact, it feels perfect.

"Hungry?" Max shouts, the breeze whipping his words around the open car.

"Nah," Liddel says. "We just ate."

"*Yeah!*" Haymon shouts, suddenly ravenous, for cars like this and more sunny days at the beach when he can do no wrong, the ocean breeze blowing the sweat dry on his face before it can fall to the ground.

Max makes a left at Ocean Parkway and drives into Coney Island, pulling to a stop right in front of Nathan's, violating every regulation in New York City's complex traffic code. Seeing the look of concern on Liddel's face, he says, "Relax, kid. I got a police card. Comes from havin' friends downtown. Lissen," he says, pulling a twenty-dollar bill out of his wallet, "get me a dog with a lotta mustard. A pastrami on rye, lean, to go. Celery soda in a bottle. Use the rest for whatever."

"We got money," Liddel protests. "We just got paid."

"*Hey!*" Max says, suddenly offended. "You're with me, right? My guests. My treat. Take it," he says, shoving the bill into Liddel's hand. "Go-*wan*. Knock yourself out."

Back at Manhattan Beach, the wind begins to come off the ocean in gusts, making a serious game an impossibility. On the third court, now empty, Reed Kreiger shoots around all by himself, knocking home jump shot after shot. No one notices. Just another skinny kid banging away with a basketball. The city is filled with them.

CHAPTER FOUR

HAYMON JACOBS' junior year in high school brings him all the attention a sixteen year old boy nearly seven feet tall could hope to attract. No longer do rival fans dare mock him. He is just too good. Teams unprepared for the change in him stand around open mouthed as he sweeps one rebound after another off the backboard and jams home point after point. In game after game, he easily dominates smaller men who try to stop him on court. At the end of the season, both the *Post* and the *World-Telegram and Sun* make Haymon an Honorable Mention All-City selection. By spring, the scouts start coming around.

Even so famous a person as Max Trapp gets in touch through Liddel to let Haymon know he is willing to do what he can to grease the skids so that Haymon can get the "full boat" he'll need if he is going to be able to afford college. Haymon is honored. The great Max Trapp offering him help. But the first time he mentions Max's name to Charlie Oceans, he gets a kind of reaction he did not expect.

"This guy is a *bum*," Osh hisses through clenched teeth, violently clutching at Haymon's forearm with thick fingers until the pain starts to run up into Haymon's shoulder. "Nothin' more, nothin' less. You lissen to me on this, Haymon. Stay away from him. You want Columbia, you don't need Max Trapp. I'll get you Columbia. I'll get you *Harvard!* You don't believe what I'm tellin' you, ask Liddel. Ask him to ask his old man. Ah, shit . . . just forget you ever heard about him, all right? Just let Charlie Osh cover you on this. I ain't fucked up yet, have I?"

Haymon accepts Osh's advice without question, never even bothering to find out what it is that makes Max Trapp such a threat. All around him now, things are happening at a rapid clip.

At home, Sam Jacobs has given up on reading his newspapers in order to concentrate on fielding calls from people who want to know if Haymon is interested in attending college in the Midwest, California, or the Deep South. Does he prefer a school in a rural setting or a large city? He has only to indicate his preference. Visits can be arranged.

Quickly, Sam Jacobs becomes an expert in the field of college selection, as knowledgeable as any high school guidance counselor or scholastic adviser. Acronyms like SAT and CEEB dot his conversation at the dinner table. Often he talks of grade-point average, tuition fees, and grants-in-aid, frankly expressing the view that he personally would like to see Haymon go somewhere in the Ivies so he can get himself the kind of real education that will set him up for life.

A month before Haymon begins his senior year in high school, Charlie Oceans sees to it that the troublesome problem of his virginity is disposed of. Along with a carload of other ballplayers, Charlie arranges for Haymon to visit Rose, a large black woman who plies her trade in a rundown apartment building in downtown Brooklyn, not far from the construction site where Haymon has spent the summer doing manual labor.

A quiet woman from the West Indies with breasts as soft and comforting as old feather pillows, in her time Rose has accommodated most of Charlie Oceans' boys. She knows they must be treated gently like the oversized children they are or they will lose themselves instantly to the washrag and the wet towel.

After his boys have had their pleasure, Charlie Oceans himself always comes around to pick up the tab. Paying is but part of the ritual. Forcing Rose onto her back, he puts his mouth where his boys have only just been, an act that is his single concession to a longing buried so deep within him he would not name it if he could.

The mystery of sex having been revealed to him in the most direct and perfunctory manner, Haymon becomes even more confident and self-assured. The coming season will be the one he has been waiting for all his life, the year when Miller sweeps through Brooklyn like a house on fire and then goes on to play for the city title. Only once the schedule begins, Miller loses its first three games.

The word on Haymon Jacobs has gotten out. Miller can be beaten by rigging special defenses designed solely to thwart their big man. The triangle-and-two. The diamond-and-one. The fearful box-and-one. Exotic zones designed to surround Haymon wherever he goes on court.

Since he spends the majority of his time during a game right underneath the hoop, waiting for easy tap-ins and garbage baskets, there is no more effective way to shut Haymon down than by playing a box-and-one against him. Team after team goes to this defense, assigning four men to play a rigid, box-shaped zone while the fifth shadows Haymon everywhere, playing him head-to-head all over the court.

Whenever Haymon gets the ball beneath the basket, the entire zone collapses around him, four men waving their hands in the air, challenging him to shoot, while the fifth, the man playing him one-on-one, slaps away at his hands trying to force a turnover. Harried, confused, trapped within a tangled forest of grasping arms and hands, Haymon can only stumble wildly, heave mad passes no one can get to, and humiliatingly dribble the ball off his own leg. Once again, he becomes the hapless giant of earlier years.

Even when one of his teammates shoots, Haymon is powerless to pull down the rebound. Two and three man cadres form before him, human walls that keep him boxed out far from the backboard, a helpless, stranded bystander.

Like Gulliver tied down by the Lilliputians, Haymon is constantly besieged, ensnarled, and frustrated. On one court after another, smaller, quicker men dog his every step, buzzing around him like gnats. Long before a game begins, Haymon already knows what awaits him. The hated box-and-one, the defense from which he can never escape.

Truly a man of limited ability, the Miller coach can find no way to beat the zone other than to instruct Haymon to stay away from the ball completely and let his teammates work the offense without him.

By now, Haymon knows enough to realize that he will win no college scholarships by being unselfish. Hitting the open man while he himself averages six points a game will get him nowhere. After a month of utter frustration, with Miller having managed only to split its first six games, Haymon turns to Charlie Oceans for help.

"I been tellin' you about him all along," Osh says of the Miller coach. "This man is dangerous. He is an im-ped-iment to your entire career."

"So, tell me what to do."

"You won't like it."

"Try me."

"You wanna play ball in the Ivies?" Osh says. "Get a nice education and big name all at the same time? Dump this *shmuck* of a coach. Go somewhere you'll learn *basket*ball, not stupid ball. Trust me. I know a place."

Two months after the season begins, readers of the scholastic sports column in the New York *Post* are apprised of the fact that Haymon Jacobs has left Miller High School in order to finish out his senior year at a private academy in the rolling hills of western Connecticut.

"He's goin' where?" the boys in the schoolyard say, questioning Liddel with unceasing ferocity. "To some academy? To do what? Become a cop? Is he cray-zee? With him, Miller woulda won the city. Who's gonna see him play out there? Geese?"

But Charlie Oceans has planned the move carefully, Sam Jacobs giving it his full approval once it has been explained to him. Pennbrook Academy is a pipeline for ballplayers who need a final year of preparation in the classroom or on the basketball court before they can go on to star in the Ivy League. Going there now is a percentage move, no matter what the wise guys in the schoolyard think.

For Haymon, Pennbrook is much like camp. The food is bland, the nights cold, the days long and solitary. He has only his radio for company. Reveling in the luxury of having his own room for the very first time, Haymon often stays up late at night with the tiny radio pressed between his ear and the pillow, dialing in distant stations to listen to the patter of fast-talking all-night disc jockeys. He makes no friends.

Rather, he goes to classes, works out daily with the basketball team, and spends his spare time reading. The incredible luxury of being able to just sit on the toilet bowl for as long as he likes with a book before him more than makes up for the loneliness. Haymon is already accustomed to being alone.

On the day before the Easter vacation begins, Pennbrook holds its annual sports banquet, to which Haymon is invited. The pouring of pints of Seagram's and Canadian Club into the ginger ale and Seven-Up served with the meal is a Pennbrook tradition, as are the after-dinner skits and speeches. Soon Haymon finds himself laughing along with everyone else, drunk.

At two in the morning he winds up at play on one of Pennbrook's perfectly manicured, lush green practice fields. All in his drunkenness, it seems to him that the chalked white stripes that divide the field into five-yard increments glow with a luminosity of their own, shimmering and vibrating in the stark white moonlight.

On this eerie, dream-like plain, two great armies are locked in mortal combat. Thirty varsity athletes, all of them drunk, intently maul and tackle one another in the vicinity of the midfield stripe, battling for precious territory, continuing a tradition that began long before Haymon was even born.

This is the Cup Run, a simple struggle in which the only goal is to move a battered brass drinking cup from one end zone to the other. Generation after generation of Pennbrook scholar-athletes have competed in this strange midnight ritual, one so fraught with deep private meaning that no one from Brighton can rightfully be expected to fully understand its significance.

And yet Haymon Jacobs eagerly joins in the game, ready and willing to give it his all. Although no one has managed to move the cup more than ten yards in nearly half a century, Haymon somehow emerges from a pileup with the precious trophy in his hand, heading for the far goalposts on a dead run.

For one glorious moment, Haymon Jacobs is completely on his own, out in front of the pack and running for glory, outdistancing his pursuers with every stride. For that one moment, he imagines that he can hear the crowd calling out to him, cheering him on to greatness.

More likely it is the rush of blood through his ears, a sound he heard regularly, when he ran home from school each day to avoid being humiliated by his tormentors.

With but twenty yards to go before he reaches the end zone, about to become a true Pennbrook legend at long last, Haymon glances back over his left shoulder. Tacklers are closing in on him from either side. He can hear them panting as they come. Their breath hangs in steamy clouds in the cold night air.

Executing what he imagines to be a brilliant maneuver, Haymon flings out his left hand in a stunted approximation of the straight arm Red Grange used so effectively in his heyday. Haymon Jacobs is no Red Grange. The sudden, awkward gesture throws him off balance. Placing one foot in front of the other, he tries to complete the move by sidestepping in the other direction, certain that this maneuver will leave his pursuers open mouthed in his wake.

Instead, one big foot entangles the other. Haymon's forward motion carries him on, over himself, one leg twined around the other like a grasping jungle vine. The left leg slowly gives way beneath the right, an inch at a time, bending until it seems it can bend no more, then bending still more. Then something snaps.

First, Haymon can feel his leg functioning as a connective system of bone and sinew and tissue straining to speed him on his way. Then there is only pain. Pain so astonishing it seems to Haymon that some tiny soldier has just fired a miniature mortar into the back of his leg. For the shell has conclusively found its target, detonating just above the heel, in the very spot where Hector's arrow felled the mighty Achilles.

For a long moment, Haymon lies gasping on the ground. A cold sweat drips off his forehead into his eyes, making them smart and sting. Somehow, he manages to rouse himself to his feet. He stumbles and stutters along for another yard, then forgets himself and places all his weight on the now-shattered left leg. This time the pain is too much to bear. Haymon pitches face forward to the ground, unconscious.

When he comes to, Haymon finds himself in a bed in the Pennbrook infirmary. His left leg is bound in plaster and suspended by traction from a pulley. A week later, a private ambulance paid for by the school takes Haymon back to Cropsey Avenue to recuperate. Pennbrook grants him his high school degree in absentia.

When they remove the cast two months later, Haymon's left leg has become a shrunken replica of what it once was, the muscles of both calf and thigh having withered by more than half in the time it has taken for the Achilles tendon to heal. The doctors assure Haymon that they have done all they can, giving him an old man's cane to use until the leg comes around completely. It does not seem possible to Haymon that he will ever be the same again.

For the very cord that once held together Haymon Jacobs' left leg has been severed. Although it has knitted itself back together now, Haymon's left ankle is still thick with pain, swollen, stiff, and unresponsive. Far worse the left leg itself is a full inch shorter than the right. No one will ever be able to miss Haymon Jacobs now. He has become a seven-foot monster with a permanent limp. Haymon Jacobs. The gimp.

"What the fuck," they say in the schoolyard when they hear of his misfortune. "If he'd stayed at Miller, he'd still have two good legs and a future, right? So what's he got now? A lifetime fuckin' pass to Cropsey Avenue? Right? So what?"

In sum, God has punished Haymon Jacobs for the ultimate sin—aiming too high too fast and forsaking those who knew him when. He has been struck down, yes, but not without reason.

At home, Sam returns to the *News* and the *Forward*. He stacks and bundles all the college catalogues and files away the letters. Who knows? Maybe they will be of use someday to Mase, when he is ready for college.

Haymon sits by the window. He goes out for long, rambling walks that lead nowhere and back again. Although Liddel stands by him and Charlie Oceans goes so far as to break down and cry when he gets his first good look at Haymon's shrunken leg, Haymon knows no one can help him now. He is alone, back at the starting blocks and less of a runner than he was when the race first began. His good left leg, the passport that was going to get him out of the neighborhood has been voided, stamped invalid.

The demand for a one-legged ballplayer being only slightly less than that for a dancer with the same affliction, Haymon Jacobs is free once more to stalk the streets, the *mishima*, the geek, the *golem*. Having been given a glimpse of other shores, the weed-choked lots of Cropsey Avenue, stinking with shit in the hot summer sun, smell only that much the worse to him. His exile among them becomes only that much more galling. Like a quart of milk left for too long on a back shelf, something inside Haymon Jacobs sours, never to be palatable again.

Reed Kreiger's dream of escaping from the cattle cars of the BMT that he rides each day to and from school ends not long after Haymon's return to the neighborhood. Having convinced himself for two and a half years that once he graduates from Tech he will be able to leave the stations of the BMT behind him forever and go on to some small college in the country where thrilling blond coeds slowly walk their bicycles to a stop by the ivy-encrusted redbrick library, Reed learns otherwise one night over supper.

Having told his father of all the colleges to which he intends to apply, and of the fees they charge just to consider those applications, Reed watches as Honey looks over at him with a mouthful of food and says, "Save your money, buster. 'Cause I ain't got what to send you with. Besides, you ain't gonna get a better education anywhere than at CCNY. For free. When you're ready for graduate school, you can go anywhere you like. Till then," Honey shrugs, "you can rest assured . . . we ain't gonna rent out your room."

Reed is stunned. For a week, he rides back and forth to school telling himself that his father will reconsider. There are ways to get around having no money, loans and scholarships. Reed has read about them in the college catalogues he keeps stacked on a shelf in his bedroom. If only his average were higher. If only he played the violin or threw the discus. If only he had run for student body president. If only. The truth is that there is really nothing very special about him. He is just another kid from the city. Perhaps CCNY is where he really belongs after all.

"Now you're talking," Honey says when Reed tells him that he will give up on going out of town. "Great men have come out of CCNY. Judges, lawyers, doctors. Everything."

"If I go, I wanna join a fraternity. . . ."

"How much?"

"Couple hundred a year."

"Why?"

"To have a place to go. . . ."

"A home you got," Honey says, "you want a clubhouse too, all right with me. You're not a kid anymore. You go to City, you do what you want and come home when you're finished. Live here like a *mensch*, and we'll have no troubles. All right?"

Reed shakes his father's hand to seal their contract. Honey

beams. "And your mother said you'd be so disappointed," he says. "Rhoda, you hear? He knows how to deal with these things. He always did. Didn't he take the rubber dump truck? Hah?"

Having had his mind made up for him, Reed Kreiger enrolls in CCNY in September. The train ride each day is never-ending. The only thing that keeps him from losing his mind is Beta Tau, the fraternity he pledges.

At CCNY, Beta is best. You can see it in the way the brothers dress, their khaki twill pants hiked up just far enough over Bass Weejuns polished positively orange to show a glimpse of powder blue sock. Between classes, Beta's brothers stand on the steps of the liberal arts building as though they're posing for the back-to-school issue of *Playboy* or *Esquire*. To look at them, you'd never guess that CCNY is just another stop on the subway where the student body arrives en masse every morning and then departs at night, just like the army ant workers who people the office buildings of midtown Manhattan and Wall Street.

What Beta Tau is truly best at is reproducing the kind of collegiate atmosphere that just cannot exist when you still reside at the same address your parents call home, hoping for a seat on the train each day in the heart of the rush hour. Aside from Raymond the Bagel Man, who has stood outside the front gate since time immemorial hawking his wares, CCNY has no traditions, no code of being, no philosophy at all to impart save for what fraternities like Beta Tau can manufacture.

Reed picks up quickly on the Beta ethic. Stated simply, if someone who pledged before you had the good sense to walk out of an exam room with a complete set of questions in his pocket, you'd be a fool not to take advantage. The basement of the fraternity house is crammed to bursting with files, old tests, and mimeographed sets of notes. They are there to be used. The point is to chip away at it every day in every way so that one morning in the middle of your senior year you wake up to find that the mailman has succeeded in forcing the thick envelope containing your med school acceptance letter through the front door slot. That's the only gold ring up for grabs at this particular merry-go-round. The point is to get out, and up. Everything else finishes a poor second.

Reed goes out for the freshman basketball team. He is more surprised than anyone when he makes it. By his sophomore year at City, he is spending all his spare time in the cafeteria, where the sharpest brothers go to cut classes so that everyone will see them, spending long hours over the *Morning Telegraph* before making their daily pilgrimages out to Aqueduct to test their latest, foolproof theory. Each morning, Reed sits at the fraternity table in a knit cardigan and a candy-striped shirt, working at the New York *Times* crossword puzzle as black men who long ago joined the brotherhood of heroin nod out over steel trolleys laden with dishes on which spaghetti reds and egg-yolk yellows have dried like the caked layers on an artist's palette.

It is in the cafeteria that Reed gets his first look at the new freshman girls who form the pledge class of Alpha O, Beta's "sister" sorority. The glances exchanged between tables are more than casual. Many an Alpha O sister and Beta brother have already begun the natural progression that leads from being "pinned" to getting engaged to the wedding ceremony itself, with the wine glass broken beneath the groom's heel. Both organizations regularly take out ads in the interfraternity newspaper to proclaim their marital successes, each new union a further proof of their high social standing.

In the autumn of Reed's sophomore year, Alpha O pledges twelve girls who look so much alike it seems possible that they are all truly sisters, related by blood as well as sensibility. Uniformly small, dark, fragile, and fine-boned, they possess great, luminous eyes and pert, little noses, some of which are even God-given.

In years to come, as cafeteria-made marriages fall apart, the new pledges of Alpha O will shear their hair and slash at their wrists with rusted razor blades. Some will go mad. Others will grasp desperately for salvation in radical politics, avant-garde sexuality, or advanced forms of psychotherapy.

For the moment, they are at the peak of their power, pure, perfect, unattainable. Twelve almond-eyed princesses in knee socks, Peter Pan collars, plaid skirts, and shoes from Fred Braun in the Village, they rule the new and exciting collegiate world in which they now find themselves.

Every witty remark that drops from their orthodontically perfect mouths is repeated in the cafeteria. Their entrance as a group into the ancient school gym during Friday night basketball games is more of an event than the outcome of the game itself. Since few Beta brothers can muster up enough courage to ask any of them for a date, rejection being too crushing a prospect to consider, the new sisters of Alpha O turn naturally to one another for comfort and companionship.

Like everyone else, Reed is first drawn to the most perfect of the lot, Adrian Albaum. Adrian has never been seen to eat, eating being a bodily function which entails digestion and then excretion, vulgar acts of which she is not capable, being too finely made to have come equipped with plumbing. Protected by a coterie of adoring fellow pledges, Adrian is never alone. She is the princess among princesses, the stuff of a thousand wistful daydreams.

The closest Reed can get to Adrian is her best friend, Lauren Sklar. A shy, pretty girl, with less than perfect features and a hesitant way of carrying herself that betrays all the insecurity that comes with being handmaiden to the queen, Lauren is delighted to be seen talking to Reed in the cafeteria. A varsity athlete, a Beta brother in good standing, Reed is universally considered a "catch." Adrian's countless conquests, her icy, unassailable virtue, and her total disdain for those who so desperately pursue her provide Reed and Lauren with material for a thousand conversations.

One Wednesday evening, at precisely the hour prescribed for calling up girls and asking them out for Friday night dates, Reed phones Lauren and invites her to accompany him to the event of the season, the annual Alpha O-Beta Tau Christmas dance.

Since Reed must first play in the big game that precedes the dance, they make arrangements to meet afterward in the Alpha O house. Reed knows that Lauren will be at the game. Should he actually get in once the outcome has been decided and score a point or two, there is no telling what may happen afterward.

Although the Friday night games at CCNY are often laughed at by those in the stands, Reed can never take them lightly. Having never played at all in high school, when to be on the team meant everything, he has to squeeze every precious drop from it now that he has made the grade in college. Little things count. Before the game begins, he takes special care to make sure the knots on his sneakers are tied, doubled over, and then tied again. His uniform jersey must be spotless so that when he yanks it from his shorts in the heat of the battle, it will hang just so when he runs downcourt. Two pairs of extra thick socks hide his still-thin ankles.

All of it must be perfect so that when he plays, if he plays at all, it will look casual, thrown together. Reed is the kind of self-taught player who would rather look good and miss a shot than appear awkward and have a lucky basket fall for him.

During a game, should he be fouled, he will take his time at the line, carefully accepting the ball from the referee only after having made sure the silver mezuzah he wears only when he plays is safely tucked inside his jersey. Then, squinting carefully at the hoop, he'll raise the ball over his head and shoot, following through with an exaggerated motion that leaves him corkscrewed at the line like some ancient Greek athlete who has just flung the discus. It is an anti-climax when the ball goes in. Form is everything.

On the Friday night he is to meet Lauren after the game, Reed gets in with time to spare in the second half and cleans up on the court, scoring a lifetime high of eight points. When Honey, who takes care to attend every game, finds Reed after the final buzzer, the first thing he says to him is, "Hey, Sherman White. You were open twice in the corner for jump shots. What is it? You're shy?" Reed can only laugh and shrug helplessly. Honey is more demanding than any coach.

After he has showered and dressed, Reed drives over to the Alpha house. Still buzzing from the game, he stands by the punch bowl, accepting congratulations, waiting for Lauren to find him. "Nice game," she says, sidling up to him through the crowd. "Twice you were open in the corner for jump shots. You need a note from the coach to shoot from there?"

Reed groans. "Jesus," he says. "You should talk to my father."

"Why? Does he know?"

"He said the same thing."

"Obviously a man who understands the game."

"Come on. Let's go eat."

Together they make their way into the street, Lauren stumbling once on the steps outside the house, reaching out naturally for Reed's arm to steady herself. When they are settled in the front seat of Honey's old Chevy, rock and roll playing softly from the radio as the old engine revs itself into life, she suddenly leans boldly toward him. The warm smell of the alcohol on her breath envelops him a moment before she puts her mouth on his, her tongue wriggling forth like some tiny cobra sticking its head out from its basket lair.

Shocked at this violation of the rules that govern all first dates, Reed is about to reciprocate when Lauren pulls her head back, giggles, and moves away from him. "So," she says, "let's go eat."

At dinner, in a restaurant he has never eaten in before that Lauren "highly recommends," Reed drinks more of the strange thin wine they bring with the food than he realizes. By the time the waiter presents the bill, Reed is feeling light-headed, strangely elated. He realizes he is enjoying himself. He makes it a point to take Lauren home the long way, through Central Park. The romantic effect of driving through the park at night is well known, yet Lauren seems immune to it all, restless, as though she is suddenly anxious to get away.

On the corner of Ninetieth Street and Riverside Drive, she says, "I can just jump out here and walk, if you don't mind."

"Oh. Okay."

"Well," she says, putting out her hand, "I really had a nice time."

Reed reaches out for her hand and draws her toward him. She comes unwillingly, an inch at a time, and he actually has to tug at her wrist to get near enough to kiss her. All in his haste, he misses her face, his lips brushing a single wisp of perfumed hair as she turns her head at the very last minute. Gathering herself up, she vaults out of the car onto the street outside.

"Call me," she says, once she is safely out of range, "I'm always home. You know the number. Bye."

Then she disappears into the maw of an old redbrick building. Reed watches, certain he has muffed a cue or missed a connection somewhere. Otherwise, why would she run off like this, especially after having fallen all over him earlier in the evening?

Turning the old green Chevy around, he heads uptown toward campus. Maybe there will be someone up in the Beta house willing to bullshit for a while. Reed needs to talk. Many half-formed questions are buzzing in his head. Certainly someone there will be able to tell him the things he needs to know. After all, what else is a brother for?

CHAPTER FIVE

IN THE months after his accident, the boundaries of Haymon Jacobs' universe quickly shrink to what they were before he ever touched a basketball. From the little house on Cropsey Avenue he dares venture only as far as the Italian candy store where the guy behind the counter refuses to hold a *Post* for him even after he asks. Too ashamed ever to appear in Hirsch's, feeling as though he has let the entire neighborhood down, Haymon hibernates, never once even thinking of going near the schoolyard.

For the first time, Haymon understands the pleasure his father gets from reading the daily paper. Walking for it along the empty streets around Cropsey Avenue kills a good ten minutes. Then there is the walk back, another ten minutes, with the freshly inked paper rolled beneath his arm. Then a good twenty minutes spent lost within its reassuring borders, reading from back to front so that he gets all the sports news first. Going for the *Post* each afternoon marks the passing of another day.

Having given up all hope of ever being a ballplayer or even going to college, Haymon passes his days in a somnolent haze, a state of non-consciousness that he carries with him into the dollar theater at the end of Kings Highway where old men sit in the balcony jerking off to the flickering light of grainy nudist films, on to the subway train that takes him to the great library in Grand Army Plaza where he spends hours with an unread book before him, staring out the open windows at the endless bird-filled trees of Prospect Park across the way.

At night, as he lies in his bed unable to sleep, Haymon keeps his tiny transistor radio wedged between his head and the pillow. At the far end of the FM dial, he has discovered WKCR, the student radio station from Columbia University. It gives him a kind of perverse pleasure to listen to confident student deejays talk about a campus he knows he will now never get to use. An entire life has been denied him.

Only Liddel keeps coming around, refusing to give up. Two or three times a week, Liddel and Haymon take long walks. Liddel talks at him, urging him not to quit. "We come too far to stop now," he says again and again. "Osh knows a guy who knows a guy. Let him fix it up for you to see a real doctor. What can it hurt?"

In October, as a favor to Liddel, Haymon journeys uptown by subway to see a Park Avenue specialist. The doctor probes in painful places with skilled fingers. The leg is traumatized. Of that there is no doubt. But Haymon is still a young man. The muscles will heal. What the doctor cannot tell is precisely how much damage has been done to the tendon itself. In all likelihood, he says, within a year Haymon will regain full use of the leg. An extensive program of physical therapy may even restore it to its original length. In any event, it will be a long, slow, painful process.

Charlie Oceans is optimistic. He sends word out along his network of old boys. Haymon needs a job in the city. A ballplayer's job. One of Osh's schoolyard wonders of old, now assistant to the director of sports programming at one of the television networks, comes through with something. Osh relays the offer.

"You go to work for this guy," Osh explains, "as a page. The money is good, the hours nothing. Spend your free time workin' on the leg. Whirlpool, weights, the whole thing. The leg comes around, this guy's got a friend in the admissions department at Boston University. He went there. Not much of a program now but they're goin' big time next year. He'll get you in. If not, what the hell, least you got a foothold where you can make some real money without a degree. What's it gonna hurt you to try? Anythin's better than this, layin' around the house, goin' crazy. No?"

Haymon takes the job. Since most of the men he works for have played basketball or football at the college level, they are a sympathetic, friendly bunch of guys. All Haymon has to do is show up at the office each morning by nine, go out for coffee, and then make sure everyone's got all the aspirin and typing paper they need.

Afternoons, they send him over to a theater on West Fifty-eighth Street where they tape a game show. Haymon's job is to stand out under the marquee in a poorly fitting network blazer and hand out free tickets so they can fill the place up with passing tourists. He's a natural shill. Who's going to walk past a seven-foot page without looking up?

Out on the street, people cannot restrain themselves. Often, after accepting the tickets he thrusts at them, they look up and say, "Hey, you're a big guy! Jesus, you're big."

"Hormones," Haymon says, developing an attitude. "I got a gland problem."

"How big are you?"

"Eight-six. When the sun's out."

"You a ballplayer?"

"Nah. I work the circus when it comes to town. I hold up the tent."

"Really. Mary, did you hear that? . . . This young man is a circus performer."

"Tickets . . . free tickets," Haymon chants. "Get 'em while they last. Show's goin' on right now, inside."

When winter comes, they take Haymon off the street and make him part of the unit that travels each weekend to whatever city the pro basketball game of the week is coming from. His duties include making sure the high-priced hooker the director spends every Saturday night with is out of the hotel before the director's wife calls on Sunday morning to check up on him.

Often Liddel goes with Haymon to the game city, most often Boston or Philadelphia. Running straight D's at a local community college, Liddel is unsure about his future. The weekend trips are a welcome chance for him to generate a little pocket money of his own. For wherever Liddel Gross goes on the weekend, a phone call back to Brighton is sure to follow.

Each Sunday at eleven A.M., Cookie Gross makes his slow, torturous way from his apartment to the phone booth on the corner. As soon as the phone rings, he slides in and picks it up. Rarely is the message of great duration. Sometimes Liddell will say only, "Go against it," indicating that the big bettors on the TV crew who make it their business to know exactly what is going on inside both dressing rooms do not think the favorite is worth the points. Other times, Liddell will report back some piece of gossip, noting which nationally known player was seen in the lobby of the team hotel at four in the morning, shot glass in hand.

Though it may not seem like much, Liddel's reports allow Cookie to refine his position at the last minute and decide whether or not he wants to lay off some of the action he always carries on the heavily bet televised games. For Liddel's trouble, Cookie pays him twenty dollars a week.

The information is also a service Cookie supplies to his old friend, Max Trapp. Max and Cookie have known each other forever, the beginnings of their friendship buried so deep in time that even Liddel cannot unearth the story of when it began.

On any given weekend, Max may be in Vegas or Miami Beach. Being able to make some phone calls and tell people all over the country who will *not* be starting in the nationally televised pro game only enhances Max's burgeoning reputation as *the* man to see when it comes to betting basketball, be it pro, college, or high school.

Although Haymon knows Liddel is feeding information back to Brighton, he sees nothing wrong in it. Everyone gambles on the game of the week. It makes Sunday a sporting proposition. Why shouldn't people back in the neighborhood know as much as the sharpies who work for the network? He himself never puts down a nickel. Betting is not something that interests him. He has his bad left leg to worry about.

All through the dark days of January and February, weeks when the light vanishes along Sixth Avenue at four in the afternoon and the cold wind whistles down the canyons of midtown Manhattan, Haymon leaves work early with his shorts and sneakers in a bag and goes to a nearby gym to work out. He strains with the weights, struggling and sweating, doing squats and leg raises with the barbell across his shoulder, trying to get his left leg to bend an extra inch more than it did the week before. Unconsciously, he begins rocking from his heels up on to his toes whenever he has a spare moment, flexing and bending his ankle in tight, painful circles. At night, his calf throbs. The ankle aches. The foot itself often cramps up just as he is about to fall asleep. Haymon welcomes the pain. Pain is progress.

Just as the doctor predicted, the rebuilding process is slow. Sometimes it seems to Haymon that it has never been any other way. He has always walked around on a bad left leg, an unwilling fence post that refuses to become a sapling once again. Day after day, just as he once worked to make himself a ballplayer, Haymon puts all his energy into the leg, imagining that he is getting somewhere even when he isn't.

By the time the playoffs begin in March, Haymon has taken to shooting around with the ex-ballplayers from the TV crew who play pickup games in the still-empty arenas before the crowds arrive. He finds the leg is still not right. There is a stiffness there that will stay with him for life, giving his every movement on a basketball court a curiously lifeless, robot-like appearance. One of the men on the TV crew takes to calling him the Hulk. The name sticks.

In June the assistant to the director of sports programming at the network gets in touch with his friend in the admissions department at Boston University. The basketball coach there lends his support for Haymon's application. The school decides to take a chance. On a provisional basis, it grants him admission and a scholarship. Having already lost a year because of the injury, knowing that he has no other choice, Haymon gratefully enrolls in B.U. It is a far cry from the glamorous institutions of higher learning that came clamoring around him when he was whole. Still, anything is better than Cropsey Avenue.

AT CCNY, basketball is on the upsurge, the Beavers starting to play the way they did before the point-fixing scandals of the early Fifties wrecked their program. As a junior, Reed Kreiger leads all the scorers in the Knickerbocker Conference. At the end of the year, he is elected team captain. Heady stuff indeed, for one who spent his Saturdays staring at the real ballplayers from his seat on the schoolyard steps.

Nearly everything has started to come Reed's way. The pledges of Beta Tau and the newly minted sisters of Alpha O look up to him and his steady companion, Lauren, in awe. He is suave, collegiate, and pre-med. She is bright, bouncy, undeniably cultured. There is not a Greek on campus who would not happily exchange places with either of them.

In the two years they have been seeing each other, Reed and Lauren have become *the* couple. They are so obviously the perfect match, headed down that blissful path that leads to marriage and then the big house in the suburbs, that their relationship is taken for granted, as solid as one of the old granite buildings that has stood on campus forever.

In truth, they are held together by something more desperate than love, although the love is there, now and then. Reed clings to Lauren like the last survivor of a shipwreck in the open sea holding on to a life preserver. Her buoyant certainty in all matters of style and taste and sensibility keeps him afloat, no matter how high the waves. For Lauren is the absolute arbiter. "Rank" she will declare something to be, and so it is. A rank film. A rank person. A rank performance by Reed and his teammates on court. "Boring" is even more final, a purgatory from which there is no escape.

Lauren's influence rapidly extends to every area of Reed's life. She takes him to Brooks Brothers for the very first time and explains the mystery and significance of raincoats, the pecking order of loops, buckles, and epaulets that makes Burberry far superior to London Fog. For his birthday, she annually buys him three silk ties that cost more than any shirt he has ever owned. She introduces him to a world in which he is sure he wants to live.

For herself, Lauren has long sought confirmation that she has become a young woman of great beauty and intellectual power. With Reed rapidly becoming the closest thing CCNY has to a campus hero, she founds a little kingdom of her own, one that rivals the duchy Adrian rules in terms of popularity and respect.

What goes on between Reed and Lauren when they are alone together is less glossy and hardly inspirational. For when it comes time to say goodnight, date after date, as they sit together in the front seat of the old Chevy with the motor running and time slipping away, there is still awkwardness, fumbling, indecision, uneasy compliance, mumbled apologies, and then . . . nothing.

It is a difficult, querulous business, this knowing what to do with your hands when you are with someone like Lauren. Always, when they are locked in some less than immortal embrace, Reed fears that Lauren is only putting up with it all out of a sense of duty, because it is what she "should" be doing. Some nights he is certain he is causing her actual physical pain.

"Am I hurting you?" he will ask, and although the answer is always no, Reed cannot help but feel she is lying to him. For Lauren is so fragile really, her bones right there to be felt beneath her skin, that he is terrified that some night he will lose control when he is with her and hear them snap. Lauren is not Adrian's best friend for nothing. They are two of a kind, delicate figurines never intended for sweaty makeout sessions in the front seat of an old car.

Then too, in Reed's mind there is always the hidden fear that some night Lauren will leave the car with that little sneer on her face and pronounce final judgment on him. "Rank," she will say, and that will be it, the last word on his abilities as a lover. Sex is not the problem. The problem is love. Or so Reed thinks. For if he did not love Lauren, why would their failed attempts at lovemaking be so painful for him? There is no one to whom he can go for the answer.

Instead, he takes to showing up alone at the Beta House on Friday nights with a pint of Jack Daniel's or Southern Comfort for company. Swilling it quickly, all in his drunkenness, he will pick up some hard mouthed high school girl out for a night of adventure along Fraternity Row. Taking her upstairs to the room reserved for such activities, he will do things with her he would never dare try with Lauren, then go home feeling empty and thoroughly disgusted with himself. Every Saturday night, like clockwork, he sees Lauren for what has become their very tightly structured evening out together.

At CCNY, the veneer is very thin. Reality laps at the campus like an unrelenting sea. No matter how well Reed does on the basketball court, no matter how lionized he becomes in the cafeteria, when it is all over, he still must ride the subway home alone. He knows that there has to be something more. But no one can tell him what.

It is with a profound sense of indifference then that he applies to thirty-four medical schools during his senior year, hoping to get in somewhere. After all, no longer is he just another faceless student. He is Reed Kreiger, captain of the CCNY basketball team, a campus celebrity, with grades respectable enough to win him admission someplace.

By spring, Reed has been rejected thirty-one times and placed on two waiting lists. He has no illusions. Should a plane filled with pre-med students from Yale or Columbia go down in the foothills somewhere, he may have a chance to slide into the profession. Otherwise, forget it.

Then a letter arrives from the Medical College of the University of Brussels. The board of admissions is pleased to inform Reed that, along with nearly every other American applicant with money enough to afford the outrageous tuition fees foreign students must pay, he has been accepted as a member of the fall entering class, provided he presents himself in Brussels by July 15 for a three-month intensive preparatory course in French, the language in which all instruction is given.

Is this the gold ring or only a lousy fourteen-carat phony? Far into the night, Reed and his father thrash it out, Honey insisting, "Go. What other offers you got? Brussels or Buffalo, what's the difference? It's medical school, right? You get out, you're a doctor."

Reed is less sure. Brussels is a world away. The cost is outlandish. He tells his father he's not certain they can afford it. "Wait," Honey says on the third night of their discussion, which like all other issues ever decided between them, has become a marathon test of wills. After charging into the bedroom, Honey Kreiger comes back into the dinette with a green burlap bag in his hand. Dumping it on to the table, he pours out money, more money than Reed has ever seen, tens and twenties and fifties flooding the table like a mountain of dead fish dumped out on to a dock.

"*Here!*" Honey cries, fingering the bills, making them crackle. "You need money? You got it!"

Piles of bills form hillocks that slide and subdivide into hollow valleys. Money lies everywhere, on the table, the chairs, the floor. The little dinette has gone green with its reflection.

"You know how much is here?" Honey challenges Reed. "Guess."

"Ten thousand," Reed ventures.

"*Pisher,*" Honey laughs. "Thank God an accountant you'll never be. Guess again."

"Fifteen?" Reed says.

"*FIFTY!*" Honey howls. "FIFTY THOUSAND DOLLARS *CASH* SAYS YOU'RE A DOCTOR."

"Shh," Rhoda importunes. "Not so loud, Honey. You want the world to hear?"

"Let them *hear*," Honey cries. "I stole it? I made it, every penny, by myself. Twenty years throwing pennies into a *pishka*, saving, taking lunch to the store. When did I ever buy myself a new car, a suit of clothes? We went to movies and spent it in nightclubs? We saved it . . . for *you!*

"Twenty years of my life says you're a doctor," Honey Kreiger shouts. "Who are you to say no?"

"What if I don't make it?" Reed asks.

"You'll *make* it!" Honey cries, enveloping his son in a bear hug reminiscent of the one he gave him on his sixth birthday. "*Surgeon!*" he cries. "It's a loan. You'll pay me back. Every cent. Don't worry. Rhoda, you're my witness on this. Every penny he pays me back, and in addition, I demand . . . *I demand* . . . free medical care for a lifetime. So long as I live. Head to toe. The best. Nothing less. Is it a deal? Come on, Reed, shake my hand. Tell me it's a deal."

Reed stares at the money and then at his father. There is no choice at all, not really. "It's a deal," he says, giving Honey his hand.

Tears well up in his father's eyes. "Twenty years I waited for this," he shouts, "*twenty goddamn years!* My son . . . a doctor!"

The issue has been decided precisely the way everything in Reed's life has been worked out, with Honey Kreiger pushing from behind. Reed Kreiger must cross the great water and become a man of medicine. It is his destiny.

Before he can board the plane that will take him to Brussels, he and Lauren play out the final act of a drama he thought was already long finished. On a warm summer night a week before he is to leave, they go to a small restaurant in Chinatown for a farewell dinner. After the meal is over, Lauren looks at him in a funny way and says, "I've got a surprise. Only you can't ask me any questions about it. Okay?"

"Okay."

"Let's go then. . . ."

She directs Reed up Eighth Avenue to a midtown motel and leads him into the lobby. They ride upstairs together in silence. It is not until they have walked down a long hallway done up all green, white, and gold that Reed realizes what is going on. Lauren takes a room key out of her bag, inserts it into a door, and swings it open.

There, in the middle of a quiet, carpeted room, is the double bed of the dreams he no longer has. Lauren leads him into the room. She goes over to the bed, pulls down the covers, and steps out of her jeans. Naked, her body is boyish, slight. Her little shoes lie in the middle of the floor.

"Don't say anything," she says, reaching out for his hand, "I know it's right. I know it."

Reed knows how it will be before they begin. In turn he is angry, embarrassed, and finally just exhausted. He lies on the rumpled, sweaty bed, listening to the traffic hum in the street below.

"I can't," he says helplessly.

"You don't want to. . . ."

"It's not that."

"You're a virgin," she says sarcastically. "You could have fooled me. . . ."

"Lauren, look, I. . . ."

"What is it then?"

"I don't know."

"Some people find me attractive," she says defiantly. "You'd be surprised how many. But no, I've been on some kind of crusade for you. People laugh at me, you know? Adrian does. You think I don't know about your Friday nights? I know. People tell me. They love to tell me. . . ."

She begins to cry then, her thin shoulders quaking pitifully. For the first time, Reed realizes how complete her nakedness is. He has no idea what to do. "Don't," he says. "I thought we were friends. . . ."

Lauren leaps out of bed, the sheets tangling around her ankles like strands of seaweed. *"Friends fuck!"* she sobs. "Friends fuck. Oh," she moans, tears rolling down her face, "go home, Reed, huh? Go to Brussels. Go anywhere. Just go. Now. I mean it. I'll take a taxi home."

Grateful to get away, he is half dressed before he looks over at her and says, "You're, uh, not going to kill yourself here, are you?"

"OVER YOU?" she shouts, her pinched white face growing red with anger. "You asshole! You ace prick. I must have been crazy. *Get out!"*

Reed leaves her there, knowing he will not see her again before he goes. On the night his plane is scheduled to leave for Brussels, without having heard from her, he allows his parents to take him to the airport.

Bags checked, all possible conversation long ago exhausted, ("You got the passport? You got the money? You promise you'll write?"), the three of them sit in silence on a poured plastic bench. All around them, young kids about to embark on a summer of adventure in Europe squat on their knapsacks, laughing and talking, apparently able to depart without having to bid their parents goodbye at the terminal gate.

Half an hour before the flight is called, Lauren and Adrian appear, carrying a bottle of Dom Pérignon and a stack of plastic glasses. There are awkward introductions all around and then a toast to Reed's good health and future success. Lauren takes him to one side and gives him her going away present, an ancient silvered stethoscope no doubt worn by the venerable Dr. Gillespie himself. Reed's initials are engraved on the bell, along with the date. Class, right to the bitter end.

Reed and Lauren kiss goodbye primly, their mouths properly closed, as his mother and father watch. Then, all by himself, Reed walks off through the departure gate to the flight that will take him to his future, half a world away, to a city where he has never been before.

BOOK TWO · **City Boys**

"All the box players will try to match up as well as possible with the other four offensive players. They try to avoid guarding empty space."
    DELMER HARRIS, *Multiple Defenses for Winning Basketball*

CHAPTER SIX

No SOONER do Reed Kreiger and Haymon Jacobs take their first, tentative steps outside the comforting womb of the neighborhood than they are deposed from their positions in the intricate hierarchy of the schoolyard. Although Liddel Gross stays behind, untouched by the sudden wave that sweeps nearly everyone he knows out of Brighton, the same is true for him. Shoved to one side by an entirely new generation of kids eager for a chance of their own on the first court, three more city boys must lurch toward manhood. The city offers them no alternative.

No longer can Liddel spend his days in the schoolyard hanging out and feel good afterward. Basketball is not going to make him a living. With Haymon away in Boston, Liddel is on his own totally, with no real purpose or direction. After a long winter spent not doing very much at all, needing money and desperate for work, he decides to become a peddler.

Although it is low work, more suited for beasts of burden than men, Liddel throws himself into it, trying to prove a point. In the vacuum that the old neighborhood has become, it makes no difference. All directions seem the same.

Each day from ten in the morning when the beach begins to fill until five at night when it starts to empty, from the basketball courts at Manhattan Beach along the esplanade to Brighton and then as far down toward Sea Gate as he dares go without having the old and crazy bastards who have worked the beaches in Coney Island for years attack him, Liddel Gross plies his new-found trade.

"HEY, *YOU! KNISHES! COLD SODA!*" is what he hears all day. "THREE TIMES I CALLED YOU, YOU DIDN'T HEAR? I LOOK INVISIBLE TO YOU?"

The *yentas,* with rolls of flesh bulging out from around the seams of their ancient one piece black bathing suits, the veins all purple and broken in their thighs, are his steadiest customers. Day after day they see him, and day after day they shout at him as though he has no other name but the product he is selling. To them, he is not human. Peddling on the beach is not a job done by humans.

The work itself is hot and brutal, the rag he wears tied around his forehead never keeping the stinging sweat out of his eyes for long, the two brown paper bags filled with merchandise growing heavier with every step. The sun is a constant fire. If he takes off his T-shirt and works bare chested, the skin on his back peels away in great strips, like the layers of an onion after it is boiled. If he keeps the T-shirt on, it soon becomes so sodden with sweat that Liddel feels as though he's suffocating. Put on the T-shirt, sweat. Take off the T-shirt, burn. There is no happy medium.

Only sand. Miles and miles of burning sand that sift through his cut-down sneakers, caking and breading his sweating feet like veal cutlets about to be fried. The braided handles of the brown paper shopping bags cut welts across his palms. The "cold" bag is loaded with cans of soda and frozen Milky Way bars layered between bricks of dry ice that burn like a fire if he touches them with his bare hands. The "hot" bag is full of knishes, each tucked securely into its own grease-soaked wrapper, a single slab of heavy kasha or mashed potatoes sandwiched between two layers of crusty dough.

All day long, children come running toward him, quarters clutched in their tiny fists, snot running from their noses. They drop whatever he sells them as soon as the money changes hands. Then their mothers charge over, *tsitskas* flapping, faces red with anger, screaming, "I TOLD HIM NOT TO TAKE IT HIMSELF! HOW COULD YOU SELL TO AN INFANT LIKE THAT? YOU'RE BLIND, YOU CAN'T SEE HOW YOUNG HE IS? GIVE HIM A REPLACEMENT . . . THERE'S A COP ON THE BOARDWALK I SWEAR I'LL CALL HIM. . . ."

"Enough," Liddel says as soon as they pause for breath, "enough. Here's another one. Enjoy it."

It is an old game. Many times, Liddel has watched the women send their children over to him. They wait until the kid drops whatever he sells them and then come on the run. As soon as they think he's out of sight, they pick up the sand-ruined knish or frozen Milky Way bar, take it to the water fountain and wash it clean. Then they feed it to a younger child, crooning, "See? All new. Good as new. A little water takes care of everything."

Liddel cannot afford to argue the point. Without a peddler's license, which no one has, the cops can give him a summons every time they catch him selling on the beach. Another old game. Twice a week, the cops come on the sand, three and four at a time, uncomfortable in their short sleeve summer uniforms and shiny black shoes. The peddlers run for the ocean, ducking down behind people so as not to be seen. The cops leave, cursing, and the peddlers re-emerge, chanting their litany once again, "HEY, COLD SODA! HEY, KNISH! COLD SODA, KNISH! OVER HERE!"

So Liddel never argues with the women who *kvetch* and complain. Service, with a smile. Always. But when they come back to him a day or two later, they find that his prices have gone up. By the end of August, Liddel is getting thirty-five cents for a can of soda and half a buck for a knish. Not bad considering that he buys the soda by the case for a nickel a can and the knishes at a stand under the boardwalk for fifteen cents each. The profit margin is unreal. On a good day, he can clear fifty bucks. Over a long weekend, he makes three times as much.

Liddel learns quickly. If he has to give a cop five or ten bucks to avoid a summons, he never hesitates. None of them wants to take a day off to go downtown and testify on a peddling violation. He even throws in a free soda and a knish now and then. Anything to keep the people happy.

The other peddlers, the old sacks of bone, the ancient crones with rags on their feet and babushkas tied around their heads, would rather stand their ground and argue, as though the cops have been sent by the Czar to deprive them of their land. "*SS*," they hiss, "*Gestapo!*" Liddel sees them daily, screaming like banshees, as the cops lead them off the beach.

By the end of August, Liddel Gross is virtually the last peddler left working the beach. On the Friday before the Labor Day weekend, he invests five hundred dollars in inventory, hiring ten young black and Puerto Rican kids to carry for him. Even with what they steal and drop, he still comes away from the weekend with over a thousand in cash, boosting his total earnings for the summer to nearly two thousand dollars.

With the summer over and the beach closing down for winter, Liddel takes all his money home, putting it on the table between him and his father.

"See?" he says. "Two thousand bucks. Made it this summer. You understand? I ain't a kid anymore. I can go out and make it on my own."

"How?" Cookie Gross asks, pushing the money away from him. "By peddling on the beach? Can't peddle in winter."

"I don't wanna peddle. Don't have to. I can open a *shlock* store on the avenue with what I got."

"True. You got the patience to put up year-round with those women?"

Father and son look at each other. "Go to college, Liddel," Cookie counsels. "Try it one more time. Be smart."

"College sucks."

"Maybe. But you need a trade."

"I want the one you got."

Eighteen years old now, Liddel is still not much bigger than he was as a boy. Cookie knows well enough that his son has a mouth on him that would throw the fear of God into anyone.

"For someone like you, this is no trade."

"I wanna learn how to work the points," Liddel insists. "You teach me."

"That's what you really want?"

"That's it."

"All right," Cookie says, puffing up his cheeks and blowing out a blast of stale air. "Let's talk money then."

The two men hammer out an arrangement. If Liddel agrees to enroll again in college, any college, Cookie will buy him a car and let him make his collections for him. He will take Liddel into the business. So long as he goes to school.

"You're gonna teach me, right?" Liddel asks suspiciously.

"Every Monday you go out and make pickups," Cookie assures him. "You'll learn by doing. It's the only way."

In the old Ford coupe Cookie buys him, Liddel goes out each Monday to pick up what Cookie's clients have lost to him during the previous week. He pays off what few winners there are at the same time. As part of his arrangement with his father, he enrolls in another community college and sits through boring lectures he knows have nothing at all to do with him. Liddel Gross has already chosen his life's work. Commerce. The science of buying cheap and selling high.

Then one of his old buddies from the schoolyard turns Liddel on to this great new thing. Reefer. After he gets high for the first couple times, Liddel realizes he can get right in on the ground floor on this. There is big money to be made on the street by peddling something no one can buy in any store.

Many other schoolyard boys come to this identical conclusion at the very same time. Suddenly, losers who could never get picked to play on the first court blossom into full-blown flower children, Brighton variety. Their hair gets long, a string of cheap plastic beads replaces the Jewish star around their necks, they exchange their straight-leg Levi's for flared bell-bottoms, and *presto!* they're dealers, the stoned super salesmen of the new generation.

Which doesn't mean that they really know what they're doing. Most of them get so high with their customers, they're lucky if they can remember what they've done with their scales, much less give honest weight.

Liddel never mixes business with pleasure. He sells good weed, gives a straight count, asks top dollar in return, and then goes home to get stoned on his own time. He's seen the way his old man runs his business. Like a pro. Liddel does the same.

Community college ends much the way it began for him, without making much of an impression. More as a joke than anything else, he applies to a pharmaceutical school downtown. The idea of a dealer going to school to learn about drugs seems pretty funny to everyone who hears about it but Liddel finds that the work interests him. It's real, no bullshit about it, and if he graduates, he knows he'll have a trade to fall back on. Filling prescriptions will always pay the rent.

One thing is sure. He's not going to become a member of his father's profession. Although he is still making pickups for the old man on Mondays, Cookie has yet to show him the first thing about setting up a book. The old man has kept the business of the business strictly to himself. For as much as Liddel now knows about the fine points of bookmaking, he could just as well have been delivering eggs for two years.

What with dope and dealing having replaced sports as his primary interest, Liddel can't even get very pissed off about it. He's been conned by an expert. He has to give the old man credit. What an operator. Bullshitting his very own son.

As soon as he banks enough money from dealing to feel comfortable about it, Liddel moves out into an apartment of his own in one of the new buildings that have gone up around the train station in Sheepshead Bay. Still close enough to Brighton to make pickups every Monday for his father, he's far enough away to be completely on his own.

So long as Liddel drops by once a week, the old man doesn't even seem to notice that he's gone. No reason he should. The way Liddel looks at it, they're both businessmen now, supplying people with what they can't get anywhere else. Like father, like son. How else could it be?

WITH HAYMON having found his own way into college, Liddel never hears from his father's good friend Max Trapp anymore. Although Max is still around, it is the new generation of kids shooting around in the city's schoolyards that interest him now. Max must know them all. Like the city itself, he is constant, steadfast in focus and direction, never changing no matter how dramatically life alters around him.

In a luxurious apartment in the best building on Ocean Parkway, surrounded on every floor by judges and lawyers and the owners of prosperous firms, Max Trapp lives surrounded by his past. On every wall in every room are mementos of a career nipped in the bud, framed high school and collegiate All-American citations, gleaming brass statuettes of basketball players with arms outstretched perched atop marble columns, silver bowls engraved with the names of tournament-winning teammates, scrapbooks thick with clippings laid out on the tops of bureaus.

In the thickest of the scrapbooks, one Max rarely bothers to open even for visitors he is trying to impress, is a picture of himself clipped from the old New York *Herald Tribune*. In it, Max Trapp stands with basketball in hand, his feet encased in what look like the high black sneakers now used only for handball. Max's dark and curly hair is waved high in a pompadour, his face a skeletal arrangement of shadows and hollows. From within the picture's frame, sixteen year old Max Trapp stares out at the world with his game face, a serious mask betrayed only by eyes as large and liquid as those of an immigrant fiddler.

Everything about Max Trapp, his style of dress, his hard street accent, the way he carries himself on and off the basketball court, speaks of an earlier time. The Fifties, when the game of basketball meant more in the Jewish neighborhoods of Brooklyn and the Bronx than it has ever since.

Back then, when Max Trapp sauntered down the Grand Concourse at night, making his way toward the corner where only those who were quick with their mouths or their hands could find a place around the lamppost, no one had to be told that he alone was different. Smart, certainly. All the sons of the hardworking immigrants who had hustled their way uptown from Hester Street to the Bronx were smart. They had to be. But Max Trapp was something more. From adolescence on, his ability with a basketball had made him special, an authentic local resource who would carry the hopes and dreams of the entire neighborhood into battle. Even so prestigious and *goyish* an institution as Columbia had come looking for Max Trapp, full scholarship in hand, eager to trade him an Ivy League education for a hook shot so deadly it could not be stopped by anyone.

All of it was gone now, an entire world vanished in less than twenty years. The Herald Tribune Fresh Air Fund game in the Garden where as a high school senior Max Trapp had scored thirty-five against the city's best. The very corner on which he had spent his every free moment, standing around the lamppost with friends whose names had become such Jewish stereotypes that parents no longer even bestowed them on their children.

Solly and Shelley and Kappy and Arky. The crowd. The crew. The gang, all of whom believed in a single gospel. "Without a scheme," Kappy would say in that high, nasal voice of his, rolling a toothpick from one corner of his mouth to the other as he talked, "you're a *shmuck*. Like all the rest of the *shmucks*. You see 'em on the Lexington Avenue Express at night, the paper under one arm, the mouth is open, and right away you know . . . un-*huh* . . . here's another *shmuck* who spent the last twenty years on the Lex Ave Express . . . with his mouth open."

To the boys on the corner back then, life was a simple proposition. Nine to five, against. The *goyim* had all the pcwer, the money, the good jobs. But they were soft and fat and stupid. It was time for the yids to get their share. There wasn't a guy in the neighborhood who didn't swell with pride every time John Garfield swaggered across the movie screen. John Garfield. Hah! Jules Garfinkel. In their most secret dreams every last one of them was a junior John Garfield, sneering and fighting and pistol-whipping his way up the ladder.

What really mattered for them all was having an in. Knowing a guy who knew a guy. Playing the angles. Getting it straight from the horse's mouth. Making a buck without having to sweat for it. On Friday nights, they'd pool their money and send Arky one neighborhood over where the line was better to get a bet down. When they hit, which they usually did, every last one of them would show up on Monday wearing a pair of shiny new cuff links, a silk shirt, a freshly blocked hat.

In summer, the scene shifted naturally to the Catskills. All-night poker games in hotels that maintained staff basketball teams made up of ringers from the city who got paid big money under the table to play. Some nights, there'd be more cash riding on a game between the Laurel and the Flagler than a man could make honestly in a year.

None of this had anything to do with Max Trapp. He alone was different. Kappy and Shelley and Arky and Solly went out of their way again and again to make this clear to him. There was no need for Max Trapp to dirty his hands by scrapping for nickels in the gutter. He was going to make it on talent alone, like some great violin prodigy whose humble origins were an accident of birth. For Max, Columbia would be just the beginning. After that he could go on to become anything he wanted. A rich and famous man. And every one of the boys on the corner would be able to tell his kids that he'd known him when. His triumphs would give their lives more meaning than they could ever generate on their own.

But when Max Trapp takes up residence in the rarefied atmosphere of Morningside Heights, no more than a half hour ride by subway from the corner, he finds himself suddenly thrown into a world he knows nothing about. All around him are the smooth-talking sons and grandsons of Columbia graduates, prep school products to whom everything has always come easily. Compared to them, the boys on the corner are absurd, nickel-and-dime *shnorrers,* the very *shmucks* they spend their time laughing at.

Max Trapp does not have to be told where the money and power are. For two years he does his best to fit in, wearing the right clothes, mouthing the proper phrases, smiling back at those who tolerate him only because of his ability on the court. He is making his way, the best he can.

By the end of his sophomore year, Max has sufficiently ingratiated himself with the powers that be to get invited to a prestigious gathering of graduating varsity athletes in a fraternity house near campus. To celebrate the end of their glorious athletic careers, virtually everyone gets so drunk that they cannot even be bothered to avail themselves of the black whore hired for the occasion. Instead, they begin bombarding the street below with empty whiskey bottles. One happens to shatter the windshield of a professor's car. Someone calls the police. The police arrest the whore. The next day, the dean of students begins an official inquiry into the matter. Curiously Max Trapp's name is the only one that comes back to him.

Since the code of honor by which the gentlemen of Columbia live and die applies only to actual gentlemen, no one bothers to come forth and speak in Max's defense. There are too many complicating factors, the undeniable presence of a prostitute hired to take care of Columbia's All-American quarterback making the entire incident too grimy for anyone to be involved in. No, it's far better to remain silent and graduate with a gentleman's "C," accepting a degree on the steps of Low Library in hot June sunshine. After all, it's not as though any one of them will actually ever have to see Max Trapp again. He comes from another planet entirely. The Bronx. No one can even figure out who invited him to the party in the first place. For sure, he did not belong.

That summer, Max Trapp is suspended from Columbia for a year. The newspapers carry the news of his shame. Only the boys on the corner rally around him. Max's time of exile among them teaches him more than he has ever learned in any classroom. Like them, he too is just another *shmuck* from the corner. He will never be anything else. Whatever he gets in this world he will have to fight for. His inheritance has already been handed him. A quick brain and a quicker mouth. The time has come for him to begin using them.

By the time Max Trapp returns to Columbia for his junior

year, he has already made the acquaintance of a crippled Coney Island bookmaker named Leon Gross who knows more about survival than the well-bred gentlemen of Columbia will ever understand. He is a masterful teacher.

Max learns that it really makes no difference whether the Lions of Columbia win by twelve, as most bookies think they will, or by six, the way Cookie Gross has it bet. By the time he graduates, having been named Columbia's outstanding varsity athlete as a senior, Max Trapp has more than five thousand dollars in the bank, ample reward for having led the Lions to two consecutive Ivy League championships. Let the ex-prep school stars content themselves with a niche in the Light Blue Hall of Fame. Max Trapp must have something more, something concrete. There is nothing quite so real to him as money.

Still, when it comes time for Max to begin his professional basketball career, he is but another number in the hopper, an additional entry on the list. In the lotteries of manhood, Max Trapp must take his chances like everyone else. It is enough to make a gambler out of anyone.

The first drawing in which he is involved is conducted by the National Basketball Association, the newly formed pro league that is still struggling to establish itself in cities all up and down the East Coast and across the Midwest. In the pro draft, Max would seem to be the logical first-round selection of the hometown New York Knicks. A local boy all the way, Max will be a natural attraction, certain to fill the Garden every time he runs out for the opening tap. But the Knicks consider him too small to play under the basket in the NBA. They decide to pass him by. Instead, Max becomes the property of the Minneapolis Lakers.

The second lottery in which Max is involved is one in which all the boys from the corner have already drawn losing numbers. In turn, Arky, Shelley, Solly, and Kappy have taken that long subway ride from the corner down to Whitehall Street to persuade Uncle Sam that the fighting Army in Korea will be better off without them. So far as they can tell, there's no real reason for them to get involved in this one. Since there's no Hitler or Mussolini anywhere threatening their people with extinction, the boys from the corner decide that the only smart move is to sit this whole thing out.

"Some war," Kappy says, chewing his toothpick into moldy ruin in one corner of his mouth. "You can't tell the North from the South. All Chinks."

With the help of Cookie Gross, who happens to know a guy who happens to know a guy who works at Whitehall Street, Max Trapp is found to be unfit for military service. For five hundred dollars, Cookie's Whitehall Street connection sees to it that a ruler is bumped half an inch. Forever more, Max Trapp's medical records will list him as standing seventy-eight and one-sixteenth of an inch tall, precisely one-sixteenth of an inch over the acceptable height limit for men eligible for the draft.

With the Army no longer a factor, Max journeys west to begin his pro career. To him, Minneapolis seems no more than a couple of streets, a bunch of small stores, and a lot of blond hair thrown down into the middle of an endless prairie. On all sides, the land rolls out toward the horizon without even the outline of a single comforting skyscraper to reassure him. The monotony is phenomenal. Five minutes in any direction and the city's grid of streets disappears, giving way to open, empty landscape.

The men Max plays with are much like the surrounding countryside, blank and calm, totally without emotion. Some are a good fifteen years older than him, aging remnants of a time when the game of basketball was played only in dank YMCAs and poorly lit church gymnasiums. Yokels of the first order. *Putzes,* who on the corner would not last out the night. Max finds it possible to make contact only with the team's other rookie, a burly black kid from the streets of Chicago named Blake Marion.

On court, when Max is given a chance, there is no one who can contain him. Basketball, in all its aspects, is his game. When he is on, the ball becomes an extension of his personality, an object he can will to do whatever he desires. In game after game, when he is allowed to play, Max pours in points and pulls down rebounds, performing like a man twice his size. And yet the Lakers consistently lose more than they win. It takes Max a long while to figure out why.

Regularly, he checks in with Cookie Gross back in Brighton to let him know how things are going. If Max thinks the Lakers are better than the spread, he puts a little money down on them. If not, he lays off. Since he's betting only on his own team to win or not at all, Max knows he's doing nothing wrong. After a month he's up four hundred dollars.

When the Lakers journey back to New York to play the Knicks for the very first time, it is a signal event for Max, the homecoming he has dreamed about night after night in Minneapolis. The sports pages of the New York newspapers take note of his arrival, speculating that he has a good chance to be named rookie of the year, chiding the Knicks for ever letting him slip through their hands.

Right away Max gets in touch with Cookie Gross. He has only just discovered something he still has trouble believing can be real. His aging, balding teammates, all of whom would look more at home walking behind a plow than coming downcourt on a fast break, are in business for themselves. They have a very tight little setup going to shave points and make money on the side.

"Can't be," Cookie says flatly over the phone after Max tells him what's going on in Minneapolis. "I don't hear no talk."

"Cookie," Max insists, "it's the *emmis*. Me and this other rook, Marion, the *shvartzer*, we're the only ones left out in the cold, playin' on the level. A New York yid and a colored guy from Chicago . . . why bother lettin' us in for a piece, right? Cookie," Max hisses, the words snaking over the phone, "these guys are *crooks!* *Gonifs*. And me and Marion are supposed to go out there night after night and bust our asses so it'll all look good in the box score the next day. No more. Tonight it's my turn."

Long before the Knick-Laker game begins that night in Madison Square Garden, there is no way anyone can get a bet down, not for love or money. The bookies who work the stands and arena at the Garden have watched the price on the Lakers drop all day long until they're forced to take the game off the board in order to protect themselves. No one knows exactly what's going on, but for sure something stinks.

As the crowd starts to wedge itself into the Garden, those with money on the game are already starting to bitch. A low, continuous roar wells up from the stands, a nervous rumble that comes from fans with money on the line and no idea what will happen next. The entire Garden is feeling the pressure. Clouds of nervous cigarette and belligerent cigar smoke roll out from the balcony, billowing up under the overhead lights so that the distant floor below can be glimpsed only occasionally, a lode of precious yellow metal glinting at the bottom of a steep ravine.

When Max runs out for the opening tap, the fans stand to scream his name, kicking over the cups of beer they've set so carefully down by their feet. A thousand tiny rivers foam down the steps of the old Garden for Maxie Trapp, the hometown boy. The noise, the smoke, the excitement—it all starts to get to Max. His body begins to vibrate like a tuning fork pitched to the frequency of the crowd. He knows he is going to put on a show for these people.

In the first half, as his teammates stand around unwilling to help, Max single-handedly beats the line to death. He hits his first shot from the corner. Then his second and third. His own special overdrive kicks in, and he storms up and down the court, oblivious to everything, conscious only of the ball and any opening that will allow him to break through to the hoop for sudden, thrilling layups and impossible running hooks.

With only Blake Marion helping him out under the boards, Max runs wild in the first half, scoring eighteen points, collecting a dozen rebounds. Every last head fake, every last single lightning move to the hoop remains etched in his memory forever. Max Trapp has just enjoyed the finest moments of his life on a basketball court.

At halftime, Max is cornered by a teammate in a bathroom stall and told to lay off. His message has gotten through. Although no promises are made, Max knows that no one on the Lakers will ever again be able to work a scheme on a basketball court without him. He is just too good.

Having gotten what he came for, Max commits three quick fouls at the start of the second half and spends the rest of the game on the bench. When the Laker lead evaporates and the Knicks come back to cover, it is no fault of his own. Max Trapp has done all he could to lead his team to victory. Never once does he think about the boys back on the corner who have been wiped out by their hero's sudden cold spell in the second half. Max Trapp has more important things on his mind.

Within the week, word gets back to the NBA commissioner that when the Knicks and the Lakers played before a sellout crowd in the Garden, all was not kosher. Although rumors are circulating freely among the New York press, they begin somewhere else. The Laker veterans, who have been making good money all season long by seeing to it that their team loses politely, have no desire to cut Max in for a piece of their action. It's far easier just to throw him to the wolves. Let him take the heat off them. For Max is a rookie in more than one way. He has badly miscalculated these men for whom he has no respect.

The NBA commissioner, a short, round man who smokes expensive cigars, knows that his first duty is to protect the new league's reputation at all costs. The collegiate basketball scandal that has only recently put the game back into tiny campus gyms is still fresh in everyone's memory. The slightest hint of a similar scandal in the NBA and the game of pro basketball in America will go the way of roller derby and professional wrestling. The fate of the sport itself is on the line, not to mention all the money the owners have invested in their new franchises.

When the commissioner flies out to Minneapolis, he goes armed with telephone records showing that Max Trapp has called a certain phone number back in Brooklyn seventeen times, always just before a Laker game. The commissioner summons Max to meet with him in a downtown hotel suite.

Knowing that without a signed confession, his evidence will not mean very much at all, the commissioner informs Max of the clause in the standard league contract that prohibits a player from betting even on his own team. Although everyone certainly likes to bet and it is betting itself that makes the game so exciting to the fans, NBA players themselves must be beyond reproach. Especially when word of a scandal has already filtered down to the press.

Like some grand inquisitor playing on the emotions of the accused, the commissioner first appeals to Max's better nature. Then he threatens him outright. Total amnesty is promised him one hour, a stiff jail sentence the next. For hours, Max sits surrounded by a cloud of thick blue cigar smoke, unwilling to admit a thing. The lesson he learned at Columbia is firmly imprinted in his brain. It is only when the commissioner offers to dial for himself the number back in Brooklyn that Max seems so fond of calling that he gives in, realizing that the game is over.

"Awright," Max says flatly, still not convinced he has done anything wrong. "Get me some paper. I wanna write my own statement."

Two days later, branding Max Trapp an "undesirable element in the sport," the NBA commissioner suspends Max from the league for life. Without benefit of a public hearing or a jury trial, Max is tried and convicted in print by newspaper columnists who only recently were lauding his talents. Now he is called "arrogant and ungrateful," a "reckless youth" who is a "discredit to his Ivy League education."

Never again will fans scream Max Trapp's name in an arena so blue with smoke the hardwood floor seems to be covered by fog. Never again will he vibrate with the crowd before a big game. Twenty-one years old, Max Trapp has an entire lifetime before him in which to find a new profession. Playing professional basketball for a living is out. The NBA has seen to that.

Never for a moment does Max believe that the suspension will stick. He enrolls in law school and spends three years studying the law in order to be better able to understand his own case. For he is still a consummate player, throwing in thirty and forty points a game in the meaningless Eastern League contests in which he plays each weekend.

When he graduates from law school, having fast-talked his way past the bar's character committee, Max files his first legal brief, a three million dollar lawsuit against the NBA for preventing him from earning a living as a professional basketball player. The NBA offers him an out-of-court cash settlement to drop the suit. Max turns them down cold. Max Trapp wants more than money. He is on a holy crusade now, one he is convinced he cannot help winning. His good name will be vindicated. Once the NBA is ordered in court to reinstate him, some pro team will immediately offer him a spot in its starting five. It is his destiny, the reason for which he was put on earth.

Although Cookie Gross tells him more than once, "Max, let it rest. Goebbels got a better chance of gettin' a seat in temple on Yom Kippur than you do of gettin' back in the NBA," Max cannot give up the fight. He knows in his heart that he is as good as any of the NBA's famous big men, Pettit, LaRusso, Yardley, any of them. A six-six forward who can throw in hook shots from all over the floor? There has to be someone interested in him.

But when his case comes up in court, the NBA produces a string of witnesses who swear that the league never had an official policy to keep Max Trapp from playing pro basketball. Team owners anxious to protect the league's good name fly in from all over the country to testify that the reason they never offered Max Trapp a contract was his size. He just wasn't big enough to make it in the league. From the witness stand, Blake Marion, now a weathered veteran in the NBA, lies straight-faced that no such thing as a blacklist ever existed, much less one with Max's name on it. Extensive testimony is offered about Max's strange performance in the Garden that night against the Knicks.

Max himself finally takes the stand in a desperate attempt to save his case, only to be admonished from the bench for being a hostile witness. The judge then throws the case out of court and orders Max to pay all legal fees.

Max is crushed. This is the final defeat. Even he must now admit that his career as a ballplayer is over, ended in a court of law by men who will never love or understand the game of basketball nearly as much as he. The frustration he feels is total, his bitterness constant. He begins to drink heavily, seriously considering suicide as he sits at yet another dark bar staring into his drink.

The practice of the law means nothing to him now. For it is the law itself that has failed him, totally. Within a year, he has forsaken his practice to go into what will become his real business, the buying and selling of college players to ensure that he will be able to predict the outcome of games being played all across the country.

It is more than a desire to make money that drives Max Trapp to do this, although money comes to him in job lots. Every single game he can fix, every last player he can buy is further proof of the ease with which anyone can be corrupted. It is a corrupt world all right, one in which only those on top are safe from prosecution. This is the lesson Max Trapp's life has taught him. Game by fixed game, he begins to buy back his self-respect.

Not even Cookie Gross can keep up with him, the mad bets Max places on games both fixed and unfixed too large for any one bookie to handle. For Max can no longer feel good with a couple hundred bucks riding on a game. It has to be a thousand. Then two thousand. Then five. The basic unit gets bigger and bigger.

Cookie soon ceases to be a business partner, becoming an old and trusted friend instead. Max begins to earn far more from fixing and betting on college basketball than he could have ever made as a player. Much of the money goes for women and whiskey and cigars, for drunken weekends spent in Havana, for good suits, and for a never-ending series of crazy horse and baseball bets. No matter. When the basketball season comes round again, Max Trapp will be back in business once more, buying and selling college players who come remarkably cheap considering how much Max makes by selling fixed games to other gamblers. For five hundred and a thousand and fifteen hundred, Max can find players willing to throw any contest. To a man, they are eager to earn a little money on the side. The final outcome means little to them. For Max alone, it is an all consuming passion.

Each night, in his good apartment on Ocean Parkway, Max Trapp cannot feel satisfied unless he has a little something going for himself. A little action. For Max Trapp, a night without action is like a week in the country, so boring it is hardly worth being alive.

Action is all that matters. Action makes Wednesday evening into Saturday night, transforming Max's nightly walk to the candy store on Church Avenue for the early edition of the *Daily News* an authentic adventure.

Did North Carolina cover? How about Clemson? Duke? Bowling Green? There is no game so unimportant it cannot be bet. Action colors all of Max's nights and gives meaning to his days. Action is all there is. Action forms the very core of his being.

Able to get by on only three and four hours' sleep a night, a habit he picked up on the road in the Eastern League, Max the Lawyer always has time on his hands. Often after he goes to see a game in the Garden, he rounds up four or five local ballplayers and takes them back to his place for a little party. A few French films, a blonde in the other room who takes everyone on, and then it's out to Chinatown for shrimp chop suey and sweet and sour spareribs, to sit bullshitting until the night is finally and conclusively dead.

Some nights Max can do no wrong. Bet after bet comes through for him and he is a winner, all across the board. These are the moments he lives for, the times when he is seized with an overwhelming sense of omniscience, a godlike clarity that he has known before only in his best moments on a basketball court. There is nothing else in life that compares to it, no combination of expensive sex, good whiskey, or imported cigars that even comes close.

For as Max's phone rings off the hook, one winning result following another, on games fixed and unfixed, he can actually feel his body begin to swell and grow until he becomes a colossus, a giant untouched by the petty complaints that trouble those who scurry around his legs far below.

It is then that Max Trapp knows he can unzip his pants and piss on them all. All of them. The poor dumb *shmucks*. All across the country, fans who think they've seen an honest game go home hoarse and satisfied, most of them five or ten bucks poorer for having backed the wrong team.

Max Trapp sits in his good apartment on Ocean Parkway, surrounded by his past, laughing to himself. They are all puppets on his string. The boobs. The poor dumb *shmucks*. Max cannot even feel sorry for them. He is too far ahead.

Which is not to say that he is being smart. With his everburgeoning reputation and the Federal laws against interstate gambling growing tighter every year, Max ought to be content to lay back and keep his operation small. But he can't. There's money crying to be made. So he goes looking for a big money backer, one eager to take chances Cookie Gross is unwilling to risk.

As soon as he finds one, his network grows bigger still, runners flying all around the country to distribute "ice," the money needed to ensure that a player will lie down during a given game. Max channels his bets through a series of known gamblers in various cities who get down with bookies of their own. On a good night, his money criss-crosses itself several times before surfacing in some national layoff center like Cincinnati, New Orleans, or Las Vegas.

With so much cash going down in so many cities all at once, it takes only a little while for word to get out on the street. Once again, something is fishy with college basketball. Only no one knows exactly what, or who is to blame. Bookies everywhere are taking a brutal beating. While they can't pull all the college games off the board, they can squawk like crazy when they get burned. The people to whom they pay protection money see to it that word filters into the office of the Kings County District Attorney. Certain families in the city are very annoyed at how much money their bookmakers are losing. They demand protection.

Detectives are detailed to college towns all over the country to question suspected athletes. Without warrants or corroborative evidence, they badger and browbeat frightened players into making full confessions. The trail soon leads back to Max Trapp's luxurious apartment on Ocean Parkway, where Max is confidently assuring his close friends over a tapped phone that the probe will never touch him.

When the District Attorney announces the list of indictments handed down by the grand jury called to hear the case, Max Trapp's name tops the list. Max confidently predicts they will get him for no more than associating with known gamblers. Then he goes to the trouble of helping out one of his "boys" who has been summoned to testify. A week later the tape of his advice is played in open court. The charge of subornation of perjury is added to the bribery and conspiracy counts already lodged against him. By shooting off his mouth when he should have kept it shut, Max hangs himself.

On the day the judge is to hand down a decision in the case, the courtroom is packed with reporters. The judge calls Max Trapp "an immoral man, who left to his own devices, would have single-handedly destroyed forever the ideal of honest athletic competition in the colleges and universities of America." He hits him with a stunning ten to fifteen year sentence, later to be reduced in Superior Court to from seven to twelve. Haymon Jacobs reads about it in the Boston *Globe*, finally understanding why Charlie Oceans warned him away from the man so vehemently.

After all his appeals are exhausted, Max goes to prison. For all his godlike fits of power, his deep-seated conviction that he is above the law and, in fact, has still done nothing wrong, he settles in quickly as a prisoner, becoming Attica's leading inmate pointmaker and bookie. All told, he does nearly four years, hard time. When he gets out, New York is no longer a city in which it is possible for him to live. The law has seen to that.

CHAPTER SEVEN

HAYMON JACOBS lies in his dormitory room in Boston, trying for
sleep. The corded muscles in the back of his bad left leg ache
faintly from another day spent pounding up and down a hardwood court during practice. The extra long bed seems too small.
The little room feels as though it will at any moment fold over on
top of him.

When he finally drifts off, a familiar dream unravels behind his
eyes. A younger Haymon Jacobs sits alone in an empty subway
car with sunlight streaming in through dirt-encrusted windows.
Neighboring coaches rattle in and out of view, swaying in counterpoint to the rocking, disjointed motion of the train as it makes
its way along the elevated tracks of Brooklyn.

Each of the stations of the line appears in perfect order, Neck
Road, Avenue U, Kings Highway, Avenue M, Avenue J, Avenue
H, Newkirk Avenue, the doors sliding open for no one, the air
that rushes in at every stop as crisp and polished as a brand-new
McIntosh apple.

A golden Saturday morning in October. In the pocket of the old
and faded Miller jacket Haymon wears is a pass that will permit

him to watch Columbia and Princeton renew their annual football rivalry at Baker Field. As an authentic prospect, a possible future star for the Light Blue, he has been invited up to take his first look at the school where he may spend his next four years, if he so chooses. It is like journeying to a foreign land.

And yet he is completely confident, as self-assured as only one who has never before left the confines of the old neighborhood can be. So far as he knows, Brighton is the world. Columbia has come looking for him. He has nothing to fear.

As the train rattles down into the dark pit of DeKalb Avenue and Fulton Street, Haymon sits waiting for the part of the journey he likes best, the thrilling ride over the bridge. When the train bursts forth into streaming sunshine, he sits open mouthed, staring at the rippled water far below. Like some long beaded mechanical thread being put through the eye of the needle, the train is pulled across the bridge. Then it descends into darkness once again. Above Haymon now lies Manhattan, an alien land, a place he does not know.

The train rushes uptown, taking on and discharging passengers, none of whom disturbs his reverie. So far as Haymon can tell, he is riding toward his future on a train made specially for him. At a station where the words "COLUMBIA UNIVERSITY" are spelled out along the wall in blue-and-white stone chips, the car in which he sits is suddenly flooded with a throng of laughing, talking people who confidently help themselves to seats as though they had reserved them long ago. Everyone is going to the game. This has suddenly become the game train. Haymon has never before seen one like it.

Entire families arrange themselves along worn wicker benches, men in good tweed suits holding briar pipes settling in next to well-dressed women with cameos affixed to their blouses. Angelic, rosy-faced children poke at picnic baskets crammed with gingham cloth-wrapped food. The smell of expensive after shave, good perfume, gin, talcum powder, and old tobacco drifts toward Haymon where he sits. The car is suffused with the odor of money. Who the hell are these people?, Haymon wonders. Where have they all come from?

His outfit, worn jeans, faded team jacket, old sneakers, and a madras shirt, which only an hour ago seemed to him the very essence of collegiate attire, now looks shabby, out of place. Although no one takes any notice of him at all, Haymon does not have to be told. He does not belong.

Across the car from him sits the most beautiful girl he has ever seen. Her brown hair is streaked all vanilla by sun, her pale and perfect ice cream face sprinkled with chocolate freckles. Her short tartan skirt rides up every now and then, revealing an electric flash of firm brown thigh above her argyle socks.

A young man not much older than himself slides in next to the girl, as though invited. Between them there is some kind of mutual understanding Haymon does not recognize. It is as though they have always known each other. The young man's oxblood loafers are polished to mirror perfection. A gold key hangs from the slit pocket of his vest. His three-piece suit is a work of art. The girl begins to talk. She has missed her bus and then a train and lost her suitcase somewhere only this morning. It is still early in the day. The girl is very drunk.

The young man approves. Grinning, he reaches into his jacket and withdraws a silver flask. The girl takes it and tips it to her mouth, letting the whiskey run down her throat in a long, gurgling slug.

The train slows to a stop at 125th Street. "Heart of Harlem," the young man says, as though he were a tour conductor. "My stop," the girl says dreamily, standing up and wandering through the doors just before they slam shut.

Haymon wants to stand, to shout and call out to her to come back but he is unable to move. These people will surely laugh at him if he does. So he lets her go. As the train begins to pull out again, Haymon clears a porthole on the grime-caked window with the edge of his hand. The girl with the ice cream face sits on a bench on the platform, her short skirt riding up over her thighs. Black hands and faces surround her. The young man with the serpent smile lifts his flask in tribute, toasting the entire car's good health. Everyone laughs. Haymon does not understand the joke.

Where are the people of the city that he knows so well?, Haymon wonders. The harried stock clerks in white short-sleeve nylon shirts, the fat old women carrying their lives around in wrinkled shopping bags from A & S, the mad, grizzled bums mumbling of Joe DiMaggio, Albert Einstein, and the Club Baby Grand on 125th Street, three drinks for a dollar before noon? Where are the winos, the derelicts, the lunatics who ride this train back and forth day after day without ever going anywhere?

It all grows choppy then, Baker Field very green in the cold late autumn sun, long shadows forming on the field as the bass drum booms and the home crowd sings a single refrain over and over. "OH, WHO OWNS NEW YORK?/OH, WHO OWNS NEW YORK?" the people carol heartily, responding to their own question without waiting for an answer. "OH, WE OWN NEW YORK!/OH, WE OWN NEW YORK!/C-O-L-U-M-B-I-A!"

Indeed. Never once does Haymon wake up from his dream without knowing that truly these are the people who own New York, just as they own everything. Haymon Jacobs has boarded a train on which he can never be anything but another grimy stranger, awaiting the arrival of a station he recognizes so that he can stumble down the steps and go back to where he belongs. Which is . . . nowhere.

In Boston no less than Brooklyn, Haymon Jacobs is an outcast. The social and political protest movements sweeping the nation's campuses interest him not at all. Although upon occasion he can be seen at this or that on-campus rally, towering over the bearded guerrilla horde, he never once seriously contemplates joining their struggle. As he stands listening to the shouted rhetoric, his oversized hands shoved deep into the pockets of his jacket, his long horse face screwed up with concentration, his mind is elsewhere.

Haymon's politics extend to the limits of his oversized body and no farther. Let others join radical groups and march in circles, carrying picket signs. Haymon runs laps, working on his leg. Let others occupy buildings, demand amnesty, and then angrily build bombs when they are expelled from school and made suddenly eligible for the draft. Haymon builds his body in the weight room, knowing that he is already exempt from the draft because he is seven feet tall, the Federal government having somehow grasped most of what his classmates never intuit.

Haymon Jacobs is not like any of them. Not in any way, shape, or form. He fights only his own wars, on the basketball court. Never will he kill another man, except perhaps if that man gets between him and the hoop when his team needs a crucial basket. It is a peculiar form of pacifism perhaps, one that has more to do with the politics of his own odd personality than of principle. Considering some of the wild-eyed killers Charlie Oceans has turned out, it is accomplishment enough. At Boston University, Haymon Jacobs goes his own way, expecting only the same from everyone else.

Only with his black teammates does Haymon make any real contact. Street hustlers every one, out for themselves, they are, like him, eager to get everything they can lay their hands on.

From them, Haymon appropriates an attitude. The principle of cool soon becomes his guiding credo. Real cool, as a philosophy of life, has nothing to do with race, religion, color, or creed. It is a faith open to all, enabling those who practice it to run their game on everyone all the time without copping to anything, ever. Take what you need when you got to have it. If they catch you with your hand in the cookie jar, just smile and explain that you were trying the bottle on for size. Your ass was put there for the world to kiss.

Haymon picks up quickly on what his black teammates are putting down. Behind a facade of mumbled one-liners, mad hipster logic, and dark sunglasses, he begins to float free and easy, untouched by everything going on around him. S'happenin'? Same old. Thass raght. T'ain't nuthin' to it. Uh-huh.

My, my. Got to be. Yeah. Got to keep on keepin' on. Shore. T'ain't nuthin' to it.

The way Haymon figures it, they are paying his way through college for only one reason, his ability to put the round ball through the metal hoop. Who he becomes on his own time is strictly private business.

More out of boredom than anything else one night, Haymon wanders into a faculty cocktail party. On his way to the bar, he nearly stumbles broadside over a girl who seems to be crawling across the party on her hands and knees.

"Too much," he says, stooping over for a better look. "Let me guess. You're searchin' for your identity, right?"

The girl stares up at him with great, nearsighted eyes. For a moment, Haymon thinks he is going to lose it. The freckles that cover this girl's face and the marshmallow streaks that color her thick brown hair are exactly like those of the girl from his dream. The girl with the ice cream face has finally found him.

"Dig," he says, trying to sound sincere, "I mean . . . like you lost somethin', huh?"

"My sense of humor."

"C'mon. You can tell me."

"It's a contact lens. Move your foot. God, you're just like him."

"Like who?"

"Darrel Lucas."

"Do I know him?"

"You should," the girl says. "Darrel Lucas was only the greatest big man in the history of Revere, Massachusetts. Led Revere High to three state championship finals, all of which we lost . . . because of Darrel. Okay? Now, go away. Please."

"Hey," Haymon says brightly, putting it all together, "I got it. You lost your contact lens, right? Couldn't have happened at a better time. I set an NCAA record last year for findin' 'em."

Having crawled across many a hardwood court in search of the non-existent lens one of the team's starting guards manages to lose whenever the club is winded and badly in need of a free time-out, Haymon gets down on all fours and begins combing the floor with his fingers.

"Got it," he says after a minute, coming up with the tiny lens perched on the tip of his finger. "Blew your mind, didn't I?"

"Congrats," the girl says coolly, taking the lens from him, licking it slowly all over and then inserting it back into her eye as he watches.

"Uh," Haymon says, trying to come up with something to say, "where's Darrel playin' ball these days?"

"In the yard outside my father's factory. He puts dowels in easy chairs."

"That good, huh?"

"You're joking. I *dated* Darrel for two years."

"And all I want is one night," he says, smiling. "I'm Haymon."

"I know," the girl says, finally giving in, "I've seen you play. I'm Linda. Linda Eller. Pleased to meet you, I'm sure."

Among her many assets, Linda Eller happens to be the very first girl ever to come up past Haymon's armpits when they dance together. Her father, "Big Gordo" Eller, is the owner and president of New England's largest discount furniture department store. Several times a day in Boston, Big Gordo can be seen on local television, saying, "It may seem funny/But I'll save you money/So put the kids in the car/Wherever you are/And make that midnight ride to Revere/Where the bulge on your hip/And the smile on your lips/Comes from the money you save/Shopping/The Big Gordo Way."

Having grown up with a father who is demonstrably larger than life, even on the tube, Linda has no trouble at all understanding Haymon. She too is big, nearly five feet ten inches tall in her stockinged feet, a trait Big Gordo passed on to her apparently without the benefit of discount.

She is also Jewish, though not in any way that Haymon can associate with the faith that his father abandoned. Having been born a member of Revere's ruling family, the crown princess herself, Linda has the hard, flat accent of a New England matron, as well as total command of all the attending social graces.

Linda plays piano. She rides horses. She skis. She knows which fork goes where when you're using more than one. She can also drink and get stoned and hang out with anyone without ever losing that regal bearing that makes her so irresistible to Haymon. For a boy still not yet so far removed from Cropsey Avenue to have forgotten the shit-stink smell of its decaying weeds in summer, Linda Eller is irresistible, an upper-class rose sprouted in soil that for years has been tended by flinty-eyed Daughters of the American Revolution.

Half expecting her to be a virgin, Haymon is at first pleased and then a bit confused when she offers no resistance the first time they go to bed together, making perhaps more noise than he feels it is proper for one with her background and breeding to make.

By the end of Haymon's junior year, they are seeing each other regularly. Without telling Linda of his plans, Haymon decides that she will become the centerpiece of his new life. No longer will he be always alone, an outcast, the outsized, freakish rider on a train taking him toward his future. Linda will demonstrate for all to see that he is conclusively worth knowing. She will complete him.

His personal life taken care of, Haymon Jacobs turns his attention to more important matters, the pursuit of a professional basketball contract that will set him up for life.

With the bidding war between the old, established NBA and the brand-new ABA just heating up, a seller's market exists for those with talent. Players with half his ability are being signed out of college for huge bonuses. Haymon is hungry for his piece of the action. In the spring of his junior year, as the campus agonizes over yet another student strike, Haymon makes a political statement all his own.

Without telling anyone, he files for eligibility in the NBA hardship draft, a curious fiction which allows any college player to turn pro before his class graduates merely by claiming he can no longer afford to remain in school.

During the summer, it is announced that Haymon Jacobs has decided to forgo his final year at Boston University in order to sign a three year, no-cut contract with the Boston Celtics for a sum said to be in excess of three hundred thousand dollars. Two weeks later, stoned on some very fine strawberry mescaline that he receives in the mail from Liddel, Haymon Jacobs and Linda Eller are married by a justice of the peace on Cape Cod.

Although Linda's parents are shocked by the marriage, their disappointment is insignificant compared to the venomous abuse the B.U. student newspaper heaps on Haymon's head when the news of his signing with the Celtics becomes known. Haymon Jacobs has betrayed the only college willing to give him a chance when no one else would. He has bitten the hand that fed him and walked out cold on a team that might have gone places with him in the starting lineup as a senior. Curiously, only Haymon's black teammates understand what he has done. To a man, they congratulate him for getting the money when it was there to be had.

To make sure the entire student body understands the magnitude of his treasonous act, the B.U. newspaper prints a long statement by the Celtics' general manager outlining the terms of Haymon's lucrative contract.

But what the statement does not say, and what the student body cannot know, is that Haymon's contract is largely conditional, based on his staying with the Celtics past his first and only no-cut rookie season. Only then will the big money start to come to him. The bonus itself, some thirty thousand dollars, is placed into a trust fund not to be seen again until Haymon is in his forties.

Never quick with a buck, the Celtics have bought themselves a lot without giving up much at all. Should Haymon fail to make the grade as a rookie, his contract will be worth little more than the paper it is written on. Should he blossom into a center who eradicates the memory of the great Bill Russell from the minds of Celtic fans, everyone will go home happy, most especially those diehards from Dorchester and Charlestown who have never been overjoyed at seeing five black men race up and down the court wearing Celtic colors. For them all, Haymon will be the great white hope.

In a press release that is reprinted in many newspapers, the New York *Daily News* among them, Haymon is described by an inspired Celtic PR man as a "concerned and colorful individual, known to those who have played with and against him as the HULK, after the comic book character of the same name, who possesses superhuman strength."

In the schoolyard in Brighton, where Liddel hears the news, Haymon's signing is much discussed and debated. The consensus is that Haymon has done it once again, walking out of college just as he walked out of high school to get all he could when he could. The nickname, which no one has ever heard before, is the subject for much laughter. Opinion is nearly equally divided over whether it refers to his still less than lifelike left leg or his curiously phlegmatic and increasingly unpredictable personality. No one, not even Liddel, can say for sure.

REED KREIGER learns of Haymon Jacobs' good fortune from a two line blurb on a back page of the *International Herald Tribune*. His tiny room in Brussels is littered with yellowing copies of the newspaper, which has become his sole extravagance as well as his only real link to all he has left behind. The news both pleases and disturbs Reed. Another schoolyard boy is making his way up. But a bit too quickly. With one giant step, Haymon Jacobs is already *there,* at the top. Reed Kreiger's path seems considerably more tortuous.

From his rusted iron frame hospital bed, salvaged by a former tenant from the scrap heap, Reed can look out across a concrete cell of a room to a window so ancient it cannot be opened. A scarred wooden desk emblazoned with the initials of all who came before him and a rusted gooseneck lamp complete the furnishings, standard fare in the "Zoo," the name given to the old, rambling apartment house in a working-class section of Brussels where most of the foreign students live.

On every floor of the Zoo there are encamped other refugees from the greater New York metropolitan area who are trying to become doctors. Reed shares his flat with two émigrés from the moneyed suburbs of Long Island who make it a point always to ignore him. Obvious members of a higher caste, they have long since given up on the dream that has brought them here. Instead, they will spend their year in Europe seeing the sights and getting laid, to return happily to Hungry Harbor Drive in Hewlett to enter into whatever wildly prosperous businesses their fathers founded thirty years ago. No such option is available to Reed.

Reed's only friend in Brussels is Mike Abrams, called the "Apeman" by all who know him. Short and dark, with the simian gait and thick barrel chest of a major league catcher, Mike Abrams sports a black beard any caveman would be proud to call his own. His head is suffused with a corona of thick, frizzy hair the Belgians cannot believe is real. Mike's southern accent defies belief. To hear him attempt to answer in class, in French, is an exercise in lunacy.

"Hold on, son," Mike says one morning as he and Reed rush out of the Zoo for an early class, "*Ah-tan-days, mon amee.* I don't see no tie. You gotta have a tie, son, or these Frog profs'll get frightened you're bringin' the revolution to Brussels. Lemme lend you one. Ah got millions. Know why?"

"Why, Mike?" Reed asks, humoring him.

"'Cause ah went to Centenary College. Evah hear of it?"

"Nope."

"Course not, you bein' a fuckin' Yankee. The teams there are named the 'Gentlemen.' Can you believe. Huh? The fuckin' 'Gentlemen' of Centenary? Think they loved me there, boy? Sure, they did. Like a princess loves a wart."

"Get me the tie, Mike. I'll take a history later."

As the weeks pass, Reed gets to hear all about Mike Abrams' life. There is little else to talk about in the city to which they have been exiled. In Brussels, the sun disappears at the end of September, to be replaced by steady, falling rain that never lets up. The Zoo turns cold and dank, water seeping in behind ancient walls so that the dark, badly plastered hallways fill with the stench of age-old rot and the stale smell of old Gauloises and Gitanes, the hard, acrid odor of crushed butts, dead smoke, and age.

In Reed's tiny room, the gooseneck lamp stays on through the night. Its jagged imprint burns itself into Reed's retinas so that he can see it even with eyes closed. The rain falls. The work load increases. Bone chains and nerve endings and the finicky pathways of the blood as it courses through the human body. Work that is as overwhelming as the weather. Like foot soldiers mired in the muck of basic training, Reed and Mike Abrams struggle to keep step.

"Kreeg-or," Mike asks one day, "can you believe livin' lahk this?"

"Like what?"

"Lahk a fuckin' baboon in a cage, boy. Studyin' by kerosene heater. Goin' to do the laundry for rec-reation. That yore idea of a good time?"

Reed shrugs. His father has sent him to Brussels to become a doctor. A doctor he will be. He has never considered the alternative.

"Shit, Mike, the Belgians like it here. That's why you see so many of 'em on the street."

"Yeah? You know that for a fact? You ever actually talked to a

Belgian? Uh-uh. You can't, boy. The're too busy eatin' chocolate and tryin' to stay outta the rain. No wonder they got the shit kicked out of 'em in every war. They never noticed. They were too damn wet."

"So go home," Reed says, "like Albano."

"Albano went home?"

"Yesterday."

"*Shee-yit!* That little scumsucker. Ah loaned him ten bucks last week. Damn . . . well, fuckit. Ah tell you boy, ah'd go home if ah could. Ah surely would." The Apeman laughs. "And ah could too, 'cept for my old man. He's a doctor, you know?"

"Yeah? Hey, Mike . . . you never told me."

"Shit, yeah. Thoracic surgeon. A major. On staff at Walter Reed no less. Can you imagine havin' a Regular Army surgeon as a father? Mah ass won't be worth sittin' on if ah don't last out two years here so he can get me in somewhere in the States. He tells me so. In every letter the fucker writes, *typed* on Army stationery. Imagine *typin'* letters to yore own son? Can you believe?"

"Yeah, well," Reed says, trying to offer his sympathy, "I got a pretty thorough old man myself."

"Got to be," Mike says. "We all little cripples here, tryin' to make our parents love us and say, 'Good boy, you done real good, son. Have a Tootsie Roll.' Shee-yit," Mike says, snorting through his nose, "nine years of therapy at government expense to find that out. Ah'm fucked up 'cause of mah old man. What else is new, huh? Now that ah know."

Reed can say nothing. There is only work and rain, the gray, misting sea fog and steady downpour that make the Belgians a dense, implacable people, impossible for a foreigner to know. En-isled by work, cut off from everything and everyone save for his fellow inmates, Reed knows only that he is pursuing a goal so distant that it seems imaginary.

When midterms approach, the pressure increases. Night after night, Reed sits across a bed from Mike Abrams, feeding him questions, poring through books for answers, checking indexes to search for etiology and historical references.

"Ah'm blowin' it," Mike says two nights before the exams begin. "Ah can feel it."

"Lack of sleep," Reed says blearily. "You're hangin' in, Mike, like everyone else."

"Nice of you to say so, buddy, but ah know it ain't so. Ah can't even sleep no more without thinkin' about what it is ah ain't had the time to read. Ah am fuckin' *blowin'* it."

"Not you, Mike. You're a rock."

Reed can think of nothing else to say. The Apeman looks bad all right, pale and thin and nervous. A mysterious rash Mike has contracted on his face is visible even through his beard. But then

Reed himself is feeling none too good. The clothes he has not had the time to wash lie in a fetid pile in the middle of his room, smoldering like a compost heap in summer. Often, as he sits studying at his desk, he can hear the Apeman in his room directly above, farting and grunting and mumbling to himself. "Soon," Reed tells himself. "In a week. It'll all be over."

By the middle of exam week, Reed gives up on trying to study in the Zoo. The Apeman has taken to swallowing bennies and pacing non-stop around his room both day and night. Reed can no longer bear the sound of his steps, each heavy footfall another reminder of all he himself still has not read.

Reed goes to his last test directly from an all-night study session in the library. The Apeman is nowhere to be seen. After he has turned in a blue book filled with information he forgets as soon as he writes it down, Reed catches a streetcar back to the Zoo. If he can get there quickly and rouse Mike from whatever stupor he has fallen into, there may be time for the Apeman to present himself at the exam room with some elaborate excuse and demand a make-up.

After climbing each step of the building's five winding flights on the run, Reed pushes his way into Mike's cold and darkened flat. "Mike?" he calls out, gasping for breath, his voice echoing in the long, empty railroad corridor. "You here? You missed the fuckin' exam, man. You oversleep or what? C'mon. You gotta call 'em or something, make 'em give you a make-up."

There is no answer. Reed pushes open the Apeman's door. No Apeman to be seen. He walks slowly into a room littered with the tangled debris of weeks spent studying beyond the point of distraction. To himself, slowly, Reed whispers, "Can . . . you . . . believe?"

The Apeman has taken the easy way out. From the tattered remains of a knotted bedsheet thrown over a heat pipe, the Apeman dangles in a quiet circle in the corner, eyes bulging out, face already purple in the gloom. Numbly, Reed notes that there is no smell of death in the cluttered little room, no odor at all save for the stench of dried sweat and old, soiled socks. Then he stumbles into the hallway to notify the dean in charge of foreign students.

Although he later has no memory of it at all, in the incredible confusion of having to answer questions posed by both anxious school officials and bored policemen, Reed calls home. If he can get to talk to his father, the nervous pounding in his chest will cease. The vague and unnamed fears he is feeling will go away. Honey will be able to tell him what to do.

But it is his mother who answers the phone. Honey is at work. Where else would he be at this hour of the day? Everything's all right, isn't it? Unable to find words for all that he is feeling, Reed begins to sob over the phone.

Fearing that he will opt for Mike Abrams' final solution and further disgrace the medical school's very tenuous reputation, the dean in charge of foreign students sees to it that a place is found for Reed in the university clinic. Led to a clean white bed screened off from the view of other patients, Reed is given something to make him sleep. He is tired all right. Very tired. It is as though someone has pressed him flat with a hot iron. After waking, he can find enough energy only to fall back asleep again.

After waking and sleeping and waking and falling back to sleep again, losing all sense of time in the process, Reed feels a gruff hand on his arm, shaking him awake. Unwillingly, he opens his eyes to find his father before him. A dream, certainly.

Reed blinks and stares. The dark sweat stains under the arms of Honey's shirt cannot be denied. The grizzled cheeks and hard, flashing eyes are just as they have always been. It is no dream. No distance is too great for Honey Kreiger to travel. He is here in Brussels, standing by the bed of his only son.

"Reed?" he says. "You're all right? The school called. French they talked. Like we could understand. I came right over. All-night flight. You're all right?"

"S-sure," Reed says, not very sure at all.

"We tried calling back. No one knew. Your mother was worried sick. 'My kid,' I said, 'hell, I seen him play with pain. He's a soldier.' I came anyway. You look pale. You're sick?"

"I don't think so."

"You don't *think* . . . or you *know*. Which?"

"I'm fine, I'm fine. Just tired."

"Tired is nothing," Honey snaps. "I just spent nine hours on a plane. You think it was a picnic? The food was terrible."

Reed tries to assemble the jagged pieces of what has happened into something his father will understand. Mike Abrams is dead. Why, he isn't sure. He stares at his father. As a concession to the continent of Europe, Honey Kreiger is wearing his one good suit. His tie is loosely knotted and pulled away from the collar of his best white-on-white shirt.

"Bad flight, huh, Pop?" Reed says.

"I heard about your friend," Honey says, ignoring the question. "He was a sick boy, no? A mental case, from way back."

"No. . . ."

"That's what a doctor here told me. The one who speaks English. A very disturbed boy. That's what he said. Why else pull a move like that?"

"He was . . . depressed," Reed says. "From the work, I guess."

Reed's tongue is thick and furry in his mouth. He knows what it is his father wants to hear but he cannot bring himself to say it. I'm okay, Pop. I'm gonna take it to them in the second half. Just give me the ball.

"It's so bad here?" Honey says, the hands that have smashed thousands of no-bounce killers to the base of the wall in Brighton fluttering in his lap. "Don't look so bad to me."

"It rains a lot. All the time."

"Depression," his father says, not listening. "The doctor here, the one that talks English, he says depression. Not uncommon among first-year med students, he says. Foreign country, strange surroundings. Depression, he says. *Hey,*" Honey says, rubbing a hand along his grizzled cheek, "I lived through it, *boychik*. A real Depression. People on the ropes. Eatin' potato skins and apples. Beggin' for work at a dollar a day, and you couldn't get any if you tried. So what kind of depression can there be when there's money. *Hah?* You tell me."

Father and son sit staring at each other. Although they are both in a foreign country, Reed realizes that Honey has not yet left Brighton. He never will. Jet lag, language barriers, there are no problems too great for him to solve. Tell him who to tip. He will throw the head doctor a twenty and tell him he's Honey Kreiger from Brighton Fifth. Give the kid a bed down front. Only the best always for the Kreigers from Brighton, no matter what.

We're all little cripples, trying to make our parents love us. So the Apeman said. So Reed remembers now and for the next three days as he and his father struggle to find something to talk about besides the quality of the hardware on display in local shops.

When the school year ends, Reed decides to stay on for the summer, working as an aide in a psychiatric clinic in downtown Brussels. At the end of his second year, he does well enough on the boards to be granted admission to a medical school in upstate New York. Reed Kreiger leaves Brussels on the same shuttle train that brought him in from the airport two years earlier, knowing one thing for sure.

Like Mike Abrams, he too is scarred, the incredible wounds inflicted on him in childhood by his overbearing father just starting to become apparent to him. No longer can he go back to him for help or advice. Instead, Reed resolves to keep away from the scene of the crime, the tiny apartment in Brighton where he now knows he will never be anything but that frightened little boy who was loved and congratulated for having chosen a lousy rubber dump truck over the expensive wooden hobbyhorse he so desperately wanted for his own.

If you can't take the heat, stay out of the kitchen. Hardly words to live by. And yet until he can come to grips with having been born and raised a pauper in a place like Brighton, Reed promises himself he will live his life elsewhere. There is a world entire outside of the old neighborhood. That is where he will make his future.

CHAPTER EIGHT

THE VERY first time Haymon Jacobs draws on the cool green-and-white home jersey of the Boston Celtics for pre-season publicity pictures, a kind of silent shiver runs the length of his oversized body. From toes as big around as radishes along the bunched muscles of his thighs up into his groin flows an electric current of pleasure that warms him the way no orgasm ever has. Still three months shy of his twenty-first birthday, a boy in law as well as actual fact, Haymon Jacobs has reached the very top of the game.

He has only to look at his jersey to know this to be true. Haymon Jay, the almighty Hulk, is not beginning his pro career as the property of some hapless team that will languish at the bottom of the NBA for years. He has been spared the agony of having to play for an ABA club that will not last out the season. Instead, he is a newly crowned member of the greatest dynasty ever to rule the sport.

The Celtics are a team with a winning tradition so long and awe-inspiring that even when they lose, they do so with a kind of class that does nothing to detract from their dignity. Seasons after which yet another championship banner has not been put up to hang with those already fluttering from the rafters of the Boston Gardens are rare. Merely by affixing his name to a Celtic contract, Haymon leaves behind him the ordinary citizens of the earth and becomes one of the truly chosen, an oversized Moses parting the Red Sea of poverty to pass over into the promised land beyond.

The benefits are immediate. Friends of the club who dabble in real estate are only too glad to help Haymon and Linda find that perfect little apartment in Brookline. Haymon's tax consultant and business manager informs him that he is now the part owner of a laundromat in Newton as well as a shareholder in a new singles condominium being built on the banks of the Charles River.

Does Haymon need a car? One can be leased from a rental agency associated with the Celtics at rock-bottom rates. Can he use some extra folding money? Local businessmen and civic boosters are falling all over themselves to have a Celtic, even one as newly minted and publicly inarticulate as Haymon, speak at their awards dinners and fund-raising luncheons. Just say a few words, Haymon. Anything. A check will follow in the mail.

Quickly, Haymon learns how intoxicating it can be to have an organization behind him guaranteeing his credit. The magic phrase "Charge it!" becomes a byword with him, his new apartment filled with furniture Big Gordo would never dream of selling to his bargain basement clientele.

All at once Haymon has embarked on a delirious double honeymoon with both Linda and this marvelous organization, neither of whom can apparently do enough to make him happy. His bigamous little heaven is upset only by Linda's refusal to join in the fun. No stranger to credit cards, charge plates, or stereos that come in so many components it takes an entire day to assemble them into a working unit, she is curiously unimpressed with all the wonderful things Haymon's newfound money can buy.

When she returns home from the first meeting of the association of players' wives, Haymon knows immediately from the look on her face that her debut has been less than a resounding social success. "They weren't nice?" he asks apprehensively.

"Nice?" she says. "Haymon, they were *so* nice I was afraid their faces were going to fall off from smiling. They were all *paralyzed*, from the neck up." Sitting bolt upright on the sofa, Linda creases her eyes into slits, pursing her lips like some old, dried-up society matron.

" 'Linda,' " she says, mimicking their squeaky little voices, " 'Linda Jacobs? Haymon's wife? Oh, dear, he *is* big, isn't he? I'll bet you have a special bed. But then you're big too, dear, aren't you? I've heard you're *talented*. Do you really play piano?' Thumb piano, I should have said. Honestly, Haymon, you should have seen it. It was *gross!* The black wives were the worst. They must have all taught Aunt Jemima how to bake. If I'd asked any of them to smoke a joint, they would have called the FBI."

"Maybe they were nervous," Haymon suggests. "Afraid I'm gonna put their old men out of a job."

"Whatever they were, they can collect old clothes and help orphans this year without little Linda. I mean . . . that's all right with you, isn't it?"

"Sure," Haymon says, "sure. I signed the contract, not you."

But Linda's decision not to join the exclusive social club the Celtics like to see their employees form disturbs Haymon. It is disquieting, a first return on what he himself begins to feel after he meets the team's veterans. Most are ten or twelve years older than he is, and suspicious. A kid his size, who's already been given a big bonus and a fat contract that's been written about in all the papers, there's just no way they're going to greet him with open arms. Let him work his way up, the way they did.

After the first month of the season Haymon has to look down at his team-issued sneakers to make sure he isn't just some lucky fan favored with a choice seat at the end of the Celtic bench. If the starting five were a powerhouse, a bunch of world-beaters, he might be able to understand his status as a lowly sub. But this year the Celtics will win no championships. They may not even make it into the playoffs. They are a bunch of old men who lose as much as they win. Haymon does nothing but sit and watch, growing more frustrated with each passing week.

"They're playing guys ahead of me," he tells Linda, "who shoot their outside shots with two hands. I mean, they should be in a rest home somewhere taking digitalis. I see 'em in the locker room during halftime. All they want out of life is to be able to take three deep breaths in a row without passing out."

On those few occasions when Haymon actually does get into a game, the Celtics are either ahead by twenty or losing by the same margin. He has to battle other unknowns for meaningless rebounds in arenas already deserted by fans rushing to get to their cars in the parking lot outside.

"Why'd they sign me if they ain't gonna let me play?" he demands of Linda, who can offer no answer. "I can't learn sittin' on my ass. All I do is sit."

"It's because you're Jewish, Haymon. All right? Does that make you feel better?"

"They can all pull my chain," he grumbles. "*Assholes.*"

What should have been Haymon's glorious rookie season in the NBA soon resolves itself into a mind-deadening routine. Show up for games, get dressed, take layups, sit down, go home. Sitting on the bench night after night is more than just a blow to Haymon's sizable ego. It's something more basic, a primary dislocation, as unsettling as a strain of exotic flu or a low-grade fever that does not register on any thermometer.

The game of basketball is the only religion Haymon really has, its rules the only ones he truly accepts. Forty-eight minutes of playing time divided neatly into four twelve-minute quarters. A twenty-four second clock ticking off the time a team has in which to launch the ball to the hoop. Ten seconds to cross the midcourt stripe. Three seconds, counting one-one thousand, two-one thousand, three-one thousand, in which to linger in the lane under the basket on offense.

These are the neat, well-ordered boundaries of Haymon Jacobs' universe, the simple bylaws of the only trade he has ever taken the time to master. Not that he ever thinks about it that way. All Haymon knows is that when he plays, he feels good. When he doesn't, he has trouble sleeping. It's that simple.

The imperial Celtic manner soon crystallizes all the resentment he has carried around within him ever since his accident, giving it focus and direction. Like some unusually high-spirited adolescent who becomes an authentic juvenile delinquent only *after* his parents send him off to military school, under the weight of the oppressive Celtic yoke, Haymon becomes a stoned, sulking version of himself, a giant cardboard figure who rarely smiles or ever has a good word for anyone.

Since he has to sit on the sidelines all the time, watching others play, Haymon figures he might as well stay high. Dope cuts the boredom and makes the time pass more quickly. Stoned, nothing really matters to him.

"Is it smart to smoke this much during the season?" Linda asks him. "Our long distance phone bill is gigantic. One day the mailman's going to open one of those packages your friend in Brooklyn sends you and we'll all go to jail."

"You don't say no to the shit when it's here," Haymon says.

"I'm still a student, Haymon. I'm *supposed* to be stoned all the time."

"Ah," he says disgustedly, "I'm in shape. You should see some of those fatheads suck down beer after a game. They can't even talk until the first six-pack hits. I could get high forty times a day and still take them to the cleaners, one-on-one."

Haymon will do only what Haymon wants to do. As his love affair with the Celtics wanes and becomes something more real, so too does his relationship with Linda settle into a pattern neither one of them could have anticipated before marriage.

Linda knows for sure that the honeymoon is over when Haymon takes to spending the first hour of every day in the bathroom alone with the door locked, come what may. His body is his business, he explains more than once, and simple processes like elimination take on a mystical significance for him that she can never plumb. Never the quickest of men when it comes to thinking on his feet, Haymon is made that much slower by his wholesale dope smoking. Even the simplest decision can become a matter of state when Haymon gets stoned and sits down to ponder it.

Not unreasonably, Linda expected that even after she was married, she would still occasionally be seen in public after dark. But going out of the apartment is no longer easy for Haymon. Every potential public appearance must be smoked on, carefully weighed, and then rejected. As a Celtic player in a city filled with basketball fanatics, Haymon can take no chances. In public, he is an easy mark. There is no telling who will come up to him to ask for an autograph or inquire after the health of some teammate he hates. There is no knowing what kind of dumb and insensitive questions they will throw at him. Just because *they* follow the team like the Celtics were Knights of the Round Table questing for the Holy Grail, they think *they* have the right to grab for his hand, his time, his attention.

It is far better just to stay home at night, get high, and watch the tube. Call Chicken Delight or the Colonel and eat in the living room. Stay home and stay high and hide.

Haymon's circle of intimate acquaintances soon narrows to his wife, his parents, and Liddel Gross, to whom he speaks once a week by phone. His parents are bound to him by blood, Linda by law, and Liddel is his connection, supplying him with the weed he must have if he is to go on with the charade the Celtics have forced him into.

It is not long before arguing comes to replace sex as the only activity from which Haymon and Linda derive mutual pleasure. Cooped up constantly in their apartment, they discover that it is possible to argue about anything. No issue is too small, no slight too imagined. Haymon's increasing insecurity and constant paranoia extend in all directions. If Linda takes his side against the Celtics, Haymon rails at her. What does she know about the game? If she tells him to be patient and wait them out, he suspects her of deserting him in his time of need. When she comes to games, he is mortified that she must watch him sit on the bench. When she stays home to concentrate on her studies, still having one semester left before she graduates from B.U., he's hurt and quick to accuse her of not caring.

Haymon takes everything out on Linda. Without warning, he can become the worst kind of bully, as though the years he spent walking Cropsey Avenue in mortal fear of the gypsies have taught him only the advantages of having the upper hand. Together, they ride a furious roller coaster of anger and rejection, terrible fights followed immediately by tearful apologies.

In the middle of the season, Haymon gets the bright idea that some of the tension between him and Linda can be eased if he asks a friend up to spend a weekend with them. Since the grass level in his stash box is reaching the drought stage, Haymon decides to combine business and pleasure and get in touch with Liddel. There really isn't anyone else he can call. Generously he even offers to pay Liddel's plane fare up to Boston, where the Celtics and the Knicks will be playing a home-and-home series on Friday night and Sunday afternoon.

"Nah," Liddel says, "I can drive. Do me good to get out of the city for a day or two. I got this fuckin' ghinzo drivin' me crazy. Wants me to take a thousand ups off his hands. Can you imagine? Me with a thousand fuckin' bennies? I'll open my own drugstore."

"Is it good stuff?"

"Do I know? Have I tasted it?"

"Bring some up. Maybe I can move it for you."

"Yeah?"

"I just said so, didn't I?"

"Okay. I see you Friday."

Although dealing in pills is something that attracts Liddel not at all, grass and hash being more his style, it's easy enough for him to say yes to a guy named Momo and cop ten grooved white tablets that look to Liddel like bootleg five milligram Desoxyns. One of the benefits of going to pharmaceutical school by day is that when Liddel buys on the street at night, he almost always knows exactly what he's getting. The way Liddel figures it, ten ups is a cheap enough price to pay for spending a weekend in Boston with Haymon and his new wife, whom he's never met.

When Liddel gets up there though, he's surprised. In many ways, Haymon is set up just the way he thought he would be, in a good apartment with a view that knocks your eye out and a load of furniture that looks as though it just came out of a showroom. The big guy's got a clothes closet with more suits in it than Field Brothers on Kings Highway, plus at least twenty pairs of shoes lined up beneath them.

But Haymon isn't happy. Liddel can see that right away. The first thing the big guy says to him after they tour the apartment is, "You bring the shit?"

"Sure. Two ounces, tops. Very fine smoke."

"How about the pills?"

"I got 'em, yeah."

"Give," Haymon orders.

"What is this?" Liddel asks. "You a pillhead too these days? Smoke ain't good enough?"

"Ah," Haymon says, "I figger maybe behind a couple of ups I can take some guy's head off in practice. Maybe then they'll have to give me a run. Know what I mean?"

"Just so long as you make sure you take it easy with this shit,"

Liddel cautions. "God knows what fuckin' hoo-yeah threw it together, or where."

Haymon takes the pills from Liddel, pops a couple, and an hour later he's wired, pacing the apartment like a caged animal, talking a blue streak. According to Haymon, the Celtics are fucking him over, but good.

"Cruise with it," Liddel says. "All the big guys put in their time on the bench. You'll get your shot."

"Easy for you to say," Haymon mutters. "It's their attitude, man. Like I can't be trusted to bounce the fuckin' ball during a game. It's juvenile, you know? Like high school. It's insultin'. . . ."

"You don't like it?" Liddel says. "Quit. Take the fuckin' civil service exam, go to work in the post office in Brighton, and we can have lunch together in Hirsch's every day. You'll be the biggest fuckin' mailman in the history of Brooklyn. You can deliver two-story houses without walkin' up the stairs."

"Funny," Haymon says.

"Yeah." Liddel grins. "I thought so myself. Where's your old lady?"

"We gonna pick her up, then go to the Gardens. Wait till you see where you're sittin', man. You'll shit."

"Downtown, huh?"

"Best fuckin' seats in the house."

"Hey," Liddel says, "guess who I see on my way outta the neighborhood, I'm drivin' by the yard. . . ."

"Who?"

"Charlie Oceans."

"No shit," Haymon laughs. "That fuckin' *spook*. What's he doin'?"

"What should he do?" Liddel says. "He sits on the schoolyard steps, waitin' for another seven-foot miracle to fall into his lap. You should see him, Haymon. Fat. No shit. He looks old. But he's comin' to the game in New York on Sunday. He wouldn't miss it."

"Yeah," Haymon says bitterly. "He can watch me sit on the bench, countin' the house. C'mon. We gonna be late. I rolled some joints."

As they ride through Boston in the brand new car Haymon's leased, the big guy goes on and on, complaining about the way he's being treated. Liddel can't help thinking that with this kind of attitude, there's no way Haymon's going to be around the Celtics for long. They'd have to be crazy to let someone who feels the way Haymon does take their good money. It's almost like the big guy's doing *them* a favor by showing up for games. He says nothing about it to Haymon.

When Liddel meets Linda for the first time, she's all smiles and *very* interested in talking to someone who knew Haymon before she met him. Liddel can see what Haymon likes about her. Class. Something in short supply on the streets of Brighton.

After an expensive dinner, the two of them sit behind the Celtic bench watching the teams warm up before the game. Linda leans over toward Liddel, her face all flushed, her large brown eyes shining.

"This is the best part right now," she says, "*before* they make him sit down."

"Yeah," Liddel says, puffing out his cheeks and sighing, a habit he picked up from his father, "I can dig it. I tell ya, it still blows my mind that he's playin' for the Celtics. If you'da seen him in high school. . . ." He shakes his head. "What a fuckin' stiff he was. Couldn't tie his own shoelaces. . . ."

"He's told me. You helped him, didn't you?"

"Ah. Yeah. Maybe, a little. He did it himself, really. Worked his ass off. Made himself a ballplayer, bad leg and all. Plenty guys with more natural ability are workin' in their father's fish stores now and here he is, a fuckin' Celtic. Excuse my language. It still blows my mind."

"Is that why he's so paranoid?"

"Is what why?"

"Because he's afraid he'll have to go back and work in his father's fish store?"

Liddel laughs. "You ever meet Haymon's parents?" he asks.

"Only once. In a restaurant in New York after we got married. He's very protective of them."

"He should be," Liddel says. "His old man don't own no fish store. He sits guardin' the fuckin' sidewalk, day in, day out. His old lady still works, you know. Even though he sends her money. She doan wanna stay home with the old man. You ever seen the house he grew up in?

"Cropsey Avenue," Liddel says without waiting for an answer. "The all-time fuckin' neighborhood. Gypsies and and junkyards. Niggers won't even live there. It's a miracle he even speaks English. Ah," he says, "I'm talkin' too much. Must be that fuckin' up."

Linda giggles. "I've been rushing for an hour. What is this stuff? It's wonderful."

"Speed," Liddel says. "Believe me, you don' wanna get to like it too much. Right," he says, looking down at his program, which he has creased down the middle and cracked open to the starting lineups as though it were a racing card. "Line says the Celtics by two. At home, I gotta think they're better than that, no?"

"I don't know," Linda says.

"Player's wife who don't follow the line, huh?" he says. "Good thing my old man ain't here. He'd be upset."

"He likes to bet?"

"He likes to know who's gonna win. It's like a hobby with him."

"Some hobby."

"Yeah, well. You know. You come from Brooklyn, you pick up all kinda strange habits. Believe me, you don' wanna really know about it. Not any more than you already do, bein' married to Haymon and all."

After the game is over, Haymon meets them in the alley where the players leave their cars. He has played not at all and is angrier than Liddel has ever seen him, white-faced, his teeth clenched, his lips bloodless. On the way back to the apartment, he swallows another pill.

Once they get home, Haymon disappears into the bedroom and stays there, watching TV. The noise from the television is lost in a torrent of music coming from the piano, where Linda sits with her hair falling over her eyes, playing as though there were no one else in the room. Liddel falls asleep on the couch to Liszt's "Hungarian Rhapsody." When he wakes up the next morning, Haymon is gone. Linda sits in the breakfast nook alone, red-eyed.

"He went out," she says, her voice flat and tired, "before you got up. I don't know where."

"That was really nice last night," he says. "The music, I mean. . . ."

"Do you play?"

"Me?" Liddel says in wonder. "You kidding? Only the radio. *When* it's plugged in."

When Haymon comes back, his arms are full of brown paper bags stuffed with groceries. He seems happy. Linda goes into the bedroom with him and they close the door. Liddel knows everything is going to be all right now. Only when the door opens again, Haymon has his team bag in his hand. "She wants to go to New York," he hollers. "*You* take her." On his way out, he slams the front door back on its hinges.

"He's so *crazy*," Linda moans helplessly after he's gone, shredding a crumpled Kleenex in her hands. "I can't believe how crazy he is." Tears roll down her face like the familiar notes of a piano concerto she has played much too often.

That afternoon, Liddel drives back to New York. By the time he and Linda reach the city, it is dark. They are both exhausted, talked out, conversation between them having died halfway down the Mass Pike. Liddel takes her back to his apartment, where she calls the midtown hotel in which the Celtics are staying. Haymon isn't there.

"Could he have gone home?" Liddel asks. "Nah," he says, answering his own question, "Cropsey Avenue. Why would he go there?"

In his old bed in the gray clapboard house on Cropsey Avenue,

Haymon spends a restless night. Linda falls asleep on the couch in Liddel's living room. She wakes up in the middle of the night and goes into the bedroom, where it is warmer. Several times she whimpers in her sleep.

Then, as though it were the most natural thing in the world for her to do, Linda rolls toward Liddel. For a long moment, he does nothing. Then he feels her hand reaching out for him. In their drowsiness, it all seems logical, if a bit lifeless and mechanical.

In the morning, Liddel Gross lies across his rumpled bed, his small, thin body outlined beneath the sheets. In the last few gray moments before the dawn, Liddel looks more impressive than he will ever seem in broad daylight. The dull twilight softens and smooths his too-sharp features. It lends an air of mystery to his dark, arrogant face, creating the illusion of life in his too-small eyes. For a moment, he actually appears to be handsome, with the kind of somnolent Latin good looks that are always in vogue in dim nightclubs and too-dark discotheques. Then the moment passes, and he is just plain Liddel Gross once again.

"Can you drive me to Madison Square Garden?" Linda asks plaintively, as though he owes her at least that much. "I know he'll show up for the game. I should be there."

"Sure," Liddel says. "Where else would you go? Myself, I think I'll catch it on TV."

After he drops her off in the city, Liddel drives home alone thinking how sad it is that this girl cannot understand what it is like to have something inside you that will not let you rest until it turns everything you touch into shit. When he gets home, he calls his old man and gets ten dollars down on the game, against the Celtics. The Knicks run them ragged. All things considered, for Liddel, it's been a pretty good weekend.

At the end of the season, the Boston Celtics trade Haymon Jacobs to the Phoenix Suns, getting really nothing for him in return, happy just to be rid of this troublesome rookie and his expensive contract. Liddel reads about the deal in the newspaper. He gets in touch with Haymon in Boston, who tells him that he and Linda are going to Phoenix together to give it one more try.

"Why not?" Liddel says. "Maybe the desert air'll do you both good."

What else can he say? It's not as though he can go out and steal Haymon a basketball and a pair of Converse and make everything all right. Those days are long gone. Sooner or later, no matter how big you are, you have to learn to walk by yourself. So far as Liddel Gross is concerned, that's the bottom line. On everything.

CHAPTER NINE

EACH MORNING in Phoenix, Haymon Jacobs awakens to the soft thwocking sound of golf balls being driven skyward at the driving range next door. Leaving Linda where she sleeps on her side of their extra-long queen-sized bed, he pads silently to the bathroom window to stare out at the lady golfers of the city as they stand silhouetted against the rosy desert dawn, so many bronze figurines all in a row, clubheads held high above their shoulders on the follow through.

Haymon cannot help marveling at these women. Although they are all aged and wrinkled, their hair tinted a uniform shade of silver blue, their golf game gives no sign that they are not all as young as they feel.

Having risen like phoenixes from the ashes of their husbands' funeral pyres to come here to the valley of the sun, they now play the game of golf day in, day out all year round. After whacking out a prescribed number of balls, they depart all at once, a frightened flock of crows in motion across a meadow. Then the young kids who work the range for money begin making their way across the manicured grass, stooped over in the hot sun, gathering up a crop of scuffed Dunlop Maxflis and DT Titleists.

First the women and then those who work the field for money, morning after morning, week after week. Some days Haymon spends as much as half an hour watching from the window, as though he expects to learn something about the city from this unchanging ritual.

It is the weather that has brought everyone to Phoenix, the unceasing sunshine, which increasingly can be seen only through a fog of smoke brown smog. Despite new shopping centers and towering condominiums that threaten to block out the sky, the wind that whistles off the desert still blows an occasional pinwheeling clump of sagebrush down traffic-choked Camelback Road, as though to remind everyone of the wasteland surrounding. Empty lots strewn with stillborn weeds and garbage dot the streets of Phoenix, standing out like the toothless gaps in a barfly's whiskey grin. Air conditioning seems the answer to all local problems. On his way to work, Haymon often sees the children of the city in A and W parking lots, pooling their money for dope and gas in order to make runs into the desert.

As a city, Phoenix belongs to the dead and dying, the aged and ailing, the retired, and the rich. Haymon sees them in the stands at the Veterans' Memorial Coliseum on McDowell Road. Out for a night on the town, they sit in rows next to the tanned and turquoise-laden young women of the city. From the playing floor, they look to Haymon like a string of wrinkled trout hooked through the gills, waiting to die.

The team for which they root, the one on which Haymon now finds himself, is an unparalleled collection of castoffs, rejects, and malcontents. To a man, the Phoenix Suns have been banished to the desert from other places, cast out and sentenced to wander the burning sand like Simeon Stylites in search of mercy and forgiveness. "The Flake Five," Bran Johnson calls them.

It's not hard for Haymon, standing half-naked in the dressing room after a particularly disastrous practice, to see why. Big Reggie Masterson, the sometime center, has twice narrowly escaped being arrested for knocking over liquor stores. Reggie keeps his .38 tucked ostentatiously in his equipment bag so that no one will "mess" with his stuff while he's showering. Red Carruthers, who is totally bald, is a gaunt, aging veteran of fifteen years of NBA wars. Red takes most of his meals on the rocks, with a water chaser in back. Gnat-sized Montie Williams boasts of being the only man in the league with one testicle, its companion in crime having been shot off during a gang war back in his native city of Moline, Illinois.

Haymon is able to communicate successfully only with Bran

Johnson, a player who belongs in this hellhole no more than he does. Selected by the Suns on a lucky first-round draft pick the year before, Bran regards the city and everything connected with it as an affront to his considerable dignity.

"Dig," he will say as he and Haymon sit smoking weed together after practice, "Arizona ain't no place for a man of color. Understand? Now if I was a piece of turquoise. . . ."

"Or a driving range," Haymon offers.

"Or a yucca plant, I'd be set. As is, I'm playin' for a coach who thinks Jesus cares whether we switch on defense, a front office so tight with the dollar they squeeze it till the eagle screams, and a bunch of fans who can't relate to nothin' less they be half-drunk, three-fourths mean, and positive it's your fault the job drivin' the brewery truck ain't workin' out."

Although Bran needs no answer when he launches into one of his nonstop monologues, when the smoke is good and the capillaries in Haymon's brain become engorged with blood, he will half-close his eyes, put on what sounds to him like an English accent, and inquire, "Mr. Johnson? Pardon me? But are you referring to this club? The Suns? The pride and joy of Scottsdale, Tempe, and points surrounding? The Marauders of Maricopa County?"

"Damn straight, Hay-mone. Shit, I got to go to South Phoenix some days after practice in order to find me a real run. If it wasn't for our illustrious team physician, none of these turkeys would even bother turnin' up at night for games."

"Ah. The good team doctor."

"Bless his prescription-writin' ass, baby. When he talks, *everybody* listens."

Around the league, the Suns are said to have deep-rooted personality problems. This means that whenever the coach calls a time-out to plot some last-minute piece of strategy, conversation in the huddle comes to resemble a play for many characters, with dialogue supplied by whoever's angriest at the moment.

"Kin you see me out there?" big Reggie Masterson will scream in Montie Williams' tiny face. "Or ain't ah big enough?"

"I kin see you all right, mother, do I want to is the question," Montie will answer. "Las' time I let you hold the pill, you was lookin' at it like you expected a formal introduction. Ball, this be Reggie. Reggie, the ball."

Guffaws all around. Open palms flashed upward to be slapped, as Reggie stands glowering, trying to think of something salty to come back with. "People, *people!*" the coach will cry, chalking plays on the hardwood like some schoolteacher gone mad at the blackboard. "Let's listen up now! We're trying to overload the weak side, the *weak* side, and hit the forward cutting through. . . ."

"This whole team be the weak side, baby," Bran will offer, doing his bit to help. " 'Less you get the ball to the Muffin soon, we all gonna walk outta here losers."

"You the coach now?" Reggie will demand.

"Uh-uh. I jes' tryin' to interpret what *he* say for you . . . Afro-Americans."

On and on, people jabbering at one another as Haymon stands helplessly, unable to believe the incredible chaos that swirls around even the simplest out-of-bounds play. "Hey," Bran Johnson sometimes yells as the team trots back on court, "let's caucus. We all gonna talk, we might as well *vote*."

Some nights, the active dislike the Suns have for one another, the coach, the front office, and the city they find themselves in manifests itself in magnificent individual efforts that power the team to victory. More often, the Suns lose ignobly, winding up at the wrong end of scores that would embarrass a junior high school club. For Haymon, suiting up night after night becomes an exercise in masochism.

Since the starting lineup is always subject to such unpredictable factors as Red Carruthers' relative sobriety, Reggie Masterson's anti-social attitude, and whatever player the front office is demanding be played or traded, Haymon and Bran often find themselves together at the end of the bench, watching.

To help pass the time, they establish the Cake Award, given nightly to that Sun who does the most to let his man humiliate him on offense or defense. Falling out of bounds for no reason while in possession of the ball or dribbling it off your foot on an uncontested breakaway layup counts heavily for points when award time comes around. "Way to *cake!*" Bran will scream from the bench after some incredible Sun misplay has helped the opposing team increase its already awesome lead. With one clenched fist brandished in the air and his body poised as though he were ready to spring into action from where he sits, Bran looks for all the world as though he were exhorting his teammates to victory. Several local sports columnists salute him for his undying competitive spirit.

One night after Reggie M. throws up five hook shots in a row that caress only the air in front of the net, Bran and Haymon battle over what to call him. "King Cake," Bran suggests.

"Pope Cake," Haymon says, going him one better.

"That there . . ." Bran says, waiting for it to come to him, "is the *HOLY ROMAN CAKE!*" Wildly they slap five on it.

Soon enough, the rest of the team picks up on it. A bad loss becomes a "cakewalk." All team hotels are "doughnut shops," their lobbies filled with "day-old pastry and hard rolls." Sex with more than one camp follower becomes a "pie contest," an all-out orgy with participants numbering in double figures, the "Grand National Pillsbury Bake-off."

Cake that chick. Cake your mouth. Cake, cake, cake. "Hey, blackout cake!" Montie Williams will yell to Reggie in a crowded airport.

"What say, cupcake?"

"Check that frostin' by the newsstand. Go on, brother, ask her. I bet she'd cakewalk your face till your nose froze."

Were it not for Dr. Armand Parest, all of it would be as Bran Johnson so aptly puts it, "almost like working, God forbid." A small wiry man with flecks of gray in his dark black hair, Dr. Parest begins the season as a well respected orthopedic surgeon, his small Salvador Dali mustache as well waxed as the gleaming floors in the exclusive medical building in downtown Phoenix in which he maintains a suite of offices.

The first time Bran Johnson goes to see the doctor about some lower back pain, he makes this wonderful discovery. The doctor has a thing about professional athletes. He wants to be their friend. Even the most casual visit by a Sun is enough to set his mustache a-quiver. No matter how many patients sit waiting in his outer office, Suns players are ushered immediately into the inner sanctum through a side door reserved solely for their use.

Dr. Parest is a quick man with the prescription pad. You want Valiums? He'll give you Valiums. Quaaludes? Sure. Demerol? Desoxyn? Desbutol? Sure, sure, sure. Whatever. All you have to do is name it and it's yours. Bran takes to spending an occasional afternoon in the university library in Tempe, searching for new and exotic drugs for Dr. Pep to prescribe.

Considering the quality of the weed just in from across the border that Bran cops in quantity in South Phoenix, with Dr. Pep's kind assistance neither Bran nor Haymon is without psychic insulation of one kind or another for long. The grass they smoke is usually so strong and resinous that it becomes a matter of necessity for them to drop a couple of ups before gametime so that they will be able to put on their sneakers without becoming unduly fascinated by the intricate canvas weave of the fabric and the perfect, twining symmetry of the laces.

There seems no limit to how high a man can get in Phoenix. For Haymon, home stands and road trips fuse one into another, becoming long, weird midnight excursions from room to room in motels that look exactly like the apartments in which most of the players live. The Suns soon become known around the league as *the* team to see for anything, much of what Dr. Pep prescribes eventually being sold elsewhere for a tidy profit.

The way Haymon figures it, when he bothers to think about it at all, he can just naturally get higher than most people and keep on functioning. Because of his size, it takes more of everything to get him off. He sweats so much during a game that by the time he gets back to the locker room all the speed and smoke he's put inside himself is caked along the corners of his mouth in a fine white froth. Some nights he comes back to shower looking like a thoroughbred that's driven the final quarter in record time.

Since the Suns move him from city to city like a piece of freight, transferring him from team bus to chartered airplane and then back again, there are no niggling everyday responsibilities to keep him chained to ordinary reality. So long as his body does what it's being paid to do, no one gives a damn about the location of his head.

Since he is constantly stoned, adrift in airplane terminals and motels, Haymon's never-sharp perspective on the way things work changes radically. Ideas that bounced off him in college now suddenly take seed in the soft redwood mulch of his cerebrum. He grows a beard. Night after night, he and Bran, his main man, spend their time rapping it down. Two pilgrims embarked on a search for meaning that extends beyond the numbers posted on a scoreboard at the end of a game, they alone are exempt from everything.

With Bran pointing the way, Haymon comes to realize how totally he is being exploited. The bosses, the men who own the teams and the arenas, shuttle players around as if they were cattle. They make millions while Haymon has to pound his body into jelly for pennies. The fact that the Suns regularly lose money at the gate and pay their players an average of seventy thousand dollars a year enters into his thinking not at all. The point is still valid. Haymon knows injustice when he sees it.

A beat or two after the more progressive elements of his generation have abandoned such beliefs, Haymon comes to identify with the great thinkers of his age. Marcuse. Adelle Davis. R. Crumb. He gives up meat, starts wearing bell-bottom jeans and cowboy boots, and smokes more dope than he ever did in college.

Never once does he consider letting go of the game of basketball itself, now virtually the only stimulus that can rouse him from the heavy-lidded disdain with which he views the "straight" world, i.e., everyone but him and his cosmic companion on the road, Bran Johnson. Behind a good joint edged with a couple of dexies, the fine focus knob on the world tightens up for Haymon Jacobs, events taking on a clarity and meaning they never have before.

Playing before crowds in Phoenix that would turn out in equal number and with more interest for a demolition derby, he ceases to worry about anyone but himself. As he never could before, Haymon begins to float freely in the game's liquid suspension, sliding through cracks in patterns on the court he's never seen before.

Stoned, Haymon plays like a smaller, more coordinated version of himself, faking with his head and pumping with his shoulders before putting the ball on the floor to go around his man for a dipsy-doo, now you see it, now you don't stuff layup.

Some nights, out of the forward spot, he becomes Super Haymon, the stud he always knew he could be. Pounds lighter than he was in Boston, he is both quicker and faster, a tiger on the boards, an authentic presence on fast breaks. Women take to calling him at the team hotel after games, asking if they can come up to "talk" to him.

"Be your johnson they wanna talk to, brother," Bran tells him. "Cat like you, they figger you jes' naturally better endowed. You dig? My man, you got yourself caught up in that black sexual myth. Ain' nothin' for you to do but groove wit'it. Shit, that stuff been keepin' me up late at night for years now."

But Haymon remains faithful to Linda, as though his constancy might ever make up for their dismal life together in Phoenix. Like a passenger on an amusement park bumper car, Haymon careens wildly from the hell of their shared unhappiness together to the despair he feels when they are apart. He cannot live with or without her or reconcile himself to accepting either reality.

Linda hates Phoenix, its broiling sun and barbecue-by-the-swimming pool social life being something she cannot relate to on any level. Bored and restless, she is unwilling to spend her days shopping with the other wives. Yet, despite her boredom, so far as Haymon can tell, she never once turns her attention to the little things he expects his wife to care about.

"Do I have to always tell you what to do around here?" he asks, fingering the dust that gathers on tabletops and pictures when he is away. "Am I your father?"

"Don't make me laugh, Haymon. One thing you certainly aren't is my father. He *never* yelled at my mother."

"I'm not yelling. I'm asking. Is it so hard to go to the store and shop? Is it an insult?"

"Get me a maid," she says flippantly, although she refuses to allow one in the house, "just like all the other wives."

It's not that Haymon wants Linda down on her hands and knees mopping the floor for him. He'd just like to know that housekeeping, as a topic, holds some interest for her. In his mind is a picture of his mother, attacking the sink in their house on Cropsey Avenue after coming home from a full day's work, as though a single dirty dish would threaten the well-being of the entire family.

Arguments that petered out and died in Boston are reborn in Phoenix, bursting into flower in the desert heat. As a peace offering one night, Haymon brings Bran Johnson home for dinner. At first, Linda is charmed by him. When she sees that the names of the black heroes that roll easily off her tongue, Fred Hampton,

Mark Clark, George Jackson, Eldridge, Bobby, and Huey mean little to him, her infatuation with him fades.

"Why you so hung up with *those* brothers?" Bran asks her point blank. "You think they any different from me? We all tryin' to get our piece in a white man's world. They got their thang, I got mine. How come one be more important to you than another?"

"You've got it all figured out, don't you?" she says, her anger flaring. "Prince Charming," she says, looking at Haymon, "and his criminal sidekick . . . Boston Blackie. You both make me sick."

"Woman is fearless," Bran says of her the next day. "Woulda made J. Edgar go for the Hoover." But he never comes to dinner again. Once again Linda has cut Haymon off from his friends and teammates.

By the time the final road trip of the season begins, the Suns are hopelessly buried in last place. Bran and Haymon party their way cross-country, swallowing anything and everything they can get their hands on, smoking and snorting as though the only purpose in life worth pursuing is total annihilation.

In city after city, they sit up together through the night rapping, blurting out all the fevered insights that whirl through their wired brains. Haymon's hands begin to tremble violently after games. On the rare occasions when he does try for sleep, a weird pachanga beat plays nonstop in his head, as though there were a Latin station broadcasting only for him with fifty thousand watts of clear-channel power and no way to turn it down.

His belief that everything will be all right once he and Linda get their marriage together keeps him going. It is the rock on which his church is built. "I know we can make it," he tells Bran, night after night, " 'cause we got the love. Am I right? Some people never even get that far. I love her. Everything else can be negotiated. Right?"

"What you want me to say, man?" Bran asks helplessly. "You already run this down for me a million times."

"Say what you think."

"I think it ain't no story book, man. Folks who can get their shit together do it behind closed doors. Rest of the world be three drinks behind, playin' the jukebox and bullshittin' in some bar." Haymon's face collapses. Suddenly he looks old, tired, dried up. "Nah," Bran says, reconsidering, "I guess you right, man. You and Linda, you different. You'll get it together. In time. Like my mama used to say. All things come together in time."

By the time the Suns return to Phoenix, with but a single home game left before the season ends, Haymon's face has gone that dead-white color peculiar to those who never go to bed before the sun comes up. He stumbles off the team plane at the airport and takes a taxi home.

But the car the Suns have leased for him is not in the carport. The apartment is dark, empty. Haymon sits in darkness listening to the air conditioner hum, waiting for the cold knot in his gut to unravel. Linda's clothes are still in the closet. She will return. He must be ready to face her when she does.

Linda comes in at four A.M., her face flushed, her hair hanging loose around her shoulders. Once again she is the girl he knew in college, the girl with the ice cream face who sat helplessly on the subway platform as the train pulled out in his dream. Something long imprisoned within her has been released. She is so obviously happy that he can hardly bear to look at her. He has to fight the urge to reach out and crush her grinning face between his hands.

"Where the *fuck* have you been?" he demands through clenched teeth.

"A concert," she says, her face telling him nothing.

"Brahms? Liszt?" he asks sarcastically.

"The Dead," she says. "Honestly, Haymon, you should have been there. They played all night. It was like being in Cambridge all over again. . . ."

"Who with?"

"Who with what?"

"Who were you with?"

"Oh, this nice boy who works at the driving range had an extra ticket and needed a ride. I wouldn't say I was *with* him exactly. Not really. What's the matter with you? I didn't even know you were coming home tonight. . . ."

"I CALLED," he shouts, "I CALLED. But you weren't home, you fucking bitch. . . ."

Snatching the car keys out of her hand, he storms out of the apartment. Wanting only to get away, he leaps into the car and heads for the desert, nearly standing on the accelerator until the inevitable red light comes up in his rearview mirror and the sound of a siren fills his ears.

For the price of two passes to the final home game of the year, Haymon buys his way out of a speeding ticket, driving home at a speed well below the limit with the cop as his personal escort. When he gets back inside the apartment, Linda is gone, her clothes closet cleaned out, her suitcase missing.

The train is pulling out. The girl with the ice cream face sits on the platform. Just as in his dream, Haymon feels paralyzed, unable to act, a kind of cold numbness taking possession of him so that all he can do is crawl into bed and pull the covers to his chin. Waiting for the two sleeping pills he has swallowed to take effect, he cradles a pillow to his chest for company.

When he wakes in the morning, there is a note on the dresser he did not see the night before. "Haymon," it says, "the season is over, for both of us. I wanted to tell you last night, but you never gave me a chance. I'm going back east to stay with friends for a while. Please. I just need some time, and a little space."

Time. Haymon could use some himself, to get back into a routine that even faintly resembles the one the rest of the world follows. A little space. To get away from the blaring music that now plays twenty-four hours a day in his brain. The merry-go-round season has suddenly ended, dumping him flat on his ass in an empty apartment in Phoenix.

Without reason or purpose, he ransacks the apartment, emptying drawers and overturning cabinets as though there were something hidden that he must find. When he finishes, everything he owns is strewn across the apartment, all his fine suits, good shoes, and expensive shirts laid out in mad disarray. He rampages through them like a child in the grip of a temper tantrum, ripping the shirts, spitting on the jackets, flinging highly polished loafers to all corners of the room.

Only then does he crawl back to bed. He lies staring up at the ceiling. A drop at a time, liquid fuel is being pumped into his brain. He can feel his forehead starting to swell as the pressure builds behind his eyes.

The tiny holes in the acoustical tile of the bedroom ceiling create a pattern he has never before noticed. In their random, perforated swirl, there is a face, sometimes faint and indistinct, then suddenly large and animated with laughter. The girl with the ice cream face, dotted all over with chocolate freckles, looking down at him with scorn.

Gathering himself together, he gets unsteadily to his feet, swaying on the precarious perch the bed has become. For a moment, he is back at Pennbrook before his leg gave way, that end zone open and inviting before him, his entire future still in the balance. Then he is punching madly at the ceiling with his right hand, knocking out the tiles one at a time, systematically destroying the face so that it can never look down at him with scorn again.

By the time he has finished, his knuckles are bruised and raw. A gaping row of holes runs the length of the room, as though awaiting a crew of carpenters to seal it all back up. Droplets of sweat course down his face, mingling in salt profusion with the tears dripping from his eyes. Gagging, he sinks down onto the bed. He is just too tired to go on any longer. The game is over.

A voice he does not remember asking for help refuses to leave him alone. "Haymon," it says again and again, "are you all right?"

"Liddel?" Haymon says, noticing he has the phone in his hand.

"What's going on, man?" Liddel demands. "You call me . . . and then lay the fuckin' phone down for ten minutes? You stoned?"

"Huh? Uh . . . lissen, Liddel. I think I'm comin' home."

"Where? When?"

"Now . . . I'll take a plane."

"With Linda?"

"I'm gonna take a plane. . . ."

"Listen," Liddel says, taking command, "go to the airport and get on the next flight to New York. You can stay at my place till this thing blows over, whatever it is. Okay? I got you covered, Haymon. Just put your ass on a plane and come home."

"Okay, Liddel," Haymon says dully, glad to have someone to obey. "Whatever you say."

The Phoenix Suns play their final game of the season without Haymon Jacobs. After it is over, they officially suspend him so as to be able to withhold his final salary check. One more basketball team has decided it can get along very well indeed without his professional services.

Carrying a bag that contains nothing but pills, Haymon Jacobs boards a plane bound for New York. Behind him lies the city of Phoenix, a tiny encampment in a desert littered with the sun-bleached bones of animals driven to ground for lack of water.

Although there are no mourners in attendance and no stone to mark the site, somewhere in that barren wasteland, the corpse of his marriage has been quietly laid to rest, half-buried in blowing sand. At the driving range next to his old apartment, the lady golfers go on with their play, the soft thwocking of golf balls being driven skyward the only indication that yet another day has dawned in the valley of the sun, now just the latest graveyard along the tombstone-choked path he seems to be traveling.

BOOK THREE · A Plain Pine Box

" 'What's gone out?' Mrs. Morgenstern said. 'The law? The law doesn't go out. The law says the plainest possible box. It's not a question of expense. That's the whole Jewish idea, a plain box. Dust to dust.' "

HERMAN WOUK, *Marjorie Morningstar*

CHAPTER TEN

THE VIEW from Max Trapp's living room window was expensive in the cheapest kind of way, a vista peculiar to the moneyed, tawdry slopes of the Hollywood Hills. Invariably, it awed those new to the city who were unaware that the truly expensive panoramas in Los Angeles lay tucked away behind curving iron gates in Holmby Hills, Benedict Canyon, and Bel Air. Many who negotiated the narrow, winding road up to Max's house spent a good five minutes stunned into reverential silence staring out the window, drink in hand.

There, out beyond the cracked and rotting sill Max had never bothered to replace, was the dream city they had all come west to find, the real life model for the orange, airbrushed picture postcard that was up for sale in every last tacky souvenir shop in Los Angeles. Sooner or later, it was this card that would find its way home to friends and relatives with some simplistic message scrawled on the back and an arrow scribed on the front to show precisely where in that throbbing purple basin of lights beneath the great white toothy grin of the HOLLYWOOD sign another pilgrim had come to rest, seeking fame and fortune on the coast.

From Max's living room, each letter of the HOLLYWOOD sign

was large and distinct, apparently near enough to reach out and touch. To the right of the final *D* stood a large white wooden cross that regularly ran blood red in the last light of day. The symbolism and simple melodrama of the choice, HOLLYWOOD or the cross, was inescapable. For most of Max's visitors, the choice was purely academic, those who came to see him at home having long since made their decision.

Directly beneath the living room window, where the stiltlike support timbers of the house itself stood encased in a foot of concrete, a small red flagstone patio surrounding a cracked blue kidney-shaped pool had been laid into the ridge so as to conform to its gentle slope.

Below that there was nothing, the hill falling away rapidly until it flattened into the cross-hatched grid of streets and boulevards along which the dirty bookstores, pizza parlors, and all-night movie houses of downtown Hollywood stood. At night the basin of streets became a hot, glowing bowl of light through which all kinds of iridescent creatures moved, seeking adventure.

Like virtually all of his neighbors in the Hollywood Hills, Max Trapp had managed to pull himself from the sleaze on the streets below to a higher level. Never did he have to experience for himself the seamier aspects of Hollywood by night, while continuing to make a healthy profit from much of what went on down there.

By day from Max's house, the city retreated and the hills, green in winter, sere and parched the rest of the year, emerged. It took the eye a while to make out the other houses but as soon as one was accustomed to finding them, they were everywhere, low, sprawling structures roofed with tile and sided with shingles, half-hidden among the creepers and the vines.

Not being one subject to the reveries of middle age, Max never thought of his house and its magnificent view as a fitting reward for all his many long years of struggle. The Bentley he kept safely locked in the two-car garage to the right of the pool and the large black Doberman without a name that barked fiercely whenever anyone got near the house were to him only a very good car and a reliable watchdog and nothing more. Max Trapp had been down to the bottom of the well too many times to think he was too old not to fall in again. Anything was possible, even out here, in sunny L.A.

It was to Los Angeles that Max Trapp had come after getting out of prison. Four long years in Attica, that cold stone shithole where the food had tasted like rat shit and the cells had reeked from dog shit and the crappers had never really worked at all. One shower a week. Armpits and assholes and sheets that never got any cleaner than a sorry shade of gray. Attica, before the riot that had made it famous.

He'd served as prison librarian, of course. It was almost automatic if you had white skin and a college degree, much less one from the Ivy League. Every Saturday for four long years, Max Trapp had given out his line for the Sunday games, both basketball and football, with every book he'd stamped. If you liked a team, you held out a finger for every pack of cigarettes you were willing to bet. If you didn't like the spread, you could go play with yourself. Max's line was the one and only. Soon enough, he'd had enough people owing him money and favors to keep the animals off his back. A man with a head for figures always found a way.

Even now there were times when Max wondered how he had ever made it through without banging his head into a bloody pulp against the bars some night. Tougher guys than him had gone under, guys who could stick a shiv into someone's back in the exercise yard and then walk away without breaking stride.

Even now he would walk into a john somewhere and get a whiff off an open crapper and it would all whirl back on him suddenly, the cloistered smell of animals in cages, rack on rack. Armpits and assholes.

After getting out, he'd actually tried to start all over again on Ocean Parkway, only to soon realize that it was not possible. New York could be one very small and uncomfortable town when they had your name and address on file in the DA's office downtown and a million questions to ask about every case they couldn't solve by themselves.

L.A. was another story entirely. It had taken Max awhile to get established out here but the nest egg he'd stashed away for himself before going inside had helped, having grown into a very comfortable sum by the time he'd hit the street again. A man with money to lend in Los Angeles could always find interested partners.

These days, Max Trapp was completely legit. He'd gotten in on the ground floor of a thriving industry, bankrolling hard-core flicks for theater release nationwide. Strictly quickie jobs, the films had cost no more than thirty or forty grand to make. Some had brought in nearly twenty times as much on rentals alone. Using the money he had made from the films, Max had branched out into a series of dummy corporations that put out hard-core magazines, loops, and mail-order products.

As to what was truly pornographic or really obscene, Max Trapp had no opinion, legal or otherwise. To keep himself abreast of the very precise, ever-changing, court-ordered definition of these terms, he had for years retained a Beverly Hills lawyer named Avery Fishback. Had Fishback not been so very fond of the good life, Southern California style, he might well have been a judge by now. Instead, Fishback's great gusto for the erotic, in both his personal and his professional life, had made him America's leading authority on pornography and the law.

Unlike Fishback, Max himself had never gotten any kind of special charge from the merchandise in which he dealt. To him the business had never been anything more than a quick way to make big money. Never had he allowed it to take over his personal life. Any magazine that cost a buck to put together and then retailed in the bookstores along Hollywood Boulevard for six-fifty was an item he would gladly distribute. On such items he had grown wealthy.

For one who could never again live in the only city in the world where he felt at home, Max Trapp no longer even had much difficulty with L.A. There were constant annoyances of course, obstacles and distractions that would not go away, but on the whole L.A. pleased him in a way he would not have thought possible after first settling in there.

To a great degree, this was because it had never been part of his nature to strive for a life so smooth and simple it soon came to resemble a baby's bottom, all pink and fragrant with powder. As a young man, Max had liked the ups and downs, the swerves, the bumps, the blind curves. He had liked getting them and giving them. Now that he was older, whenever possible he still took the Bentley off the freeway and headed for the downturning two-lane roads that ran through the box canyons of L.A., driving at speeds that would have stopped the heart of any experienced Grand Prix driver.

Today, at noon, he was scheduled to have lunch with Fishback at an exclusive tennis club in Beverly Hills. They had serious business to discuss. For the past two months, Max Trapp had been experiencing what was known in the industry as a severe cash flow problem. In real terms, this meant that he had a warehouse stacked to the rafters with product that was ready to be shipped. Until the newly elected Los Angeles County DA toned down his highly publicized war on porn, the product would be going nowhere. At lunch, Fishback was going to tell him precisely how much it would cost to convince the DA to convert his "war" into a negotiated peace.

Before going to bed last night, Max had carefully laid out the clothes he would be wearing today. It was a habit that had stayed with him since childhood, when he had always known the night before what he would wear to school in the morning. The suit itself was hand-tailored. The material had been boosted from an exclusive men's shop on La Cienega and was worth twice what he had paid for it. The shirt came from Turnbull and Asser in London. The tie was from Sulka's. The shoes were oxblood wingtips, the raincoat he liked to wear looped over his shoulders a gentle shade of cream. Looking prosperous, in a very East Coast, almost English manner, had served him well in Los Angeles, where nearly everyone dressed as though they would at any moment be forced to leap into a swimming pool as a sign of good faith.

When he was completely dressed, Max padded into the bedroom to take a long last look at himself. What he saw in the full-length mirror mounted at the foot of the bed pleased him mightily. As a final touch, he slid a handkerchief made of the finest Irish linen into his breast pocket, folding it in the old tricorner style that was no longer in vogue. Without turning to look, he knew that behind him Victoria was awake and watching him.

Twenty years younger than Max, with a body that might well have been hacked from stone, Victoria Marrow was hard all over, inside and out. It was the quality Max liked best about her. She had an insolent mouth, tiny eyes, long fake fingernails, and the smallest nipples Max had ever seen on a grown woman. Her large, hard breasts rode defiantly atop her rib cage like a set of overdeveloped biceps on a weight lifter's arms.

Victoria's real last name was far more Italian and difficult to pronounce than Marrow. Although they had been seeing each other regularly for almost a year now, Max often went for long periods without being able to remember exactly what it was. Then, in the midst of some intense business meeting, it would suddenly come back to him and he would have to struggle to keep from laughing out loud.

For a girl from the farm country of Northern California outside Sacramento, Victoria was something special all right. An actress of sorts, she had walked through her young life so far as though someone had carefully scripted and blocked out every move in advance. Many people that Max knew in L.A. were like that. It was part of the local charm. Only Victoria had made a science of it.

"Hey," Max said softly, looking into the mirror, "I'm goin' to see Fishback in Beverly Hills. You need a ride?"

Like some large, expensive cat coming slowly awake, Victoria stretched and moaned. Beneath the thin blankets, her legs parted, a mechanized parking barrier automatically swinging open for the bearer of the proper card.

"A ride in the *car*," Max clarified, wondering if she'd go to all this trouble for someone who wasn't helping pay her rent.

As though she had sensed what he was thinking, Victoria sat up in bed and let the covers fall away from her. Naked, she was perfect, as confident and fully dressed as he could feel only after having spent an hour on himself and then checking repeatedly in the mirror to make sure everything was in place. With her eyes still half-closed, she reached out to the night table for the tightly rolled joint they had both been unable to finish the night before. Sticking it into her mouth, she fumbled for a match and got it lit, sucking the smoke down into her lungs like Bette Davis working on a cigarette in an old-time movie.

"Jesus," Max said, although he had seen her do this many

times before, "how can you smoke that shit *before* gettin' out of bed?"

Victoria ran a careless hand through her tousled hair. "How can you get outta bed *without* smokin' it?" she asked, mimicking his hard, flat accent perfectly. Although he had also heard her do this many times before, Max smiled in spite of himself. "Give me a minute, Max," she said. "I've got a little surprise for you."

Max stepped aside and let her squeeze past him to the bathroom. After she had closed the door behind her, he moved toward the rumpled bed. On the night table lay one of those women's magazines Victoria never seemed to be without. A banner headline on the front cover caught his eye. "*REVEALED!*" it said. "The Male Menopause: What Women Should Know About Men Over Forty."

Max shook his head and began to laugh. Then he picked up the magazine, turned to the story, and found himself getting lost in it. When Victoria came back into the room, she was wearing only a pair of sheer black bikini panties. Her hair was freshly brushed. Max could smell the sweet perfume she had used to "freshen up" with.

"Mmm, Max," she crooned, grinning professionally, her teeth so perfect that when she ran her tongue over them it was like an ad on television, "that new toothpaste of yours tastes exactly like a stinger. I just know I'm kissing sweet, baby, all over. Ready? HAPPY BIRTHDAY, MAX!"

Squealing like an adolescent girl, Victoria came toward him in a cloud of sweet perfume, her bare breasts preceding her like a pair of expensive calling cards. Enveloping him in a hug, she playfully grabbed for him through his pants with her right hand, on which the fingernails were painted the color of blood.

"Forty-five." She giggled. "And I bet you didn't even think I knew today was the day. Go on, honey, open it. I had it made special for you. It's solid gold."

Max looked down at the small white Cartier box Victoria had put in his hand. It was his birthday all right. Number forty-five in a long and unbroken string. He had almost given up counting. After opening the box, he took out a pleated gold chain of the kind they were just starting to wear in Hollywood. From the chain hung a jumble of gold letters arranged in a square.

"What's it spell?" he asked, unable to make out the word the letters formed.

"*OUTRAGEOUS!*" Victoria laughed, bouncing excitedly from foot to foot. "I know you'll never wear it in public, baby, but please, Max, just for me, try it on. That way I'll get to see it."

"*Outrageous!*" she howled after he had reluctantly draped it over his head, letting it fall over his tie. "Suits you to a T."

Wondering what Fishback would think if he showed up for

lunch looking like some superannuated Beverly Hills hippie, with a chunk of Cartier gold swinging from around his neck, Max loosened his tie and slid the chain underneath the collar of his shirt. Then he smiled and patted Victoria on the head with fatherly affection.

"Go on," he said. "Get dressed. After Fishback makes me pick up the check, we'll catch the last couple races at Del Mar. Then we'll shoot down to La Jolla for dinner. Make it a birthday celebration all around."

Victoria bounced some more and kissed him wetly on the cheek. Then she went to get dressed. After she had closed the bathroom door behind her, Max picked up the magazine from the bed. Without thinking, he furled it in his hand and put it on the night table so that he could read the article on male menopause when he had a chance. There was no denying that he was older than he felt. Still, he was doing all right. The chain Victoria had just given him had to have cost her five hundred bucks, if it had cost a penny.

Decked out in his best suit, with the gold chain swinging beneath the collar of his shirt, he was about to drive into Beverly Hills to do a little business. And it was his birthday. All in all, things could have been a lot worse. The suit, the house, the girl, and the present she had just given him were all very expensive. In the cheapest kind of way.

CHAPTER ELEVEN

REED KREIGER pushed open the front door of his apartment. He walked briskly across the thickly carpeted living room floor, drew back the heavy purple drapes shielding the large plate glass front window, and stared out at the beach below to reassure himself that he was home at last, his working day finally over.

The view pleased him in a way no one actually born in California could ever understand. Because it looked out over the beach, his three-room apartment with wet bar and built-ins was the single most expensive unit in the complex of condominiums in which he had lived ever since coming to Los Angeles. As far as he was concerned, it was well worth the price. This secant of blue and sparkling Pacific belonged exclusively to him. It was his to look at, for as long as he liked, twenty-four hours a day.

Without having to check, Reed knew that everything in the apartment was precisely where he had left it this morning before going out to work, and exactly where it would be tomorrow. It was one of the great benefits of living alone. No object ever moved of its own accord. Had he been asked, Reed could have located everything in the entire place without having to search for it, down to the precise position of every last bit of food in the small refrigerator behind the kitchen counter.

It was a kind of stir craziness more commonly associated with prisoners than with residents of this plush suburb by the sea but Reed no longer wasted his time worrying about it. Having discussed the matter with several of his immediate neighbors in Marina del Rey, he knew that they too suffered from the disease. Apparently, it came with the territory.

Switching on the small color portable he had been given for Christmas, Reed draped himself over the couch and began examining his mail. It was the usual stuff, exciting four color ads for new and improved anti-depressants, copies of psychiatric journals he no longer had the time or energy to read, offers to buy impossible sums of life insurance at bargain rates. A doctor's mail.

Much like the weatherman who was now peering at a barometer on the tiny TV screen, trying to predict whether the balmy weather L.A. had been enjoying of late would continue, Reed made a regular practice of keeping a close check on his own mental climate. Without taking his eyes from the screen or letting go of the mail he was holding in his hands, he monitored the way he was feeling just at this precise moment. Steady, but not bright. Par for the course after a long day spent doing work that no longer excited him either spiritually or financially.

Like some mechanic who always listened with half an ear to the sound of the engine while driving his own car, Reed could never relax when it came to his own state of mind. Every good mechanic would tell you that his first responsibility was to keep his own vehicle in perfect repair. Since there never had been a mind in that kind of shape, Reed tinkered with his own constantly. Fortunately, he didn't bill himself at the end of the month.

In Los Angeles, self-analysis was a hell of a lot cheaper than foreign auto repair, a fact confirmed by the outrageous bill his own Italian-born mechanic had just sent him. The aging green Fiat roadster Reed had owned for years was becoming a very expensive habit. Whenever he complained about how much it was costing him to keep the car alive, his mechanic would simply smile and shrug and point to his own vehicle, a shiny, monstrous Cadillac. No better car had ever been made anywhere by anyone, his mechanic insisted. So why bother driving anything else?

Reed Kreiger would never drive a Cadillac. That was the car *they* drove, the fat, pink-faced, well-barbered physicians who maintained offices on Park Avenue and drove home each night to palatial estates in the soothing suburban hills of New Jersey.

As soon as the New York State Board of Medical Examiners had granted him the certificate attesting for all to see that he was a licensed physician and the Motor Vehicle Bureau had eased the basic tension of his life by giving him the magical M.D. license plates enabling him to park wherever he pleased, Reed had left New York and emigrated to Los Angeles.

Eagerly, he had undertaken a residency in psychiatry at a university as famed for its undergraduate athletic teams as for its advanced research programs. That he had made the right move at the right time was something he never doubted. Although living in L.A. was not without its drawbacks, it was still infinitely preferable to being stuck in the city of his birth.

Within the confines of that greater metropolitan area, a doctor was expected to be priest, healer, and rich man all rolled up into one. Reed Kreiger had no desire to fulfill either of the first two roles. Out here no one demanded that he even try. Not that parts of L.A. were really all that different from the New York he had experienced as an intern.

On a busy Saturday night the emergency wards of the great public hospitals in Los Angeles were as littered with gunshot victims and the bloody losers of knife fights as Bellevue. The only difference was that in Los Angeles no one gave a damn. No newspapers came leaping off the newsstands out here with stark, black headlines crying out about the latest inner-city atrocity. There were no newsstands. So far as Reed knew, there was no inner city. The Action Seven news team brought him all the information he needed, again and again, until any event, no matter how grave, became no more than a subject for their easy, jocular banter.

Like nearly everyone else who had come from somewhere else to live in L.A., Reed now tended to ignore everything that did not actually touch his own life. It was not until the Action Seven reporter started running down the sports news that he began to pay attention to the tiny screen before him. Only last month, the university's basketball team had won its third NCAA championship in a row. Not unreasonably, Reed felt that much of the credit still being given to the aging coach for having again led them to the title belonged rightfully to him. As the team's psychiatric consultant, he was the one who had soothed the egos and settled the arguments, keeping the machine well oiled and running smoothly.

He had fallen into the job nearly three years ago simply by being in the right place at the right time. Bran "Muffin" Johnson, who had since gone on to a successful professional career with the Phoenix Suns, had then been the mainstay of the university team. No more than a month after Reed had begun his residency, Johnson had been busted for possession of marijuana and then busted again a week later for the very same offense.

Terrified that their consensus All-American would have to spend his final season as a collegian in a municipal court rather than on one designed for basketball, the coaching staff had eagerly agreed to allow Reed to counsel Johnson on a regular basis. Anything to keep their number one boy out of jail. In retrospect, having become a member of the staff himself, Reed now knew that they would have just as readily given some gypsy fortune teller permission to set up his booth at midcourt so long as the gypsy kept Johnson in action.

Although at no time in his own career had Reed ever shown one-tenth of the ability with a basketball that Johnson possessed, the two had come to a quick mutual understanding, not the least of it being their shared belief that the game itself was as fundamental to life as drawing breath. Bran Johnson was no one's fool. Coming in once a week to talk to Reed about his impoverished childhood had been infinitely preferable to reporting to a parole officer.

It had all mushroomed quickly then, one "blue chipper" after another dropping by to see Reed to rap about the problems that just naturally came up when young black men were let loose in the relaxed, smoggy atmosphere of casual Los Angeles. Reed had kept them all in school, for which the alumni were so grateful that the university had gone ahead and funded an entire program for him to run.

Although he now had more athlete-patients than he could handle and a growing reputation as one of the pioneers in the field of sports psychiatry, the study of athletes under stress, Reed was not content. That first season had been the best, Bran Johnson returning dramatically in midseason to lead the team to the Pac Eight title and then the NCAA championship. The season just ended had been no better than a pale reflection of that first go-round.

Much like a mountain climber who had slogged through miles of treacherous brush to reach a distant, snow-covered peak only to discover much more brush and a thousand higher mountains, Reed knew now only that he could no longer afford to stay where he was. Going back down the way he'd come up was something he never considered. The time had clearly come for him to step out on his own and establish a private practice. All he needed was the money.

Getting up from the couch, Reed paced over to the window. The setting sun was putting oranges, pinks, and purples all along the sand down by the ocean, wire-brushing the beach a thousand shades of pastel. In Los Angeles, another long and boring weekday night was about to begin. Reed knew of no one he could call to help pass the time. So long as he could find something to eat in the little refrigerator behind the kitchen counter and a movie to watch on TV, he'd be all right. He could go to sleep knowing that in the morning the sun would definitely rise once more outside his picture window, the way it did every day in L.A. Then he could go to work again.

THE NEXT MORNING Reed woke to the sound of the telephone ringing by his bed. He had slept fitfully, dreaming that his father wanted to talk to him. In his hands, Honey Kreiger had held a videotape of Reed bringing the ball up against Hunter. Honey was convinced that if Reed switched hands on the dribble as he came over the midcourt line, he could make the pass to the far corner without having to stop and look. Honey Kreiger had been dead now for nearly a year, the same period of time in which Reed had been having this dream.

Putting the phone to his ear, Reed mumbled a sleepy hello. A familiar voice giggled from the other end and said, " 'A telephone bell rang in the darkness. When it had rung three times bed springs creaked, fingers fumbled on wood, something small and hard thudded on a carpeted floor and a man's voice said, 'Hello . . . Yes, speaking . . . Dead? . . . Yes. Fifteen minutes. Thanks.' " There was a slight pause, more giggling, and then the voice said, "Guess who, Reedie?"

"Uhm," Reed said cleverly, reaching for the digital clock he kept by the bed. Seven-sixteen. "God, Callie," he moaned, "why so early?"

"Why not, Reed? C'mon. Guess who wrote that. . . ."

"Mark Twain."

"Wrong."

"Clair Bee."

"Uh-uh."

"Carl Jung."

"One more chance, sweetness."

Reed opened his eyes to the day. "Raymond Chandler," he said.

"*Wrong!*" Callie cried out triumphantly. "Dashiell Hammett. Chapter Two of *The Maltese Falcon,* entitled 'Death in the Fog.' Now guess where I am. It's a two part question."

"Malta," Reed said glumly, rubbing at his sleep-filled eyes with his free hand.

"San Francisco, home of Sam Spade. They've swung me on to a turnaround to L.A. Only I'm not turning around. We can have breakfast together."

"That's funny," Reed said. "Most people I know work on Fridays. In fact, I'm one of them."

"That's the point, kiddo," Callie insisted. "We'll have a *working* breakfast together."

"You never give up, do you?" Reed said.

"Would you love me if I did?" Callie trilled.

Reed rubbed his eyes.

"Do you love me 'cause I don't?"

Reed swung his legs out of bed and felt the carpeting with his bare toes.

"Listen, you bastard, this is a phone conversation. That means you talk sometimes."

"Right," Reed said. "Only I was looking all over for the small, hard object that thudded on the carpet when I answered the phone."

"Silly," Callie laughed. "That was your heart. Or what little was left of it when you realized who it was calling. Your one and only. Breakfast, right? At the Apple Pan on Pico at nine-thirty. See you there, ace."

Then she hung up before he could say anything more. Reed replaced the receiver and walked into the living room, automatically turning on the little television for background noise as he crossed over to the big front window for his first look at the day. A gray pall cloaked the beach. He made a U-turn, headed into the bathroom, and turned on the shower. As he stood under its hot needle spray, he thought about Callie. She was starting to take this whole thing entirely too seriously.

He had been seeing her for nearly six months now. Cathy Compton, called Callie since childhood, had the long, willowy body of a dancer, great blue eyes the size of sand dollars, and a sheaf of corn silk hair that made her look like one of those girls in the commercials who laughed madly as they bounded across a meadow in slow motion.

To look at her, you would have thought she was the ultimate *shiksha,* as long and cool as a Ramos gin fizz on a hot summer's day. In truth, all kinds of turmoil boiled beneath that diamond-sparkly surface. Callie was one very nervous girl. It was as though her biological clock had stopped suddenly midway through her final year in high school. The hysterical adolescent concerns that had driven her then were all that still mattered to her.

Reed had picked her up on the beach one day, winning her heart forever by looking out across the collection of peroxide beach bums and deeply tanned off-duty stewardesses who were her friends and saying, "What is this? The local dry hump center?" He had gone home with her that very night, an instant courtship made that much easier by the fact that she lived no more than a mile away in another beachside complex of buildings.

Annoyingly, Callie's apartment boasted an even better view of the ocean than his. Having put in so much time with the same airlines as a stewardess that she was now some kind of in-flight personnel supervisor, Callie earned nearly as much each year as he did.

It was not exactly inspiring work for someone who had studied seriously to become an actress but it did pay the rent. L.A. was full of girls who looked and talked as though they should have been on one of those televised game shows sitting inside a lighted neon square. Most of them were collecting unemployment. Long ago, Callie had decided that until she found someone willing to pick up her credit card charge slips for more than a month at a time, she would have to work for a living.

Considering the way the girl liked to spend money on herself, Reed thoroughly approved of that decision. Their present arrangement suited him just fine. Callie was blond and very beautiful. Never once had he fooled himself into thinking that there was any more to their relationship than that.

After turning off the shower, he stepped out onto the mat and reached for a bath towel. Quickly, all thoughts of Callie Compton vanished from his mind. Using the towel, he cleared a circle of glass in the steamy mirror and inspected his face. It was a daily ritual. Carefully, as though adolescence might reoccur at any time, he searched his skin for pimples and blemishes. Although it was quite possible that squeezing such pimples could lead to skin cancer, it gave him no end of pleasure to do it.

Sooner or later every doctor made his or her own little deal with what they knew to be true as physicians and what they liked to do as people. Smoking cigarettes, eating junk food, drinking one too many at a party might certainly help put you underground. Still, under the aspect of death's ashy permanence, Reed had long ago decided that to refrain from giving the occasional zit a satisfying squeeze was patently absurd.

Having completed his inspection, satisfied there were no new dermatological developments this morning, Reed slapped on some body powder that had been lying around the bathroom for more than a year. Its label proudly noted that its only active ingredient was hexachlorophene, a substance now suspect as a cause of skin cancer. Lately, even good old Phiso-Hex had become Phiso-Derm. Nothing was sacred.

Wherever you looked these days, cancer beckoned, crooking its long and bony finger. Cancer of the phiso and cancer of the hex. Creeping cancer all around. Reed bared his teeth in the mirror and began to brush. Good old teeth. At least, they were cancer-proof. So far as he knew. In minutes, he was dressed and in the parking lot, warming up the Fiat, on his way to a "working" breakfast with Callie.

Only moments after he left his apartment, Reed Kreiger's phone began to ring. It rang for a long time and then grew silent. In an office some miles away, the very large man who was trying to locate him swore mightily when informed by his secretary that not only was Dr. Reed Kreiger not at home, but he also seemed to have no answering service to field calls in his absence.

"Is this fucker kiddin'?" Blake Marion said, more to himself than the mini-skirted secretary who awaited his further instructions. "Try his office then. I want this guy in here *today*. Shit, *everyone* in L.A.'s got an answering service. Even hookers. Keep tryin' till you find him."

CHAPTER TWELVE

A WEEK after his birthday, Max Trapp was sitting up in bed alone watching the late news on television when a report came on that made him turn up the volume with the remote-control switching device that he always kept within arm's reach. A chain of angry mothers armed with picket signs was making noisy circles in front of a newly opened dirty bookstore in Van Nuys. The new DA was right there with them, collecting as much free air time as he could get by making appropriate comments into a brace of microphones the TV reporters had shoved up into his face.

That the new DA was actively bucking for lieutenant governor and eagerly seeking any and all contributions to his political war chest was something that Fishback had told Max over lunch only last week. What Fishback had neglected to mention was what Max now found so fascinating. There was something very real and terrifying behind the DA's "Clean Up the Streets" campaign. These mothers. At the moment, they were making so much god-awful noise that no self-respecting customer would dare show his face within half a mile of the store, much less ever go inside to drop five or ten dollars on the kinds of magazines and filmstrips Max had made available nearly everywhere these days.

Max knew right away that he was looking at something far more significant than just the latest outbreak of San Fernando Valley fever. An authentic ground swell of opinion was building up on the streets. People had gotten their fill of porno and were finally making angry noises about it.

For a year now, the hard-core market had been glutted with product. Profits were still there to be made but the margin was getting smaller all the time. Production costs had skyrocketed. To bring people into the hard-core theaters in number now, you had to give them something they hadn't seen before, real actors decked out in expensive costumes with background music and fancy lighting, all of it in focus all of the time. Much the same was true for loops and magazines and books. Everything had to be a production nowadays. It was all getting to be too much like art for Max, whose artistic instincts were still restricted to what he could do with a basketball when the mood was upon him.

Over lunch last week, Fishback had half chewed Max's ear off about getting into hard-core video discs for private libraries. It was the coming thing, Fishback had said. Software. The technology of the future. It was not something Max pretended to understand. Having been born into an earlier generation, most of whose sons had gone into the garment center to buy and sell *goods,* Max Trapp was truly comfortable only with a product he could actually touch when it changed hands for money. In that respect at least, he was very old-fashioned.

Ever since his birthday, Max had found himself thinking more and more about what had once been instead of what now was. Perhaps he was truly getting old. Not that he doubted his powers. His mind was as sharp as it had ever been. Sharper. It was only that there now seemed to be another clock ticking for him, one on which the sweep second hand kept making nervous circles. More pressing matters than the hard-core business had been occupying his mind. For although he had accomplished nearly everything that he had set out to do back on that corner just off the Grand Concourse in the Bronx, he could not pretend that his life had been totally successful.

In his time, Max Trapp had come out on top against nearly everyone except the NBA. That the league had screwed him, as thoroughly and heartlessly as only a multi-million dollar concern could screw a young kid just out of college, was something Max had never doubted. He still could not find it in himself to forgive or forget any of them. The owners who had flown to New York to testify against him, the fat, nervous commissioner who had marshaled evidence that had told only half the story, and Blake Marion, now general manager of the Lakers, who had come shuffling into court like some faithful household servant intent on protecting his master's estate at all costs.

Only a few months before the trial had begun, Blake Marion had absolutely refused to step on a basketball court with Max up in the Catskills for just a pickup game. Despite that, Marion had felt no qualms about lying from the witness stand that no blacklist with Max Trapp's name on it had ever existed. Marion's skillful acting job in court had driven the final nail into the coffin. His reward had been a lifetime job in the Laker organization. And now Max Trapp and Blake Marion and the Lakers themselves had all come to Los Angeles to try their hand in a new marketplace.

Max sighed and switched off the television set, realizing that he had long since stopped paying attention to the news. Victoria's magazine still lay on the night table, open to the article on male menopause. That was it all right. He was having a simple problem with his biology. Hormones were short-circuiting all over his body. Glands were drying up and becoming useless. The male menopause had taken hold, with a vengeance. Max Trapp was undergoing a mid-life crisis.

Alone in his luxurious bedroom, Max Trapp laughed out loud. The idea was that absurd. Then he settled back into his bed to go to sleep. Perhaps the time had finally come for him to cut the hard-core business loose and try his hand at something else. For far too long he had pretended that he was content with his life, satisfied to lie peacefully in the sun by his pool without the mad input and output that had always been as natural to him as a heartbeat. To be sure, he was older. But if he was not still a gambler, then he was nothing at all.

For a month, Max took no action, conscious that all he was feeling might prove to be just a meaningless flutter, no more significant than a momentary dip in the price of some favored stock. One of the great lessons he had learned in prison was that patience was a virtue of the first order, an asset that always returned a far greater profit to its investors than its initial cost.

Then, after coming home one night after a long day spent arguing over the phone with distributors in the Midwest who were terrified to bring any new product into Ohio or Kentucky because a newly appointed federal prosecutor out there was waging a war of his own on porn, Max called his answering service. A "Mr. Jack English" had left him a message. Although Max was fairly certain that he knew no one by that name, the number he was supposed to call back seemed strangely familiar. After staring at it for a couple moments, Max realized that it belonged to one of his ex-partners. Jack Engels. Jack had changed his name again. It was probably a lot easier than paying his bills.

Back in the Sixties, Max and Engels had put out a tame little nudist magazine that had sold like crazy for a couple of years at three-fifty a copy. Then the emergence of true hard core had caused the bottom to fall out of the straight nudist market. The magazine had folded, allowing Engels to go back to his two real loves, photography and crystal Methedrine.

Max had continued buying pictures from Engels now and then. When he could keep his habit under control, Engels was both a competent man with a camera and an intelligent businessman. Then one day last year Max had come home to discover Jack Engels, whacked out on speed, using his pool to shoot a gay porn loop. Three guys with rods like timbers, oiled and brown with sun, had been putting it to one another in every conceivable position, with Engels getting it down on film from every possible angle.

"Jesus," Victoria had snorted, "what a waste of good cock."

Max had been less amused. He'd gone straight to his bedroom safe and taken out the small, unlicensed Walther PPK he kept there for protection. Shoving it right up into Engels' face, where he could not possibly miss it no matter how high he was, Max had thrown him and his friends out on their asses. He hadn't heard from Engels since.

Dialing the number the service had given him for Jack English, Max held on until a familiar thin and syrupy voice came on the line.

"Max?" Engels said. "Nice of you to call back."

"Nice of you to notice, Jack," Max said. "Unlike the last time we talked. What is it? You scouting locations again? Wanna use the pool to do some underwater stuff? Girl Scouts and fish?"

Engels laughed too hard. When he was finished, he said, "I owe you for that, Max, for sure. That's why I call. I'm into something now that's stronger than *dirt*. The hottest hard-core book in town. Or so all the dealers tell me. They can't keep it on the shelves. I'm looking to talk some business with you. I need glossy stock and ink and glue. Lots of it. Strictly cash on the barrelhead. I thought maybe you could connect me with your suppliers."

Max rubbed a skeletal hand across his forehead. For all he knew, Engels was on the stuff again. As far as Max was concerned, you could not get much lower than Engels in Hollywood and still be classified as human. The guy was like a boil, looking for a place to rupture. And yet Engels was not coming to him for money, as he had so many times in the past. Instead, he was talking about a capital transfer. Paper, glue, and ink. Max had all these things stockpiled in the warehouse. Maybe he and Engels could come to some kind of arrangement. They had before, many times.

"You wanna come over, Jack?" Max asked. "We could talk."

"When?"

"Whenever. You home? Drive over now."

"All right, Max. Half an hour."

Engels made an unintelligible little noise at the other end of the line, as though he were sucking on a lozenge. Then he hung up. Less than half an hour later, Max heard the sound of an engine being shut off in the driveway. The dog went crazy by the side of the house, and Max got to the door before Engels could ring the bell. Engels was wearing his hair long now, razor cut in layers over his ears. Behind him was a new black BMW Max was sure Engels had leased in order to impress his customers.

Max ushered him into the living room. "Jeez," Engels said, pacing nervously over to the big picture window as though he had never seen it before, "what a fuckin' view you got here, Max. Worth a million. Hey . . . have I got some stuff to show you?" A tiny gob of spit appeared in one corner of Engels' mouth. The whites of his eyes looked like a pair of Triple A road maps, a series of fine red cotton threads winding through them, going nowhere at all. A small gob of dry white spittle sat perched in the cracked corner of his mouth. There was no doubt about it. Jack was wired again. Higher than a kite.

"I can't tell you how this thing is movin' for me, Max," Engels said excitedly. "I can't find enough stock to print it on. Shit, I already pulped all those back issues and returns you let me have when we went outta business. I had thousands. All gone. And I'm still short. I could move five thousand a day if I could print 'em."

Max walked slowly across the room to the bar. He poured himself a large one, a healthy dollop of Chivas over a single ice cube. He had everything Engels so badly needed. For a price he could unload it all on Jack and come out ahead of the game.

"So whatta you got, Jack?" Max asked, taking a sip of the heavy whiskey and letting it burn its way down the back of his throat. "Feelthy peectures? French postcards? Eiffel Tower and all that shit?"

Engels laughed nervously and handed over the large black leather zip-up portfolio he had been carrying beneath his arm. "First three issues are in there," he said proudly, "plus all the proofs for the fourth, which the dealers are already cryin' for. Go on. Take a look."

Max laid the portfolio on the couch and unzipped it. The first thing that caught his eye about the magazine inside was the cover price. Ten dollars. Involuntarily he let out a long, low whistle. At ten bucks a throw, Engels' profit margin would be unreal, no matter how many copies he sold.

Carefully, Max flicked the magazine open and began thumbing through the inside pages. A wave of nausea and revulsion swept over him. Engels had found himself a new bag all right. Kids, some of them no more than four or five years old, bent over and bareass naked, standing with their legs spread so that their still undeveloped sex organs were up for public inspection. Max felt as if he were looking at a bunch of baby lambs that had been split open with a cleaver and hung out in the hot sun to dry. Little kids. That was the name of the fucking magazine, for Christ's sake. If this was where the hard-core business was headed, Max knew for sure he no longer had the stomach for it.

"How can you shoot this shit, Jack?" Max asked, fighting to keep himself under control.

Engels grinned crookedly. "With a Leica, Max." He grinned, as though he had come up with a brilliant line. Making like a photographer, he crouched down with an imaginary camera held to his eye and said, "Click-click-click. You know? Smile for daddy."

"Where do you find the kids?" Max asked, curious in spite of himself.

"Find 'em?" Engels said. "Shit, Max, I had to hire an answering service just to field all the calls I'm gettin' offerin' me models. Their parents, Max, where do you think? The Valley is filled to the brim with weirdos looking to make a buck off their kids. Hey, I got people tellin' me I'm performin' a public service by puttin' this thing out. You know, keepin' crazies on the street from grabbin' some eight year old into an alley. Now for only a double sawbuck, they can get off lookin' at this.

"I got other stuff too, Max," Engels said quickly, the gob of spit that had been riding up and down for so long in the corner of his mouth finally falling on to his shirt. "Stuff you wouldn't believe. For private collectors only, of course, but it'll blow you out of the box. Four year old girls makin' it with fifty year old businessmen. Whole families freakin' together, and it's the real thing, I swear. I tell you, Max, it's a whole new day out there. And this is the coming thing. It makes anything you got for sale look like wet noodles. And it sells. Believe me, whatever price I put on it, it still sells."

Max turned away and looked out the window. He could believe what Engels was telling him. This was the future of the hard-core business. Of that there could be no doubt. That it made him want to puke was irrelevant. Sick people had their hand on the throttle everywhere these days. From the magazines alone, Max could tell that Engels was raking in the dough. There was no way to estimate how much more he was taking in on films. Then there were all the fees for introducing perverts with money to their prey.

Max turned toward Engels. "Myself I got no interest at all in handling this book, Jack. But I do have a warehouse filled with stuff you can use. Printer's ink, paper, glossy stock, whatever you need. And I'm willin' to sell it all."

"Max," Engels said, "who has that kind of cash on hand?"

"Well, Jack," Max said, closing his eyes for a moment to visualize what the lowest offer he could accept would be, "you catch me at a weak moment. Just when I feel like unloadin' the entire operation. For, say, ten cents on a dollar in cash now, I could let you have it. The rest you pay on time."

"Sure, Max, sure." Engels grinned, thinking that was the entire deal.

"By cuttin' me in for a piece of everything you take in on this," Max said. "That way your credit is guaranteed and I don't have to worry about you makin' payments. The operation itself is all yours, Jack. I don't want shit to do with it. Just a percentage."

Engels sighed. "How big a percentage would that be, Max?" he asked, knowing for sure now that he was not going to get away cheap.

"Sit down, Jack," Max said. "Take a load off. We got numbers to discuss."

Four hours later, Max Trapp's bedroom safe was filled with fifty-dollar bills banded into thousand-dollar stacks secured with bank-issued wrappers. The money would take care of Max's cash flow problem for the time being and for a long while to come. As Jack English's new silent partner, Max knew the money would come to him. Even better, he would now be out of the hard-core business on a day-to-day basis. The move could not have come at a more opportune moment. Something far more important was reaching out for him now. Before he got too old and tired, he had one last score to settle. Now that he had the money on hand to operate with, all he needed was a plan. In time, Max knew that too would come to him. It always had in the past. In many respects, he was just a lucky man.

CHAPTER THIRTEEN

REED KREIGER stared out the single window to which he was entitled as a junior member of the university's clinical staff. Despite the constant stream of shot putters blown up beyond human proportions by anabolic steroids, foreign-born soccer stars suffering from continuing sexual identity crises, and varsity volleyball players who had grown up abusing every drug ever the rage on Staxe Beach in Santa Monica who came to see him, his office was no bigger than one occupied by some bespectacled instructor of freshman English who saw maybe one coed a week for a breathy knee-to-knee conference on "The Whiteness of the Whale," Chapter Forty-two, *Moby Dick*.

In the university's scheme of things, office space was strictly a matter of seniority. The longer you stayed on the payroll, the larger and more airy your working quarters became. As one of the newer additions to the staff nearly three years ago, Reed had been assigned this eight-by-eight concrete box tucked away one floor below ground level in an obscure little building that also housed the clinical behavior labs and the group therapy workshops. It was only one of the reasons he had to get out.

His single window commanded a startling view of yet another box, a large underground waterworks conduit that someone had tried to landscape into a garden. At approximately three o'clock each day, depending on the season, a single shaft of sunlight fell into the box through an open stone grating that sliced it into rectangles long before it could nurture the curling tendrils of the single vine that was the box's only other living inhabitant.

While it was reassuring to know he could always repair to his office for shelter if the A-bomb was ever dropped on campus, Reed would have preferred something a little less subterranean. At times, he felt like an integral part of the Southern California scene, Doc-in-the-Box, the walk-in shrink who put therapy on a seeded sesame bun and kept the chipped ice out of the root beer upon request.

Lately, he had not even been that, the conclusive return of the sun to the greater Los Angeles basin having sent most of his potential patients to the beach. Barring an epidemic of something truly weird, like last spring's run of Chinese pre-engineering students convinced they were becoming impotent from eating dorm food, he could look forward to spending the rest of the school year in comparative quiet.

Which was fine with Reed. For what the university was paying him each month, it had already gotten more than its money's worth out of him. In his large, white office at the Fabulous Forum in Inglewood, Blake Marion, general manager of the Los Angeles Lakers, had made this very salient point only a week ago while explaining that Reed would just be helping himself by coming in to advise the Lakers on a deal they had been offered by the Phoenix Suns.

Haymon Jacobs and a guard named Hamid Malik were on the trading block. The Lakers could have them for not much more than a brace of future draft choices and some cash. A big white center who could back up Arvin Williams and a backcourtman who might be able to slip into the starting lineup alongside the immortal Cliff Summers would be worth far more than that, Marion had said, if not for their peculiar personality problems.

To hear Marion tell it, Hamid Malik and Haymon Jacobs had done everything but tear the Phoenix franchise apart with their bare hands. Both were suspected of being heavily involved with soft drugs. Jacobs had problems at home as well, having recently separated from his wife. Reed had been surprised to hear that, having not even known that Haymon was married. It had been years and years since Reed had seen or thought about Haymon Jacobs. Hamid Malik he didn't know at all.

"One thing seems sure," Reed had told Marion after the big general manager had run down a list of both players' quirks. "Neither one of them seems like a candidate for the Fellowship of Christian Athletes."

"Nice understatement, doc."

"Can they still play ball?"

"You got it there. That's all we care about. They didn't like Phoenix. They're city boys, flakes of the first order, they wanna grow beards and eat vegetables and give their money to some storefront swami, more power to 'em. So long as they put out on court. All we care about is . . . will they stick the round ball through the hoop for us and fall back on defense?

"See, doc," Marion grinned, shifting around in his oversized chair so that the silver bracelets on his massive wrists jangled in time. "We damn tired of making the playoffs every year only to get the shaft in the championship series. We want it all this time and these dudes could get it for us. *If* they can be motivated."

"Who says they can't?" Reed had asked.

"Who says they can?" Marion answered quickly. "Who knows jack about what goes on inside their Swiss cheese brains? I know they ain't gonna go out there and kill for old alma mater like college kids. Still, you'd be surprised how money can motivate a man. Almighty dollar. You can move mountains with it, if need be. Only we wanna make sure what we'd be gettin' *before* we open up the vaults. Which is where you come in. If they had bad knees, we'd send 'em to the best orthopedic man money can buy. Their knees is fine. It's their brains we wanna know about. So we callin' on you."

"To do what?"

"Test 'em. Poke 'em. Talk to 'em. Do whatever it is that you do and then let us know if you think they're worth havin', headwise."

"You're shitting me," Reed had blurted out, unable to believe what he was hearing.

"Like hell I am," Marion answered. "You been doin' this kind of stuff for a while now. Your team gone and won it all twice in a row, right? That's credentials enough for us. We think you can tell us what we want to know about these two. Of course, there'll be a fee involved."

"Almighty dollar, huh?"

"Coin of the realm. Got to be."

"I've known Haymon for years, you know," Reed said, growing more confident. "I grew up with him. We used to play ball in the same schoolyard."

"You know Malik too, doc. Under his old name. Bran Johnson. One of your first patients, no?"

"Yes. Yes he was. Bran's a Muslim now?"

"Hell, doc, I don't know what all he is. All I know is that you're the one we want to look at them both. What say?"

Reed had accepted Blake Marion's offer on the spot. The way the Fiat had been sounding lately, he knew he was going to need a lot more money than the university was paying him in order to just continue riding to work. Three days after his sitdown with Marion, Reed had gotten a call from the big general manager to alert him that Bran Johnson was on his way over to see him. "Try not to be shocked when you get your first look at him, doc," Marion had warned. "The boy's heavy into it." Marion had not been exaggerating.

Bran Johnson, fast talking product of the streets, he of the wide-brimmed purple hats, stacked high-heel alligator boots, tightly fitting body shirts and wide-wale corduroy bell-bottoms, whose first move upon receiving his bonus for signing with the Phoenix Suns had been to purchase a shiny Winnebago trailer and affix it to the back of an equally shiny Cadillac convertible, had obviously found himself a new tailor. The one who'd clothed the Riff leader in Sigmund Romberg's *The Desert Song*.

Hamid Malik had swirled through the door of Reed's office in a cloud of orange water and incense, a beaded leather bag swinging from one shoulder, a magnificent brown-and-white djellaba scraping the ground around him as he walked. On his head was a square red pillbox hat encrusted with gold. His bare feet were shod in intricately woven leather sandals. His fingers dripped rings of every color and description: moonstone, jade, turquoise, amethyst, and ebony. Around his neck was a string of camel beads. His hair, which had once blossomed forth in a natural the size and shape of a hawthorn bush was now neatly cultivated into a landscape of cornrows.

For a long moment, Hamid had stood framed in the doorway, fully aware of the magnificent picture he was making all by himself. Then he'd brought his palms together below his chin and bowed solemnly from the waist, whispering, "*Salaam aleikum.*" He'd put forth his right hand for Reed to shake, then quickly drawn it back, balling it into a fist and thumping it against his heart.

"Old desert custom," he explained. "From hand to heart to mind. All one. United in thought and deed."

"You're putting me on," Reed said, tipping so far back in his chair that he nearly fell backward on his ass.

" 'Hearken,' " Hamid whispered, his great eyes shifting from side to side, " 'Hearken to the reed forlorn/Breathing ever since t'was torn/From its rushy bed, a strain/Of impassioned love and pain.' "

"Holland-Dozier-Holland?"

"Rumi," Hamid said. "Took him forty years to write the poem those words came from and he had you in mind. I do not doubt it."

"When did he write it?"

"Well, he died in 1273."

"Kind of a distant relationship we had, huh?"

"He was a great man, Reed," Hamid breathed. "Founder of the Mevlevi order. Which you might know as the whirling dervishes. It is from that order and, of course, the Prophet Mohammed that we claim our lineage. As well as the patriarch you and I both share . . . Abraham."

"Bran," Reed said helplessly, "what is this?"

"A way to cope, without being blown to pieces."

"You call this coping?"

Hamid shrugged. "What I call it matters little. You knew me before. You have the right to hear the story entire."

"Hold on," Reed said. "I'll set up a tape recorder. Just in case the Lakers want to hear it, too."

To listen to Hamid Malik tell it, Bran Johnson had been a typical product of the ghetto, wandering lost and angry in a world he had never made, distracted by drugs, women, good clothes, and expensive cars. Reed could not argue with the analysis. He himself would have been content with a tenth of the constant distractions Bran Johnson had enjoyed just as an undergraduate. The man had always had a talent for drawing people to him.

"Then," Hamid Malik said, "after the season ended in Phoenix, I met a friend I had not seen since we were kids together in the street. He is now Hadi, the guide, the personal assistant to the man I count as my teacher, Sheikh Ali Baraka. He took me under his wing and gave me instruction. His presence was a beam of light in the darkness surrounding."

"And he recommended that you give up the game. . . ."

Hamid looked surprised. " 'The life of this world is but a sport, and a play,' " he said ingenuously. "So the Koran says. 'Whithersoever ye turn, there is the face of God.' No need to give up anything, so long as you recognize what is real and what is not."

Hamid motioned for Reed to turn off the tape recorder. "The reed," he said, his great eyes brimming with laughter, "one end between the lips of the Prophet, from the other the voice of God. Separated from its stem and wandering the earth in the sandals of Moses, looking for union. How are *you*, brother?"

Having never known Bran Johnson to inquire after anything except some girl's telephone number and address, for a moment Reed was speechless, too surprised to answer.

"Oh," he said finally, "not bad . . . you know what it's like here."

"A factory. That cares little for its workers."

"Shit, Bran . . . uh, Hamid," Reed said. "Whatever this is, you're lookin' good. I got to give you that."

"I feel good. I see things. Who knows where this new association with the Lakers will lead us both."

"Me?" Reed laughed. "This is a one-shot deal, man. A consultation."

"Who is to say? Really?" Hamid said, letting it go at that.

Reed let him go on talking. He had long since administered every personality inventory and multiple-choice test that he kept stockpiled in his filing cabinet to the old Bran Johnson. None of them had ever revealed anything about Bran save for an ego so strong it caused the sun to rise and set on whatever he was into at the moment. God seemed to be the current thing.

"Okay, Hamid," Reed said after a while, tipping back in his chair and switching off the tape recorder. "We're through."

Hamid had gotten slowly to his feet and smiled. Without asking Reed how he had done or when the results would be forwarded to the Lakers, he'd reached out for his hand. Closing his eyes, he'd bowed and mumbled what sounded like a little prayer. Then he'd smiled and turned for the door, his djellaba swirling slowly around him like the imperial robes of a desert chieftain. " 'Wouldst thou learn how lovers bleed,' " he said from the door, " 'Hearken, hearken to the reed.' " Then he'd closed the door behind him, bringing the curtain down on a masterful performance Reed could not remember having asked to see.

Although he had listened to the tape of the interview again and again since Bran had been in, none of it had made any more sense to Reed on replay. Either Bran Johnson was putting on the world at a level he himself had never before approached or he had truly found refuge in God.

Reed was considering this possibility when the phone rang. He picked it up immediately and was treated to the introductory static of long distance, followed immediately by the sound of his mother's voice.

"You forgot the number, Reed?" she boomed, as though she had to shout to make herself heard. "Or maybe you called when I wasn't home, hah?"

"I've been really busy the last couple weeks, Ma. Things have been coming up right and left."

"Too busy to call I know you were. This I don't have to be told."

Reed swiveled around in his chair and put his feet up on his desk. His mother had never really needed a telephone to contact him. She just used one so as not to upset the physical laws of the universe. She could have easily spoken to him without the benefit of Alexander Graham Bell's genius at any time, projecting her voice three thousand miles cross-country through the ether. For a while, they discussed the weather, which had been terrible in Brooklyn and wonderful in L.A. Then she got down to cases.

"Reed," she said, "it's coming to a year."

"What is?"

"A year to the day . . . you know . . . your father. The unveiling."

On a hot Saturday in June nearly a year ago Honey Kreiger had gone out and played his usual three hours of handball. He had just turned to say something to a defeated opponent when a massive myocardial infarction had felled him. He'd died right on the court. It had been a *shtuch* all right, one of those sudden and inexplicable thunderbolts that come out of nowhere to pierce the heart. Only lately had his mother even begun to sound like her old self again. Now the unveiling was coming up. Another chance to mourn and wail.

"I'm expecting you'll be here, Reed," she said point blank. "No excuses this time. For his only son to be at a conference somewhere in Colorado and miss the funeral was bad enough. Not to be here for the unveiling is. . . ." She let the sentence trail away, her silence the final indictment.

"I'm going to try," Reed said. "That's all I can say now, Ma. Give me the date. I'll write it down . . . and I'll try."

They talked for a while longer. Reed hung up knowing that although he had no desire to go back to Brighton for any reason, it would virtually be impossible for him to avoid showing up for the unveiling. He had just replaced the phone in its cradle when it rang again. "Zoo parade," he muttered, picking it up.

"Dr. Reed Kreiger?" a voice at the other end asked.

"Right here," Reed said wearily.

"*Doc!*" the voice said, warming to its subject. "Left a message for you last week with a secretary. Guess you never got it, huh? Secretaries can be funny that way. Am I right?" The voice plunged on, without waiting for confirmation. "Don't know as you'll remember me," the voice said. "Liddel. Liddel Gross. From the schoolyard."

"Liddel," Reed said, "from Brighton?"

"The same, doc. You got it."

"Well," Reed said conversationally, as though it made sense for him to be speaking to someone he hadn't seen or thought about in years, "what's up?"

"Got someone here wants to say hello to you. Hold on."

The phone clanked down on to a hard surface. Reed could hear the swelling tide of some kind of dance music in the background.

"Reed Kreiger?" a deep voice boomed.

"Still here," Reed affirmed.

"Far out. Haymon Jacobs."

Reed blinked. "Where are you, Haymon?" Reed asked, as though he were talking to one of his patients.

"Liddel's place. If they want me to talk to you, it's okay with me. Okay?"

"You mean the Lakers?"

"Yeah. Fine with me. Only . . . hold on."

There was the sound of clanking disconnection and giggling. Then Liddel got back on the phone. "Look, doc," he said, "we been goin' around on this for a week with Marion. They want Haymon, they don't want Haymon. They want him to fly out to the coast for an interview. Haymon can't fly out anywhere right now to sit down on this. We told Marion to pop for a ticket and send you here. How's that feel to you?"

"Uh, I might be able to see my way clear," Reed said, remembering his mother's request, "in a couple weeks."

"Good enough. Way I understand it, there's no great rush. I'll get back to Marion, tell him it's all right with you, and let him make arrangements from his end. That okay?"

"All right."

"Great," Liddel said. "Call me as soon as you hit the city and we'll set the whole thing up. Where do you stay when you get in? East Side, where?"

"With my mother," Reed said. "The small room in the back."

"All right, doc," Liddel said, laughing heartily. "Good to know you ain't changed all that much. What the fuck, ain't none of us ever outgrown the schoolyard. Am I right? You hit the city, you look me up. Liddel Gross. I'm in the book."

Reed mumbled his assent and Liddel Gross chuckled one final time before clicking off the line. Reed put the receiver down, and the little office grew quiet once again. It was unbelievable, really, the way people could still find him when they needed him. Despite all the distance he had put between himself and Brighton, they could just stick their hands through the continuum of time and space and grab him by the coat whenever they felt like it. First his mother, and then Liddel.

Listening to Liddel now, Reed could have almost believed that they had once been friends. Nothing could have been farther from the truth. Reed had never forgotten the exalted position Liddel had occupied in the schoolyard. Haymon Jacobs' best friend. A pretender to the throne. The world had turned itself around several times since then. Now he was the one with the power, and Liddel was . . . who the hell could say? A hustler certainly. Always that.

On his way out of the office, Reed made a mental note to pick up the latest copy of *Mad* magazine at the bookstore near the campus. He had nearly a complete collection, stretching all the way back to the days when he'd rushed out to buy each new issue as it had arrived in Hirsch's, carefully counting out the pennies he'd saved all on his own so he wouldn't have to ask his father for money.

No longer did Reed Kreiger ever bother to count out his pennies or even glance at the change handed him in stores. Earning a regular salary, even so meager a paycheck as the one the university handed him twice a month, had cured that nagging neurosis once and for all.

Whistling between his teeth, Reed closed his office door behind him and went home for the weekend. Money could not buy you happiness. He knew that for a fact. Still, so far as he could tell from his own experience, it could enable you at least to suffer in comfort.

CHAPTER FOURTEEN

ALTHOUGH HONEY KREIGER had lived and died in Brooklyn, the borough of churches, they had laid him to rest in Queens, where the diner was king and the Van Wyck and Grand Central expressways coiled their asphalt cloverleafs toward one another in serpentine greeting. Did it matter once you were dead, Reed wondered, if they put you down where the traffic rattled unceasingly and the sky was always leaden with noxious gray smoke? Could you tell the difference?

Honey Kreiger had never had much use for Queens. Riding toward it now in the back seat of a car driven by his mother's best friend, Ceil Kapstein, Reed could understand why. His father had been a citizen of Brooklyn first and foremost and only then circumstantially a resident of the city of New York, which to him had meant Manhattan. Queens was another country entirely.

Dressed like a schoolboy on graduation day, with a tie he had not worn in years knotted tightly beneath the collar of a starched white shirt, Reed squirmed uncomfortably and stared out the window. The diagonals of hot morning sunshine slanting in through the car's windows promised that before this day was over in the city of New York, murders would be committed on street corners. Couples would scream at each other and go their separate ways. Former friends would come to blows in barrooms. Had he been alive, Honey Kreiger would have had the good sense to turn this car around and head straight for the beach, to spend the day there slamming around a handball.

"A scorcher," Mrs. Kapstein said from behind the wheel, as though the day might become something else if she did not name it now. "This kind of weather in June I don't remember. Not for years."

"Honey's kind of weather," Reed's mother said in a voice as tightly knotted as the handkerchief she held in her hand. "The kind he loved."

As always, Reed wondered where she found the strength. Rhoda Kreiger had always been a tiny woman, small boned and fragile, but in the year since Honey's death she seemed to have shrunk yet again. Grief had sucked the marrow from the bones of her face and withered the little flesh that had once padded its angular slopes. Now she gazed out at the world with a fierce, almost Slavic glare, as though she was perpetually angry. There were gray hairs over her temples that Reed did not remember. Only her eyes had remained unchanged, quick and penetrating, like those of a sparrow perched in the highest branch of a tree.

She had insisted that he come home for this, the unveiling of the stone that marked his father's grave, and he had not argued very much at all, as though by coming home he might actually be able to discharge final payment on a debt that he had long left unpaid.

He knew now that was not possible. The old neighborhood was no place to make amends of any kind. Although he had only been back since Friday night, the weekend had been an authentic eternity, the minutes refusing to become hours, the days passing slowly in the quiet, empty tomb the old apartment had become. Seeing it all once again, smelling it, feeling it, he was not now sorry he had refused to come home for his father's funeral a year ago and the week of sitting *shiva* that had followed it.

A week spent mourning in a living room crowded with relatives he would have barely known, each one having brought the requisite basket of fruit wrapped in glazed yellow paper, the box of candy from Barton's, the string-wrapped cake from whatever bakery had taken over from Ebinger's. Let one Jew die in Brooklyn and the entire history of the race had to be aired and re-examined. Breasts had to be beaten and flesh gouged. Nothing less would do.

Having only recently re-read all the relevant chapters in the standard texts, Reed knew that even in the most finely honed members of the human species, grief had a definite half-life, lessening considerably after six or seven weeks. The textbooks' authors had no doubt failed to include anyone from Brighton in their testing sample. Here, grief was a fine old wine, to be saved and savored one sip at a time until the bottle was empty so that it could then be smashed into shards with which to pierce the heart. The mourning never ended.

The car picked up speed, then slowed to a dead stop in traffic. Honey had battled this rush hour five days a week for twenty years. By the time he'd found all the little shortcuts, the apparently dead-end streets that ran for miles along the shoulder of the parkway, the intersections where fabulous time could be made simply by bearing away from the main flow of traffic, he'd died. It was but one aspect of his tragedy.

Reed leaned his head back into the overly upholstered seat and closed his eyes. He was here on business. Blake Marion had provided him with a first class round trip ticket so that he could travel in comfort while looking out for the Lakers' best interests. As soon as he had done what he had been sent here to do, he could leave. Already he was anxious to be home. Anything was preferable to being adrift in this city where he no longer knew a soul.

He had spent most of the weekend walking the streets of Brighton, the prodigal son returned, seeking what it was that had driven him away in the first place. Brighton had changed all right, but only for the worse.

The schoolyard was now filled with kids who wore their hair long. They seemed to prefer sitting on the steps to playing ball. There was an inordinate number of Chinese takeout places, *shlock* stores, and synagogues on and around Brighton Beach Avenue. The subway still rattled along the el at regular intervals. All of it was somehow smaller and tamer than he'd remembered it, as though some Hollywood set designer had created his own plastic vision of what a folksy little Jewish neighborhood should look like. It wasn't real. Perhaps it had never been.

Mrs. Kapstein, who'd insisted that he call her "Ceil," stamped her foot on the accelerator. The car lurched forward in traffic, only to slow down immediately as cars coagulated around them once again. "Won't be long now," Mrs. Kapstein said brightly. "Here we are at the double gas stations already."

She swung the steering wheel to the right and the car came around like a fat-bottomed whaler bellying into the wind under full sail. It spun off the parkway onto a broad boulevard lined on both sides with automotive wrecking firms and junkyards. From behind fallen down wooden fences, great hubcap mountains rose majestically, towering over terminal moraines of ancient differentials and stripped transmissions. Bodies by Fisher, rusted now, rotted, caked and pitted, lay alongside ridges of bald and blackened tires, hillocks consisting entirely of cracked windshields and crazy-quilt patches of metal twisted beyond all use or description. The boulevard of junk led directly into a large graveled parking lot where Mrs. Kapstein rolled the car to a stop.

When he stepped outside, the heat of the day rushed up at Reed as though it were being pumped from some subterranean furnace. Shading his eyes against the glare, he followed his mother and her best friend along a pebbled path that led to the cemetery's various sections.

Reed had not spent much time in graveyards, but then who had? He did not believe there could be many that looked like this. The Jews of Brooklyn and Queens had been laid out here in job lots, buried wholesale like the cars nearby that they had kept so carefully washed and polished in life. Accumulated union dues and death benefits had gone to purchase monuments guaranteed to stand until the very last of days, when it would all become a charnel house.

Until then, these markers would endure. They were quality goods, row on row, expensive tombstones blazing with reflected light in the morning sun, one more garish than the other, competing in death as their owners had in life. Monuments of white marble and mica-flecked rainbow granite stood next to minor Taj Mahals with white chalk domes. Ridged stone houses, weighty slabs, massive blocks, towering plinths, and great obelisks cried out, "*I was prosperous! I gave heavily on the High Holy Days!*"

As far as the eye could see, there were glittering monuments and markers, interrupted only by occasional patches of sad green ivy, the tired pointed little leaves already hung with the dust of summer.

Gravel clicked and rolled beneath Reed's feet as he dutifully followed his mother along a path bordered by a low black chain. The hot, sere smell of earth with no moisture left in it rolled up behind them, filling his nostrils. In the middle of an empty section awaiting future tenants, Reed saw a single chunk of ash-gray marble swathed in white, as though it had been wounded in action and then hastily bandaged in some battlefield clinic. The name on it could not be read. Rhoda made straight for it, and Reed followed.

Around the stone stood people Reed did not know. They nodded at his mother and then at him. A young rabbi dressed in black robes with a white prayer shawl draped over his shoulders and an embroidered black velvet yarmulke perched on the back of his head handed out tiny paper prayer books. Someone gave Reed a black crepe skullcap with a silvered disk on top. Without thinking, he placed it on his head.

The rabbi, whose trimmed goatee and tinted glasses spoke of a more liberal doctrine than Orthodox Judaism, cleared his throat.

He bobbed his head and the ceremony began. For convenience sake, the words of the mourner's *Kaddish*, the prayer for the dead, had been spelled out phonetically in the booklet. Even someone like Honey, who had never mastered the Hebrew language at all, attending synagogue but once a year to say *Yizkor* for his own parents on Yom Kippur, could have followed along.

Reed realized he was looking at his father's grave for the very first time. Much like the apartment, it was small, ordinary, and unremarkable. That they actually had put a man like Honey Kreiger inside a plain pine box under this patch of curried earth beneath a gray stone marker that had rolled off some assembly line came as no real surprise to Reed. Such things were done all the time, as a matter of course. In death, all things were possible, so long as arrangements for perpetual care were made in the gatehouse by the parking lot.

The AMA furnished no Trip-Tiks for visits to the beyond. There were no coordinates available to plot journeys that went off the edge of the graph. Having seen many corpses, first in medical school and then as an intern, Reed had few fantasies about what went on after life ended. The heart pumped one final time, the brain underwent clinical death, and the motion of the molecules in the individual cell slowed to a stop.

Then one called in those whose business it was to care for the dead, the morticians and funeral directors and this rabbi, who had never known the man he was now speaking over, commending the dead man's soul to rest with all the righteous men and women in paradise, Abraham, Jacob, Sarah, Rebecca, Rachel, and Leah.

Reed looked up from his father's grave and stared across the cemetery. Some rows away he could see another knot of people gathered around yet another rabbi. Another box laid beneath the earth. Another final post-mortem for someone who had lived and died in this crowded city.

Perhaps ranchers and cattlemen who had spent their lives riding the high country got to witness eternity from a quiet slope where sunset purpled the horizon and the trees whispered one to another in the evening breeze. Those who had lived out their lives here, on hard asphalt, never knowing there was another way, wound up scattered like pins along a bowling alley, awaiting the moment when the great automatic pinspotter would descend to restore them all to an upright position.

As the rabbi mumbled his way through a long Hebrew prayer Reed could not understand, he found himself drifting, unable to pay attention. Mrs. Kapstein stood by his mother's side, supporting her, smelling salts at the ready should she topple over and lose control. The rabbi broke into English, noting that the body of the deceased was going back. Orthodox law decreed that to be buried in such a cemetery, the mortal envelope had to be in the same condition in which it had been received. No tattoos or other defacements. No cancellations or postmarks, or it would be rejected, unfit for burial.

What a joke. After a lifetime, the toenails hardened and turned to stone, curling over the toe. The eyes glazed, and the brain grew weak. The fingers refused to bend and the skin grew cold and clammy to the touch. Clinical death staked its claim no matter how you had lived or who you had been. Then they shoved you so deep inside the earth there was no way you would ever trouble anyone again.

Someone nudged Reed and he saw that his mother was moving toward the stone. He moved with her, coming to her side just as she reached out for the white cheesecloth covering the marker. She tugged at it and it came away in her hand. The words "HAROLD KREIGER, DEVOTED HUSBAND AND FATHER, 1920–1971" leaped forth. Harold. Not even Honey.

People began shuffling forward then, placing tiny stones on the gray marble marker, stones on stones on stone, little pyramids of pebbles forming along the fluted ridges to affirm that Honey's friends and relatives had come to bear witness and share the grief. Someone pressed two pebbles into Reed's palm. They were hot and smooth to the touch. He wiped them free of dust and added them to the growing pile on the gravestone. Then he turned and walked away from the grave toward a small table on which an open bottle of Canadian Club stood surrounded by tiny Dixie cups and a plate set with slices of sponge cake. He reached out for a cup and saw that a single piece of cake had fallen to the ground below.

Stooping to retrieve it, he realized that it was already spoken for. A persistent line of dark black ants had it encircled in cavalry fashion. No doubt the ground here was rich with insect life. It figured to be.

His once dark loafers, purchased in Beverly Hills, were caked with dust, nearly white. Reed did not bother to wipe them clean. What for? His last responsibility to the man who had given him life had been discharged. He felt no better. Inside him there was only dust. Ashes and cinders and bits of gravel. Dead embers long ago gone cold. Dust inside and out. A cemetery's worth, for the taking.

THE NEXT morning he woke with his old room stretched out around him like a long and narrow tube of toothpaste someone had squeezed in the middle. Against the far wall, hanging over the desk, he could see a picture of himself in his CCNY uniform. It had hung there for years, the single icon in this peculiar little chapel, the most prized piece of art in the curious museum it had become.

Nothing in the room had been disturbed since he'd gone off to medical school. Waking up in it now was like slipping back into an old and slightly too small suit of clothes. Within its cramped confines, Reed imagined he could actually feel himself growing younger, until he was once again the frail and slender college boy who had last slept there regularly.

A rough breeze blew the curtains around on the window, bringing with it the carbon monoxide smell of cars in motion on the street below. Reed got out of bed, pulled on an old terry-cloth robe, and wandered into the kitchen.

"Omelets I made," his mother said, tucking a strand of graying hair behind one ear. She slid a plate on to the table before him. "Lox and onion. I hope they're all right."

"How bad could they be?"

"Ach," she said disgustedly. "Already I burnt one bagel. I had to throw it out. I ask the man in the appetizing store for Nova Scotia, he gives me belly. Is it any wonder your father never let me shop alone?" His mother looked suddenly distraught, as though there could be no greater tragedy than this. "I ask for Nova Scotia," she said again, "he gives me belly." She rubbed her face with a wrinkled hand until the look disappeared.

"Coffee?" she asked.

Reed nodded and she bustled toward the stove, returning with a white ceramic pot on which tiny blue cornflowers were sprouting. Honey had always made his own coffee in an ancient battered tin pot he had absolutely refused to let anyone throw out. Coffee could never be too sweet for him. Reed could remember watching him dump teaspoon after heaping teaspoon of sugar into his cup, as though his squat, powerful body could not take on enough fuel before setting out for a day's work.

"You got a few minutes?" his mother said. "I want to talk to you."

"Sure. Talk."

"You remember Mrs. Kapstein?"

"She drove us out yesterday."

"Right. She also lost her husband a year ago. I wrote you about it. Cancer of the prostate. You shouldn't know from it, Reed. By the time they finally let him die he weighed. . . ."

"Please," Reed said, holding up a hand to stop her. "Spare me."

"You're a doctor?" she said. "I thought this was your business, no? All right. The two of us . . . we've been talking. What with both unveilings over, hers and mine, and the neighborhood going the way it is. . . ." She looked at him and then spoke quickly. "We've decided we're moving out. Together."

"About time," Reed said.

"To Florida. Reed," she cautioned, holding up her hand to stop him, "don't start in on me. I know you want me to come to Los Angeles. It's too far away."

"Florida is closer?"

"As the crow flies," she said, looking at him with surprise, "certainly. It's not just distance. Between us, Mrs. K. and I know lots of people down there already. It's *haimish*."

"How do you know California isn't?" he asked. "You've never been there."

"Oh," she said airily, "I can tell. Last week Mike Douglas took his show out to Hollywood for a full week. Very phony if you ask me. Very false. I could tell."

"But Florida isn't?"

"Who knows?" she said. "I've never been there either. It's nicer. So they tell me. You want to know the absolute truth, I'm not convinced it's any bargain either."

"I don't want you staying here," he said sternly.

"*You* don't want. . . ." She laughed.

"Go to Florida," he said.

"You mean it?"

"The sooner, the better."

"It's not California."

"I know it's not."

"I was sure you'd have a fit."

"So long as you get out of here," he said. "Anything is better than this."

"*Mein feinera mensch*," she said scornfully. "It was plenty good when you were growing up." She sighed. "Only it's changed. You turn on the news these days, all you hear is junkie. Junkie this, junkie that. Who can live with that all the time? I'm supposed to be afraid to walk down the street at night?"

"Florida will be perfect," he said. "You'll see. I'll send you checks, I'll come visit now and then. . . ."

"Send me no checks," she said. "What I need to know is if you've got any books or papers here that you want. I could have them shipped or stored or . . ."

"Don't worry about it. I'll handle it when the time comes."

As though some great burden had been lifted from her shoulders, Rhoda Kreiger shrugged and smiled. Absentmindedly, she stooped and kissed her son on the forehead. "My doctor," she said. "For me, you were never a problem."

Then she turned and went to the sink, automatically going to work on the dishes she had only just dirtied to prepare breakfast. As she worked, she began to hum softly to herself. Reed recognized the tune. It came from an Alka-Seltzer commercial that ran constantly on television.

When she had finished with the dishes, she wiped her hands on a dish towel, kissed Reed once again, and went out to meet Mrs. K. for their mutual weekly appointment at the beauty parlor.

After she was gone, Reed sat at the old Formica dining table for a long while, listening to the grinding hum of the refrigerator. Once his mother packed it in, this apartment would exist only in his memory. Never again would he have to come back to it to be reminded of things that were better left forgotten. New York City as the place of his birth would exist only as a fact duly recorded on some certificate stored deep in the bowels of City Hall.

Well, why not? The Dodgers had abandoned this place long ago, back when Brooklyn had still been alive with neighborhood after neighborhood where families knew and cared for one another. Their kids had grown up together in the street and the schoolyard and then run for greener pastures. Where Duke Snider and company had gone, fools and angels alike rushed to follow. California, Florida, anywhere, so long as it was *out*. Getting out was all that counted.

For a moment, sitting at the table, Reed thought he knew how it felt to be dispossessed, to have truly lost your homeland, the very street on which you had been born and raised. Then the feeling passed and he got up to call Haymon Jacobs. Once that bit of business was taken care of, he could return to Los Angeles, the place where he undeniably now made his home.

CHAPTER FIFTEEN

WHAT WITH the stereo blasting and the TV on and Haymon and Tina rapping and giggling like crazy, Liddel had to wedge the bedroom door shut and put the phone close to his ear in order to be able to hear what was being said to him.

"Liddel?" the voice on the other end of the line said. "This is Reed. Reed Kreiger."

"Doc, *doc!*" Liddel crooned. "Good to hear from you, man. When d'you hit the city?"

"Couple days ago, Liddel. I had some other business to take care of first. How's Haymon?"

"Bigger than life, doc, and twice as mean. When we gonna get it on?"

"The interview? As soon as possible. I'm on my way back to L.A."

"What say tomorrow?"

"Fine."

"Say ten A.M., here in my place. I'll clear out, leave you two alone, and you can ask him every question in the book. What say?"

"Sounds good. Tell me where you live."

"Right. Listen, doc," Liddel said, changing the subject, "you remember Sponge from the schoolyard? I know you do. They did him in, man. But good. Just last week. Seven to ten upstate for passin' credit cards that belonged to other people and he was only frontin' for the family. Heavy, huh? Is that a bitch?"

There was no response. Liddel waited a second, then plunged on. Phones could be funny sometimes. Although Kreiger was in Brighton, no more than a mile away, he sounded distant, as though he were still in Los Angeles. Liddel kept punching away at it but the shrink didn't come around. Finally, he just gave up and supplied Kreiger with directions. Then he hung the phone up and walked back into the living room.

The volume on the stereo was jacked up to the pain level. Haymon lay spreadeagled across the floor watching Tina demonstrate this new dance Puerto Rican faggots in midtown Manhattan were making popular. Liddel watched her tight ass bob in rhythm to the beat for a while. Then he walked over to the machine and knocked down the sound. Both of them looked up immediately.

"*Hey!*" Haymon said in protest.

"Hey yourself," Liddel said. "You ain't heard this record but a thousand times, right, Haymon? You're studying it. They got a Tito Puente Regents this year. Am I right?"

Haymon made a face and reached across the coffee table for the pearl inlaid stash box that was part of the furniture. "Pull my chain, little man," he said, not even bothering to flip Liddel the finger that nearly always followed this remark.

"Nice," Liddel said. "Excuse me for living. You, Fat Mama, and Tito are gonna sew up this contract with the Lakers, right? We should all live so long. I just heard from the shrink. He's in town."

"Keegler?"

"*Kreiger!*" Liddel shouted. "Try to hold onto his name, huh? If only till tomorrow. He's comin' here at ten. Jesus," he said, "I swear all that shit you been smokin' is eatin' your brain away."

"Huh?" Haymon said, letting some spit drool out of the side of his mouth. "I can't hear you, man. Like my brain is damaged."

"Your fuckin' memory is. . . ."

"Huh? What? Say it again. I already forgot."

"Tomorrow, comedian. So if you're rolling a joint, make it a good one 'cause it's your last for today. I want you straight when he comes. So when you look him in the eye and lie about how you been liftin' weights and runnin' on the beach, he won't bust out laughin', see the jay in your hand, and call the narcs."

"I'm in shape," Haymon protested, selecting the largest buds he could find in the stash box and pinching them into a joint. "Considering."

"Yeah. Considering that you been layin' on the floor stoned since you got here. Tina, this goes for you too. You wanna see L.A. before it falls in the ocean, you gotta help me keep him straight. We gotta clean this place up, too. Looks like goats been fuckin' here."

Haymon guffawed. He pointed a large finger first at Tina and then at Liddel. "Shame," he said, waggling it, "shame, shame. What the little man said. Naughty, naughty."

Tina made a face but Liddel knew she would listen. He had been paying for her voice and music lessons for months now, which was more than her father had ever done. Just to show him that she still had a mind of her own, she went over to the stereo and turned the volume back up.

"Great," Liddel said. "Just what we need. More of the Latin Sound."

"I got a joint," Tina said brightly. "Let's smoke it."

"Smoke some reefer," Haymon said automatically, "and we'll all get straight." He said this ten or twenty times a day, usually just after he had rolled one of his three-paper super bombers. Liddel had never known anyone who could smoke dope like Haymon. He even made Tina look like a beginner.

Pulling a thin joint out of her shirt pocket, Tina grabbed for some matches and got it lit. She took a heavy hit off it and passed it over to Haymon, shaking her ass in time to the music all the while. "You want," Liddel offered, "we can all go out tonight, catch a meal, maybe see a movie."

"Let's go dancing," Tina said. "I know a place."

"Take a shower," Liddel ordered. "We'll go dancing."

"Yes, master," Tina said, bowing from the waist. "What else?"

"Use soap."

Tina bowed again and yanked at the yellow ribbon that held her hair in place. The ribbon came away in her hand and her thick brown hair fell down around her shoulders. Quickly, as though she were alone in the room, she undid the first four buttons on her faded work shirt, revealing an expanse of flesh already brown with sun. Still dancing, with her shirt flapping around her, she ran a careless hand over the taut and muscled washboard that was her stomach. "You don't think I'm getting fat, do you, Liddel?" she pouted, pulling the shirt farther away from herself so he could get a better look. "It happens, you know."

"Not to seventeen year old chicks, it don't," Liddel said.

Haymon toked silently on his joint. Then he rolled over on to his back and threw a hand over his eyes, as though to shield them from the sun.

"C'mon, c'mon," Liddel told Tina. "We ain't got all day."

"Peekaboo," Tina giggled, lacing her fingers in front of her face. "I see you, Haymon. You can't hide from me."

Then she ran laughing into the bathroom. The sound of running water from the shower began to seep into the living room through gaps in the music. It occurred to Liddel that he could use a shower himself. He strolled out of the room, leaving Haymon stretched out on the carpet behind him like some great whale that had washed up on the shoreline.

Haymon rolled slowly over on to his side, reaching out with his huge right hand to smooth the ruffled carpeting beneath him. It seemed to him that he had been lying here forever, letting Tina and Liddel decide what he would do next. It was easier that way. Why bother going out? There was no place to go. There was only this room where the music played all the time and the box of good dope on the coffee table that made one day seem exactly like another, each one passing in a boring haze.

It had been three long months since Phoenix, yet he still could not look at a woman without thinking of Linda. The pain of her leaving was stuck firmly in his throat, a wishbone wedged so securely in place that it was impossible to swallow or spit out. All he could do was gag and wait, and then wait some more.

Although he had some idea of how spaced he really was, Haymon knew that it did not matter. Not really. No matter what he did to himself, they still wanted him. Another team was willing to take a chance and pay him big money to play. He was not yet so far gone that they'd need all the king's horses and all the king's men to put him back together again. Just one would do. And he was arriving tomorrow. Tomorrow would be soon enough. He could wait. He had waited before and he could wait again. It was one of the few things in his life that had never changed.

THE NEXT morning Liddel got out of bed and began immediately straightening up the apartment. Reed Kreiger, the crown prince of the first court at Manhattan Beach, was coming. Although it had been years since they'd seen each other, Liddel could remember exactly how Kreiger had treated him the last time they'd seen one another face to face.

It had been right at the end of the summer he'd spent working the beach, *shlepping* his guts out day after day, peddling. Kreiger and his fancy collegiate friends and fraternity brothers had owned the first court. They'd spent their days playing ball and bullshitting with the girls. Loudly, Kreiger had called him over one afternoon. Making sure everyone could hear, he'd made a big production of asking Liddel for a discount. When Liddel had refused to let him have one, Kreiger had begun riding him, giving him the same kind of abuse the old women on the beach heaped on his head every day.

Kreiger's friends along the fence had laughed themselves blue in the face and slapped five, as though there could be nothing funnier than one schoolyard boy trying to bargain with another over the price of a knish.

What had seemed a hilarious joke to them all had been for Liddel an insult of the first order, one he had never been able to forgive or forget. Kreiger, talking down to him, as though he was so high and mighty no one could touch him.

So totally lost was he in the memory of that day that when the downstairs doorman buzzed to say that he had a visitor, Liddel fully expected to see Kreiger come to his door in the very same outfit he'd worn at the beach that summer, white sneakers, starched shorts, and a pressed white T-shirt.

Instead, Kreiger was wearing a brown Palm Beach weave suit, a floral pointy-collared high roller's shirt with a brightly colored kerchief where his tie should have been. Tony Curtis, making a house call.

So far as Liddel knew, everyone in L.A. went to see a shrink once a week. Kreiger was probably piling up the dough out there. He had to hand it to the scumbag. California had done wonders for him.

Then he took a closer look. On his feet, Kreiger was wearing a pair of fake Guccis, with imitation gold chains, covered in dust no less. Instead of the black silk socks he should have had on, he'd chosen a pair of thick blue ribbed sweat socks. Jesus. The Tony Curtis kerchief was bad enough. But the shoes and socks closed the deal. It was all Liddel could do to keep from laughing out loud. How casual could you get?

In New York, only ghinzos wore shoes like that. Guys like Momo, who hung out in crummy discotheques in printed shirts that were forever four buttons open to the navel so you could get a good look at their dark and muscled physiques. Not one of them ever had two nickels to rub together when it came time to pick up a check but they all smiled a lot. They had good teeth.

Liddel himself had never paid less than a hundred for a pair of shoes, not since he'd started going to a special place on the Upper East Side where you had to order them weeks in advance so that they could be custom fitted. He'd always had tiny feet, the right one a full half size smaller than the left, and the shit they sold in Brooklyn just didn't fit him. It was a lesson his old man had taught him. Buy only the best, always. Top of the line, or nothing.

Accordingly, Liddel had come to believe you could tell a lot about a man by his shoes. Only a cheap hustler would wear a pair like Kreiger had on. Fake Guccis, with sweat socks no less. Jesus. Liddel had to fight to keep the smile off his face. Kreiger hadn't changed that much at all.

"So, doc," Liddel said warmly, extending his hand in greeting, "how is it to be back? Fuckin' town is still the greatest. Am I right?"

"Well," Kreiger said, "I don't know as I'd go that far."

"Well, yeah," Liddel smiled. "Neighborhood ain't what it was when we were growin' up here but then what is? That don't mean it ain't still got heart. I been out to L.A., y' know. Coupla times. I ain't sayin' it ain't nice out there. Shit, I can't say that. But where do you go at night? When you wanna eat Chinese at two-thirty? You gotta get in your car and drive halfway to Tijuana, no?"

"It's not that bad," Kreiger said, allowing himself a polite smile.

"Nah," Liddel said. "It's all still right here as far as I'm concerned. The Apple. The way I look at it, everything else is . . . Paramus."

Kreiger smiled again. Then he took a pigskin portfolio from under his arm, withdrew some papers, and laid them on the coffee table, all the while looking around the apartment as though he were appraising it for the city. "You're a pharmacist?" he said. "Is that what you told me on the phone? This is a pretty nice place."

"It makes it," Liddel said, unwilling to concede a thing, "for now. Tell you the truth, doc, I see myself gettin' into bigger things eventually. Now I fill prescriptions a couple nights a week in the city, yeah, but that's only like a base of operations for me. Now, take your friend and mine, Haymon. He and his old lady split in Phoenix. He gets the itch to come home. I say, 'Hey! Lay up here for a while. Place is yours, for as long as you need it.' So when the offer comes from the Lakers, it's only natural he turns to me for advice."

"Where is Haymon?" Reed asked.

"Gettin' dressed," Liddel said quickly. "He don't spend the first hour of every day in the john, he don' know if he's alive or not. Now, I got a lady, Tina. Sings like a fuckin' bird. Dances. Been takin' lessons all her life. Went to Music and Art. She's gonna be another Streisand. Soon as she gets her shot, I'm gonna be right there . . . for advice."

"Sports, show biz, pharmacy," Kreiger said, "you're a regular Renaissance man, Liddel. You really know about all these things?"

"I know people, doc. And they never change, no matter what business they're in. I had Al Pacino come into the store the other night. No shit. 'Al,' I says to him, 'how is it?' 'How should it be?' he says to me. Real, you know? No bullshit about him. Just another guy from the street, who remembers. The way we grew up, I figger there ain't nothin' we can't do if we put our minds to it. Shit. Look at yourself. Am I right?"

Kreiger nodded and smiled but Liddel could tell he was barely listening. Fuck you, he thought. You'll wait till I'm good and ready, and then some. Compulsively Liddel moved around the living room, plumping up the pillows, straightening an ashtray, putting a pitcher of ice water and two glasses on the coffee table.

178 ·

"And now, *the man!*" he said dramatically before going into the darkened bedroom to get Haymon.

The big guy was sitting in the middle of the bed with his eyes closed and his mouth open, as though hoping the bedspread might at any moment become a magic carpet and take him away.

"You sleepin'?" Liddel asked.

"Concentrating my energy," Haymon said in a low voice.

"Good. Concentrate it on gettin' your ass into the living room. Dr. Stiff is here. And Haymon . . . no fuckin' off-the-wall answers, huh? Just tell him what he wants to hear. Your tongue is hangin' out to play ball for the Lakers. Right?"

Haymon hung his tongue out one corner of his mouth and panted. Then he nodded and got to his feet to precede Liddel into the living room. Kreiger stood up to greet him and Liddel watched the big guy sit down immediately, giving away his advantage. If I was that big, Liddel thought, I'd stand all the time. Make everyone look up.

"Okay, doc," Liddel said, taking note of the small pocket tape recorder Kreiger had laid out on the table, "I can see you're gettin' ready to go to work. Don't let me stop you. If I don't see you when I get back, here's wishin' you a safe trip back to L.A. You said you were leavin' soon, right?"

"Tonight."

"Okay then. All the best, and fuck the rest. Am I right?"

"Sure."

"And listen, now that you know where the place is, next time you come back, don't be a stranger. Door's always open to an old schoolyard boy."

"That's nice, Liddel. Thanks."

Kreiger put out his hand and Liddel shook it quickly, barely pausing on his way to the door. "Haymon," he called out as he left, "be good. Don't tell him nothin' I wouldn't. Which leaves you a hell of a lot of room. I see you later."

Reed took advantage of Liddel's drawn-out departure to shuffle some papers and gather his thoughts. Despite all that Blake Marion had told him, he was shocked by the way Haymon Jacobs looked. Haymon's gaunt, angular cheekbones protruded through his dark and scraggly beard like an angry pair of isosceles triangles. His eyes were blank and unfathomable and he seemed willing to look anywhere but directly at the man who had come to interview him. Reed wondered if it would make the big man feel any easier to know that he had no secrets. His life story was neatly on file in Blake Marion's office, for anyone to read.

"Nothing very mysterious about what we'll be doing today," Reed said. "I'm going to take a medical and psychiatric history, administer some standard tests, and then we'll talk for a while into the tape recorder. I want you to feel free to answer my questions as honestly as you can, Haymon. As a doctor, I'm sworn to protect anything you tell me. It's a privileged communication."

Haymon's face brightened for a moment. "Privilege be all mine," he mumbled.

Reed did his best not to look surprised. Although the voice had come from Haymon Jacobs, the rhythm and phrasing belonged to Hamid Malik, back when he had still been Bran Johnson. Reed knew that the two men had been close in Phoenix. Still, he hadn't expected a ventriloquism act.

"Is there anything you'd like to ask me before we start?"

"What kinda tests?" Haymon asked, his low and rumbling monotone rattling the baseboards of the room.

"MMPI," Reed said, "Rorschach, thematic aperception, and some word association. No blood samples. All painless. Ready?"

"I gotta vomit first," Haymon said, completely deadpan. "No, I don't, doc," he said, seeing the look of alarm on Reed's face. "Just a little humor to loosen us up."

"Right," Reed said. "But from here on in, it counts. Okay?"

Haymon nodded and Reed began working him up. Not until Reed inquired as to the status of Haymon's injured left leg did the big man seem interested. "Got me a lawsuit goin' against Pennbrook, you know," he said proudly. "If they'd had someone supervising us, I'd have been asleep that night instead of makin' a fool of myself on some football field. I'd still have me two good legs. Instead, I got this."

Haymon hiked up his trouser leg before Reed could stop him. It was as though someone had found a doll's calf and ankle lying around somewhere and bolted it in to Haymon's leg at the knee. And yet the man was still able to play professional basketball. Real desire took no notice of physical infirmity. Reed made a mental note to try to remember that. It had quite a ring to it. Then he began the word association quiz. Twice, Haymon began to answer, lost the thread of what he was about to say and foundered, apparently completely at sea as to what the question had been. The second time it happened Reed wrote the word "blanking" on his yellow, legal-sized pad.

When it came time for the interview itself, Reed turned on the tape recorder and let Haymon take the lead, allowing the conversation to wander wherever the big man wanted it to go. Haymon seemed most interested in talking about his wife, from whom he was still separated. He said he was sure that being with a team like the Lakers, in a city like Los Angeles, could only help them get their marriage back together. Reed regarded this as a very positive sign, and he noted it on his pad.

"A year with the Celtics, a year with the Suns," Reed said. "Do you think you're ever going to be able to find an organization you can stay with? A place where you feel comfortable?"

Haymon laughed. "Lotta guys get to feelin' *real* comfortable with a team only to find their asses traded in mid-season. It ain't a matter of bein' comfortable, doc. They pay me, I'll play. Money makes me comfortable."

"How about wanting to be somewhere you could feel you belong?"

Haymon laughed again. "Who's loadin' these questions, doc?" he asked, a small grin appearing on his face. "This the place we both come from, right? You feel like you belong here? I don't. I never did. Liddel now, he's different. He loves it here. It's his home. To me, it's all the same, wherever I go. I bring it with me when I come."

Reed nodded in understanding. No matter how he dressed or behaved, Haymon Jacobs would always be singled out and noticed in any crowd. He could no more escape his size than someone like Hamid Malik could avoid being black. Just sitting across from Haymon now, Reed noted that he himself was experiencing tiny flashes of fear. In comparison with Haymon's great bulk, he was dwarfed, insignificant, a bothersome little schnauzer snapping at the heels of a great work horse. There was just no way around it. Big men were a race apart.

As though he sensed what Reed was thinking, Haymon suddenly smiled and said, "World ain't built for us big men, doc. We gotta stoop through doorways, sleep across both beds in motel rooms, and listen to the assholes of the universe ask us how the weather is up here."

"What do you say to those people, Haymon?" Reed asked, sincerely interested.

"I usually say, 'Piss poor, since you got here.' The ones that want to know how tall I am, I just say, 'Six-twelve, baby, and every inch is worth five grand a year to me.' Be surprised how quick that shuts 'em up."

Although Haymon seemed to be suddenly enjoying the conversation, there was something in his face that made Reed wonder whether he was really there at all. To Reed, Haymon seemed to have become some figure out of Jewish mythology, a large and hulking peasant selected by God to be tested again and again. Bontche Sweig. That was it. Haymon was Bontche Sweig.

It was not exactly the kind of scientific data that he could put into his report or anything that could be isolated by determining where Haymon's responses spiked on the MMPI but Reed could not deny what he was feeling. This man was a victim. He had been singled out. By whom, Reed was not sure.

Reed wondered whether Haymon realized how important this interview was in terms of his very shaky career as a professional athlete. An unfavorable report and the Lakers would pass on what certainly was Haymon's last chance to make a paying career out of basketball.

It was an odd reversal of roles. In the schoolyard, Haymon had been the star and Reed just another nobody sitting on the steps. Now the big guy needed his blessing to be able to go on with his life. Reed dutifully noted that he was deriving a curious pleasure from this knowledge.

Realizing that he was beginning to think more about himself than his patient, Reed switched off the machine. "That's about it," he said. "We're finished."

"What happens now?" Haymon asked.

"I go back to L.A., evaluate the tests, file a report, and the Lakers decide."

"What do you think?"

"About what?"

Haymon grinned. "My head, doc. My goddamn head."

Reed smiled. "Seems to be in the proper place," he said. As though to rid himself of some of the misgivings he was feeling, he said, "Psychiatry's not an exact science by any means, Haymon, despite what many people think. Two experts can examine a single person and come away with different opinions. Most of the time we just listen and then try and figure out what we think is going on in there. The mind is pretty uncharted territory, you know."

"Fuck that, doc," Haymon said. "I mean . . . what do you think my chances are with the Lakers?"

"They want you," Reed said. "You and, uh, Bran. Otherwise, why go to all this trouble?"

"Yeah," Haymon said. "That's how I figure it myself."

Reed began shoveling papers back into his portfolio. When he was through, he stood up. Haymon did the same, sticking out his huge right hand. There was still something about Haymon that reminded Reed of the awkward, gangly adolescent giant he had once been. For a moment, remembering their shared beginnings, Reed was deeply touched.

"All the best, Haymon," he said, really meaning it, "and, like Liddel says . . . 'Fuck the rest.' I'll see what I can do for you back there."

"Solid," the big man said, squeezing Reed's hand in his out-sized grasp. "You tell 'em for me, doc. They want me, I'm ready. I'll even bring my own ball. Can't do no better than that, can I?"

"I guess not," Reed said, making his way to the door.

After Kreiger had gone, Haymon stood alone in the middle of the empty living room where he had been sleeping for the past few months. He stretched both of his arms up to the ceiling and rocked back on his heels. Without straining, he placed the flat of both his palms against the ceiling's nubby white surface, holding them there for what seemed like a very long time. When he took them away again, two perfect palm prints remained, the outline of all ten fingers etched in perspiration like the spoor of some legendary monster that walked upside down. Then the sweat evaporated, and the prints disappeared from view.

For days now, he had been meaning to go out and get some organic apple juice from the health food store by the station. Only things just kept coming up. With Liddel gone and the interview over, now would be the perfect time. Haymon decided he would do just that, after he smoked a joint. Since he was going to get high, he figured he might as well put on some music first. On his way into Liddel's bedroom for the stash box, he slid a record on the stereo and punched the "play" button. Before the needle found its way into the first groove of the record's shiny black surface, he was already back at the couch, building a joint.

By the time Liddel came home, Haymon was totally stoned, the coffee table in front of him littered with torn bits of rolling paper and mounds of discarded seeds. Although the health food shop had long since closed, Haymon was still thinking about going out for apple juice. One more joint and he would be ready.

"Christ," Liddel said, looking around in disgust, "d'jou wait for him to leave at least? Smells like a rock concert in here." Without waiting for Haymon to answer, Liddel marched across the living room and turned down the volume on the stereo. The arm was up over the turntable. Liddel wondered how many times Haymon had listened to the same side without changing the record. When the big guy got really stoned, he could be useless.

"Pull my chain, little man," Haymon said, experiencing a sudden rush of good feelings. "You talkin' to an L.A. Laker."

"Says who?"

"Number one, right here."

"You got it on with that *putz*?"

"Damn straight," Haymon said. "Why not? He knows his business."

"Yeah? Good thing his business ain't shoes."

"Huh?"

"Never mind. What'd he say?"

"Said he'd do what he could for me. Can't ask for more than that, can you?"

Liddel didn't answer right away. "And you waited till he left to start smokin'?" he asked.

"Fuck you," Haymon said. "Sure."

"You think it's set, huh?" Liddel asked nervously.

"All the way. Money in the bank."

"All right!" Liddel cried exuberantly. "Smoke a pound of the shit then! Lemme get you some of the good stuff."

Laughing, Liddel went in to the bedroom where he kept some very expensive Colombian hidden in a box in the closet. If Haymon was right and Kreiger could be counted on not to mess things up, the Lakers would soon have to come through with a real money offer, something in the neighborhood of seventy thousand a year.

For now, it was enough for Liddel to know that Haymon was headed for a spot on a championship team. A high-rent connection like that could open up all kinds of doors. Before the season was over, he might even go to the coast himself. Being out there obviously hadn't done Kreiger any harm.

Of one thing Liddel was sure. Money came only to money. You had to have some to make more. Without a business manager or a wife to get in the way, Liddel was positive he could give Haymon some solid advice about putting his money to work where it would do the most good for everyone. Humming tunelessly, dope in hand, he went back into the living room, where his oldest friend was waiting to get higher still.

BOOK FOUR · **At Home in the Box Canyons of Los Angeles**

"The more you struggle, the more the box, like an extra outer skin growing from the body, creates new twists for the labyrinth. . . ."

Kobo Abé, *The Box Man*

CHAPTER SIXTEEN

On a hot Tuesday in October, in the midst of a heat wave that made it seem more like midsummer than early fall, Reed Kreiger drove his old green Fiat roadster to the campus of Loyola University. The blazing Santa Ana wind coursing through the box canyons of Los Angeles was blowing most of the traffic the other way, toward Santa Monica and beaches already crowded with sun-scorched flesh. To his great surprise, Reed found himself making amazingly good time on the freeway. By the time he left his car in a lot jammed with student vehicles, he was actually humming happily to himself.

He could not deny that he was excited. Hardly anyone in Los Angeles even knew that today the Lakers would begin training for the upcoming season. Fewer cared. In weather like this, getting near the ocean was all that mattered to most people. As the newest member of the Lakers' super efficient organization, Reed would not have dreamed of being anywhere else. For him, this was an occasion.

In the months since his return from New York, Reed's life had changed radically for the better, an obvious by-product of his having bothered to go back and touch home base again. The quality of his work on the Jacobs-Malik deal had convinced Blake Marion to offer him a full-time position with the team. Naturally, he had accepted. The salary it would bring him each month was so reassuringly large that he had gone ahead and opened an office of his own on Rodeo Drive in Beverly Hills.

Today, he was going to get his first look at the powerhouse of a team most experts thought could not help winning an NBA title this year. Reed could not deny that he was nervous. The high-salaried world of big time professional basketball was a far cry from anything he had known at the university or as a ballplayer at CCNY. Although he was confident that his professional credentials were in order, Reed could not help wondering if he was really good enough to make it among ballplayers whose talent was super human.

His first glimpse of the little gym in which the Lakers practiced was a blur of assistant coaches in tattered sweat clothes rolling basketballs along the floor, chanting, "Piggup, piggup, piggup." Several outsized men in reversible jerseys and multicolored shorts were sprinting to the foul line and back, to the midcourt line and back, and then all the way down to the far wall and back, scooping up loose balls as they ran. Reed knew the drill well. At CCNY it had been called the "puker."

It was the smell that hit Reed hardest, whirling him back to his own days as a ball player. The gym smelled like peanuts, a heavy, cloying odor made up only in part of the scent of bodies in motion. Far more noticeable and considerably more oppressive was the aroma of cleanliness, the hot air smell of clean socks still warm and fluffy from the dryer. Every gym he had ever played in had smelled like this, the institutional odor of socks and jocks and organized athletics, with a faint trace of melted butter thrown in somewhere for good measure.

Reed looked around for a familiar face. All the way up in the deserted bleachers, sitting with his back against the wall, was Blake Marion. Blake motioned for Reed to join him. Taking care not to lose his balance, Reed made his way up into the swaying stands.

For a long while, the two men sat in silence, watching. The only sound was the pounding of feet on the polished floor, the squeak of rubber on hardwood, and an occasional grunt. Between drills, this year's Laker team stood with their hands on their hips, sucking for air with their mouths hanging open as beads of sweat rolled down their necks and foreheads. Dressed in a random assortment of athletic equipment collected during lifetimes spent playing for various pro teams and institutions of higher learning, there was something sleek and expensive about each and every one of them.

Individually, the Lakers had the attenuated air of whippets specially bred for the race, the solemn and positively Egyptian look of men who knew that they were the absolute best at what they did. It was as though they were all privy to another level of physical reality, one Reed himself had never reached. Reed was reminded of a collection of Grand Prix drivers before a big race or a flotilla of powerboat captains preparing for a Gold Cup run.

In his own way, each of these men was a legend. Reed found it hard to believe that they too had to suffer through the same mindless drills he himself had run so many times in college. He would have thought them exempt from such activity.

Had he been asked, Reed could have easily supplied a curious questioner with a surprisingly accurate list of each player's particular skills and idiosyncrasies, culled from careful, religious readings of the sports sections of both Los Angeles newspapers as well as *Sport* and *Sports Illustrated.*

Hamid Malik, whom he had known for years, seemed certain to move into the starting lineup at guard next to the immortal Cliff Summers, the man they called "Western Union" for his uncanny ability to launch long distance bombs to the hoop. At center, Arvin Williams, the man mountain known simply as the "Big A," was so dominant a performer that even now, in his twelfth year in the league, he was still the hub around which the team was built. Haymon Jacobs would have to go a long way before he could displace Arvin from that spot.

At the forwards, Dexter Mathorpin and Edgar Weekend were two solid, reliable performers. Wendell Milk, the "Arkansas Strongboy," would again be the first man off the bench in any game or on-court brawl. The other Lakers, many of whom could have started for most other NBA teams, were "Wee Willie" Whitman, Haywood Music, Sticks Hooper, Wilton Felder, and a promising rookie from LSU, Larry Carleton.

As far as Reed was concerned, every single one of them was an authentic celebrity. Cliff Summers and Arvin Williams, neither of whom was present today, were actual national heroes, who could often be seen shaving their faces and spraying their underarms on network television.

For Reed, who had played the game himself, albeit on a far more rudimentary and less glamorous level, their names had a magical, almost incantatory quality. *"SUMMERS!"* he had heard many an undersized guard back in Brooklyn shout after launching a long-distance jump shot toward the rim. Every big man in the land had seen pictures of Arvin's specially designed mountaintop house, with a bed hewn from the trunk of a redwood tree. As the Lakers huffed, panted, and puffed their way through practice, it was all Reed could do to keep himself from asking for autographs.

"This ain't shit," Blake Marion said after a while, re-arranging his great bulk into a standing position. "Let's you and me get us some lunch, doc. We can always come back later, if you're interested."

Reed looked up hesitantly, happy to be where he was. "C'mon, doc," Marion cackled. "You ain't on a time clock. I'll see to it the owner don't hear."

Reluctantly, Reed followed Marion out of the gym into the hot and super smoggy autumn sunshine. Blinking constantly to clear his smarting eyes, he walked with the general manager to his car, a brand-new Mercedes Sedan. Marion drove to a restaurant not far from the airport where a waiter led them to a back table.

"For some reason," Marion grinned, "they got themselves a cellar full of old Pouilly-Fuissé here that no one drinks. 'Cept me."

After the waiter had brought the food, the big man settled in and said, "You ever think how come it is grown men come to be running around with kids' nicknames?"

"How do you mean?" Reed said.

" 'Western Union,' 'The Big A,' 'The Hulk.' "

"Part of the game, no?"

"Maybe once," Marion allowed, "but no more. You got a product you wanna sell these days, you gotta hang a handle on it people can grab hold of. L.A.'s one bitch of a market, doc. We out there competing for the entertainment dollar like everyone else. On any given Sunday, people got their choice of a thousand things to do, from hang glidin' to sittin' at home watchin' movies on cable TV. Yet we gotta pull 'em into the Forum to watch us."

"Seems the best way to do that would be to win."

"Shit, yes!" Marion cackled. "That's all. Just win. We been so close these past couple of years, we could taste it, only to blow it at the end. We let that flag go back to Boston one more time and we're gonna be up shit's creek, *sans* paddle. You dig? We'll all have to get us nicknames or flood the damn Forum and bring in the lions." Marion took a long swallow, emptying his glass. He refilled it and said, "Understand what I'm talking about?"

"The team is serious about taking it all this year," Reed said, parroting a statement Marion had been quoted as making in this morning's *Times*.

"Shit, yes. And we're all gonna have to do whatever it is we have to do in order to get there. All of us. I just wanted you to know, right from the gitgo. End of lecture. Let's eat."

During the week that followed, Reed had little time to reflect on why Marion had chosen to single him out for a rousing preseason pep talk. His fairly well-publicized association with the Lakers was doing wonders for business. In the suite of offices he'd rented in Beverly Hills, both the appointment book and the plush, oversized waiting room were filled to capacity. Apparently, if you were a young and troubled high school sprinter from Brentwood or an anxiety-ridden Olympic swimming prospect from Canoga Park, the only head doctor in town worth seeing was the one the Lakers had endorsed by putting on their payroll.

Reed found himself constantly at work or in his car, going toward it. Three afternoons a week, he spent a few hours at the Loyola gym, making himself available to the Laker players, none of whom seemed to notice he was alive. Then he returned to the office to see patients, staying there some nights until eight-thirty. Commuting from the beach to his office to Loyola and then back again, he put more than a hundred miles a day on his beleaguered little Fiat.

It was well worth it. The way things were going Reed was certain it would not be long before he could trade the Fiat in on something older and a little more precious. Something like the gleaming 1959 Porsche convertible "D" with roll-up windows that grinned seductively at him every time he passed the showroom of Beverly Hills' leading used car dealer. The asking price was a cool ten thousand.

Each day, when Reed pulled into the parking lot outside the gym where the Laker players were going through their paces, he could not help noticing their cars: cool, sleek racing machines standing one next to the other in rows, a brace of expensive thoroughbred horses waiting at the gate for the race to begin.

In Los Angeles, more than any other place Reed had ever been, what you drove was who you were. Never was this more apparent to him than on the day Arvin Williams finally took it upon himself to begin training for the upcoming season. On that afternoon every other car in the parking lot was dwarfed by the magnificent two-tone magenta Rolls-Royce parked so near the players' entrance that Reed had to sidle around it in order to get inside the gym. The bar and the television set in the back seat of the Rolls spoke of untold wealth. The large golden "A" monogrammed on the driver's door in old English script left no doubt in anyone's mind who owned the car. Arvin Williams. The king himself, who could afford to leave his royal carriage parked out in the hot sun while he took care of more pressing business inside.

Standing anywhere from six-eleven to seven feet three inches tall, depending on to whom you talked, weighing in at no less than two hundred and seventy-five pounds, no matter whom you questioned, the "A" was easily the strongest man in the league, if not the free world. By reputation, he was also the strangest, one of his better-known peccadilloes being a large stuffed teddy bear that he carried around with him everywhere. Arvin had christened the teddy bear "Odin" after the ringing cry Tony Curtis had sounded so often in Arvin's all-time number one favorite movie,

The Vikings. For some reason, the "A" loved Tony Curtis. Odin himself often occupied a seat of his own on team flights. The "A" sometimes carried Odin into hotel coffee shops for breakfast, ordering a complete meal for each of them, eating all of it, and then asking for separate checks. The two were inseparable.

A millionaire a few times over from various real estate holdings and financial speculations, the "A" no longer played basketball for money. Rather, he had returned to the Lakers for this, his final season, for the express purpose of adding a world championship ring to his already-impressive collection of personal jewelry, much of which he wore all at once on his fingers, wrists, and outsized neck.

Although he reported to camp a week late, the "A" seemed in no hurry at all to round into shape until the Lakers began to scrimmage. Then, whenever he took the floor against Haymon Jacobs, something short-circuited inside his brain. He did everything he could to make his new teammate regret that he had ever come West to challenge him for a starting berth.

Their continuing one-on-one was a state of armed conflict no one could avoid noticing. Its ferocity fascinated Reed and he found himself turning up day after day to watch it, if only to follow the awesome battering Haymon was taking. Barrage after barrage of elbows found their way to Haymon's head. He accepted knees to the groin that would have killed a smaller man. Any time a knot of players tangled under the hoop, two of them were guaranteed to be Arvin Williams and Haymon Jacobs, with Haymon usually lying on the floor, cradling some new injury after the knot was undone.

For his part, Haymon never complained. He took the unremitting physical abuse day after day, answering back only with his curiously effeminate jump shot from out beyond the perimeter of what Arvin considered to be his turf. After a particularly grueling session midway through the third week of practice, Haymon hobbled over to Reed holding an ice pack to his forehead. "Got a second, doc?" he asked. "Like to talk to you."

"Sure," Reed said, eyeing Haymon's head. "You okay there?"

Haymon peeled the ice pack away to reveal a blue lump the precise size, shape, and color of a robin's egg. "Sure thing," he said. "I've had worse. What I wanted to ask you was . . . what's team policy here on pills? Clue me in."

"What kind of pills?"

"Greenies, doc."

"Greenies?"

"Ups. See in Phoenix, we had us a doctor who kind of looked out for anyone who needed a boost. Which this week is me. Williams is gonna break me in pieces if I don't get myself a little edge going. Know what I mean?"

"I'm not sure I do, Haymon. What did this doctor in Phoenix prescribe the pills for?"

"Uh," Haymon said, his brow furrowing and unfurrowing like a hillside of long grass in the wind, "depression?"

"Really? Hadn't he ever heard of lithium?"

"That an up?"

"Actually, it's a salt."

"He never heard of it. Besides, ain' no salt gonna help what I got. I wake up some mornings knowin' there's no way my body can make it outta bed. I been pissin' weird colors too, doc. That's how banged up I am. Soon as the regular season starts and Arvin gets to work out on guys on other teams, I'll be fine all on my own."

"I don't know," Reed said, running a nervous finger around his shirt collar. "That stuff can be murder on your body."

"And this ain't?" Haymon said, mopping at the sweat that was coursing down his face. "Tell you the absolute truth, doc . . . I'm gonna get my hands on 'em one way or the other, either from you or by takin' my chances on the street like everyone else."

"I wouldn't like to see you doing that, Haymon."

"Solid. That's why I ask. Maybe you could ask around, see how the breeze blows, and get back to me. No names, of course. I wouldn't want to get either one of us in *shtuk*, doc. Not this early in the season, 'specially after what you done for me already."

"Ah, that was nothing, Haymon. You make me look good out there every day. Tell you what. Let me check on it and I'll get back to you soon as I find out."

"Great. Whatever you say."

Reed made it a point to seek out Blake Marion for advice on the matter. After he asked him about the club's policy on drugs, the general manager just stared at him as though he were talking a foreign language. *"Greenies?"* Marion said. "That's a funny word."

"You're putting me on, right, Blake?"

"Me?" Marion said, his large eyes growing wider. "I'm not even here. I don't hear you talking . . . so how can I put you on? But if I was, and I did, I'd tell you to go easy on that stuff, doc. There's all kinds of rumors around the league about players who won't suit up without swallowing all kinds of pills first. If we had any of those on this team, I'd want to know about it. Once I did, I'd have to inform the league office and the commissioner. Assuming I was here to hear about it. Of course, as general manager, I sure as hell wouldn't want to let a little thing like a pill truckdrivers all over Interstate Five are popping by the handful stand in the way of my team having a winning season. You read me?"

"No."

"I know you'll come to your own conclusion on this thing, Reed, but my motto is . . . never give a man anything he can't handle . . . but don't deny him what he needs to be a winner. Hope that helps some, seein' as how I wasn't here to begin with. Clear?"

"Like mud."

"Great, doc. You got it now."

Realizing that no one was going to stick his neck out and take a position on the problem one way or the other, Reed wrestled with his conscience for a few days before deciding that he would only be on the side of humanitarian concern if he gave Haymon something to help prop him up in his continuing struggle with the "A." The Red Cross would have done no less. Besides, Reed had no desire to encourage anyone to go out looking for dope on the street. Grudgingly, he wrote Haymon a two-week prescription for amphetamine sulfate in capsule form, which could be refilled once and then only with a doctor's permission. The big man seemed grateful and the next day the Lakers packed up and set out for their first pre-season exhibition games of the year in San Francisco and Seattle.

Reed was not sorry to see them go. What with his new practice and their practices, he had been in motion for a solid month, going flat out from freeway to freeway with never any time for himself. Although Callie would be working all weekend, he was actually looking forward to spending a blissful Saturday and Sunday at home, planted in front of the television set. To make sure that he'd be able to remain there, Reed made a Friday night pit stop at an unfamiliar supermarket to lay in a weekend supply of taco chips and beer.

With nothing more on his mind than the Muzak humming in the background, Reed pushed his wire-rim cart down one aisle and up another, humming contentedly to himself. As was his habit, he paused by the vegetable counter to check himself out in the long mirror running above it. He often looked at himself in mirrors in public places, as though to confirm the continuing fact of his existence even in a crowd.

At the far end of the counter, a young woman was arguing intently with a clerk who looked as though he would have been more at home perched on the nose of a surfboard than stenciling price changes on bottles of ketchup and cans of creamed corn. Every time the girl spoke, her dark, shirred hair shook with indignation. Judging from her tone of voice, Reed guessed that he had already missed the opening salvo in their little battle.

"Lettuce?" the girl said scornfully, holding up a head of well-drenched leaves in her hand. "This is watercress. This is seaweed. Any wetter and I'd need a snorkel to eat it. . . ."

"*Heeey,*" the clerk said easily, shrugging his shoulders as though he were not responsible for anything but surf conditions at Malibu. "The manager tells me to water the lettuce. I water it."

"Water," the girl said, shaking the lettuce so that droplets of water pinwheeled from it like the spray coming off the back of a large dog shaking itself dry after a dip in the ocean, "not drown."

"I put too much on, huh?" the kid said. "Tell you what. Lemme bag one for you and stamp it paid. Okay?"

"How disgusting," the girl said. "Bag two and we'll call it a deal."

The kid laughed and slid two butter lettuces into a plastic bag that he stapled shut with a conspiratorial wink. Reed wondered whether he could use what he'd just seen to shake the kid down for a can of jalapeño dip when the girl wheeled her cart in a circle and made straight for him. It took him a moment because of her hair, which had been clipped and styled. Her eyes and smile were unchanged.

"Jesus shit," he said. "Lauren?"

Uttering a small cry of delight, Lauren Sklar skipped out from behind her wagon and came running toward him.

She hugged him and the familiar smell of her sweet, heavy perfume drew him back in time. Once again, he was the adolescent boy he had been back in New York City, thin and frightened, little more than a pale reflection of his father's hopes and dreams. When she stepped back to look at him, Reed realized that Lauren's pinched white New York prettiness was gone. It had been replaced by something more native, a kind of glossy local protective coloration that made her look as though she had been born and raised in the Golden State.

That Lauren Sklar was here, standing in a supermarket on the Pacific Coast Highway, was undeniable. How it was that he came to be standing across from her he did not yet really comprehend.

It was impossible, certainly. Higher powers had to be at work. The particular set of circumstances that had brought him to just this market at precisely this time, down the very aisle in which she'd been standing, could not be traced. There was no rational explanation for it, save for the fact that certain people were tied to one another for life, no matter how much time and distance came between them. He and Lauren were such a pair.

"Hey," he said, appraising her as though she were a prospective patient, "you look . . . great."

"Aha," she laughed. "My Hollywood haircut throws you off. You miss my long and flowing locks. The end of innocence. I cut it off last year."

"Looks good," he said, voicing more enthusiasm for the change than he was feeling. "Really. Looks damn good. I guess I knew you were out here. My mother told me. What happened to grad school?"

"I dropped out," she said, her face darkening, "just after my father died. . . ."

"Mine too," Reed said. "Last year."

"Oh God. What of?"

"Heart attack. Very quick. Yours?"

"Cancer," she said. "Very slow, and expensive. I'm afraid there wasn't much left of anything at the end. My mother's moved to Arizona. She's working in a clinic. We're all working. . . ." She batted her eyelashes. "And I'm in Hollywood, an orphan of the storm, trying to make my way. Look."

Reaching into her shoulder bag, Lauren pulled out a cerise business card with a white bird in flight across it and the words "Skylark Films" etched along one wing.

"Skylark?" he said.

Lauren giggled. "It was Skyler Productions for a while, but that sounded too much like I was in the garment center. In half sizes. So I made it Skylark Films. You know . . . Percy Bysshe? 'O noble bird thou wert? . . .' A little class, all around. Lauren Skyler of Skylark Films." She giggled, "On a good day I pass for a Wasp."

Reed laughed. "Not you, kid," he said. "Not ever. Not with that face. What kind of work do you do?"

"You name it," Lauren said, "we do it. Whatever we can crank out to sell."

"You've got partners?"

Lauren made a face. "Have I got partners?" she said. "Don't ask. My partners have partners. It's a commune. All you have to do to join is drop out of the UCLA film school."

"Damn," Reed said, feeling suddenly guilty at having never even made the effort to find out precisely where in Los Angeles Lauren had been all this time, "I could have at least looked you up in the book and given you a call."

"Please," Lauren said. "Spare me. First of all, I'm not even listed. Secondly, even if I was, it would be under my new name. So I'm afraid we're just fated to go on meeting in supermarkets. Vegetable karma."

Reed grinned and threw up his hands. "I surrender," he said. "Just promise you'll be with me."

"Where you're going now, Reed?" Lauren said, adopting a heavy Brooklyn Jewish accent. "You've eaten? No? I thought so. You look very . . . t'in. Too t'in is no good. You'll come home with me, I'll make us supper, you'll tell me everythin'. No?"

"All right," Reed said. "So long as it's not boiled chicken."

"No boiled chicken. You can buy the wine. So long as it's not Manischewitz."

"A deal," Reed said, feeling very happy. "Good stuff. At least ninety-nine cents a half gallon."

"What class," Lauren laughed. "But then I always knew you had it in you."

Hooking her arm in his, she led him around a pyramid of wine vinegar bottles down an aisle lined with cans of freeze-dried coffee, jars of large green olives stuffed with ruby colored pimentos, and boxes of exotic wafers from foreign lands. Reed let her steer him to the wine section, conscious only that his past had once again reached out for him. He had come all this way only to meet himself, again and again, coming back.

Were it not for the undeniable fact that he had just carved out a place for himself with the Lakers and founded a private practice that gave no sign of becoming anything but a resounding success, Reed would have felt frightened. There was something positively pathological about constantly going back in time. The old, musty cellars of memory and the dank, cobwebbed basements of years gone by were no place for anyone to make a life, much less someone like himself, who had struggled so long and hard to find something better.

CHAPTER SEVENTEEN

IT HAD long been Haymon Jacobs' deep-seated belief that all across America, from the dressing rooms in the new Madison Square Garden atop Penn Station in New York to the ramps that led to the playing floor in the Fabulous Forum in L.A., there stretched a long green corridor running from coast to coast. Specially marked doors and smaller corridors led off the main hallway to a series of identical airlines terminals, cinder-block motels, and apartments like the very blank three room suite in Inglewood he now called home.

Within the corridor, it made not a damn bit of difference where you were. All along its green neon length, things were always exactly the same. So far as Haymon was concerned, Los Angeles was nothing more than its western terminus, the place where all the creosote and sheetrock came together to form the biggest quick-lunch Copper Penny of them all. Since he was a prisoner in the city, he was forced to amuse himself with whatever came to hand. Fortunately, when it came to providing a source of cheap entertainment, the locals never failed him.

Sitting in some plastic and Formica coffee shop after yet another practice in which the large black asshole he was forced to guard every day had brutally worked him over once again, Haymon would lean casually toward a rouged waitress who had only just come on duty and inquire politely, "Ma'am? Excuse me. What's this place made of?"

"How do you mean, dear?"

"Oh, you know, the walls."

"Brick?"

"I don't think so."

"It's not wood, I know that. Masonite?"

"You mean like wallboard?"

"Like plasterboard, dear."

"Could it be stucco?"

"I guess." A nervous laugh. A flick of the pencil used to record orders. "Tell ya the truth, dear. I never thought about it much myself." A glance at the vinyl-coated menu. "Now, you want those eggs scrambled or sunnyside?"

During his years on the road as a professional athlete, Haymon had discovered that there was virtually no one who could not be drawn into a conversation about the technical aspects of a building's construction. The long green corridor was filled with fools who liked nothing more than to thump their fists against the wall of a motel lobby and point out where the fake beams came together over the phony fireplace to form a cathedral arch. Although no one had ever been able to tell Haymon exactly what stucco was or whether cinders were actually pressed together to form the blocks that were then stacked into the stores, restaurants, and banks that ran all across the contiguous forty-eight, they all gave it their best, blathering away stupidly as he reeled them in.

It was a way to stay sane on the road. Bran Johnson, back before he had become Hamid Malik, had made a practice of walking up to good-looking women on the streets of strange cities and saying, "Hi, there. I wonder if you can help me. I seem to be having trouble finding *your* house."

Not unreasonably, Haymon had expected that even in Los Angeles they would continue their search for truth and the occasional joint together along the long green corridor. He had even thought that the two of them might share an apartment for a while until Linda came out to join him.

But the free spirit he had known as Bran Johnson in Phoenix had vanished, to be replaced by a religious zombie he had no desire to befriend. The first time he had tried to draw Hamid Malik into one of their old routines, Hamid had stared at him as though he were crazy and then walked away.

Good enough. Haymon Jacobs had been alone before. He could go his own way easily once again. As a club, the Lakers seemed to encourage that kind of behavior anyway. Players did their thing on the court and then went home. The veterans seemed more interested in stocks and bonds and sowbelly futures than basketball, the blacks spent their time on planes playing poker, and the newcomers kept their mouths shut, waiting for a chance of their own at the big money that came with a starting berth.

More than any other team he had ever known, the Lakers were serious. God, were they serious. Total professionals, they never displayed any real emotion even on the court. No one wildly slapped five or shouted congratulations to a teammate after a good pass. It would not have been professional. Every Laker was being paid top dollar to perform, and the impossible was routine to them, to be done casually, as though none of it were any more difficult than tying the laces on their sneakers.

Compared to Phoenix, the level of competition was incredible. Although the Lakers' heads were nowhere, their bodies were murderously efficient. Had it not been for the vial of pills he'd fast-talked Kreiger into giving him, Haymon doubted whether he would have been able to make it through the pre-season scrimmages. As it was, he'd taken to spending a couple of hours in the bathtub each night, soaking away the pain so that he could get up the next morning and start all over again.

Despite his dedication, no one had yet grabbed his hand and told him how much he was going to help the club this year. Blake Marion, who'd been all smiles and encouraging winks when it had come time to talk money and sign a contract, seemed oblivious to the fact that he was even around. A cold fish, that man, riding herd on a school of equally cold and smaller fish. Welcome to Los Angles, Haymon Jacobs. Home of the chili dog and the dirty bookstore.

If only the Celtics hadn't given up on him so quickly, things might have been different all around. Oh, he had hated their we-are-champions trip all right but Boston was a hell of a lot easier a city to live in than Phoenix had been. He now blamed that place for a lot of things. The breakdown of his marriage, the rotten shape his body was in, the confusion he still felt some days once practice was over and he was on his own. Many things had blurred so badly there at the end of the season that the time he had spent with Liddel in New York now seemed to him no more than a long stoned weekend.

Of one thing he was sure. Los Angeles was a miserable place to be alone in. The apartment he was renting on a monthly basis didn't have a thing going for it save that it was virtually within walking distance of the Forum and so close to the airport that he could pick up anyone who might come to visit him without having to battle freeway traffic.

Most nights, Haymon just stayed home, staring out through the living room's sliding glass doors at the rows of unblinking lights from identical apartments across the way. He spoke to no one and no one spoke to him. He ate most of his meals in antiseptic coffee shops and bought both L.A. papers each day, though neither was as time-consuming to read as the *Daily News* or the *Post*. Once a week, he forced himself up to go and sit through a movie in Westwood. He soon found that the young hand-holding couples from UCLA distracted him, so he took to catching the early shows, when the theaters were still relatively empty.

He brooded constantly about Linda, missing her at the strangest times, waking up some mornings convinced that she was still lying next to him only to realize that nothing had changed and he was still alone. The pain was constant and unremitting, sometimes as sharp as an elbow to the gut, more often just dull and throbbing, like some pulsing migraine headache that would not go away. The only thing that made it stop was when he pushed himself beyond his physical limits at practice and came home so exhausted he could do nothing but lie in the bathtub, more dead than alive.

Linda had asked him for time to think. He had given her that. The fat contract he'd signed with the Lakers would enable them to live well in Los Angeles, where there were concerts and movies and apartments for rent within spitting distance of the blue Pacific. So long as he took care of his action on the court, Haymon believed that everything else would eventually fall into place for him. It always had in the past. Although he had no hopes of replacing the "Big A" (for asshole) in the starting lineup right away, he knew he had a real chance to see some action once the regular schedule got under way. Over the course of a season that would take the team through fall, winter, and most of next spring, nearly anything was possible. No matter how mighty he seemed in practice, the "Big A" was not indestructible. No one was.

By phone from Brighton, Liddel let Haymon know that the prescription he'd wheedled out of Kreiger could probably be refilled indefinitely once it had been doctored. As soon as the Lakers hit New York, Haymon would see to it that Liddel did the doctoring. The same road trip would take the team to Boston. It was there that he intended to make his case to Linda.

For he'd changed. He knew that even Linda would be able to see that. This move to the coast had been the best thing for him really, removing him from everything and everyone he'd known back east. Out here, he was truly alone, and taking care of himself for the very first time. There was now no reason for them not to start it up all over again. The more Haymon thought about it, the more sense it made to him. Nothing had ever come easy to him, ever. He had willed himself into becoming a ballplayer by never giving up, ignoring a crippling injury that would have ended the career of a man with less desire. He felt the same way about his marriage. It could be mended.

For now, he was content to live within the confines of the long green corridor, spending each day putting out maximum effort on the court, then sinking blissfully to sleep on a bed that was too small for him. It wasn't much of a life but he was accustomed to it. He could take another month or two of it. He was Haymon Jay, the almighty Hulk. He could take anything, so long as he knew that somewhere down at the far end of the long green corridor there was a door marked "Linda" that would swing open for him into bright sunshine.

AFTER THE first six weeks of the season, Haymon was no longer so confident. More out of desperation than anything else, he had begun quietly chanting weird voodoo curses and black magic imprecations at Arvin Williams from his spot down at the far end of the Laker bench. Night after night, he would run through an entire medical dictionary of athletic ailments in Arvin's name: strained knees, pulled ligaments, torn cartilages, hip pointers, floating bone chips, thigh bruises so deep and painful they'd take a week to heal. Nothing worked.

In city after city, in Cobo Arena, Hofheinz Pavilion, and the Coliseum in Oakland, Haymon put the shit on Arvin Williams' head and the man remained in perfect health. Some nights, with the Lakers leading by as much as twenty points, the "A" went so far as to argue with the coach about coming out of the game. He loved to play. If they'd only let him, he'd stay out there until the janitors came in to sweep up the arena.

Night after night, Haymon dressed for games in which he knew he would see no action. The familiar feel of the elastic in his shorts, the comforting woolly texture of his extra-heavy socks, the smooth swish of the silken fabric of his jersey as he pulled it over his head all promised what would not be forthcoming—a chance to play.

Being on a team that won all the time was exactly like being on one that lost with the same dunning regularity. Sitting on the bench was sitting on the bench, no matter who you were doing it for, the most frustrating life a ballplayer could face. Once again a lowly reserve who never got to sweat out his anger during the game, Haymon moved from one motel room to another without reason, having to rely on yet another Magic Fingers massage unit to buck him to sleep for a quarter.

With Hamid Malik having now become a total stranger, there was no one at all with whom he could share his total disdain for the life his fellow Lakers seemed to love beyond all bounds.

Cliff Summers, who had been in the league for more than a decade and should have known better, liked nothing more than to browse in airport curio shops. His collection of plaster gnomes holding golf clubs with the inscription "Old Golfers Never Die— They Just Lose Their Balls" was said to be the world's largest. Wendell Milk, the team's redoubtable sixth man, could sit down to a pre-game meal of ground gristle on a frozen roll with a side order of french fries doused in ketchup that came from one of those little Rinse-and-Dri packets and go away smacking his lips as though he'd enjoyed a gourmet feast. Haymon felt himself surrounded by men who *believed*, fully grown adults so square they actually closed their eyes during the singing of the national anthem and hummed along.

Dexter M. and Edgar W., as the weak and strong side forwards liked to be called, were no better. They spent their time and money assembling a collection of fox-fur vests and Borsalino hats no self-respecting pimp would have worn anywhere but to his own funeral. The "A" spoke to no one at no time ever, often going so far as to book himself into a deluxe suite at a hotel other than the one the rest of the Lakers were in, as though being in the same building with the field troops would affect his status as the game's reigning superstar. Often, as Haymon sat morosely pulling on his socks in some locker room before a game, the "Big A" would sweep in at the very last minute, his stuffed teddy bear cradled in one hand, three hot dogs he'd purchased on his way through the arena for dinner balanced in the other.

Although he had no use for any of them, most especially the "Big A," Haymon saw that there was a certain method in Arvin's madness. The "Big A" did not want to be hassled. In order to make that clear to everyone, he had put some real distance between himself and the rest of the team. While Haymon could not afford to do this in as flamboyant a manner as Arvin Williams, he could let his teammates know he wanted nothing at all to do with any of them.

The men he had to work alongside every day could stare at him all they liked. They could ask him questions. He didn't have to answer. Safe within the comforting, climate-controlled confines of his own loneliness, Haymon was exempt from participating in any of the mindless rituals that made traveling from city to city with the Lakers such a total waste of time and energy.

The team's first extended road trip of the season took them cross-country, zig-zagging madly from Atlanta to Philadelphia to Chicago and Kansas City, then into New York and Boston, all in the space of seven days. Cities rushed by so quickly Haymon didn't even attempt to leave his motel room before games. In New York, he had time only to make his way down Fifth Avenue, which was crowded with holiday shoppers, to buy Linda an expensive piece of Steuben glass for Christmas before showing up at the Garden to watch as the Lakers ran the Knicks off the court.

Thankfully, Liddel appeared at the players' entrance after the game ended with two fat ounces of nearly purple weed that he let Haymon have for a rock-bottom price of fifty bucks. With Tina in tow, they headed to Chinatown for a post-game meal, Liddel working on the prescription Kreiger had given Haymon in L.A. right at the table so that it could be put on file at the pharmacy where he worked.

"You're good on this," Liddel said, "for the season. *If* you go easy. I figure I can refill it three or four times without makin' anyone nervous. Okay?"

"Cool," Haymon said. "Good enough."

Although both Liddel and Tina looked as though winter in the city was squeezing the color out of their faces, Liddel seemed happy enough about the way things were going. "Fuckin' Lakers keep winnin'," he said, "I promised Tina we'd hit the coast for the playoffs. I might even take a little dust with me. You think I could move that stuff out there?"

"You givin' up on grass?" Haymon asked.

"I sell what I can sell," Liddel said. "This winter, if you ain't got a snowstorm goin' on inside your nose, you ain't hip. So I deal a little coke. It don't bother me. 'Cept when I gotta go to Coney Island to cop. Fuckin' nightfighters there are cray-zee. It's gettin' heavier all the time too." Lowering his voice so that Tina wouldn't hear, he whispered, "I even got me a piece now. The fuckin' yahms and the Italians own Coney Island. They're all the time sellin' to one another, only they hate each other so much somebody else has got to be there in the middle to move the stuff. Yours truly."

It had been a long time since Haymon had heard Liddel say anything at all about the mechanics of his trade. "You high?" he asked suspiciously.

Liddel laughed and rubbed his nose. "It shows, huh?" He laughed. "Yeah. I take a little pop before we leave the house. For Tina, you know? She don't feel like she's dressed for a night out unless her nose is filled. Next week, she'll be eighteen. Nice, huh?"

Tina grinned in a slow sunshine-y way, her eyes half-closed from all the wine she had drunk with dinner. "Liddel," she said, "do me a favor, huh? Take a flying leap at yourself."

Liddel laughed louder than anyone. "What a bitch, huh?" he said admiringly. "She was born a fuckin' star."

After the meal, they went back to Haymon's hotel room and smoked until Tina fell out on the bed. When Liddel stood up to leave at four A.M., he put on his coat and made for the door as though he had come by himself.

"*Hey!*" Haymon said, gesturing to the bed. "You forget somethin' maybe?"

Liddel shrugged. "She wouldn't mind," he said, "and I know I don't. . . ."

Haymon looked from Liddel to Tina and back again. She was out cold, her mouth open, her hair falling over her face. He sighed and shook his head. Although he wasn't sure what one thing had to do with the other, he knew he would soon be seeing Linda. He had waited this long. He could wait a little longer.

"I'll give you a hand with her," he said, getting slowly to his feet.

"Nah," Liddel said, "I carry her all the time. She's the fallout queen. It's her move."

Liddel got Tina to her feet and wrapped her coat around her. Halfway across the room, she managed to get her eyes open. "Lemme say goodbye first, Liddel," she said sleepily, lurching over to where Haymon was sitting to give him a very wet kiss on the mouth. Liddel raised his eyebrows, as though to say the offer was still good.

"Well," Haymon said, going to work on another joint, "I got me some serious smokin' to do before I listen to the new Al Green album. You know. Smoke a little reefer. . . ."

"And we'll all get straight," Liddel said automatically. "Yeah. You call me when you get back to the coast, man. You know I always dig to hear what's goin' on inside the locker room. Play good. I see you. Later."

"Later," Haymon said, getting up to close the door behind them.

BY THE time the Lakers hit Philadelphia, Haymon was so thoroughly whacked out on the weed Liddel had sold him that he couldn't get it together to show up for the 76'ers game but moments before the Lakers were scheduled to take the floor. Fortunately, Arvin Williams chose just that precise moment to sweep into the locker room in a full-length sable coat. Haymon took advantage of the ensuing confusion to tear off his clothes and pull on his uniform, not noticing the single joint that rolled out of his shirt pocket onto the carpeted floor by his locker.

"This belong to you, I believe," Hamid Malik said, coming up to him with a wheatstraw wrapped bomber balanced between his fingers, "or am I mistaken?"

Haymon looked at the man who had once been his friend for a long moment before grabbing the joint. "You mistaken all right," he said, tucking it away, "but your mistake'll be my good fortune. I know it ain't yours."

Hamid wrinkled up his nose like a rabbit munching on a carrot. He sniffed the air around Haymon and said, "They makin' cannabis cologne these days, brother? Or did you blow up in the taxi on the way over?"

Haymon looked at Hamid in surprise. As a matter of fact, he had shared a joint with the black cabby who had brought him from the motel, the two of them getting so fucked up they'd circled the arena twice without noticing it.

"How the fuck . . ." he said. "Oh. The smell."

Hamid reached into a locker for a can of Right Guard and sprayed the stuff in circles in the air. "Coach got a nose too, you know," he said.

"Thanks, man," Haymon said coldly, shoving his feet into his sneakers. "I'm touched. I didn't know you cared. Seein' as how you found God an' all. Didn't think you bothered talkin' to white folks no more."

"Says who?"

"You still get high?" Haymon demanded, as though Hamid's answer would furnish some proof of his sincerity.

"I might, if the time was right."

"Don't shit me, man. You wanna smoke, you know where my room is."

"I might drop by," Hamid said, clasping his hands together prayerfully beneath his chin. "Now that you asked me." Giving Haymon a sweet smile, he bowed from the waist and then walked away.

"You ain't gotta pray, huh?" Haymon mumbled behind him, making a mental note to try to sweat during layups so that the odor of the grass would be conclusively gone by the time he sat down to watch the game.

The game itself was no different from all those that had preceded it. Arvin Williams did everything to the 76'ers except rip the rims off the backboards for souvenirs. As was his habit, Haymon was the first one out of the locker room and back in the motel. As soon as he got inside his room, he turned on his cassette player and rolled himself a post-game number, smoking it down to a glowing roach. If Hamid Malik was going to come by, Haymon wanted to be ready for him. Let Hamid try and lay some shit on his head now. There was no way. He was long gone.

Giggling, he turned on the color TV with the sound off so that he could goof on Johnny Carson's face while listening to Smokey Robinson get down on side two of *A Quiet Storm*. By the time Hamid knocked on the door, Haymon was feeling no pain. Hamid came in wrinkling his nose and sniffing.

"You still in that same old groove, huh?" he said, shaking his head sorrowfully. "Come back, get high, go crazy. Wake up, stay high, *be* crazy. Smoke smoke smoke. Toke toke toke."

"I wanna hear a sermon," Haymon said defiantly, "I'll dial a prayer. You wanna smoke or not?"

"Definitely," Hamid said, "but let's use this. A brother in Detroit laid it on me."

From a slit pocket in the red-and-black striped djellaba he was wearing, Hamid took out a gray stone chillum. He slid a pebble down it to block the smoking hole and stuffed it with four fingers of the good purple weed Haymon had bought in New York. Then he stood up and went into the bathroom. When he came back, there was a wet washcloth wrapped around the bottom of the chillum. Hamid squatted down, said something in a foreign language, and offered the chillum to the four corners of the room before putting it to his forehead.

"You smokin' it up there?" Haymon asked. "No wonder you ain't gettin' high."

Hamid said nothing. He struck two wooden matches against the rough surface of the match box and held them to the grass, which caught fire immediately, turning a bright red orange, fragrant seeds and stems crackling in the flame. Hamid took three mighty hits, holding the smoke deep within his lungs for what seemed like a very long time.

Haymon had to hand it to him. Whatever the fucker did, he did with style. When it came his turn to smoke, he tried to emulate Hamid but the stinging smoke caught him deep in the lungs and he had to give it up quickly, coughing and choking.

After the chillum was dead and the cassette had run out, Haymon tried to get to his feet to put on some more music. A wave of dizziness rolled over him, and he sank back to the floor, giggling. What weed. "You wanna hear something?" he asked. "Spinners? O'Jays? Harold Melvin and the Bluenotes?"

"I *am* hearing things," Hamid said, closing his eyes. "Just listen."

Haymon listened. All he heard was the rumble of traffic outside the motel window and the padding of footsteps down the corridor outside the door. For a second he got paranoid, thinking that maybe Hamid had heard someone coming. He'd always had superhuman powers when it came to detecting the approach of agents of the law. No, there was no one on the way. Just Hamid, sitting cross-legged on the floor with his eyes closed, listening to the traffic.

"You meditatin'?" Haymon asked.

Hamid opened his eyes and smiled. "Just thinking," he said. "It's not the dope, you know. Dope is just dope. Sometimes it gets you high, most times you get you high."

"Heavy," Haymon said sarcastically.

"When I look at you these days, brother," Hamid continued, "all I see is pain. Your face goes through a thousand changes a minute. On the bench. In the locker room. You want to know these men you work with, but you refuse to open up to them. It must be very hard for you here."

"Same as Phoenix," Haymon said flatly. "No better, no worse."

"How sad," Hamid said, "for things always to be the same. I thought I might play some music for you tonight, Haymon. But now I think there'll be a better time. When you decide you want to hear it."

"Yeah. I'll leave a note on your door."

Hamid sighed and smiled. "It's about love," he said, "with a capital 'L.' "

Haymon had no idea what Hamid was talking about. The dope continued to rise on him. After what seemed like a long and uncomfortable silence, he said, "You ever check out Summers before games? He's got this trip he does with his contact lenses to make sure they're in. Looks in the mirror, covers one eye, slams his hand against the other, then changes off. First time I saw him do it I nearly bust out laughin'. Motherfucker is weird."

Hamid said nothing. "If I'm hassling you," Haymon said, "let me know."

Hamid smiled. "All right, Haymon," he said. "I have to get some sleep now. Many thanks for the smoke. What I want you to know is that I'm still here, brother. If you ever really need me, you won't even have to call. I'll know. Till then. . . ."

Abruptly, Hamid got to his feet and walked silently out of the room, leaving Haymon behind to wonder how he could smoke such dynamite shit without even bothering to ask where it had come from. The old Bran Johnson would have been all over him to score an ounce for himself. Hamid Malik couldn't be bothered. Haymon turned up the volume on the TV and got out the bag of corn chips he kept stashed for such emergencies. When the bag was empty, he fell asleep.

The next day, on a plane headed for Chicago, he sat writing the letter he had long been composing in his head. The Lakers would be in Boston in a week. Could Linda see her way clear to come to the Gardens for the game? He was enclosing a hundred dollar check to cover her expenses. Tickets in her name would be left at the box office.

"It has been six months now," he wrote, "and much water over many bridges. I am completely set up in Los Angeles with many leads on quiet houses by the beach. Although so far I have not seen much action, I feel the attitude of the front office here is one of grooming me to take Arvin Williams' spot when he retires. (I know you've heard of him.) The Lakers are a first-class organization all the way, and although no one talks about it much, twenty thousand (20-0-0-0) dollars in playoff money is a bonus no one wants to pass up.

"I know you'll remember how to get to the Gardens. I'll meet you after the game in the players' entrance in back. Looking forward to seeing you again. . . ."

It took Haymon a long while to decide exactly how to sign the

208 ·

letter. After wrestling with his choices, he settled on, ". . . Your loving husband, now wearing the double-three's for L.A. Haymon."

He had already licked the envelope shut and addressed it to the post office box in Vermont where Linda was getting her mail these days when he thought of something he wanted to add. On the back of the envelope, in a curiously cramped and girlish hand, he wrote, "P.S. All I want is for us to talk."

He mailed the letter that afternoon from the Holiday Inn on the Lake in Chicago. Putting his head on automatic pilot, Haymon resigned himself to waiting until he would see Linda again. Then and only then could he begin patching up the cracked seams of his never waterproof personal life.

CHAPTER EIGHTEEN

MAX TRAPP's plan did not occur to him all at once. Rather, like all things of real worth, it came to him bit by bit, one piece falling perfectly into place next to another like the separate sections of the large and complicated jigsaw puzzles he had so often put together in prison to pass the time. Patience was the key. Patience, and an overwhelming desire to see what it would all look like when every last puzzle piece was finally stuck in place.

At forty-five, Max Trapp was starting over, though definitely not from scratch. He had time on his hands and enough cash locked away in his bedroom safe to stake him for however long he'd need to put his plan into operation. There was no great rush. He had waited nearly twenty years to pay back those who had kept him from making a name as a professional ballplayer. He could easily afford to wait a little longer. Beyond that Max knew nothing, save that in time all the information he needed would come to him, bit by bit.

By paying close attention to the sports pages of both Los Angeles newspapers before the pro basketball season began, Max had learned that the current owners of the Lakers were about to sell the club to a cartel of big businessmen from the Midwest. Blake Marion, who for years had kept the team at the top of the Western Division of the NBA by making one brilliant deal after another, was said to be in line for the top job when the deal went through. If Marion did indeed become club president, it would earn him a place in the history of pro basketball. Marion would be the first black top executive in the game at the major league level. Max carefully filed the information away in his mind.

Then, with nearly everyone else in L.A., Max read the news about Blake Marion's latest coup, a deal that would bring Haymon Jacobs and Hamid Malik to the Lakers in return for some cash and a few future draft choices. The host of a local sports phone-in show on the radio called it the biggest pro basketball steal since the Detroit Pistons gave Dave DeBusschere to the Knicks in return for Howie Komives and Walt Bellamy. Certainly, this would be the year when the Lakers finally went all the way.

Although it had been many years, Max remembered Haymon Jacobs clearly from the first court at Manhattan Beach. A gawky, gangly, horse-faced teenage giant, Jacobs had never shown one-tenth of the ability with a basketball that he himself had demonstrated as a schoolboy. And yet Jacobs would get a chance to play before sellout crowds at the Forum while Max Trapp sat watching from the stands.

As soon as Max had digested the news of the Jacobs-Malik deal, something clicked inside his head. He decided to give Cookie Gross a call in Brighton, just to find out how things were. During the course of the conversation, Max inquired casually after Cookie's kid, Liddel.

"Huh?" Cookie said, obviously surprised that Max would even bother to ask. "Kid's fine. Livin' in the neighborhood. Like always. A good kid."

After talking for a while longer, Max hung up on Cookie and got Liddel's number in Brooklyn from directory information. Although it had been a very long time indeed since they had seen or talked to each other, the kid seemed authentically glad to hear from him.

"Liddel," Max said, after they had bullshitted for a while, "I see where your old friend Haymon is gonna be out here at the Forum this year. Nice break for him to finally be with a winner."

"For us all, Uncle Max," Liddel said. "Local boy makes good at last."

Max laughed. "I tell you," he said, "even though I don't follow the sport like I used to, I still keep a season box out here. Go to the game every chance I get. You ever hear from the big guy anymore?"

"Like clockwork," Liddel said. "He checks in with me regular. Two, three times a week. Shit, I'm his main man. Why?"

"Well . . . I was wonderin' . . . see, back in the old days, me and your old man used to have a regular little communications network goin'. Maybe you and me could get into that same habit now. . . ."

"To tell you the truth, Uncle Max," Liddel said, "since last we talked, I been gettin' into a few things myself. The game don't mean all that much to me anymore."

"I can understand that," Max agreed. "I'm talkin' about a business arrangement. See, it would be nice for me to know what's goin' on with the Lakers. Inside stuff. Who's hurtin', who's puttin' out, who hates who this week, who don't really give a shit no more. Small stuff, you know? Gossip. Anything you can throw me that you get from the big guy. So if I lay down a bet, I'll have an edge. What I'd do is start you with a thousand and then put down a little every time I like the line. When I win, you win. It'd be like having yourself some stock. Money in the bank."

"I heard you were in films out there, Uncle Max," Liddel said.

"I was," Max said. "I might be again. I know some people."

"I got a friend wants to break into that business in the worst way."

"Yeah?" Max said. "Well, who knows? I'm sure I could help. I know some people. One hand washes the other, right?"

"Always," Liddel said quickly. "And they both wash the face. I remember you tellin' me that back at the beach. Tell you what, Uncle Max . . . anything I hear from Haymon that I think you can use, I'll shoot you over the phone. Also, I'll send you some glossies."

"Of what?"

"My friend. She's an actress. Musical comedy."

"Sure thing, Liddel. You do that. We'll see what we can work out. Only, Liddel, this is like just between you and me, right? No one else needs to know."

"Who would I tell?" Liddel said. "Not my old man."

"Right, Liddel. You talk to me and no one else. Stay in touch."

Max hung up feeling pleased. The kid was no dummy. He had picked up on the offer right away, the way his old man had once been able to do. Over the course of a long season, there was no telling how valuable a direct pipeline into the Laker locker room might prove to be. As a source of information, Liddel would be worth his weight in gold.

Although Max hadn't worked it all out yet, the rough edges of his plan were becoming smoother. Since his time in the NBA, the league had become one high and mighty outfit. People believed with all their hearts that the pro game was totally on the level. National television brought games to eager fans all over the country, none of whom thought for a moment that what had happened many times in college basketball could ever possibly occur in the pros. A fix. The stink and scandal of an investigation into point shaving. If that kind of story ever broke about the Lakers, one of the most respected franchises in the league, there was no telling how badly both the NBA and Blake Marion might suffer. Fans would turn their backs on the game in number, like it was some kind of diseased animal. Max had seen it happen before. The Lakers themselves could go play their home games in a high school gym.

Of course, these days there was no way Max Trapp could get close enough to any NBA team to work a real fix. It just wasn't possible. Not with all the expensive and elaborate security the league maintained to keep itself simon pure. Besides, with what NBA teams paid their players now, the "ice," the money needed to persuade a player to dump, would be prohibitive. No one could afford it.

Any NBA player who was sincerely interested in making some money on the side by betting wouldn't need Max Trapp's help to do it. Las Vegas was no more than a quick plane ride from anywhere. All that player had to do was send a friend or associate to Vegas to lay down the money and then collect his winnings.

Which was precisely what Max Trapp himself intended to do. He had an old friend in Vegas named Jerry Pompano. Through him, Max could do all his betting by phone, telling Pompano precisely what to put down and when. By playing it smart and betting only on Laker games, Max realized that he could create the illusion that he was back in business again. If the Lakers took the Western Division title, as they were widely expected to do, and then proceeded into the championship finals, there was no telling how far he could run with this thing.

The idea excited him more than anything he had thought of in years. For once word got out that Max Trapp was betting pro basketball again, heavy, no one would believe for a moment that he was not getting inside information. By making it look as though he had players working solely for him, Max knew that he might finally be able to pay the league back for what they had done to him. In the process, he could make himself a nice piece of change on the side, without having to break a single law.

When it came to understanding how to bet the game of basketball, Max Trapp was an acknowledged master. His name was synonymous with the sport's sordid history. By using both his expertise and his reputation, Max could stampede the NBA. At the very least, they'd make the Lakers clean house. Blake Marion could go looking for a job on the unemployment line.

Once the season got underway, Max made it a point to show up for nearly every Laker home game. For years, he had kept a pair of seats at the Forum in the name of one of his dummy corporations. When he'd first come to L.A., he'd been careful not to buy season tickets in his own name for fear that the Lakers might not allow him into the building when they played. That's how paranoid the league had made him. Now he was going to pay back the favor in kind by creating a scandal that would cast fear into every last NBA owner's heart.

The seats themselves were perfect, in a box down front where he could see without being seen. Max had always liked a little altitude when he watched a game, a little distance. It never failed to amaze him that big Hollywood stars would pay good money for the privilege of sitting in the row of cushioned armchairs that ran right around the edge of the court itself.

As far as Max was concerned, only a pimp sat so close to the action that he became part of the show instead of a paying customer. To let everyone know he was back in action, Max made sure to take Victoria with him to nearly every home game.

Wriggling into the row behind him in a skimpy halter top and a pair of skin tight pants, Victoria was heart attack material for every horny bastard in the Forum. When she went for popcorn, everyone took notice. An immediate good credit rating, Victoria was as flashy and impressive as a crisp one-hundred dollar bill thrown down on the counter of a beer-soaked bar. She commanded attention.

The only problem with taking her to games was that she understood the sport not at all. Instead, she spent her time at the Forum picking out every last famous showbiz *shmuck* who was so busy glad-handing friends down at courtside that he never had time to watch the action. One night she topped herself by reaching into her pocketbook for a pair of opera glasses, the kind that snapped shut into a flat case.

"What the fuck?" Max said to her. "This the ballet?"

"Shh, Max," Victoria said, twisting around in her seat as she adjusted the fine focus knob with the ball of her thumb, "Jack Nicholson."

The way she said it made Max think she was looking at the new Pope or something. "Hey!" he said. "I could give a rusty fuck who's down there. I come for the play, not the players."

"God," Victoria moaned, "is he *beautiful!*" Then she twitched so violently that the guy sitting next to her nearly dropped his popcorn cone down her cleavage. "I think I'm going to come from just looking at him."

Max laughed despite himself. "At least that'll be some kind of a change," he said, more to himself than to her. "Hey, do you believe this? Game is tied up with a minute left and people are already goin' home like it's over. When it comes to assholes, this place has got the franchise."

As far as Max was concerned, the Lakers were little better than their fans, who during a game sat listening to the radio *inside* the

214 ·

arena, as though if they didn't hear the play-by-play coming to them from a transistorized box, they would be unable to follow the score.

As a team, Max found the Lakers dull and mechanical. They won all the time, especially at home, but they had no heart and simply could not be trusted when it came to points. There were teams that lost twice as much as the Lakers and still made you money by covering. And then there were the Lakers, who could reel off six and eight victories in a row and still leave you holding your crotch when it came time to collect.

More than once, Max found himself longing for the old Garden in New York, where the smoke had hung in layers over the aging yellow hardwood floor and even the dumbest stiffs in the second balcony could have quoted you the last half-point shift in the odds before gametime.

Still, being Max the Lawyer, he made money, staying off the Lakers for weeks at a time when he didn't like the line, then plunging heavily on them in Vegas with Jerry Pompano when he was sure that they would cover. On the average, the Lakers could be counted on for one big payoff during every home stand. Although Max would have liked a little more action going for himself, his batting average over the course of the entire season would be far more important this time around than trying to hit one out of the park every night. He had to make it look as though he had the club neatly in his pocket and performing only for him. Only by betting in the kind of refined, scientific manner he had never had the patience to do back in Brooklyn would this be possible. That he had gotten smarter over the years was a plain fact. This time there would be no slip-ups.

"Couple more like this," he told Victoria one night in the front seat of the Bentley as they sped away from a game in which the Lakers had made his money on them stand up like a gilt-edged bond, "and I could live a little."

"Yeah, Max?" Victoria said nasally, picking through her pocketbook for one of those killer joints without which she never left the house. "How come you get such a kick out of it? I mean, it's just a kid's game, no?"

For a long moment, Max stared at her. "Ah," he said, "you gotta be from New York to understand. Forget it." Affectionately, he reached out with his hand to ruffle her egg-beaten hair.

"*Hey!*" she cried, nimbly dodging out of reach. "Cost me fifty bucks to get that done today at Sassoon's." Smoothing a manicured finger wave in place with her hand, Victoria pulled a joint out of her pocketbook and got it lit. The heavy smell of burning weed filled the car. Victoria took a deep hit off the joint and held the smoke down in her lungs until her eyes crossed. Then she leaned over to the dashboard and stubbed out the glowing joint on the ashtray, dropping the roach into her pocketbook for later use.

Max looked over at her as she settled back into the seat. She was out there all right, somewhere beyond the horizon. In the flickering light from passing cars, she looked like a life-sized Siamese cat someone had shot up with first-class stuff.

"Here," Max said tenderly, reaching into his pocket for the roll he always carried. Peeling off a bill without looking at it, he handed it to her and said, "Go back tomorrow. Have 'em do it again."

"Max," Victoria said slowly, looking at the bill, "this is a hundred."

"Yeah?" Max said, staring into the rearview mirror to see if anyone was behind him. "That's a nice number. I always liked it myself." Then he put his foot down hard on the accelerator and swung the car into the passing lane, leaving traffic behind.

Max Trapp did not have to be told that he was getting older. No longer could he stay up three and four nights in a row gambling and drinking and whoring. Those days were long gone. No longer could he get ten thousand people up on their feet screaming his name as he rammed hook shot after hook shot through the basket. All that too was behind him now.

But if he had learned anything in his time on the planet, it was that a smart man always made his own luck. This time around the jumps he was going to make sure that he alone was holding all the winning tickets. When this long season was over, whatever happened to the Lakers, Max knew that he'd be standing all alone in the winner's circle, a glass of victory champagne in one hand. Who knew? He might even find time to wave to the suckers up in the cheap seats with the other. If it pleased him to do so.

CHAPTER NINETEEN

As soon as he stepped out onto the familiar cross-hatched parquet playing floor of the Boston Gardens, Haymon knew that he was home. The hard, flat accents of the vendors, the scattered cheers from fans who still remembered him as one of their own, the championship banners hanging from the rafters far above the court all told him that he was once again back where he belonged. Without being able to pick her out, he knew that Linda was also there, watching him warm up as she had so many times before.

As far as Haymon was concerned, nothing could touch this place. It was still the temple, where the faithful turned out in number year after year to worship those wearing Celtic colors. No one in Los Angeles could ever understand such devotion. There was just too much sunshine out there for it to flourish. The cold darkness of a long New England winter was the only soil in which it could take root and grow.

Despite all he was feeling, Haymon began the game exactly as he had every other contest during his term of service with the Lakers, watching from the far end of the bench with his warm-up jacket looped over his shoulders as Arvin Williams leaped for the opening tap.

From the beginning, it was obvious to Haymon that tonight the Celtics were motivated, running at the Lakers with all they had, trying to turn the game into an early rout. Surprisingly, for the first time all year, it seemed that Arvin Williams wouldn't have been too upset if just that happened. The strange torpor that in other seasons had often enveloped the "Big A" in pressure games had him solidly in its grasp tonight.

Throughout the first half, despite repeated instructions from the bench and shouted entreaties from his teammates on court, the "A" refused to come out from under the basket on defense, allowing the Celtics' big rookie center to bomb away at will and with great accuracy from around the foul circle.

Haymon watched with morbid fascination as the "A" sleep-walked through the first half, barely aware of where he was. Midway through the third quarter, with the Lakers losing by six, the Celts came downcourt on yet another fast break. The "Big A" backpedaled down the near side of the court, stepped out of his left sneaker in front of the Celtic bench, and sat down casually right where he was to re-lace it, allowing his man to thunder past him to the hoop for an uncontested slam dunk that left the backboard trembling in its wake.

"Jacobs," the coach said in a disgusted tone of voice, "give him a blow, huh?"

Haymon quickly pulled off his warm-up jacket, his fingers thick with excitement. His legs were trembling, like those of some high school kid about to get into his very first game. To still them, he sat down quickly on the floor in front of the scorer's table. It was just another game. He had played in hundreds of them.

At the first buzzer, he ran out on court. The game rose up to meet him in a jumbled haze of noise and reflected light. The hardwood floor was streaked with light. The translucent backboards gleamed like windows facing the afternoon sun. The entire arena glowed, a cathedral of warm, throbbing light. Individual faces in the huge crowd were impossible to pick out because of the glare.

Automatically, Haymon positioned himself in back of the Celtics' rookie center, applying pressure with his hands in the small of the rookie's back just to let him know he was around. He could count the fine red hairs on the rookie's neck and smell his cologne. Planting his knee between the rookie's legs, Haymon leaned in with all his weight, bumping the young Celtic center away from the basket, fighting for ground. Before the rookie could get accustomed to it, Haymon backed away from him and began playing the ball, arms extended, fingers pointing toward the far basket.

When the shot went up from the far corner, Haymon was in perfect position for the rebound, his ass stuck out to keep his man away from the hoop. Clawing for it in the confusion under the basket, he slapped the ball to Hamid, who rifled it to Cliff Summers, already on the run at midcourt.

As he had so many times in practice, Haymon wheeled and headed immediately for the far basket. All thoughts of where he was and who was watching him vanished from his mind. The ball was in the middle of the court. He was coming down the near sideline. At the very last moment he cut to the hoop, transcribing a perfect circle to the straight line Hamid and Cliffie had been making as they came across the ten-second stripe.

He was all alone by the foul line when Cliffie found him with a blind pass. The ball came up into his hands before he could worry about dropping it. Letting his forward motion carry him, Haymon swept the ball along with him. Without breaking stride, he shouldered his way to the hoop, leaped, and laid the ball off the glass with a soft, sure touch. His momentum carried him past the end line and it was from there that he had the satisfaction of watching it fall cleanly through the net.

Twice more, the Lakers came down and scored. The Celtics quickly called time. In the huddle in front of the bench, someone smacked Haymon on the ass and said, "Way to go, brother." Haymon turned in time to see the grinning face of Hamid Malik half-hidden behind a large white towel.

When they lifted him for the "A" at the start of the final period, Haymon had scored six points, grabbed as many rebounds, and held the young Celtic center totally in check. As he sat down, he could feel his body protesting the demands that he had made on it. A hot wind inside his chest burned at his nose and throat every time he breathed. The sweat was popping out along the grooves in his forehead. Feeling hollow and winded, yet certain he could go on playing if asked, he sank back down on the bench knowing he had finally gotten a chance to show what he could do.

But it was Arvin who finished out the game and Haymon who sat watching as the Celtics continued to burn the big man by lobbing passes over his head for fast-break layups. When it was all over, the Lakers had lost by six. The locker room was quiet, subdued. Haymon had to concentrate to keep from shouting out loud under the hot, stinging spray of the shower. They had lost, not he. Tonight, he was a winner.

After he'd dressed, he grabbed his bag and made his way brusquely through a knot of kids assembled outside the players' entrance. A short kid with tousled hair and a pair of oversized glasses perched on his nose came up to him and said, "Mr. Jacobs?"

"Yeah?"

"Linda said she'd be around in back, waiting. I'm Ted. 'In the usual place,' she said. What a swell game. Do you . . . could you . . . get me Cliff Summers' autograph?"

Although he wanted nothing more than to see Linda right away, Haymon took the kid by the hand and led him back into the arena. Summers was standing under the stands bullshitting with Wendell Milk. Although Haymon had said no more than thirty words to either of them all season long, he led the kid over and called out familiarly, "Cliff? Friend of mine would like to meet you."

Summers looked at him as though he were crazy. Then he caught sight of the kid. He put on the face he used to sell breakfast cereal and sneakers to kids all over the country on television and said, "How are you, tiger? You're a friend of the big man here, huh? He must have known you were coming. Did you see how good he played?"

Coming from the great Cliffie Summers, that was high praise indeed. The kid said nothing. Awed at being in the presence of a true immortal, he just stared, goggle-eyed. Then he stuck out a piece of lined notebook paper and held it there, as though he would faint if he had to explain what it was for. Summers took it easily, smiling. "What's your name, tiger?" he said. "I wanna make this personal."

"T-Ted," the kid stuttered. Summers scrawled something on the paper and handed it back to the kid, who grabbed for it as though it were suddenly worth money. Only when they got back outside did he start breathing normally again.

"Wait till I show this to Allan Barnes," the kid said. "He'll shit."

"Nice language," Haymon said.

"He will," the kid said. "In his pants."

Haymon walked with him to the back of the old, soot-blackened alleyway where Linda had always picked him up after home games. A late model station wagon sat double-parked at the far end of the narrow brick lane. As they drew near it, the kid broke away from Haymon and began running toward the car, hollering, "Linda! Linda! Look what I got."

Linda Eller Jacobs rolled down her window and took a cigarette out of her mouth. "What is it, Ted?" she asked. "A check?"

"Cliff Summers' autograph!" the kid said proudly.

"You should have asked for it on a check," she said, opening the back door. "Come on. Hop in."

The kid scurried into the back seat. For a moment, Haymon stood where he was, shifting his oversized bag from hand to hand, watching his breath turn to smoky vapor in the cold night air. Then he walked forward slowly to meet his wife.

Since he'd last seen her, Linda had lost a lot of weight. There had been a fundamental redirection in the shape and focus of her face so that her cheekbones now seemed more prominent. Her dark brown hair was longer and pulled back into a bun that she now wore loosely knotted at the base of her neck. She had never used much makeup but now her face positively glowed, as though the way she was living had imbued her with a kind of undeniable, radiant good health. The girl with the ice cream face had been reborn. Clad in a man's outsized flannel shirt with the sleeves rolled up at the elbow, she looked like an advertisement for the good life, as lived in L. L. Bean country.

"Hello," she said, leaning her head out the window to stare up at him. "How's the weather up there?"

"Cold," Haymon said. "Almost snowing."

Slowly, he walked around to the front of the car and got in on the passenger side, throwing his bag on the floor in back. As he slid into the front seat, he felt an overwhelming desire to reach out for her. Linda gave him no sign that this would be allowed. Instead, she kept her cigarette firmly in place in the center of her mouth.

"Nice game," she said.

"First time I played in weeks. Ruined my consecutive on-the-bench streak. Coach must have known you were coming."

Linda laughed a little. Then she put the car into gear, rolling it down the alley toward the street. "You staying anywhere?" he asked. "I think there's room at our motel."

"No need," she said quickly. "Ted's got to be back home tonight. We both have school tomorrow."

"So quick?" he said, instantly disappointed. "Jesus, Linda, it's been a long time."

"Look," she said testily, turning to face him, "I came, didn't I? Not all of us can play games for a living. Some of us have to *work* for our money. . . . Sorry," she said a moment later, "I didn't mean it to sound like that. Only . . . God, Haymon, don't you ever consider even *wanting* to grow up?"

"Meaning what?"

"That letter. On airlines stationery, with no return address. The star on the road issuing a royal command for his woman to come and watch him play . . . with a quick shack-up in the motel afterward. That's what you had in mind, right?"

"No," he said, confused. "I didn't mean. . . ."

"With a check enclosed to cover expenses. Here," she said, reaching into her shirt pocket for the money he had sent her, "I can pay for my own gas these days. I'm working."

Haymon looked at the check. "I just thought. . . ."

"I know," she said, "I know. You just wanted to see me again, and you thought the best place to do it would be the Boston Gardens. A nice, small, intimate room."

Neither of them said anything for a while. Then Haymon asked, "What are you doing up there?"

"Teaching by day and going to school at night. By June, I'll have my master's and I can start subbing as a music teacher in elementary school."

She smiled and nipped a speck of tobacco from the tip of her tongue. Haymon couldn't remember her ever smoking anything but an occasional joint. The cigarette, which was unfiltered and harsh-smelling, seemed awkward in her hands. "Is it nice up there?" he asked, not really caring.

"Wonderful," she said. "Woods and hills and it snows all the time."

"Sounds pretty cold. What do you do at night? Chop wood?"

"Read. Watch TV. It's not Siberia."

"I thought you might consider L.A."

"As what? A disaster area? It is already."

"As a place you might want to live."

"I've got a place where I live," she said evenly. "I just told you about it."

"I thought we could get a house," he said, "by the beach."

"Phoenix all over again, huh?" she said.

"Not Phoenix," he said. "L.A. By the ocean."

"It's all plasticland to me, Haymon. I live in Vermont. Where they still breathe real air. Basketball finishes a poor second to hockey up there, thank God. It's like being in Canada sometimes."

"I know things got weird in Phoenix at the end," he said. "But it wasn't just us. Everything was fucked. L.A.'s a whole new place."

"Not for me it isn't."

"It could be."

"How? With you paying my bills?"

"You could teach out there," he said. "If not, once the playoffs are over, I'd have enough so we could both travel for a while. Europe, or. . . ."

"Games," she said bitterly, "playoffs. Where do you go from here, Haymon?"

"Uh . . . back to the coast . . . Seattle and San Francisco and then home. . . ."

"That's it," she said. "Two more games and the road trip's over, right? Two more teams to beat. See, you're lucky that way. You always know who you're playing. I'm not even sure what the game is. . . ."

"Shitting in an outhouse in Vermont isn't a game?"

"Look, Haymon," she said wearily, "I didn't come down here to fight. I want us to get a divorce. No alimony, nothing. I just want my own name back."

"Whose kid is this?" Haymon asked stubbornly, totally ignoring what she'd just said.

"Teddy? His father teaches up there with me. When he heard I was coming to the game, he went crazy. He thinks Charlie Summers is God. Right, Ted?"

"Cliff," Haymon said automatically, "his name is Cliff."

"Whatever," Linda said flatly, turning around to look at Ted. "Right, kiddo?"

Haymon turned with her. The kid was stretched out along the length of the back seat, fast asleep. The precious autograph Cliff Summers had granted him was clutched tightly in his fist. "I should be so lucky," Linda said. "I've got four hours of driving ahead of me."

"You want an up, or a joint?"

Linda shook her head stubbornly from side to side. It was a gesture he remembered well. "I don't do any dope these days, Haymon. I drink a beer now and then, smoke too many of these, and I walk. I walk a lot."

Haymon looked through the windshield, searching for something to say that would crack the icy exterior Linda had apparently developed since moving to those frozen woods. Already they were in Cambridge, on the Drive. The lights of Boston reached across the water to him, leaving their shattered reflection on the dark and liquid surface of the river. She had changed and he had changed. Everything was changed, more than he had thought it ever could.

"See," he said slowly, "I've finally got a shot at it out there. And I want you with me to share it. . . ."

"But that's not what I want."

"Look," he said nearly pleading, "I can't do it myself. All this time, all these months, I never looked at anyone else. I was waiting, knowing you'd see that I'd changed, that we had. . . ."

"Haymon," she said in a low voice, "what does this have to do with anything?"

"You love me, right?"

"If I do," she said carefully, choosing her words, "it hasn't stopped me. Not ever. You wouldn't want to know some of the things I've done. . . . I'm sleeping with Ted's father. This is his car."

"I don't care," he said, refusing to give up, "L.A.'s a new place. . . ."

"God, Haymon, *God!*" Linda screamed, slamming her hands against the steering wheel in frustration. "Do you ever listen to anyone? Ever? What do I have to do to get through to you? We are finished. Closed out, like one of my father's fake fire sales. . . ."

"No," he said. "You're just angry. You're saying things you don't mean. . . ."

"You never listen to me, Haymon," she cried, the words rushing out in staccato bursts, like barrages of artillery fire. "You didn't when we were living together and you don't now. How could you?

There's always been something more important. Nerves before the game. Headaches afterward. Upset stomachs. Always Haymon first. Haymon, Haymon, *Haymon!* The truth is that it was over a long time before Phoenix. Right here in Boston. The weekend your best friend Liddel Gross came up. Haymon," she said, looking him full in the face, "I fucked him. All right? When he took me to New York that time and you disappeared to your mother's house? Although I could never understand what you saw in that little creep, he was nice to me. Can you imagine? He *listened* to me when I talked. And you didn't. And you still don't. Do you understand me now?"

Although Linda's voice had softened by the time she reached the end of her little speech, Haymon did not hear it. A chain saw shredding its way through an old and rotten stump had come into contact with a solid hunk of galvanized metal. Both the blade and the hunk of metal were going to get destroyed, yet neither gave way. The noise of one grating on the other was horrible. Haymon knew only that if he did not make the noise stop, he would go mad.

Reaching blindly behind him, he grabbed for his bag with one hand while pushing down on the door handle beside him with the other. He leaned his weight against the door, shoved with his shoulder, and nearly fell out of the moving car. When Linda saw what he was doing, she screamed and slammed her foot down on the brake.

Metal screeched against metal once again as the big station wagon foundered to a stop against the edge of the hill bordering the Drive. The kid fell off the back seat and began to wail. Haymon leaped out of the car and started to run.

With no place to go but up, he took one great step and began climbing the steep and snowy slope at the edge of the highway. The soft, muddy turf gave way beneath his feet. His bad left leg nearly went on him and he grabbed madly at the hill, seeking a handhold. Although he could hear Linda crying out to him from the car, he did not stop or turn around until he had fought his way through one tangled thicket of branches after another, emerging at last onto a quiet street lined with houses.

It was then that he began to run in earnest, pounding along the pavement with bag in hand until all he could hear was the roaring of blood in his ears. His breath came to him in stinging, icy gasps and it was not until he found himself on an avenue choked with traffic that he slowed to a walk. Then an overpowering wave of nausea hit him and he staggered to a garbage can. A series of dry heaves racked his chest and stomach but nothing came up. He could not even vomit.

"Go on, big guy," an old drunk with a battered face told him, his breath thick with the smell of cheap whiskey. "Throw it all up, and then go out and buy some more. Gowan. It's your fuckin' life, ain't it?"

Haymon straightened up and walked away without really knowing where he was headed. Without breaking stride, he took out the expensive piece of Steuben glass he had bought for Linda on Fifth Avenue and threw it to the ground. It exploded, shattering like the tendon in his leg that had never really totally healed. His lot in life was pain. Pain so total that he could not tell where it began or ended. He stumbled on along the street, looking for a cab.

By the time he got back to the motel, Haymon's hands were twitching uncontrollably, as though he had been struck with palsy. He felt cold all over but his face was flushed and hot with fever. His head buzzed as though someone had loosed a swarm of bees inside his brain.

Shutting the door to his room behind him, Haymon forced open the empty tape cassette where he kept his pills, swallowing the first two he could find. He sat down on the bed and tried to roll a joint but his hands were shaking so badly the papers would not stick together.

Impatiently, with trembling hands, he crammed some weed into an old metal pipe he rarely used anymore, toking on it like a drowning man gasping for air. He needed to be numb. Technicolor obscenities of Linda and Liddel in bed together kept flooding in on him no matter how hard he fought against them. He did not want to see. He could not bear to look. And yet the pictures came, swelling and dancing before his eyes. The two of them giving each other pleasure, Linda moaning and crying and biting the sheet as she called out for more. More. She wanted more. She could not get enough.

Liddel had taken such good care of him. Liddel had fed and housed him. Never once had Liddel let on how funny it all must have seemed to him. To offer comfort to a man you had thoroughly destroyed. What a perfect expression of total contempt. Liddel and Linda had made his life a smutty one-liner. My best friend and my wife. My wife and my best friend. It was hilarious all right. Only he was not laughing. Like a small child trying to kick free of his covers, Haymon began to thrash wildly back and forth across the bed, scattering pillows.

Suddenly, a pair of chromium steel bands formed across his chest. The bands grew tighter and tighter, squeezing all the air from his lungs. His skin grew cold and clammy. His lips turned blue. Waves of crimson pain ran out along the ridges of his arms and shoulders. His heart thudded like a jackhammer tearing up the street. He knew then that he was going to buy it. The farm in the country. He was having a full blown heart attack. He was dying.

He reached out blindly for the phone but it eluded his grasp and fell to the floor, the receiver rolling loose on the carpet. He grabbed for it desperately, his body sliding sideways off the bed so that he was lying jack-knifed with one shoulder on the floor, hammering wildly with his right hand at the phone's little plastic buttons.

"I'm here, sir," a nasal voice informed him. "No need to flash. What number would you like, please?"

Out of the dizzying fog that was rolling over him, he gasped. "Bran . . . Hamid . . . Malik."

"Mr. Malik? Room Sixteen. Just a moment, please, I'll connect you."

The pain grew worse. A throbbing fireball whirled up inside his chest. His face was bursting, the veins and capillaries in his neck and forehead swollen with blood. No matter how desperately he tried, he could not draw breath. *"Please,"* he moaned into the phone, "help . . . me. . . ."

The receiver fell from his grasp. He tried to get to his feet only to fall heavily onto his side. Crawling, he began to make his way across the room. If he could get into the hallway, he might stand a chance. He was nearly there when he heard the knocking. He struggled to his knees for a second only to pitch headfirst into the dresser, knocking it back against the wall. Somehow, he managed to get a hand on the knob and make it turn. The door swung open just as he realized he was going to be sick.

It all welled up within him then, a shower of pus-green vomit bursting from his mouth to spew across the doorjamb onto the sandals of the man who had come to help him. Despite the pain, he was embarrassed. He wanted to be dead, where it was dark and quiet and no one could see him. He felt himself being half carried back to the bed.

No matter how hard he tried, he could not force any air into his lungs. Those great sacs of membrane were shuttered, useless. He began hyperventilating madly and the dizziness grew worse, the room spinning in circles around him. Tears streamed down his cheeks.

"HAYMON!"

Haymon tried to locate the voice but his eyes would not focus. He was going. This was it. "LISTEN, HAYMON, YOU GOTTA BREATHE WITH ME. NICE AND EASY. DEEP BREATHS. ME AND YOU. ONE. TWO. THREE. FOUR."

Haymon surrendered to the voice, knowing it no longer made any difference. He was going to die in a motel room in Boston in a pool of his own vomit. It was no more than he deserved. He let the rhythm of the voice take over for him.

At first it was no more than a trickle. Then a whisper. Then the tiny sacs inside his lungs began to fill with air. The steel bands around his chest loosened. His diaphragm ceased its mad flutter.

When his vision cleared, Haymon saw that Hamid was standing over him, chanting in a language he could not understand. Still, the sound was strangely comforting. He closed his eyes and the room disappeared entirely, save for the rhythmic chanting.

When Haymon opened his eyes again, he realized that he had been asleep. Where the pool of vomit had been on the floor, there was now only a dark, wet stain. Hamid sat in the middle of the room with his back very straight and his legs crossed beneath him.

"How is it now?" Hamid asked gently.

"Better. I had . . . an attack. . . ."

"Yes," Hamid said. "What happened?"

"Linda, I. . . ." He stopped speaking, fearing that the pictures would return.

"Sleep," Hamid said. "You'll be able to sleep now. I'll be here. For as long as it takes."

Haymon closed his eyes and felt himself drifting into a light and feathery sleep. When he woke again, it was still night and dark outside. The room was illuminated by the glow of a single candle. In its flickering shadow, Hamid sat with his legs crossed and his eyes closed, looking like a holy man who had come down from the mountain to minister to the needs of those below. Haymon fell asleep again. The next time he woke, it was morning. Hamid was still sitting where he had been, apparently having spent the night there.

"Good," he said, when he saw that Haymon was awake. "I have something for you to hear. Now is the time."

Hamid slid a cassette into the tape player. Then he resumed his position on the floor. From the speaker nearest Haymon's ear there came the sound of a horn. There was no way to resist its hypnotic call. Haymon closed his eyes and let it take him away.

The horn and the man playing it were on a journey. That much was clear. The same journey he was on, the one all men took. Death and rebirth, the horn cried out. Death and rebirth, the other instruments answered. Death, death, death, and rebirth.

Haymon felt himself being drawn out of his body along fine silver wires. He was somewhere in the desert, with only the white, hot sand for company. The swirling horn carried him past barren water holes where sun-bleached skeletons lay beneath prickly tubes of cactus. The bass pulsed casualties. Another person dead. His mother. His father. Linda. Hamid. Liddel. Everyone he had ever known was in this desert, lying face up in the sand staring at the sun with sightless eyes. Everyone he had ever known or loved, laid out on burning sand, dead. Tears came to his eyes but he had no time to mourn. The music would not let him.

Even in the white hot desert waste, there were patches of cooling shade. But he could not pause. He had no time. The music moved him to the edge of a high red bluff. He grabbed desperately for a handhold but the music pushed him and he fell over the edge, his body growing light and shiny in the air, turning slow, silent circles as it plummeted toward the rocks below where certain death was waiting.

For a moment, the fear returned. His body became leaden. Then he gave up all hope and he was light once again and tumbling. At the very last moment a crystal pond appeared at the bottom of the ravine.

Haymon's body turned one final time in the air and he fell head first into the pond. Miraculously, there was no splash. The water took him down silently, soothing and caressing his blistered skin. He sank deeper and deeper without reaching bottom. Breathing water, he grew buoyant and floated back up to the surface, safe, warm, and happy.

The music surged, cried out a final time, and ended with a long and rolling drumbeat that affirmed that he had made it through. He lay in silence for a long while, quivering, awestruck. Cautiously, he said, "What was that?"

"John Coltrane's 'A Love Supreme,' " Hamid said, his eyes still closed, a peaceful expression on his face. "How do you feel?"

"Good. I feel good."

"Then you have truly understood its meaning."

"I saw things."

"Yes," Hamid said.

"Such things," Haymon said. "And the man who made it?"

"Dead," Hamid said. "But he left us this."

"God," Haymon breathed, almost afraid to speak.

"God," Hamid repeated. "Whithersoever ye turn." He got to his feet and said, "I'm going now, brother. But don't worry, I'm leaving you this." He pointed to the cassette and then silently left the room.

Haymon fell asleep once more. When he woke, he felt strong and confident, as though all the events of the previous night had been solely a product of his own imagination, no more than a fevered childhood dream. He got dressed and floated easily onto the team bus, which was waiting for him just outside the motel. As though someone were orchestrating all his movements, he drifted toward the single empty seat on the bus. Only after he had sat down did he notice that Hamid was sitting next to him.

When the shouting and rude joking that usually accompanied such rides began, Haymon heard Hamid hum the opening refrain of the music under his breath. He closed his eyes. Miraculously, the cooling, peaceful waters of the crystal pond closed over him once again. It had been no dream. Within his mind Haymon knew he had finally found a place to hide. No one would ever think of looking for him there. He was safe at last.

BOOK FIVE · **The Cold Train**

"*A person will respond in general the rest of his life the way he reacts on the athletic field.*"
DELMER HARRIS, *Multiple Defenses for Winning Basketball*

CHAPTER TWENTY

It was said that inside every fat man there lurked a thin man crying to be set free. Cookie Gross was not only fat but lame, crippled beyond repair and now growing old. His hair, what was left of it, stuck out over his ears like a clown's fright wig. It was the color of steel wool and had the same consistency. His stomach, never taut, now sloped over the belt of his old man's pants like the swelling bubble in a knotted garden hose.

He had long been imprisoned by his body, sentenced by some unknown judge to live within its confines. Only lately, prison conditions had been getting worse. His legs ached in the mornings and throbbed at night and nothing made the pain go away, not hot towels warmed over the oven nor cold compresses soaked in ice water straight from the refrigerator.

His teeth were bad too. He had never taken care of them as a kid, and the ones in back were now rotten through and through. Drinking a glass of hot tea had become a carefully choreographed series of movements designed to keep the super heated sugar sweet liquid away from the hollow molars in back. More than once he had forgotten about them only to be jolted out of his chair by a mouthful of pain, as though someone had shoved a live wire into his jaw.

Each morning, early, Cookie forced himself to go down to Hirsch's for a roll and coffee and the morning papers. Then he struggled back to the apartment and took up his position in front of the double windows that looked out onto Brighton Beach Avenue. Laying out the *Times* and the *News* before him, he turned the radio on to the all-news station, letting the steady hum of headlines being read over and over soothe him as he did his work. He liked the feeling of knowing that the city was out there pulsing, although he himself rarely got to see very much of it anymore.

In the marbled black-and-white school notebooks that Hirsch supplied him free of charge, he kept his accounts, taking care to redline any of his regulars who were nearing their limit. His list of steady customers had declined steadily over the years, death taking many of them, so that these days he rarely talked to more than eight or nine clients a week, depending on how things were going for them on Wall Street or in the garment center.

All told, they usually bet a total of forty-five thousand dollars a week. Back in the old days, he and Max had often had that much going for them on a single night. Still, the vigorish on forty-five thousand was nine hundred a week. Four times nine times twelve came to nearly forty-five thousand once again. It was quiet money, made without government supervision, untaxed and unreported, subject to no deductions for Social Security, workmen's compensation, or health insurance. So far as the government knew, Cookie Gross was unemployed and unemployable, as he had been all his life.

Most of Cookie's regular customers had been with him for so long now that they did not worry if he went a month or more without making a payoff. They knew that he was good for the money and that he never made a mistake or cheated anyone. No longer did the painstaking addition and subtraction of figures that he did each day by habit demand an ensuing transfer of cash, as it had in the old days.

Only when he was short and in need of money to pay off some bet he himself had made in order to balance the book did he send Liddel out on rounds, a route the kid had covered for him weekly back when the losers had coughed up each Monday so that the winners could be paid.

These days, Cookie Gross was content to sit by the window with the radio on, listening to the headlines and working with the points. The boys in Vegas who now made the official line were no more infallible than those who had put it together back when it had come out of Cincinnati and Lexington, Kentucky. Sportswriters and most of those who followed sports on a regular basis could still be touted on a sure loser. Unswayed by emotion, unswerving in his devotion to the back pages of the *News* and the *Post*, where small bits of sports gossip and reports of injuries could be gleaned by careful reading, Cookie had not lost the ability to translate seemingly worthless bits of information into factors that would affect a line. To be able to sit and weigh the many components that went into making up a spread that could withstand whatever pressure was put upon it was his genius, the special talent that had kept him in business so long.

Although it had been years since he'd dragged himself to work each day along Mermaid Avenue in Coney Island, Cookie Gross' work was exactly the same now as it had been back then. Numbers were his business, and numbers never changed. Three and three could always be counted on to add up to six no matter how many men walked on the moon. These days, the *Daily News* told him all he needed to know about Coney Island and what was going on there.

The Jews and the Italians had abandoned that place to the *shvartzers*, with dope having replaced numbers as the primary source of all money and power. So what else was new? As far back as 1948, Cookie had seen the cokies who'd worked for Louie the Barber. Punks, every one of them, perpetually on a jag, talking a blue streak about nothing in particular as the spit ran down their chins and their eyes grew big in their heads. Not many of them had lived to see thirty. To Cookie Gross, dope was nothing new.

It was only that the family that had always controlled everything in South Brooklyn, from the seafood restaurants in Sheepshead Bay to the more profitable concessions along the boardwalk in Coney Island, had taken an interest in the stuff. They'd always had their hand in everything anyway. Trading in dope had only made them wealthier and even more powerful.

So far as Cookie was concerned, every last *shvartzer* in Coney Island could shoot himself up and fall down dead in the middle of Surf Avenue if that was what he wanted. It was no concern of his. What drove him crazy was knowing that his kid had somehow gotten himself involved with it.

Although Liddel had never come right out and said what he did for spending money, Cookie knew that his son lived in a good apartment. He drove a big car and he had a girlfriend who was going to become an actress. Cookie knew about such women. They cost money. In order to get that money, Liddel was selling dope to the *shvartzers*. Bad enough. Even worse was that sooner or later Liddel would have to cross the people who controlled the trade, just as they had always controlled everything on the street. The *Italianers*. When that happened, Cookie dreaded the consequences.

Longie Zwillman, Abe Reles, Lepke Buchalter, all had been big men in their time. Every one of them had run afoul of the family. Now they lay buried in the expensive suits they'd had hand-tailored at Three-G Clothiers. The *Italianers* had learned all they could from the Jewboys and then gotten rid of them one by one and gone on doing business with the crowbar, the tire chain, and the baseball bat.

Again and again, the *Italianers* had tried to take control of all the bookmaking in Brooklyn. But without at least one Jewish *superkopf* to calculate the odds, their attempts had always failed. Still, they continued to try, using methods that he found repulsive.

If you stiffed a Jewish bookie, he'd cut you off and put an end to your credit. If you stiffed an Italian bookie, you'd have visitors coming for you at night, again and again, until you'd paid off every last cent with interest. It was always an affair of honor with them, a vendetta, and never just a simple question of dollars and cents. It was not a way of doing business he had ever understood.

For making book was just that, a business, and Cookie considered that he had survived at it for so long only because no one but his customers knew he was alive. He made his line and collected his winnings and put the money quietly into the bank, talking to no one about anything but the weather. He never made a show. That was their way. He was afraid Liddel could never do the same.

Not that the kid wasn't smart. He had brains enough. But there was something else there, a kind of arrogance and lack of respect that was out of place in a man who wanted to live by his wits.

Look at Zwillman and Reles and Buchalter. Nothing had been too good for them. The best suits, the most expensive cars. Two and three *kurvas* at a time to share their beds. They had rocketed through life as though they were going to live forever. Now they were all dead. Louie the Barber was dead. Cookie Gross was alive.

Despite the rotten teeth and the aching legs and the fetid breath no toothpaste could sweeten, he was still around. Born with a body no one would have bet a nickel on, save in a race for the morgue and then Potter's Field, he was still functioning, his brain as sharp and precise as ever. He had no troubles, really, not so long as he had his life. It was a lesson he wished he could make his son understand. Staying alive was all that counted. In the end, it was the only game worth winning.

CHAPTER TWENTY-ONE

LIDDEL GROSS had problems. They were nothing new and nothing he could not handle but that did not mean they weren't annoying. All afternoon and into the night, he had been waiting for Momo to call. Momo was the all-time fucking ghinny all right. Mr. Reliable. To him, time was something other people had. So long as he was holding and you needed to make a buy, he figured you'd wait on him forever.

It was now nearly midnight. Over the phone this morning, Liddel had promised some yahm he had never met that he would find him in Coney Island at one A.M. with half an ounce of coke, for a thousand bucks. Judging by the way the yahm had jumped at the deal, Liddel guessed that he knew from nothing when it came to buying dust. He was probably already out there in the street walking nervous circles, making it that much easier for the cops to spot him. With a thousand bucks cash money burning a hole in his pocket no less.

Liddel cracked the knuckle of his middle finger and then inserted the finger into the corner of his mouth so that he could chew on the nail. The yahm was a total stranger to him, a new customer sent his way by Momo, who simply could not stand selling to *shvartzers* himself. It gave Liddel no pleasure to know that he was acting as Momo's middleman tonight, in a strictly lightweight deal. Still, a thousand bucks was a thousand bucks. If Momo did not show up soon, there would be no deal at all.

Liddel knew he could probably find the asshole if he tried. Momo had a phone. Only it was in his parents' house, where he still lived. No matter how badly you needed to talk to the little scumbag, you had to go through his old man first, who always picked up on the first ring, as though it would cost him more money if he let it go any longer. Momo's old man was a sanitation cop. The last person Liddel wanted to talk to now was a cop, even if he did do nothing more than police a heap of trash out on Staten Island.

Liddel looked at his watch and made a decision. If Momo was going to be this late, he could take his shit elsewhere. Liddel had learned a long time ago that the only way you got respect from these people was to treat them exactly the way they treated you. If they fucked up, you had to let them know immediately or they would make a habit of it and start pushing you around like some shop teacher they'd learned to intimidate before being thrown out of high school.

The same was true with the yahms. Liddel never tried to come on "hip" or "cool" with them. That was shit for the birds. You had to treat them all like the jitterbugs they were, get your money, and clear out. It was the only way.

So fuck Momo. He'd do it without him. Reaching for the phone, Liddel dialed the number of the disco out on Long Island where the Whale worked on weekends.

"Gatsby's," the girl at the other end said, her voice nearly drowned out by the sound of loud electric music and the babble of a lot of stoned out people trying to hit on one another before Friday night ended. "Lemme speak to the Whale," he said, "Larry Vargas."

Gatsby's was the kind of club you went to if you owned a Corvette and liked to take pills on the weekend to relax. Whale's uncle owned the place and the Whale spent his Friday and Saturday nights out there, bouncing bodies. As it happened, the Whale owned a pale-yellow 1958 Vette in cherry condition. Liddel had seen him get really angry only once, when two hitters had made the mistake of sitting on the hood of the Vette out at Atlantic Beach one day. Judging by what was left of them when the Whale had finished, he doubted whether either one of them had ever sat on a strange car again. At least not without waxing and polishing it first before leaving.

"Yeah," the Whale said when he got on the line.

"I got a problem," Liddel said.

"Tell me about it. A prick we both know hung you up."

"Who told you?"

"He was in here half an hour ago with his nose full and his mouth goin' a mile a minute. Asked me could I take half an oh-zee. Right in front of the boss. Asshole. I had to ask him to leave."

"The fuck," Liddel said through clenched teeth. "The ghinny fuck. That's my half he's out peddling and I got people waiting on me for it right now. What can you do for me, Larry?" he asked, already knowing the answer.

"At this hour?" the Whale said, grunting and laughing at the same time so that the two sounds ran together, "You kidding?"

"What can you let me have?" Liddel repeated.

"A quarter for seven and a half."

"A terrible price," Liddel said.

"A bad time," the Whale noted. "You wanna cut it, I got manete."

Manete, also known as mannitol, could be used to cut coke if you didn't much care about the people you were selling to. Even mixed in with the real stuff, it still did its thing, drawing all the shit out of your body so that your nose ran and your eyes got all red and watery. The way Liddel figured it, his yahm probably knew from nothing when it came to coke. If he cut the Whale's quarter with manete, he could make it into a half and still come out ahead.

It wouldn't exactly be rocks but the yahm would only be stepping on the stuff anyway, breaking it down into five and ten-dollar pops to be unloaded at parties where people formed "syndicates" to snort up a line or two each. No one there would be able to point a finger at anyone else and say, "This bad coke, man. You burned me." They'd never know the difference.

"What kind of stuff is it?" Liddel asked.

"Not like what Momo is holding," the Whale said. "But it makes it."

The very real possibility that the Whale had bought up his half ounce from Momo and was now dealing half of it back to him at a higher price crossed Liddel's mind. He didn't blame the Whale. Business was business. He blamed Momo. Momo was a prick.

"Five-fifty," he said.

"Seven."

"Six-fifty and I bring it with me when I come," Liddel said.

"All right," the Whale conceded, "as you are my friend."

"In an hour," Liddel said, and they both hung up.

This time on a Friday night, Liddel knew he would do no better anywhere. At least with the Whale he was sure of getting something for his money. Still, he hated to do business like this. First, he'd have to drive to Coney Island to assure his yahm that the deal was still on. Then all the way out to Long Island to cop, with his money. He'd have to cut the shit right there and if the yahm wanted to come along to protect his investment, it would even be messier.

Sighing, he went into the bedroom and slipped on his leather car coat, taking care not to wake Tina, who was sleeping heavily on her side of the bed. He checked his pockets to make sure he had his cigarettes and car keys and then walked out to the elevator. He got in and punched the button marked "G." It was nearly midnight. His working day had just begun.

When he got into the car, it took its own sweet time coming around, kicking and coughing and making several weird and wired noises before finally coming alive. Although the GTO was only four years old, it was temperamental. The suspension and the steering were beat to shit. Three New York City winters had done that, freezing nights that turned the slush along Ocean Parkway into ice, cracking the asphalt into potholes the size of the Grand Canyon. Hit one of them late at night going sixty, as Liddel had done many times, and the pins rattled right out of the axles.

The car still had power, though, a massive, air-scoop-fed engine that made any speed limit a joke. With his right hand, Liddel reached under the seat to make sure the .38 was tucked in its usual place inside the springs. Nobody drove into Coney Island at this hour of the night without a little protection. Not if he had half a brain.

Although he had never fired the gun and didn't even much like having it around, Liddel knew it would be useful as the final argument in any discussion that got out of hand. He'd gotten it a couple months ago in exchange for half a kilo of weed. It made him feel better to know he could look out for himself now, if it came to that.

Giving the car gas, he let it roll slowly to the base of the exit ramp, where he inserted his key into the black box that made the garage door roll open. It cost him an extra fifty bucks a month to keep the car in here but it was well worth the money. Leaving a GTO out in the street at night, even one that was four years old, was like extending an invitation to every hood-in-training in the neighborhood to try his hand at popping the door lock, hot-wiring the ignition, and driving it away while you slept.

The only alternative was one of those plastic-coated police locks that fitted around the steering wheel and the gas pedal, making it impossible to move the car without either the key or an acetylene torch. The only problem with them was that they were a pain in the ass to take off quickly. Liddel didn't want to have to fuck with one some night when he was in a hurry to get his ass in gear. So it was the garage and an extra fifty bucks a month. Money. It always came down to money and the things you had to do to get it. It was a tough world all around. No one could argue that.

The streets outside the apartment house were quiet and empty. The traffic lights blinked red, yellow, green for no one. Liddel drove down Ocean Parkway to Surf Avenue past Nathan's to where the real Coney Island began. These days, Coney Island looked like a city after a war. Bombed out. Block after block of two-family houses and small stores had been razed, to make way for what he didn't know. A couple of high rises had gone up by the boardwalk, vertical slums replacing horizontal ones, but otherwise most of it was just empty lots, block after block filled with nothing but weeds, broken glass, and dog shit. Jungle land.

The yahm was supposed to meet him by the boardwalk at the end of the street where Silver's Baths had once stood. Liddel assumed he'd be there waiting. To make himself visible, he cruised the block twice. Then he pulled in at the curb and waited. He'd just gotten a cigarette lit when there was a tapping on the window. Liddel nearly jumped out of his seat. Looking up, he saw a black man standing in the street with a blue knit woolen cap pulled down low over his eyes. He was wearing a peacoat, with the collar hiked up around his neck. Liddel rolled his window open just wide enough to hear what he had to say.

"You late, man," the brother said in a high, peeved voice that cracked with annoyance at the end of every word. "You fuckin' very late. Me and Zee-man been playin' hide-and-seek with the Man for over an hour now. You got it wit' you?"

"I know you?" Liddel said.

"Shee-yit," the brother said, breaking the word into two familiar syllables. "Yeah, you do. Who you think I am? The Lone Ranger? I spoke to you on the phone, right? I'm Stone. Okay?"

"You alone?"

"Got Zee-man wit' me. Already tol' you that. What for you got to ask me all these bullshit questions, man? You takin' a survey? We here like we said we'd be. You the one what's late. You got it?"

"Get in," Liddel said. "We got problems."

"What about Zee-man?"

"I talk business with one man at a time," Liddel said, stating a fact.

Stone turned and said something to a dark figure standing in front of a building that looked as though it had taken a direct hit in the last air raid. Shadows talking to shadows, in shadows. "Open your coat when you get in front of the car," Liddel said. "I'm a nervous guy."

"Jiveass," Stone muttered. He walked in front of the car's headlights. Liddel tapped his foot on the button for the high beams and watched as Stone turned a slow pirouette in the brilliant light with his coat held away from him, one hand shading his eyes.

"Think I'd be fool enough to hold a piece this hour of the night?"

he asked plaintively. "Out here? They got Sullivan Law in this state, y'know?"

"Yeah," Liddel said flatly. "So now we both know."

He popped the door lock control by his left side and the button on the far door jumped to attention. Stone slid into the front seat bringing with him the smell of the night and whatever cheap wine he had been drinking.

"You cold?" Liddel asked, looking over his outfit.

"Mah blood is thin," Stone said, pulling off his knit cap. His head was completely shaven. In the light from the streetlamp, it glistened like a waxed brown cueball. It was impossible to guess how old he was.

"My man hung me up," Liddel said.

"You tryin' to pull some scam on me," Stone said nervously, the whites of his eyes growing very large against his pebbled skin. "I kin feel it."

"Cut the shit," Liddel said, holding up his hand to stop the rap before it began. "Would I be here if I was? I made a call. I got someone else to come up with it. Only I got to go and cop now."

"So cop," Stone said. "We still got a deal."

"I got to drive out to Long Island."

"You free."

"Thanks," Liddel said grimly. "This guy wants bread up front."

"So?"

"You want the shit, you gotta let me see some cash."

"How much?"

"Half now, half after I deliver. Five and five."

Stone rubbed a hand over his smooth shaven dome. "You think this my day off from school?" he asked. "I ain't gonna give you a penny without seein' some shit."

Liddel sighed. They were all the same. Talking to them was like banging your head against a wall. "You front me some bread," Liddel said patiently, "half now, half when I deliver, and we do the deal. You wanna come along, all right. Only you gotta stay in the car when we get there. This ain't no house party. My man got a job to protect. He gets off at four. Either we go now . . . or we forget it."

"I gotta consult," Stone said.

He got out of the car and disappeared into the shadows in front of the ruined building, moving as though he were on familiar turf. In the darkness, Liddel could make out another black man in a dark blue knit woolen cap and a peacoat. Christ. He'd look lovely waltzing into Gatsby's with these two on his arm. They were dressed like merchant seamen off some freighter bound for the Orient. Still, between them they were holding a thousand in cash on them right now. For dope, people always found the money.

Stone came back and leaned in the window, treating Liddel to a really good whiff of whatever he had been drinking. Turpentine, maybe.

"We go," he said. "Only Zee-man wants you to get out the car first so he can make sure you ain' about to take us off."

Liddel considered the request. It was no more than he'd demanded of Stone. He knew they'd never think to look under the seat where the piece was stashed. He shut off the engine and took the ignition key with him, stepping out of the car into the dank darkness. Coney Island at night smelled like cold garbage. A lot of it. "Face away, little man," Stone said. "Zee-man shy."

Liddel put his hands against the car and stared into the sideview mirror in hope of catching a glimpse of Stone's partner. He heard heels clacking on the hard pavement. Then a pair of hands moved quickly from his shoulders to his ankles with practiced precision.

"Clean," a black voice said.

By the time Liddel turned around, Zee-man was already hidden in shadows. "He's quick," Liddel said.

"Got to be," Stone said. "That's one hard man there. You doan wanna fuck with him, believe me. He even scare me sometime. That there is one bad brother. He gonna stay here and wait on us. If we ain' back in two hours. . . ." Stone shrugged. "He'll know somethin' be wrong. Then it be your ass."

"It's my ass already," Liddel said impatiently. "Get in."

Stone went around the other side of the car and slid into the front seat. "That a joint?" he asked when Liddel put his already lit cigarette back into his mouth.

"A Parliament," Liddel said.

Stone frowned and turned on the radio. He changed stations with one hand till he got to WWRL at the far end of the dial. With the other, he reached into his jacket pocket and withdrew a joint that he lit off the dashboard lighter. From the smell, Liddel gauged that it was "bush," the heavy black Congolese shit that twisted up your head but good.

"How's that smoke?" Liddel asked as they rode past Sheepshead Bay on to the Belt Parkway.

Stone grunted. "It makes it," he said, continuing to smoke without offering up a hit.

With the car stinking from weed and the relentless beat of the all-night soul show pounding from the radio, Stone and Liddel rolled out toward Long Island in the fast lane. In cars all around them, Friday night dates were blissfully coming to an end. The way Liddel figured it, there was no more unlikely couple out on the road.

By the time they hit Gatsby's, the parking lot was deserted, save for the Whale's precious yellow Vette. Liddel left Stone in the front seat and went inside to cop. Whale looked more than a little drunk and generally fucked up, and he made a big production of taking Liddel into the back room to do the deal. What with one thing and another, it took him a good half hour to get the coke measured out into a Baggie. All the while, Whale talked non-stop about Tina. What a piece of ass she was. She had to come out to the club. He could get her a job, dancing. Liddel listened without saying a word. That was just what he needed. Tina as a disco dancer.

Stringing the Whale along, he promised he'd talk to her about it when he got home. After the shit changed hands, he told him he had been able to come up only with six bills. Since they both knew this was a hundred more than the stuff was worth, the Whale bitched only a little before taking the money.

Then Liddel went into a stall in the men's room that smelled of puke and piss and aftershave and sat down on the crapper. He cut the stuff right in his lap with a butter knife and a straw Whale had gotten him from the bar.

By the time he was finished, it was nearly four o'clock. Out in the parking lot, Stone was sitting where he'd left him, still smoking weed.

"Taste it," he ordered after Liddel showed him the stuff.

"Hey," Liddel said, "I'm sellin', not buyin'."

"Hit on it."

"You think this shit is rat poison?"

"Ain' my part to say."

"Strychnine?"

"Gowan."

"This good shit, man."

Liddel snorted up two healthy nosefuls to prove his point, taking care to keep the straw on top where he hadn't cut the coke much at all. He handed the Baggie to Stone, who did the same. With all the grass he'd smoked, the manete alone would have cleared his head. Gradually, Stone's reddened eyes took on some life. He tapped a long finger against his nose, cleared his throat, and said, "*Mm*. We got us a deal."

"Next time," Liddel told him, just to let him know where things stood, "don't get in touch unless you want real weight. Aggravation at prices like this I can't afford."

He drove Stone back to Coney Island and dropped him off at the corner. His partner was nowhere in sight. Liddel figured he'd probably passed out in some doorway. Real tough guys all right. There had never been one half as smart as a manhole cover, or as useful.

It was nearly light by the time he got the car put away. Although he tried to be quiet, Tina woke up as soon as he walked into the bedroom. She refused to go back to sleep until they had snorted up nearly the entire piece he had taken out for himself. One thing led to another then, and it was nearly mid-morning before he fell out.

When he woke, it was late afternoon. He was alone, Tina having gone to her Saturday dance class in the city. The tiny bedroom was swollen with heat. Liddel got out of bed, went to the window, and popped the shade.

The street below was a patchwork of old snow, stained dog piss yellow and shit brown, the telephone wires no more than dark diagonals against a gray and leaden sky, all of it dark and dull and dirty with no hint of color anywhere. He put his finger to his nose and inhaled gently. Nothing. His nostrils were as clamped tightly shut as a virgin's knees, and not just from the heat.

He went into the bathroom and took down a box of Q-tips from the shelf, then dipped one into a large jar of Vaseline before easing it into his left nostril. Christ. Even the coke he hadn't stepped on was plaster of paris. He hated to think what the rest of the stuff was like. Putting the Q-tip away, he decided to forget about breathing through his nose for a while.

The TV in the living room was on with the sound turned off. The remnants of last night's Chinese takeout dinner lay scattered along the coffee table in aluminum serving trays. Tentatively, Liddel poked a finger into one of the trays and licked at it. Cold roast pork with Chinese vegetables for breakfast. Uch. He was trying to decide whether to go out for coffee when he remembered his dream. It had been mad, the images overlapping like layers of cheese and meat in a dish of lasagne.

As best as he could recall, he had been standing on a footbridge in a tropical greenhouse in the Botanical Gardens downtown where he hadn't been in years. Coffee trees, a parrot, and humidity so thick he'd had trouble breathing. A bunch of black kids wearing blue knit caps and peacoats had been diving off the bridge into the scummy water below, coming up with rusted pennies and leaden nickels in their mouths. None of them had possessed hands, or a nose.

Christ. What a dream. Those yahms. They had spooked him all right. Automatically, because it was Saturday, he picked up the phone and began to dial Haymon's number in L.A. Then he remembered that the big guy was still on the road. Without putting the receiver down, he called Momo. The little prick richly deserved to have his ass nailed to the wall. The way Liddel was feeling this morning, he was just the man for the job. As soon as the little bastard got on the line, Liddel began laying into him, in no uncertain terms. The nightmare slipped quickly from his mind.

CHAPTER TWENTY-TWO

So FAR as Reed could tell, in the months since their innocent and very accidental meeting in the supermarket, Lauren Sklar had done a remarkably accurate job of re-spinning the sticky web in which she had once held him prisoner. Thankfully, they had not yet slept together. Apparently the memory of that last, failed attempt was still so vividly etched in both their minds that neither of them had enough courage even to broach the subject. For such small favors, Reed was grateful. And yet he could not help feeling that sooner or later the situation would present itself again.

For the shared memories that held them together now were as powerful a brand of emotional epoxy as any available on the open market. There was no reason for Lauren not to soon begin telling him how to make his bed and whom to put in it.

Nothing escaped her notice. Furiously, she'd tried to persuade him to keep a diary of his season with the Lakers, insisting that it would make a terrific book and an even better movie. Many times, she had implored him to junk his old Fiat for something with a little more pizzazz. On the occasion of his thirtieth birthday, she had somehow convinced his receptionist to let her slip unannounced into his inner office so that she could present him with three handwoven silk ties. The ties, of course, were perfect, far more expensive and better crafted than any he would have permitted himself to buy on his own.

Every morning, when he looked into the mirror and fastened the knot on one of those ties, which soon came to be the only ones he owned that gave him any real pleasure, Reed was forced to admit that Lauren still knew. What he liked, what he disliked, what was good for him.

Although he was still sleeping with Callie and enjoying it more than ever, he knew that she could never have done as well. Maybe one, or two on a good day, but never three. Three ties that he loved spoke of an authority and a total knowledge of him that Callie would never have.

On the subject of Reed Kreiger, Lauren Skyler, née Sklar, was still the absolute arbiter, the final authority. And yet, in that knowledge, there was something that stifled Reed, something he could never accept or simply rise above.

The truth of the matter was that Lauren's re-emergence in his life was but one complication in what had become a very tangled kind of existence. With the regular season nearly over and the Lakers looking like a sure bet to sweep the Western Conference playoffs and then proceed into the championship series itself, Reed was forced to admit that his role as team consultant had turned out to be a total bust.

What Blake Marion had really wanted for the club was a prescription-writing pharmacist, not a trained psychiatrist. So long as the Lakers continued to perform as they were being paid to do on the court, the burly general manager had no interest at all in seeing that any of their very real personal problems were ironed out.

Reed had read countless season diaries penned by superstars, sixth men, coaches, referees, general managers, trainers, ball boys, and players' wives. Not one had ever told him a thing about what the day-to-day grind of being with a professional team in America was really like. Now that he had spent nearly a full season with the Lakers, he himself was unable to shed any real light on the subject.

After the nth game won or lost, the nth last minute time-out called to hurriedly diagram a play that either worked or immediately fell apart only suddenly to re-resolve itself into a bit of brilliant improvisation so effective no one could understand why it hadn't been thought of in the first place, what was there to say? Only that up close, professional sport became the business it truly was. An act of game-saving heroics meant no more after the game was over than some time-saving solution deposited in a suggestion box by an eager office worker.

So far as Reed could tell, a curious kind of ennui encircled professional sports in America. It was both exciting and boring as hell all at the same time. One had to be either a total zealot or a complete idiot to ignore the financial wheeling and dealing continually going on in the background and concentrate on the game itself.

Compounding the problem were the players, men who worked but a few hours a day for salaries ranging from sixty to two hundred thousand dollars a year. It was Reed's professional opinion that not one of the Lakers even paid an occasional visit to that neighborhood most laymen called normal behavior.

A complete listing of all their phobias, fixations, obsessive pre-game rituals, and out-and-out psychotic episodes would have filled a tome as thick and weighty as the PDR, the handy bible of drugs every physician kept within arm's reach.

Cliff Summers, on court the mildest and best mannered of men, was a wreck looking for a place to happen off it. On five separate occasions, Reed had been called upon to administer massive doses of Thorazine to combat the attacks of hysteria and anxiety Summers invariably suffered just before bursts in which he'd score thirty and forty points a game. During the season, both at home and away, Summers had continual nightmares of the kind Reed associated with eating a large and oily pizza decked with pepperoni immediately before going to bed. On the road, Cliffie sweated through his sheets at night and occasionally woke up with them so knotted around his legs that a trainer had to be summoned to cut him out of bed. He suffered fainting spells in locker rooms, collapsed from exhaustion in airports, yet stolidly submitted to a variety of pre-game cortisone and Butazolidin injections from the team physician that would have crippled a racehorse.

During the off-season, when Cliffie became an apparently very competent stockbroker, all his troubles vanished. Yet when Reed politely suggested to Summers that he consider giving up the game, the advice immediately found its way back to Blake Marion, who called Reed on the carpet to lecture him about the ethics of advising all-league guards to retire while still in their prime.

"You ain't on the payroll to help the Celtics," Marion told him. "They don't need no help. They're already kickin' ass in the East."

"Blake, my concern is Cliff. You ever talk to him at length? The man can't go five minutes without starting to stutter. He's a bundle of raw and bleeding nerve ends."

"Been like that for fifteen years, doc. Every season he looks so bad you think for sure they gonna come for him with the butterfly net and the straitjacket. Every year he leads the league in assists and scoring and demands a raise over the winter to sign a new contract. He's happy as is. Leave him be."

There was little Reed could do with that kind of logic, which permeated the entire team, right down to the players. To a man, the Lakers did not want to be saved from the demons that plagued them so much as to control them with medicinal help so as to boost their scoring average.

Unquestionably, the man who led the list for wholesale weirdness was the "Big A." One night Arvin would play so well it seemed he could scale opposing centers in a single bound. The next night he'd look like Clark Kent with a cardiac problem. The big man's obvious difficulties with the most rudimentary aspects of the game he'd played all his life fascinated Reed. No matter how many times he was reminded of them, Arvin could not remember out-of-bounds plays. He rarely made more than two consecutive free throws. Buried somewhere deep inside his brain, Arvin Williams had a mental block on the subject of basketball as big as the Rosetta Stone.

But there was no way Reed could talk to him. Blake Marion had declared Arvin Williams off limits to everyone, both inside and outside the organization. Of all the players, only Arvin was allowed to leave the dressing room after games without talking to reporters. Only Arvin granted no in-depth interviews. Only he refused to appear on television talk shows. So far as Reed could tell, Arvin spoke only to Blake Marion and occasionally to the silk and velveteen teddy bear he persisted in carrying around with him everywhere.

Reed's greatest personal disappointment, though, was Haymon Jacobs. Before the season had begun, he had considered Haymon a real friend, not to mention an important ally within the paranoia ridden Laker organization. After all, it was his favorable report that had gotten Haymon his job. He had asked the big guy for nothing in return. He had gotten precisely that. Nothing.

Ever since the first road trip of the season, Haymon had been distant and aloof, a hollow-eyed, silent, staring stranger who hid behind a luxuriant black beard that threatened at any moment to engulf his entire head.

Nor was he what you would call a great conversationalist. Just after the Lakers had returned from their first swing through the East, wanting only to be friendly, Reed had gone over to Haymon at practice and asked, "You see Liddel back in the city?"

A nod. A blank look and a nod, as though the question warranted no further answer.

"Was he okay?"

"Who?" The single word given up so grudgingly that for a moment Reed had wondered if Haymon had taken a vow of silence.

"Liddel, Haymon. How was Liddel?"

"I can't say."

"What does that mean? He's your best friend, no?"

A look Reed had never seen before and no wish to soon see again had taken possession of the big man's face. For a moment, Haymon had actually grinned. The smile had been so chilling and bloodless that Reed had unconsciously hugged himself for warmth. "Hamid's my friend now, doc," Haymon had said, looking through Reed as though he were no longer there. "I don't use words like best no more neither. There ain't no best. There just is." Then Haymon had turned and walked away, leaving Reed standing behind him, feeling like a fool. They had not talked since.

They were all crazy. Of that Reed was sure. Every last Laker, Haymon included, was like a giant safe with a secret combination that had to be mastered before the tumblers of their intricate personalities would unlock and the door to their friendships came swinging open. So they were good with a basketball. So what? There were other things in the world that mattered, a lot of them.

Still, he'd kept on pitching, trying to get through. Noting that Hamid had indeed once again become Haymon's only friend, Reed had tried to establish some contact there. During an afternoon shoot around when everyone had seemed relaxed and happy, he'd cornered the former Bran Johnson and asked, "What is it with the big guy, Hamid? He mad at me?"

"Haymon?" Hamid had said icily, his face betraying nothing. "He's cool, doc. You ain't got to worry about him no more. He's stayin' away from those pills you gave him, too. He don't put that evil shit in his body no more."

"*Hey*. I didn't give him those pills to hurt him, Hamid," Reed had said, feeling more than a little hurt himself. "He asked me for them. He nearly begged me."

"Well, he ain't beggin' no more, is he? Go help Arvin, man, he be the one who needs it now."

Trying to stay calm in the face of Hamid's incredibly hostile attitude, Reed had made a show of laughing and shaking his head. "Arvin," he'd commiserated. "How can a guy blow so hot and cold? One night he's great, the next he can't walk."

"Don't tell me you don't know?"

"Do I?"

"If not, you the only one in the league who don't. . . . Arvin gone down the stony end, man."

"What's that mean?"

"That boy got hisself a habit."

"Heroin?" Reed had said, unable to believe that anyone could be on the hard stuff and still play every night.

Hamid had snorted and made a face that had reminded Reed immediately of the old Bran Johnson. "Odin," he'd said. "That ain't no teddy bear he carries around with him, baby. That's a stone monkey. A gorilla. On his back. You dig? He oughta call it Oh-deein'.''

"Heroin?" Reed had said again, unable to believe this had been going right in front of him all season long without his having known about it. "Can't be. . . ."

"He don't shoot nothin', man. He's afraid of needles. Try givin' him a vitamin shot sometime and you'll find out how scared he is. It all goes up his nose. Coke. You can tell whether he scored or not that day . . . by the way he scores at night. Dig?"

"How much does he use?"

"*Hey*," Hamid had said, terminating the conversation, "you lookin' for data? Talk to him. All I know is he don't carry that teddy bear around with him for company. That's his stash bag. Sad, huh? Comes from tryin' to make it without help. Real help. The kind Haymon's getting now, full time."

When Reed began looking at Arvin Williams with the knowledge that Hamid's information had given him, it all finally fell into place. The "Big A's" outrageous clothes, his jewelry, his habitual lateness, his abstract and other worldly treatment of his fellow Lakers. Arvin Williams was a stone coke freak, with a habit he'd managed to conceal from everyone but those who already knew his secret.

Finding out about Arvin's problem had marked the turning point for Reed. Blake Marion's refusal to give him any guidelines when it had come time to write prescriptions for amphetamines and sleeping pills had placed him in a very precarious legal position. Just because the Lakers were crazy did not mean he was going to endanger himself professionally. He had a practice of his own to protect now.

L.A. was one tough town all right. Blake Marion had gone to the trouble of telling him that before the season had even begun. More than once since then, it had occurred to Reed that if the Lakers failed to go all the way again, he would make a perfect scapegoat. Who better to lay the blame on than some outsider with a fancy title and an extremely liberal prescription pad?

Without telling anyone, not even Lauren, whose advice he had decided to take, Reed had begun keeping a diary at mid-season. In it, he had faithfully recorded every last detail of the Lakers' less than charming foibles and odd personality quirks. If Blake Marion was thinking of sending him packing once the season was over, Reed had tons of fascinating data any publisher would be happy to put before the public. A book that would let everyone know once and for all how sick and hypocritical it all was, this religion of sport, where only winning counted, winning and nothing else.

If things got down and dirty, he would be ready. Not that he cared about coming back to spend another year with the Lakers.

Reed Kreiger no longer needed the Lakers at all. But when he left, as he fully intended to do once the season ended, it would be with nothing but lavish praise for the excellent job he had done. The diary would ensure that. It was his ace in the hole.

No matter what happened to the team once this long and boring season was over, Reed Kreiger intended to come out on top. Without doubt, it was where he now belonged, the only place where he felt truly comfortable and at home.

CHAPTER TWENTY-THREE

THAT HE had squandered the first twenty-eight years of his life in pursuit of things that did not matter was something Haymon Jacobs no longer even bothered to doubt. It was a fact, as certain as the terrible toll that pursuit had wreaked on him.

He could see clearly now how much of a near thing it had really been. He had fooled himself into believing that loving Linda had been the reason he had been put on earth. He knew better now. For the first time in his life, he was seeing things for what they were. Haymon Jacobs had been born a giant. A giant he had always been. A true giant he would now have to become. The destiny that in other times had been offered to princes and kings had been thrust upon him. A chance at greatness.

The stark white desert he had glimpsed while listening to John Coltrane's music for the first time had only been the beginning. He was still somewhere in that barren region looking for his path, lost somewhere between truth and illusion, wandering the very wilderness through which Moses and the children of Israel had passed after leaving Egypt and bondage behind.

Like Moses, Haymon Jacobs too was on a journey, a long and

involved search for meaning that went beyond the bounds of the life that other men led. As a true pilgrim, he had to first be tested and made pure in order to find what he was looking for. He had to suffer, both for his sins and for the sins of those around him. It was his destiny.

Night after night, long after he should have been asleep, Haymon would lie in yet another cold, hard motel bed, waiting. Faintly, from somewhere far off in the distance, he would hear the shrill sound of the ram's horn he remembered from childhood days spent in the synagogue. Then it would grow quiet again, the silence so thick and lustrous Haymon imagined he could almost reach out and touch it. Then the fire would begin.

Night after night, the fire came to surround him, actual lapping tongues of flame licking hungrily at his hands and feet, turning them a bright beet red. The room spinning around him, turning on its axis, its walls gone all orange with flame. The sound of his own scorched skin crackling in his ears as the horrid stink of burning flesh filled his nostrils. Alone in the inferno, he could only writhe in silent agony and pray for mercy.

The fire seared his memory, causing things he thought he had long since forgotten to rise to the surface. Often, when the pain became unbearable, he would find himself repeating phrases from the *bar mitzvah haftorah* he had recited so haltingly fifteen years before and never thought of since.

One night, all in his delirium, the words of the *Shema* came back to him, the holy phrase every kid in Brighton knew was all you had to say before dying in order to be granted entry to the kingdom of heaven. Over and over, he chanted the ancient words, until their sound drowned out the purple noise of his pain.

"Hear, O Israel: the Lord our God, the Lord is One. Blessed be the name of his glorious majesty forever and ever."

Not long after, Haymon began hearing voices. At first, they swirled and crackled just outside his ear, like the swelling, fading sounds of the distant radio stations he had so often dialed in as a teenager lying in bed alone late at night. Then, from out of the static and confusion, a single, familiar voice emerged, one he had thought he would never hear again.

"Hey, *big guy!*" the voice cried out to him in that same hoarse tone Haymon had heard an eternity ago in the back booth at Hirsch's luncheonette. "It's about time you realized what's goin' on."

"Liddel?" Haymon had gasped, unable to understand how his oldest friend could have found him, just when he needed his help so very badly.

"No, it's the fuckin' mystery guest. Wait. I'll sign in."

"How'd you get here?"

"BMT. *Shmuck.* How do you even know where I am?"

Haymon soon realized that Liddel had been sent to lead him out of the tangled wilderness he now recognized as his life. Why, it was difficult to say. Haymon knew only that he alone had been chosen. Summoned by fire, just as Moses had been called by the burning bush, he had been singled out. He was not mad and had never been. The blood of all the great martyrs, prophets, wise men, and rabbis of years past, all of whom had received this same sort of guidance, now flowed through his veins.

The message he had first heard in John Coltrane's music had been that of the *shofar* calling him back. Back to temple. Back to a God who was finally reaching out for him. Soon, he too would get to climb that holy peak and stand where Moses had stood, trembling with fear. It was just a matter of time.

In the wasteland that his life had become, God was now his only guide, and Liddel His messenger. Haymon lived each day as though it would be his last, making himself ready. One by one, he got rid of the unnecessary possessions with which he had cluttered up his life. He disconnected his phone. He gave away his precious television set, as well as nearly all his good clothes and expensive shoes. The Salvation Army was glad to come for his bed so that he could begin sleeping on the hard floor without any blankets. He was making himself ready. When the call came, he would go. God would lead him to higher ground.

Nor was this God the kind and gentle Jesus Cliff Summers had so often spoken about at prayer meetings and team breakfasts. This God bore no relation at all to the all-compassionate Allah to whom Hamid Malik had dedicated his life. This was a God only Haymon Jacobs could understand and appreciate, a fierce and avenging Old Testament patriarch more exacting than any coach. Haymon's God was the God that his father, Samuel, had abandoned without ever really knowing, a God who taught by fire, a taskmaster who demanded love and obedience above all else.

This was the God who had commanded Moses to lead the children of Israel to freedom and then caused them to wander the wilderness for forty years without ever granting Moses a glimpse of the Promised Land he had been born to find. Thousands of years later, He had condemned six million of those very same children to die in the showers and the ovens, just as Haymon was dying now. God's way was not always easy to explain but Haymon knew that it was just. For there was no in-between about it. When God acted, He did so with a certainty that Haymon had longed for all his life.

Over the course of that troubled life, he had lost his wife, his only friend, and the full potential of what had once been his good left leg. Now Liddel at least had come back to help him. It was no accident. There were no accidents. There was only God and the divine fire that came nightly to burn out the tangled underbrush of a life no one had ever been able truly to understand.

Every old and rotting branch was being torn out at the trunk so that new limbs could sprout. In order truly to live, you had to first die. No one had ever told Haymon this. He would not have believed them if they had. Now he knew it to be true. He was dying into life. He was being made over, entirely, with Liddel encouraging him not to give up.

"You on the freeway all right," Liddel told him, "with dudes drivin' by you like crazy, floorin' it hard as they can in the fast lane, killin' themselves to get where they're goin'. And all you got to do is wait for the exit sign with your name plastered all over it. You dig? It's like a game, man. You wanna win, all you got to do is stop losin'."

Haymon knew in his heart that Liddel was telling him the truth. His time was not yet at hand. Not yet. But it would soon come. His hour of triumph was approaching, the single, shining moment he had been put on earth to engineer. Then, and only then, he would be able to break the chains that had bound him to the earth for so very long and soar forth like some great eagle circling high above the world.

It was all part of God's great plan, which in every one of its many aspects was perfect. Even the name of the man who had first sounded the call to Haymon now took on new meaning. Coltrane. John Coltrane. The cold train. That was the one Haymon would ride as it began its long, whistling journey along cold steel rails, clouds of pure white smoke pouring from its blue black stacks.

The cold train was coming. Haymon Jacobs would be its single passenger, borne forth into the cold sunlight of eternity like a king. Where he was headed now, he would need no ticket, no token, no transfer. No one would dare muddy this car with their expensive laughter and well-worn tweedy arrogance. The cold train would belong to him and him alone.

He had only to await its coming to begin the final stage of his journey. Once the cold train came and went and was gone for good, everyone would know. Nothing would ever be the same again.

CHAPTER TWENTY-FOUR

ALTHOUGH LIDDEL GROSS had been going through the motions for weeks, constantly phoning people and looking to make a buy, ever since the first of the year, the city had been bone dry. No hash, no weed, no coke, no nothing. Just a pile of bills growing higher and higher in the drawer by his bed where he kept them neatly stacked until he could afford to pay them off.

After weeks of going around in circles without finding anything he could turn into money, Liddel drove out to Gatsby's one night without giving the Whale prior notice, hoping that if he just dropped in and surprised him, Larry might come up with something he could sell. Things were tighter than Liddel could ever remember. It was as though some unseen hand had turned off the faucet that kept the city supplied with drugs.

Nor could he depend on seeing any money from Max Trapp in the near future. His L.A. connections had dried up completely. Haymon Jacobs was no longer listed in the Los Angeles telephone directory. The big guy had disconnected his phone. He could not be reached through the club either. Not ever. It was but one more mystery in a winter filled with them.

To Liddel, Gatsby's on a Wednesday night looked like the out-patient ward of a methadone clinic, just show your reds at the door and go on in. The Whale's pride and joy, his precious yellow Vette, was nowhere to be seen in the parking lot. Someone Liddel didn't know was standing in the Whale's spot in the front room. Liddel walked over to the hatcheck girl, flashed her his best smile, and asked, "Larry around?"

"Uh-uh," she said, folding a dollar bill around her finger as though she were a cocktail waitress. "He don't work here no more."

"Since when?" Liddel asked, knowing it had only been a couple of weeks since they'd spoken to each other on the phone.

"Couple weeks," she said. "He had an accident."

"Anything serious?"

"Tell ya the truth," she yawned, looking past him at the clock over his head, "I don't ask. It keeps me working, y'know?"

Liddel got back into his car and drove out to Main Street in Flushing where the Whale shared a house with his ex-brother-in-law, Freaky Miltie. Miltie sold storm windows and siding for a living but what he really liked to do was to get high. He was a dynamite salesman when he remembered to go to work but not exactly what you would call reliable. Liddel had known him on and off for years. When he rang the front doorbell, Miltie wouldn't let him in.

"Hey, Miltie," Liddel said, "come off it, huh? It's me, Liddel. I wanna see Larry. . . ."

"You and everyone else. . . ."

"Just me, Miltie. F'Chrissakes, open up, will ya?"

"Try Elmhurst, man. He oughta be up and around by now. And don't come back here, huh? By tomorrow, this house is up for rent."

Figuring that Miltie was off on some weird trip of his own, Liddel drove to the nearest pay phone and called Elmhurst Hospital. Sure enough, they had a Larry Vargas listed as a patient. Visiting hours were from ten to six, every day.

The next morning, Liddel drove out to Queens. He took the elevator up to the fifth floor of the hospital, the stink of rubbing alcohol and ether thick in his nose. Larry's room was at the far end of a brightly lit corridor.

"What the fuck?" he said after he'd poked his head in through the open door.

Where the Whale's head had once been there was now a wobbly cotton ball of gauze and adhesive with one hole for his mouth and another for his right eye. Tubes ran into his arm and then out again into a bottle hanging upside down from a strap next to the bed. The Whale looked like Mr. Potato Head, before any of the features were stuck on.

"Whale? It's me, Liddel."

There was some movement and the bandages tilted so that Larry's good eye revolved into position to look at him. "Liddel," a voice croaked, "you got a smoke?"

"In here?" Liddel said. "You can't fuckin' smoke in a hospital, man. They got oxygen and shit. You'll blow yourself up."

"Fuck it," the voice said. "Gimme a smoke."

Liddel took out his pack of Parliaments and slid it along the sheet toward Larry's right hand. The Whale made no move to grab for them, so Liddel lifted the sheet. The Whale's hands were wrapped in some kind of brown gauze.

"Shit, Larry," Liddel said, "what's with the hands?"

"That's so I don't scratch myself. I itch, man," he moaned. "Christ, I fuckin' itch all over."

"What the fuck happened?"

"I got jumped."

"You? Where? By who?"

"Nightfighters. . . ."

"Guys you knew?"

The bandages shook back and forth. "Never seen 'em before. . . ."

"They take you off?" Liddel said, lowering his voice. "Coke? Money?"

"Nothin'." The Whale coughed and gagged a little. "For nothin', man. In the parkin' lot outside Gatsby's one night after work. They left me in the Vette, man . . . then they set it on fire." The coughing grew worse and Liddel wondered if he should call the nurse. "Vette's gone, man," Larry said, nearly sobbing. "Total loss."

"You got insurance," Liddel said. "They'll cover it."

"They toasted my Vette, man," Whale moaned, "for no reason."

"It's only a car, Larry," Liddel said impatiently. "You're fuckin' lucky you walked away from it alive." Then he lowered his voice again. "They didn't say why?"

"Nothin'," Larry said weakly. "They didn't say nothin'. Only thing I remember is one callin' the other off after they had me down. 'Zee-man,' he called him. Then I black out. . . ."

The icicle started in Liddel's balls and worked its way up to his stomach. He knew right away who had worked Larry over and why. If the Whale hadn't been so fucked up, he would have figured it out himself. The yahms he had burned had come back to the first guy they could get their hands on and burned him for real. After telling Larry he'd be back to visit him real soon, Liddel hurried out into the hallway and grabbed the first nurse he saw. "How's my friend in there doing?" he asked.

"Mr. Vargas?" she said. "Well, he's going to be all right, considering that he had a severe auto accident, with third-degree burns all over his body."

No wonder Freaky Miltie hadn't opened the door for him. It

wasn't every day you had a severe auto accident in the parking lot of a discotheque. Liddel knew that what his yahms had done to Larry would be only a down payment on what would happen when they got to him. He tried to stay calm.

So he had burned them. So what? It was part of the business. Dealers burned people all the time. Only sometimes those dealers got killed for it. He could always claim it had been an honest mistake, an error in judgment. Sure he could. In small claims court. Liddel knew that if he didn't get these clowns off his back right away, he'd never be able to show his face in Coney Island again.

The way he figured it, if he could get to them quickly with an ounce of righteous coke, he'd be able to buy his way out and smooth the whole thing over. After all, they weren't Italian. They were brothers, from the street, with memories no longer than his pinkie. So long as he gave them something to shove up their noses, they'd be happy. They'd forgive, and forget.

But no matter whom he called, the answer was the same. Not now. In a couple of days. A week at most. A "mule" was coming in from South America. A suitcase from Mexico was long overdue. Some shit was on its way from the coast. A guy had a boat. A plane. It was coming in by rail. Soon. Any day now. Call back. There was no telling when the shipment would hit. Call back.

In the entire city of New York, Liddel Gross could not lay his hands on a single ounce of coke, although he needed it to straighten a debt he could settle no other way. Money he had. What he needed was a deal. He called Momo's number so often that one night the little bastard's father blew up on him, screaming, "*Strunz!* You think I don' know what you call him for? He ain't home. He ain' never home no more. I got no son! I kill him, and you, if I get my hands on you bastards."

Liddel knew that if he lost his head and started acting crazy, he'd only open himself up and make it easier for them. All he could do was stay home, keep making phone calls, and wait. The idea of praying never occurred to him.

Hanging around the house all day long waiting for the phone to ring soon drove him crazy. To give himself something to do one night, he drove down Brighton Beach Avenue and paid four bucks to watch a couple of porno movies that so far as he could tell had no plot at all, just a lot of fucking. On his way to the john between flicks, he looked out through the lobby's plate glass doors to the street. Then he looked again, certain that he had caught a glimpse of a black man in a peacoat with a blue knit woolen cap pulled down low over his ears walking past the theater.

Whether it was Stone or Zee-man or just some brother on his way to the subway to go to work he didn't know. Bolting into the men's room where he had fucked around every Saturday afternoon as a kid, he jacked open the window, crawled out onto the fire escape, and shinnied down an iron ladder into the alleyway. He hit the ground running, sprinted to his car, and peeled out. No one followed him.

Back in the apartment, Liddel realized he wasn't sure if he had really seen one of the yahms who were after him or if he was just suffering from a terminal case of bad nerves. Brighton was way out of their territory, unless they were actively looking for him. He decided not to take any chances.

In order to deal with the problem full time, he couldn't afford to waste time worrying about anyone but himself. Tina had to go.

"We been talkin' about goin' to the coast anyway, right?" he said to her over the phone. "I want you to go now. I'll meet you out there."

"Is something wrong, Liddel? I've got a right to know."

"What could be wrong?" he said. "I gotta make a payoff for my old man. You come by tonight and I'll fix it up for you. Believe me, I'll be out there in a week, catchin' rays."

That night, he laid five hundred bucks on Tina, instructing her to stay with her older sister in Woodland Hills until he got in touch. Just to make sure she'd be taken care of if things took longer than he thought, he gave her Max Trapp's number. Haymon he no longer knew how to reach at all.

"This is a guy who's holding some money for me," he said. "You run short, go see him. He's an old friend of my father's . . . a movie producer, the one I told you about. You need cash, go see him."

Tina cried a little but did what he told her. She always had. Besides, she had been dying to go to the coast ever since they'd started living together. All in her eagerness to finally see California, she knew better than to ask too many stupid questions.

With Tina gone, Liddel had no one but himself to look out for. He stockpiled the apartment with food and called in sick at the pharmacy. He had some vacation time coming to him anyway. If they wanted to fire him for taking it all at once, that was okay too. The job was the least of his worries. Until he got his hands on an ounce of coke, he wouldn't be going anywhere. With a doorman on duty all the time at the front door and no back entrance, the apartment building was like a fortress. So long as he stayed put, he'd be all right.

Then the Whale called. A detective from the Sixtieth, the local precinct in Coney Island, had been out to see him. The cop's name was Latif, and he had actually gone to Miller with both Liddel and Haymon. Liddel remembered him well. Latif was Syrian. In South Brooklyn, an Arab kid had to be either stone crazy or a lunatic with his fists to survive. Latif had been both. Now he was a cop.

"I told him nothin'," the Whale said, "I swear on my life. Only when he brings up your name in conversation, social-like, I got to tell him I know you. Says he might come by to see you. To bullshit about old times. Nothin' heavy."

"Great, Whale," Liddel said, biting his lower lip. "Just what I need. You give him my address, too?"

"Nah. He said he had it already."

If Latif came to see him, Liddel knew he'd be all right. The apartment was clean. He had the .38 stashed on a ledge outside the kitchen window where no one would ever look for it. Just to make sure he would be totally covered, Liddel laid twenty bucks on the doorman who worked days, telling him he was going up to the Catskills for a week. "Look after my mail for me, will ya?" he asked. "I'll leave ya the key."

He was seriously considering having the phone disconnected like Haymon had done out in L.A., when it woke him the next day. Cautiously, he picked it up, holding it to his ear without saying a word.

"Liddel," a familiar voice said, "you there?"

"*MOMO!*" Liddel shouted, so angry and overjoyed at the same time that he nearly fell out of bed. "Where the fuck have you been, prick?"

"Ah, Liddel," he said in that annoying whine of his, "I got big troubles, man. My old man found out about me. Threw me outta the house. Beat the shit outta me, too. If my mother hadn't stopped him, he woulda called the cops. Can you imagine? Callin' the fuckin' heat down on your own kid?"

"Look, man, I ain't got no time for family counseling. I need an ounce. *Now!*"

"Can do," Momo said. "That's why I call. I'm goin' to Florida till he cools off. I'm gonna stay with a cousin down there."

"Great. Enjoy the sun. This good shit?"

"A-number one. Preemo. Never been stepped on. Well, maybe once."

"Bring it over," Liddel said. "We'll do the deal here."

Then he remembered that a cop had his address. Maybe Latif was just waiting for him to pull something stupid like doing business at home. "Hold on," he said. "I got a better idea. I'll meet you."

"Where?" Momo said. "It's gotta be today, man. I'm leavin'."

"Gimme a second, will ya?" Liddel said impatiently, "I'm thinkin'."

Liddel searched his mind for a place nearby where they could meet. It had to be very public so that they could both slip in, do the deal, and then disappear. The old confidence came back to him, warming him all over like a shot of good Scotch. He'd cop the ounce, see to it that the yahms were cooled out, and then split for the coast. He'd be high and dry and sitting in the sun at Malibu before anyone knew what had hit him. He was still Liddel Gross, the dealer. So long as he was on his feet and thinking, there was no one who could stay with him.

"Nathan's," he said, the idea coming to him all at once. "Meet me at Nathan's."

"In Oceanside?" Momo whined. "It's too far."

"In Coney Island, you prick."

"I ain't hungry. . . ."

"So you won't eat, *shmuck.*" Although Coney Island was jungle land, nightfighter turf, Nathan's would be dead quiet in the middle of the day. He could meet Momo on the side street by the roller coaster, do the deal, and then head straight for the airport.

"Meet me on the side street with the meters down the middle," he told Momo. "By the roller coaster."

"By the Army recruitin' station?"

"You got it. By the fuckin' house of horrors. Where they got the guy outside swingin' from a rope."

"The dummy, right?"

"No, you asshole," Liddel said, "a real guy. Your father. Yeah, a dummy. I see you there. In an hour."

Liddel slammed the phone down, grabbed his jacket, and made for the elevator. He'd connected for his coke. He could cop from Momo, see to it that the yahms got their share, and clear out. Once he hit L.A., he could solve his other problem by hunting Haymon down and reading him the riot act. He'd need Haymon more than ever now. Dealing was for kids, nickel-and-dime shit. This experience had taught him that. Out on the coast, he was going to get into something a little less dangerous. Like becoming a player's agent. On his way to Coney Island, Liddel ran three red lights, just for the fuck of it.

The green glass doors were still up at Nathan's, the usual collection of bums with wrinkled cardboard faces and paper stuffed inside their shoes assembled inside, each one hunched over a bowl of red clam chowder. Liddel cruised by once, made a U-turn, and swung back for another look. Very quiet and peaceful. Nathan's on a weekday afternoon in late winter, with all of Coney Island still boarded up, awaiting the Memorial Day weekend to swing into action again.

For a second, Liddel thought of running in for a dog. A last taste before leaving. Then he decided it would be better to wait on Momo, who'd never been the most punctual of men. He made a right turn on to the side street by the roller coaster and found some time on a meter halfway down the block.

Idly, Liddel watched the dummy corpse outside the house of horrors twitch as the breeze coming off the ocean blew it around. It almost looked real, as though there were really someone up there feeling the rope tighten.

Slouching down in the GTO's front seat, he lit a cigarette off the dashboard lighter and tilted the rearview mirror toward him so that he could keep an eye on all the traffic entering the street in back of him without being seen. An old black man in a gray sanitation man's uniform came walking toward the ancient Ford parked next to the GTO, carrying a cardboard plate heaped with six foil-wrapped dogs and three capped cups of orange soda. The guy got in his car and backed out, heading down the street.

The car Momo was driving must have been waiting by the boardwalk because Liddel never saw it in his mirror. The first he knew of it was when he heard the sound of squealing tires. He peeped over the dashboard in time to see an old and battered green and white 1957 Chevy Bel-Air with a bent coat hanger for an aerial pull into the newly vacated spot next to him.

Although he couldn't say much for what Momo was driving these days, there was no doubt it was the little scumbag in person behind the wheel. Liddel had to laugh. Momo and his old man. It served the prick right, for living at home. As though he had heard him, Momo twisted around in his seat and motioned to Liddel that he was coming out. Liddel popped the door lock on the passenger side, losing sight of Momo for a moment until the door actually began to swing open.

The first thing Liddel noticed was that Momo was hopping. Then he saw why. His legs were bound with a length of clothesline. Liddel did not need to see any more to know that he had been set up. Sitting bolt upright in the seat, Liddel jammed his foot down on the accelerator, twisting the key in the ignition all at the same time as he slammed the gearshift lever into reverse. The engine caught, coughed, protested, and fired into life, the GTO flying back with a sudden squeal, its back tires striking the curb with a heavy thump. Liddel pumped the gas pedal furiously, searching for first with the gearshift lever. The engine coughed. Then it coughed again. Then it died completely.

It was then that the back door of the Chevy came open in what looked to Liddel like slow motion. Two black men in peacoats and blue knit caps vaulted out, one headed straight for him, the other going toward Momo, who had managed to hop and stumble to a leaning halt against a meter in the middle of the street.

Liddel reached automatically under the seat for his piece. He came up empty handed. All in his eagerness to do the deal, he had forgotten to bring it with him. He tried to open his door and jump out, but a gloved hand caught him by the jacket sleeve. Something hard smashed into the side of his head just above the ear. He got sick all over, then his legs went weak.

"*Watch!*" a black voice commanded, wedging his head against the steering wheel so that he could just see over the edge of the dashboard to where Momo was still leaning helplessly against a meter.

The huge black man standing in front of Momo went into his pocket for something, coming out with it in his right hand. He swung his hand back and forth beneath Momo's chin with a sweeping, scythe-like motion. Momo seemed to grin for an instant, as though relieved of some burden he had long been carrying. Then two red, brimming semicircles appeared on his neck. His face went fishbelly white and he slumped out of sight.

The man who had done the cutting turned and ran toward the GTO, pulling off his blue knit woolen cap as he came. His face was horrible to look at, as though some skin doctor had tried to change its color and failed. Alternate bands of darker and lighter skin ran horizontally across his nose and mouth. Zee-man. A fuckin' natural born zebra. Liddel wanted to laugh.

"THE RIGHTEOUS INDIGNATION OF THE INVINCIBLE ZEBRA," a voice howled in his ear. Then something hard hit him, and he went down, under the dashboard, into darkness.

CHAPTER TWENTY-FIVE

IT was a good ten days before anyone thought it odd that no matter what time of day or night you called him, Liddel Gross was never home. Only Max Trapp, some three thousand miles away in Los Angeles, where it was conclusively spring, the Japanese cherry blossoms, dogwood, and acacia running riot all around his house and down by the pool, felt there was something wrong in Brighton.

Liddel, who for most of the season had supplied him with prompt and regular information, was suddenly nowhere to be found. And for the first time since they'd started doing business together, Max absolutely had to talk to him. Liddel's good friend Haymon Jacobs had suddenly become the most important man in Los Angeles.

The Western Conference playoff series between the Lakers and the Bucks was finally over. Max had been as happy as anyone to see it end. Right from the start it had been an authentic circus, one roughhouse contest following another, with fistfights breaking out under the boards and fifty-five foot rainbow shots falling in at the buzzer to send games into overtime. The Lakers had stumbled through only because of Arvin Williams. When roused, the "Big A" had played like a threshing machine let loose in a field of winter wheat. Only last night, midway through the second quarter of the final game, something had gone wrong with his machinery.

Tearing down the near side of the court, with absolutely no one near him and no reason at all for it to happen, the "Big A" had suddenly pitched face forward on to the floor. The Forum had gone dead quiet, the crowd gasping as though it had witnessed the first sports assassination. They'd brought out a stretcher and wheeled Arvin away, the body of the big guy passing in review no more than thirty feet in front of where Max had been sitting with Victoria. Max had caught a glimpse of Arvin's left leg. A knee. An injury that could put Williams out of action for the rest of his life.

Somehow, despite how badly Haymon Jacobs had played in Arvin's place, the Lakers had managed to hold on to their lead and close out the series. They would need more than they had shown Max last night to do the same against the Celtics. This year the Celtics were world beaters. With Arvin Williams missing from the starting lineup, the Lakers were just another team.

By being smart, Max had managed to make money on the Lakers in their series with the Bucks. Being smart would not help him now. Without Arvin Williams, the Lakers had no chance to stop the Celtics from running them off the court in four straight. Losing back as much as he'd already won in Vegas would make Max look like just another high roller taking his chances with the line. It would persuade no one that he had gone back into business for himself and pre-arranged the outcome of the nationally televised final series.

Max needed to get in touch with Liddel. Although it had been a while since they had spoken to each other and Max had done pretty well for himself without the kid's help, the situation now was altogether different. The way Haymon Jacobs played in the upcoming series would be crucial. Max wanted to hear about it from Liddel every time Haymon changed his socks. It would make betting each game a simpler proposition.

Only no matter how many times he tried, Max simply could not locate Liddel Gross by phone. The kid was never home. Ever. Knowing that it would be less than a pleasant conversation, Max finally broke down and got in touch with the only person he knew who might have some idea where Liddel had gone.

"Leon," Max said after Cookie Gross had picked up the phone, "it's Max."

"Long time, Max. How are you?"

"Good. Yourself?"

"Like always."

"Leon," Max said, taking a deep breath before plunging in, "what do you hear from your kid?"

"Liddel?" Cookie answered, wheezing slightly. "Nothing. I

called him a couple days ago, he wasn't home. Been a while since I seen him."

"Cookie, lately he ain't never home."

"How would you know?"

"Okay," Max said slowly, "I know you ain't gonna like this . . . but you gotta hear it sometime, so it might as well be now. We been talkin' to one another regularly lately. What with his boy Jacobs bein' a Laker and me havin' a small interest in knowin' how the team might go out here, we been helpin' each other out."

"This don't make me happy, Max."

"I didn't think it would, Leon. Look . . . what he fed me stayed right here. Only what worries me now is that I can't ever get a hold of him."

"So? Maybe he took a vacation."

"With the playoffs goin' on? It don't make sense. Could be it's nothin' . . . but do me a favor. Check on the kid for me. If somethin' back there ain't kosher, I can handle it from my end. I just need to know . . . should I start handlin' it or not?"

They hung up together, Max knowing full well how furious Cookie had to feel. His old partner and his kid doing business right under his nose without cutting him in for a piece or even telling him the first thing about it. It was an insult of the first order. Still, Max figured he could always make things right with Cookie when the time came. The important thing now was to find out about the kid.

"Went there myself," Cookie told him the next day over the phone. "Hirsch drove me. Doorman let me in. Looks like he ain't been home in weeks. Place is a mess. What is it, Max? I got a right to know."

"Too complicated to go into now, Leon. . . ."

"Where's the kid, Max?" Cookie said in a dead, flat voice. "You know?"

"No idea, Leon."

"If he's hurt because of you, Max, I ain't gonna forget it."

"Don't worry, Leon. Just gimme some time. I can find out."

"I blame you for it, Max," Cookie said doggedly. "All the way. Just so you know."

"Leon, I got business to take care of for you. I'll get back to you."

Max hung up, knowing there was nothing Cookie could do about it from his end. For all his talk, Cookie was just a fat old man now, with two bad legs and a handbook that was peanuts compared to the big money he had riding on the outcome of the final series. Cookie had no juice at all, not any more. Only he could help the kid.

Max got on the horn and began calling people back in the city who owed him a favor. If the kid was alive and walking around, they'd find him, sooner or later. Until they did, Max had to hang tough. He had come too far on this thing to let an unpredictable yo-yo like Haymon Jacobs do him in. As though that wasn't enough, Max now also had Cookie to placate. Regularly, like some sick old woman calling her doctor at night to make sure she'd wake up alive in the morning, Cookie checked in with him once a day, like clockwork.

"Leon," he told Cookie night after night, "I'm on it, all right? You think I ain't? Maybe you'd like me to put an ad in the paper, huh? I called people in New York and I'm waiting to hear."

"So how come you ain't heard yet?"

"I can't say. . . ."

"How long you prepared to wait?"

"As long as it takes. . . . Look, Leon, I got cops workin' on this. Understand? Cops who owe me favors. I got an assistant DA on it. *Emmis,* soon as I hear, I'll call you. I guarantee it."

"I give you a few more days, Max. At the most. Already it's too long. I got a feeling I don't like. . . ."

"Sure, sure. He's your kid, Cookie, you got a right to worry. But not about how I'm handlin' it. From this end, it's being taken care of."

"I'll call tomorrow night."

"Fine, Cookie, fine. Maybe I'll even have somethin' to tell you then. . . ."

"And if not, I'll still call. . . ."

"Right," Max said. "Right. I don't talk to you before I go to bed, Leon, I don't feel like my workin' day is complete."

More than once, Max had felt himself right on the verge of telling Cookie to go take a flying leap. There was no way an old man who lived by taking nickel and dime bets could understand what he was into now. Cookie was from another era entirely, a throwback to an earlier time. Unlike himself, Cookie had never been able to change. Over the years, he had grown only old and fat. Max Trapp was still out there at center court, scrapping like a rookie for the tap. His game was not yet over.

So his plan had sprung a little leak. The leak could be patched. All Max had to do was get back his edge. Had Liddel been available, that would have been as easy as dialing directory information. With the kid apparently out of the picture, Max knew he could go it all on his own. He had been on his own many times before. Right at the very end of things, it always got like this. Tough and hairy and off the wall. Shit flying at you from so many directions you didn't know which way to turn. Eventually, Max knew he would come out on top. He was still a winner, all the way. He always had been.

CHAPTER TWENTY-SIX

Cookie Gross sat by his window watching spring come to Brighton. One day, without warning, the single tree implanted in concrete outside his apartment building sprouted buds. Within a week, they unfurled into large, fine-veined leaves that glistened at night in the light cast by the streetlamp on the corner. People began returning to the beach, cruising the crowded streets of the neighborhood in search of a parking spot, then walking slowly toward the sand with canvas weave beach chairs and oversized red reflectors folded beneath their arms.

As best as Cookie could figure it, Liddel had now been missing for at least two weeks, though how long he had been gone before that was anyone's guess. Save for the constant chatter of the all-news radio station, the apartment was very quiet these days. The phone, his sole link to the outside world, rarely rang anymore. He had shut down the business.

Calling each of his customers in turn, he had informed him that his "health" was forcing him to take his annual vacation a little earlier than usual this year. He'd put checks in the mail to those few to whom he'd owed money and asked the rest to settle up with him as best they could on such short notice.

Although he knew he would see no more than half of what he

was owed, he wasn't worried. The important thing now was to get all the loose ends tied down so that when Max came through with word on Liddel, he'd be ready.

The morning after Hirsch had driven him over to his son's apartment, Cookie had sat down and tried to work the accounts, like always. Only the numbers had danced and swayed before his eyes, defying him to order them into neat columns. He had worked and worked, trying to concentrate, but it had not gotten any easier.

Instead, for the first time in longer than he could remember, tears had filled his eyes, sliding down his grizzled, unshaven cheeks on to the pages of his notebook, blurring the neatly inked columns of figures. He had broken down completely then and wept, for what reason he did not know, blubbering like the young boy who had so often cried himself to sleep in cardboard boxes in empty lots.

Afterward, blowing his nose into one of the old rags he kept around the apartment for just that purpose, he had felt calm once more, cleaned out, as though he had taken a good long *shvitz* at Silver's. It had all become very clear to him.

For too long, he had been fooling himself, pretending that the city was still his home, the neighborhood a place where he could go on living. Unlike Louie the Barber, who had held on to his shop and his grape arbor until he'd lost his very life, Cookie knew for sure now that he had overstayed his welcome in the city. New York no longer was a place he understood. Coney Island had become a jungle.

Like some spavined nag hooded with blinders who discovers that the race is over only when he is led out to pasture for the final time, he had just gone on and on without ever once realizing that the finish line was already far behind him.

The disappearance of his son had changed all that, proving to him beyond any shadow of a doubt that he could not go on like this any more. If he did, one day he would wake up looking into a gun held by a couple of junkies intent on getting all the money they'd heard the old man on the corner kept stashed in his apartment.

He was going to take his annual vacation all right, only this time it would last for more than a month. Cookie Gross was getting out for good. They could have the city, what little was left of it. It was theirs already, as it had been for years. With what he'd saved, he could afford a little place in Florida, where the hot sun and the healing salt water would do his aching legs good.

There would still be plenty left over to see that Liddel had a stake of his own so that he could set himself up somewhere else. California, Colorado, wherever it was that kids went these days, Liddel could go. Anywhere but the city. The city was for animals.

First, though, he had to find out from Max where Liddel had gone. That came before anything. No longer did he bother to go down to Hirsch's for a roll and coffee and the morning papers. There was no need. Every day around suppertime, Hirsch sent up a kid with a sandwich and the *Post*. After the paper came, Cookie knew it was time to call Max out in California. Each day Max told him exactly the same thing. He too was waiting.

But it was not the same. Max had no children. He was a cold, bloodless man who had never really given a damn about anyone but himself. There was no way Max could understand what it was like to know that someone you had raised was in trouble and you could do nothing to help.

Cookie was sure that Max was involved in something big out on the coast, something to do with gambling and fixing and the professional basketball season that was just about to end. That was why Liddel had disappeared. Someone was putting the heat on Max by taking his New York contact out of action. It was an old play. "Street insurance" they had called it back in Louie the Barber's day, an easy way to make sure someone would give you his undivided cooperation. Grab a guy's wife or his sister and you were assured that the guy would give you no trouble. None. Cookie had seen it done a hundred times.

Only this time, it was his kid. Twenty-five years he and Max had known each other and this was how Max was paying him back. By getting Liddel kidnapped.

For the first time, Cookie understood in his gut why the *Italianers* did business the way they did. An eye for an eye and a tooth for a tooth. It was biblical. For every act of treachery, there would be retribution, swift and sure, predicated on rules everyone knew in advance. Every investment, good or bad, would have its payoff. It made perfect sense.

A cold and cleansing anger had taken possession of Cookie Gross, anesthetizing him to everything save the conviction that Max Trapp owed him more than money. Once Liddel was safe, Cookie was going to make sure that Max paid for all the debts he had run up over the years with other people's lives. It was only just. A man should be made to pay his debts.

More than one grateful client had often told Cookie that they could take care of anyone who was causing him trouble, no matter who or where he was. Los Angeles was a world away, a place he had never been. Still, even out there, Cookie knew he could find someone to carry out a piece of work that was long overdue.

Money he had. What he wanted now was his son. He had never realized before just how much that could mean to a man, especially one who had suddenly realized how old and tired he really was. If he could not have Liddel, he would have satisfaction. At his age, it was one of the few things money could still buy.

CHAPTER TWENTY-SEVEN

JUDGING BY what was left of him, Liddel Gross had suffered horribly before finally being allowed to die. His body, discovered on a cold day in April that felt more like winter than early spring, had been bound with twine and wrapped in brown paper and left in back of a Good Humor stand on the sand at the bottom of the dead-end street where Silver's Baths had once stood.

An old bum who had been making the stand his home all winter long, using it as a combination living room, kitchen, and *pissoir*, found the body. A wagon from the Kings County morgue was dispatched to collect the remains and carry them back downtown for identification and toxicological reports.

Having attained that final state, Liddel Gross was permitted to rest in peace. No newspaper carried any notice of his demise. The all-news radio station to which his father listened so faithfully did not devote even ten seconds of its precious air time to reporting that yet another body had been found under the boardwalk in Coney Island. Simply, it was not news.

Not even in the medical examiner's report that found its way to Detective Dave Latif's desk in the Sixtieth Precinct in Coney Island did Liddel Gross receive the attention his twenty-eight years on earth should have earned him. The name of the deceased was listed as "Unknown Male," the blank next to his age left just that way, as were the spaces next to "Usual Residence," "Occupation," and "Home Telephone Number."

The report from the morgue, where fingerprints would have been taken had exposure to the elements not made them impossible to obtain, was more informative. Nearly every major bone in the victim's body had been splintered with a blunt instrument. The flesh on the face, hands, and genitals had been burned, possibly with a lit cigarette. There were extensive acid burns on the soles of his feet. Marked dispositional lividity on the dorsal plane indicated that death had occurred on the sand where the body was found.

The actual cause of death was thought to be a combination of shock, internal bleeding, and exposure. As a bizarre footnote, the doctor who had performed the autopsy noted that upon forcing open the victim's jaws, he'd found a plastic Baggie filled with white powder. Chemical analysis revealed the substance to be a mixture of talc and mannitol, a six-carbon sugar used as an antitonic to reduce brain swelling in cases of severe head injury.

Latif, who had looked at corpses fished out of the weeds in Jamaica Bay after having floated face down for weeks, could not remember ever having seen a human being so totally mutilated. Taking it upon himself to try and ID the body, he had sifted through what little clothing the victim had been wearing. In the folds of what had once been a shirt, Latif found a thin gold chain and a fourteen-karat Jewish star. On the back of the star, the words "For Liddel—7/11/59" were engraved.

Latif, who was working on four different and apparently unrelated cases at the time, one of them the slaying of an unidentified white youth found on a street near Nathan's with his throat slashed from ear to ear, knew then whom he had been looking at. Larry Vargas' good friend Liddel Gross, the dealer. Still, it took him two days to get an address for a next of kin. On a set of old records at Miller High School, Leon Gross was listed as Liddel's closest relative, with an address on Brighton Beach Avenue no more than a ten minute walk from the precinct house.

Latif could have called up the father and asked him to come to the morgue to ID the body. Considering the shape it was in, he decided to pay a house call.

At a red brick apartment house that looked like all the other apartment houses in Brighton, Latif pressed the downstairs buzzer next to an old and fading piece of tape with the name "Gross" inked on it. There was no answer. He rang the superintendent's bell and flashed his shield. After the super had let him in, Latif asked if there was still a Leon Gross living in the building.

"Cookie?" the super said. "Sure. Third floor. Three-G."

"He home?"

"He's always home." The super laughed. "He's a cripple. The buzzer's out of order."

Latif took the elevator to the third floor and walked down a dark hallway that smelled of old soup. Behind the door marked "3-G," a radio was playing loudly. He had to knock twice before it was turned down.

"It's the *Post*?" a voice called out. "Leave it by the door."

"Mr. Gross?" Latif said. "I'm from the Sixtieth Precinct. I wonder if I could talk to you for a moment?"

"Police?" the voice said. "A minute. Give me just a minute."

As Latif stood waiting, a dull mechanical scraping began on the other side of the door, as though someone was dragging something heavy across the floor. The sound was punctuated by labored breathing, as though the load weighed more than the person could manage. After what seemed like a long time, the door swung open the width of a man's hand, held in place by a safety chain.

"What is it?" an old man whose hair had gone gray above the ears asked suspiciously. The attitude was one Latif had grown accustomed to in Brighton, where old people often refused to open their doors at all for anyone, no matter how many times you told them who you were.

"It's about your son, Mr. Gross."

"Huh? Liddel? One minute, I pull off the chain."

The door closed. Then, free of the chain, it swung back open all the way. An old man with a thick roll of flesh around his gut and two days' worth of beard covering a surprisingly gaunt and well-lined face stood leaning on a pair of metal canes. His T-shirt was spotted, as though it had been used to clean a counter. There were dark gray sweat stains under his arms.

The old man motioned for Latif to come in and the detective followed him across an expanse of linoleum so dark with age it no longer had any discernible color or pattern. He was swallowed up immediately in the funk of the apartment, the smell of old and neglected pieces of clothing thrown under furniture in corners where no one had dusted for years. In the living room, stacks of magazines and newspapers rose up in a trembling urban skyline that threatened to collapse at any moment.

By the time they'd reached the large padded armchair that stood before the apartment's double windows, the old man was out of breath. He sat down heavily, puffing up his cheeks. Then he flattened them, the air whooshing out of his mouth with a sibilant hiss. He slid his canes together with an audible clack, stacked them by the armrest of the chair and looked up.

"So?" he said. "What is it? The kid's in trouble? Under arrest? What?"

"When's the last time you saw your son, Mr. Gross?" Latif asked gently.

"Seen him?" Cookie said, puffing up his cheeks again and letting go with a blast of stale breath. "Ain't seen him in a long time. Seen his place two, three weeks ago. Why? You got something on him? I got a right to know."

"Do you recognize this, Mr. Gross?" Latif asked, taking out the small manila envelope the department used for storing personal property. He tilted it so that the thin gold chain and tiny star within it slid on to his palm. He held this out for Cookie Gross to look at. The old man craned his neck and squinted. He reached out for the Star of David and turned it over slowly with his large, square butcher's fingers.

"This?" he said, more to himself than the police officer who was standing over him. "Sure. I give it to the kid when he's thirteen. Instead of a *bar mitzvah*. He still wears it."

"You've seen him wear it?"

"Sure."

"Then I'm afraid I have to tell you that your son is dead, Mr. Gross. We found him under the boardwalk last Thursday in Coney Island. It's taken us this long to find out who he was."

Latif did not say that the job had been made easier by the investigation he had been pursuing for weeks into the current street war raging over cocaine rights to Coney Island or that this murder and that of the young white male found dead on the street next to Nathan's were probably closely related. He said nothing at all about Larry Vargas, to whom he had talked in a hospital room in Queens, or the Baggie of white powder that had been found crammed inside Liddel Gross' mouth. What for? None of that could be of any interest to this old man. All he needed to know was that his son was dead.

For the rest of the conversation, the old man shook his head at appropriate intervals and mumbled responses. Latif could see that he was not really paying attention. No, he knew of no one who might want Liddel dead. He was only a pharmacist. He himself had been retired for years. He had been an accountant. A good boy. Yes, Liddel had been a good boy. A good son.

"If you need it, Mr. Gross," Latif said, "we can arrange for transportation downtown so you can claim the body. It's in the Kings County morgue now and will be for another two weeks. If you don't claim it by then, it will be buried at city expense in Potter's Field. That's on Hart's Island in the East River. You can get there by ferry from either the Bronx or Queens."

"*NO!*" the old man snapped. "I know where it is . . . I . . . I'll make arrangements. Private."

"Certainly," Latif said, anxious to be away now that his job was done. "Just one last thing."

"Yeah?"

"If I were you, I'd spare myself the agony of trying to look at him. He's in pretty bad shape. Let them close the box before. . . ."

"Huh? Oh, yeah, sure. The box. By the Jews, they always close the box. It's the way it works. Thanks for your help, Detective . . . ?"

"Latif."

"Right. I'll be in touch."

After the cop was gone, Cookie turned the radio back up. News flooded into the apartment from all parts of the greater metropolitan area. There'd been a three car collision on the Long Island Expressway. A young Puerto Rican had been apprehended and charged with the slaying of his ex-wife and infant daughter. A tie-up on the Seventh Avenue IRT was making commuter traffic on all northbound lines an hour late.

Cookie sat motionless for what seemed like hours, the reports washing over him like a cresting ocean wave. Finally, he roused himself and reached for the phone. Liddel was dead. He had to make arrangements.

His first call was not to any funeral parlor or mortuary. All that could wait. Instead, he called one of the men who had promised him assistance should he ever need it. The man was surprised to hear from him but able to suggest someone who might be able to help. Cookie would have to meet with that man in person. It would not be very hard to arrange. Although he was old and fat and lame and just a small time bookie, for a sum not in excess of ten thousand dollars, Cookie Gross was going to be able to buy the satisfaction that had been denied him by the death of his only son.

CHAPTER TWENTY-EIGHT

BY THE time Reed Kreiger left the gym where the Lakers were holding the final practice session for the opening game of their championship series with the Celtics, it was already dusk. The fading light of what had been a pretty day in Los Angeles was turning the buildings on campus several shades of pink and purple. The pastel wonder of sunset over the picturesque outcroppings of Loyola University notwithstanding, Reed was as angry as he could ever remember being and right at the end of his rope so far as doing anything more for the Lakers in a professional capacity was concerned. The long season was nearly over and he was back where he'd been at the start, standing outside an odoriferous little gym, wondering why he had even bothered to try in the first place.

Arvin Williams, whose moderately sprained left knee was as closely guarded a secret as any the Joint Chiefs of Staff kept locked within the Pentagon's vaults, was not around. The word in the gym was that Arvin had been sent to a clinic in Minnesota to be fitted with a wonder brace that might enable him to see some action if the series went beyond the minimum four games required to decide its outcome.

It was because of Arvin that he had made the long haul over here today, spending an hour on the freeway entertained by a rhythmic clanking noise buried deep within the Fiat he had never heard before. Although Reed had no real idea of how badly the big man's knee was damaged, he was positive that the only place Arvin Williams belonged today was in a detox ward. He had been courtside at the Forum the night Arvin went down. Players did not just collapse like that on a basketball court because their knees gave out.

The "Big A" had been so very stoned for so long a time that Reed considered it no less than a miracle that Arvin hadn't permanently crippled himself in the fall. Right then and there, Reed had decided that he could no longer stay out of it and pretend he did not know. Arvin Williams could not play again for the Lakers this year. Not if Reed Kreiger had any say in the matter.

He had come to the gym today to tell Blake Marion just this. Only before he could get to talk to him, he'd had to sit through the worst Laker practice he had ever seen. One angry squabble had followed another, the Lakers blowing defensive assignments, throwing bad passes, and committing acts of total stupidity on the court so basic a high school coach would have hidden his head in shame. All the while, they had shouted furiously at one another in the kind of language Reed had not heard since his days in the schoolyard.

The cause of most of the anger, Haymon Jacobs, seemed peculiarly immune to the chaos breaking out around him, as though he alone was unaffected by the rampant discontent from which his teammates were suffering. After the practice ended, of all the Lakers, only Haymon remained on court, shooting one methodical jump shot after another from outside the foul circle. The occasional droplet of sweat running down Haymon's nose was the only indication that his body even knew it was being put to use. So far as Reed could tell, the man was a total zombie, a seven foot robot operating on remote control, a distant satellite at the very edge of the universe revolving in its own eccentric orbit.

How anyone could feel so good about playing so badly was something Reed could not grasp. Had Haymon asked, Reed would have been more than happy to offer his help. Another prescription, a heart-to-heart talk, a fiery speech designed to rouse Haymon from the blissful contentment he was so obviously enjoying. Anything, just to bring the big guy around.

All the pressure in the world had come to rest on Haymon's shoulders. Yet to look at him, you would have thought that he did not have a care in the world. A classic case of *la belle indifférence*.

Reed had been just sitting, wondering how he could reach Haymon, when a stray rebound had bounced into the stands near him. He'd picked the ball up and walked over to the big guy with it under his arm.

"Haymon?" he'd asked. "You okay? You wanna talk or something?"

Haymon had only grunted. "Don't talk," he'd said. "Play."

Not really sure what he was hearing, Reed had stared up at the bearded, grinning giant. Sure enough, Haymon was inviting him on court to go one-on-one. Reed had accepted the challenge immediately, seeing it as a way to get through to Haymon.

The game itself had been surreal, the two of them completely alone in the deserted gym, the hollow thump of the ball smacking against the hardwood the only sound, its echo rebounding around the walls of the cavernous room.

Not for a moment had Reed expected Haymon to take the game seriously but he had, bumping him on defense, swiping at the ball with his big right hand, talking non-stop to himself all the while.

"Got to go, big guy, got to go, got to *go*," Haymon had crooned as he'd swept yet another rebound off the board. "Got to do it, got to be there, got to be *there*."

Haymon had hit an astonishing number of long distance bombs from the outside, a talent he apparently reserved for empty gymnasiums. Whirling in circles at the key, he'd launched a brace of sweeping hook shots, looping projectiles that rose to an impossible height before descending rapidly in a sure and deadly arc through the rim. With the score ten–two and Haymon needing but a basket to win, he'd added insult to injury.

"Seconds to go in the game, the series, the season," he'd muttered, parodying some over excited radio announcer, "Jacobs with the rock. Haymon Jay with the apple. Rockin' and rollin' with it where he stands. Yo-yos over the midcourt line, looks left, looks right, lays it on the floor, and goes the other way."

Dribbling out toward the no-man's land near the midcourt stripe, Haymon had turned his head and body away from the basket, seized the ball, grunted mightily, and let fly from where he was, propelling the ball backward over his head in a straight line toward a hoop that was now a good forty-five feet in back of him.

Reed had watched the ball rocket over his head, knowing full well that it had no chance of going in. Apparently Haymon knew this too. Charging in at full speed toward the basket, he'd left his feet somewhere out by the foul line. Leaping like some maddened Marine recruit attacking a wall in basic training, he'd gathered in the ball in mid-air, tucked it behind his head, and then blasted it through the basket with so much force that it had risen nearly as high again on the rebound. Hardly a shot he could use in any game.

Then, without taking notice of Reed, he'd run toward the showers, one clenched fist raised in triumph above his head. Reed had been too astonished to move. Haymon had wiped the court with him, as though it mattered, and then made an impossible circus dunk shot to prove his mastery at the end of the game. Strictly schoolyard stuff, from the old days.

In his wake, he'd left a thirty year old doctor panting for breath, worrying about whether or not he'd sweated through the shirt he'd intended to wear back to work. An impressive performance all right, for no good reason.

It was then that Blake Marion had emerged from his office.

"Waitin' on me, doc, or tryin' out?" he'd said smugly.

"You know why I'm here, Blake. We have to talk."

"Talk."

"Not here."

"All right," Marion sighed. "Come on in then. Join the fun."

Marion led Reed into a tiny concrete block office illuminated by the harsh glare of a single fluorescent fixture. The monotony of its blank stone walls was broken only by a large four-color poster of Arvin Williams stuffing the ball through the basket on a fast break. It was a far cry from the luxurious surroundings in which they had first talked. In some peculiar way, Reed felt that it accurately mirrored the long road he and Blake had traveled over the course of this endless season. If the Lakers were a first-class operation, Reed didn't want to know what things were like elsewhere around the league.

"It's about Arvin," Reed said.

"Go on," Marion said, rubbing a big hand across his face in a weary gesture. "That's all I been talkin' about all day long. He's the main topic all right. Bad knee and all."

"Bad knee my ass, Blake. We know what's really wrong with him, don't we?"

"His knee," Marion said. "He tore it every way but loose. You wanna see the orthopedic report?"

"The *reason* he tore it is what I'm interested in, Blake. The way he could just topple over like that. . . ."

"Bad luck for us all is what I see. . . ."

"How about his coke habit, Blake? How about the fact that he was so full of the stuff the other night that he could have shot himself and not felt it? There's no telling how long that knee has been hurting him, Blake, only he hasn't felt it . . . he's been too stoned."

"Is that the way the stuff works, doc?" Marion said casually, sifting through some papers on the desk before him. "I didn't know that."

"You don't *care* what he's been putting inside himself?"

"Look, doc," Marion said, really looking at him for the first time

· 279

since they'd begun to talk, "this is the real world. I ain't his daddy. He wants to snort up his paycheck, that's his business, not mine."

"But when I hear rumors that he might get to see action against the Celts if it goes more than four, I have to wonder how far you're really willing to go to win this thing, Blake."

"Well," Blake said, ignoring the question, "he might not. Haymon might get his shit together all at once. Who knows? He looked pretty good against you out there just now." Blake punctuated the remark by cackling loudly.

"You're not listening to me, Blake. I'm asking you if it concerns you that you have a . . . *junkie* . . . on your team?"

"Easy on, doc. That word could get a lot of people in trouble, you included."

"People are in trouble already, Blake. Cocaine is a federally controlled substance. It's illegal. It's harmful. If you knew he was using it, it was your responsibility to refer him to me."

"I deny knowing he was. . . ."

"What are you, Blake?" Reed shouted. "Some politician testifying before a Senate committee?"

"I," Marion grinned, "am a realist."

It was then that Reed had stomped out, slamming the door to Blake's office behind him so that the sound echoed through the empty gymnasium like the sharp, flat report of a carbine. All season long, when it had come time for him to get official permission to prescribe this or that pill, there'd been no one home in the front office. He had been on his own, totally. Now they were circling up the wagons and leaving him out in the cold.

Nearly blind with rage, he'd slammed out to the Fiat, leaped inside, turned the key, waited, and then waited some more. Nothing. The car was dead. The perfect finishing touch. To be stranded at Loyola with no car and an office full of patients waiting for him back on Rodeo Drive. Still seething, he'd charged back into the gym to use the phone only to meet Marion coming out.

"Doc," Marion said, in a soothing tone of voice that gave no indication they had just been shouting at each other, "glad I caught you. We gotta get this thing straight between us. Both of us said things in there we didn't mean."

"Fuck that," Reed said, "I need the phone. My car's conked out."

"You sure?" Blake asked. Reed nodded. The big man began to grin. "When it comes," he said, "it comes in bunches, don't it? We all bein' put through the wringer this week for sure. Lemme go back in and call this guy I know. He'll tow it for you, anywhere you say, for free. He owes me a favor."

Reed let Marion make the phone call. The Lakers owed him

more than money for all that he'd done for them this season. Let them foot the bill for towing his car.

After the call, Marion drove Reed back to Beverly Hills, his large, capable hands encircling the wheel of his large Mercedes sedan like those of a strangler on the neck of a victim. In a soothing voice, he said, "We're all in the ditch together on this one, doc. See, the league's been sniffin' around Arvin for two years now, knowin' what his thing was, tryin' to get real proof. Man was a pitiful mess when he came to me about it, snortin' coke, speed, smack, anythin' he could get his hands on. I been workin' to get him straight is all, tryin' to control that habit of his. Now, if you're angry because I didn't include you in the program, I can relate to that. It's a positive attitude. I guess I just didn't know how far I could go with you right away is all. You gotta see that."

Reed looked over at the big man in surprise. The idea that Blake had known about Arvin's problem and had been working to help him defeat it had never occurred to Reed. He had just naturally assumed that the Lakers were covering for Arvin Williams to keep him playing, the way the owners of a plantation might throw an outstanding field slave a jug of corn whiskey after the harvest was in and then look the other way when he got falling down drunk.

"Thing is, you bein' a doctor and all, you gotta keep records of everyone you treat, right?"

"Of course. But they're confidential."

Marion grinned. "Anythin's that's on paper ain't confidential, doc. Not in this league. The commissioner would love to get his hands on somethin' he could use on us to stop the transfer of the franchise. See," he said, lowering his voice, "there's a lot of people in this league who ain't too anxious to see a man of my color make it to the top. That's the way it's always been for me. Play, but don't coach. Coach, but don't become a general manager. Stay a general manager forever. It's been down and dirty at every turn."

"I didn't know about that," Reed said, honestly surprised.

"No way you could, doc," Marion said. "No way you could. It ain't your thing. It's . . . corporation politics and all tied up with money. Big money. And it can get *mean*. So if you're holdin' some stuff now you think they might be able to use against us at all, I'd say take a good look at it. A good long look. You might even wanna find a safer place to keep those records stashed."

"Like where?"

Blake spread out his big hands before him and smiled. "Give 'em to me, doc. I'll know where to put 'em. I been through this kinda shit before. They investigate us, I'll see to it you come through smellin' like a rose. You think on it, let me know how you feel."

Reed didn't know what to think. Perhaps Blake suspected that he had been keeping a diary all along and was trying to get his hands on it. Perhaps he had just been too hasty in judging the man. Perhaps it was time to reconsider. While Reed turned the problem over in his mind, Marion drove to a rent-a-car agency in Beverly Hills and went inside, leaving Reed alone in the car. When Marion came back out, he was grinning. From his hand hung a set of keys to a rented car.

"On the club," Blake said, tossing the keys to Reed, "seein' as how you lost yours in the line of duty. Least we can do is keep you covered till they fix it. You think about what we discussed, Reed. Ain't no sense in jumpin' to no conclusions till you know how far you might have to fall. Meanwhile, enjoy the car. The Lakers always take good care of their own."

Feeling like one of the high-priced hookers who worked the cocktail lounges of the nearby hotels, Reed took the keys and drove the rented car back to his office. He had a long line of patients waiting for him and no time at all to work out the moral implications of working for a living in a city where money talked and only those without it walked or took the bus, a choice he himself had never seriously considered.

That night, when Callie called him just to talk, he thought nothing of it when she asked whether or not Arvin Williams would be playing for the Lakers again this year. It was a question all Los Angeles wanted answered.

"Not for a while, kid," he told her, "not so far as I can see."

The answer seemed to satisfy her and they went on to speak of other things. On the spot, Reed invented an involved explanation as to why he would not be able to take her to any of the upcoming games. For all her interest in Arvin's health, Callie seemed curiously unaffected by the news. The truth, Reed feared, might have caused her more concern. Lauren already had a lock on his spare ticket. Lauren knew all there was to know about the game of basketball. She *deserved* to go.

CHAPTER TWENTY-NINE

MAX TRAPP sat in sunshine rolling his first cigar of the day around in his hand, wearing only a pair of checkered boxer shorts and a floppy white tennis hat to protect his bald spot in back. Every now and then, the warm early morning breeze obliged him by shaking the bushes around the pool so that the rich, sweet odor of their blossoms drifted to him where he sat.

Across the patio, in the full glare of the sun, Victoria lay spread-eagled on a chaise lounge. Her million-dollar body was coated with a varnish of suntan oil and sweat so that she gleamed all over. A pair of purple-tinted sunglasses was the only concession she had made to putting together an outfit suitable for lounging by the pool.

Max shielded his cigar from the breeze, got it lit, and puffed a ribbon of blue smoke into the bright sunlight. So far he was still a winner. He had hung in there against all comers primarily by staying off the Lakers at home as they'd split the first two games of the final series.

The Lakers had then journeyed to Boston without even taking Arvin along. They had blown two in a row. Max had watched both games on television, grateful that he had once again kept his money away from them. With the Lakers down three–one in games and hanging on the ropes, the series had revolved back to the Forum. Max had gambled that the combination of the home court advantage and Cliff Summers' hyperthyroid shooting would breathe life back into the team. He'd put a bundle down on them in Vegas and held his breath. Somehow they had managed to win *and* cover all at the same time, sending the series back to Boston.

So far, so good. His winning streak was still intact. Anyone looking at Max Trapp's betting record over the course of the season would be forced to admit that the Lakers did seem to be inextricably tied to his purse strings, coming through for him always when he had money on the line. During the regular season, Liddel Gross' information had helped him run up a string of consecutive winning bets. Ever since the playoffs had begun, Liddel Gross had been totally out of the picture. Max had done it all on his own, by being shrewd and figuring the percentages in a way most of the suckers who followed the game on a regular basis could never have understood.

With the sixth game coming up and the newspapers filled with speculation about whether or not Arvin Williams would even be able to suit up for the game, Max realized that the Lakers had to either let the "Big A" play or to forget about the rest of the season. He had gotten down on them in Vegas, figuring that even if they did not win, they would at least do better than the six points the line said they would lose by.

Then, like everyone else in Los Angeles, he'd sat down in front of his TV with a beer to watch the game. When the "Big A" had come limping out on court midway through the first quarter, it was all Max could do to keep himself from pounding the set black and blue. Bad leg, knee brace, yards of tape, and all, Arvin had inspired the Lakers. They had reacted to his mere presence on court like some high school team ready to go out and kill for the memory of a departed teammate. In this case, that teammate was Haymon Jacobs, who, before being sent to the bench, had been on his way to another remarkably unconscious performance. Max had to hand it to the big stiff. He was remarkably consistent. Bad all the time.

Even though Arvin had spent as much time on the bench as on the court, the Lakers had pulled together to eke out a miracle two-point win, sending it all back to the Forum for the final go-round tomorrow night.

Max Trapp was going to get the seven game series he had so desperately wanted in order to rivet the nation's attention on the final contest. Tomorrow night, every working stiff in America would be glued to his television set to watch the Lakers and the Celtics go at it for the very last time. When they found out in a couple of months that there was evidence pointing to the fact that the Lakers had been in the bag all season long, they'd scream bloody murder. The NBA would have to give away green stamps to attract paying customers.

Max also knew that he had to be very careful. If a grand jury ever got hold of his name and enough corroborative evidence to issue a subpoena for him, they'd have no trouble at all putting him away for violating the Federal laws prohibiting gambling across state lines. Then Max Trapp would get to spend his old age in a prison cell, working with the weights and guarding his asshole from the faggots.

If it all came down to judges and juries once again, Max knew he wouldn't stand a chance. Not with his record. He'd be the fall guy all over again, as he had once before. He had to make sure things never got that far.

He had run up a small fortune in Vegas on the Lakers with Liddel's help. Now even Cookie Gross had stopped calling him from Brighton. Nor did Cookie ever answer the phone when Max called him. It was just as well. Max liked the peace and quiet. It was a refreshing change. It would help him plan his final move.

For Max, it had all become an intricate chess game now, one in which he had but a single move left to make. He knew that he had to go for a big score in Vegas on the final game in order to make it seem as though he had always known its outcome. All at the same time, he had to cloud the legal waters around him so that the league would never feel confident enough to single him out as the target of a grand jury investigation. He had but a single bet left to make. With any luck, he could use it to cover himself in every direction.

To lay the groundwork for that bet, Max began calling every bookie he knew in L.A. in order to shop for points. Casually, in the course of conversation, he just let it drop that he was planning to get down in a big way on the final game of the season. Each bookie let him know how much of his action they thought they could handle. All that remained now was for him to decide how he wanted to play with his money, considering that far more than money was on the line.

Across the patio, Victoria got up slowly from the lounge. Her body seemed to unfurl, each finely polished section shining like a soft piece of well-oiled leather. Although it was still only early spring, she was already brown all over, every hard crease and muscled wrinkle tanned so perfectly she looked as though she had been dipped in a vat of cocoa.

Moving as though there was a camera focused on her, she padded slowly to the edge of the pool. Max had enough time to take a good, long look at her before she did a nice little dive into the clear blue water. As she went over the side, the last thing Max saw were the muscles in her ass knotting like a pair of angry fists. He grunted in spite of himself.

Then he turned his attention back to the sports section of the L.A. *Times* and forgot all about her. The prospect of hitting it big on the final game while at the same time finding a way to checkmate the league's chances of ever pinning a thing on him excited him more than anything Victoria could have ever come up with. Even in her wildest dreams.

CHAPTER THIRTY

On the morning of the final game of the championship series, Reed Kreiger hit his office running late with a million things on his mind only to be told that his mechanic had called. The Fiat was a total loss. It would be cheaper to go out and buy spare parts and build a new one from scratch than repair what was left of this one.

"Shit," Reed said out loud, right in front of his startled receptionist, "that's a hell of a way to start the day."

Over the years, he had grown very fond of the little rattler. In L.A. your car was just about your best friend anyway. Life without the old green Fiat would just not be the same. Then a vision of the gleaming Porsche that was still sitting in the showroom window around the corner filled Reed's mind and he relaxed. He would have to buy it now. He had no choice. Lauren would be delighted.

By the time Callie called, he'd already seen a full slate of patients, all of whom had problems more serious than his. The two of them talked for a while about nothing in particular; then she asked him whether it was true that Arvin Williams might play tonight. Lately, the question had become a habit with her.

"What is it, Callie?" he asked plaintively. "You runnin' a little handbook on the side these days? For airlines personnel?"

"Reed," she said, "I'm just asking you a simple question."

"I never realized you were such a fan."

"Tell me, Reed, I want to know. Whatever interests you interests me."

"He's playing, he's playing. All right? He's hurt, but they're gonna take a chance. See, he won't even warm up before the game or anything. When it's time for the center jump, he'll come straight from the dressing room onto the floor. Even the rest of the Lakers don't know about it. The crowd'll go insane. The Celtics'll be six points down before they know what hit them." Reed giggled. "It was my idea," he said proudly. "Thought it up all by myself. The ultimate pre-game psych. A masterpiece, no? Now," he said briskly, "since I've given away the store, tell me why it's so important for you to know."

"Because, dear," Callie said in a low, even voice, "I just happened to watch one of those lousy games from the Forum on TV. You looked so happy in your little seat behind the Laker bench, you and that dark-haired friend of yours, that I decided to become a fan."

"Callie, listen. . . . It's not what you think."

"I don't think, Reed. It's not what I'm good at. You're the big thinker. The famous sports psychiatrist. Reed . . . what you really are is a fucking lowlife. As low as they come, and in this town, that's saying something. You make Charlie Manson look like a Boy Scout. Thanks for all the manufacturer's samples. From now on I'll buy my own pills, you *shit*." She slammed the phone down so hard that the echo rattled through Reed's office.

Although he had been expecting it for the longest time, Reed felt sad that it had come like this, over the phone. In bed, Callie was the best thing that had ever happened to him. No one could ever replace her there, Lauren least of all. She would have looked tremendous in the new Porsche, too, with her long blond hair streaming out in the breeze. Maybe she'd reconsider. Reed believed in second chances for everyone, himself most of all.

He was sitting at his desk eating a soggy tuna fish sandwich for lunch when his receptionist buzzed him to pick up the phone.

"It's Blake Marion, doctor," she said. "He says it's urgent."

"Blake," Reed said through a mouthful of food, "what's goin' on?"

"*Doc!*" Marion shouted down the phone at him. "You got to get over to Arvin's house right now."

"I've got two more people to see. . . ."

"*NOW!* I got a dyin' man here, doc. And I can't call no ambulance. You don't come, I won't be responsible. Bring your bag and get over here, *pronto!*"

Reed grabbed his little black bag and ran to his rented car. It was but a short drive to Arvin's house. To make it even shorter, he ran the red light at Sunset and Doheny.

Save for the sound of small birds crying to one another from the grove of eucalyptus trees surrounding Arvin's massive house, there was no sound at all behind the scrolled ironwork "A" on the huge gates guarding the Williams estate. Reed left his car in the graveled driveway and knocked at the front door. A Filipino houseboy in a white coat opened it and looked him up and down. "Doc-tah?" the boy said. When Reed nodded, the boy stepped aside to let him in, pointing toward the curving marble stairway.

Reed was halfway up the first flight of stairs when Blake Marion came toward him on the run. Grabbing him by the arm, Blake pulled Reed with him into the master bedroom at the head of the stairs.

There, on an elaborately carved redwood bed suspended by silver chains from the ceiling's center beam, under a canopy of flowing golden silk, lay Arvin Williams, stretched out on his back.

"What the hell is this?" Reed asked. "He asleep?"

"You tell me," Marion said. "Listen to him breathe."

Reed bent over the big man. His breath was rising and falling in the classic pattern of Cheyne-Stokes respiration, shallow, more shallow, very shallow, then deep, deep, deeper, only to become shallow once again. Reed rolled back Arvin's right eyelid. The big man's pupils were pinned.

"What'd he take?" Reed asked.

"How should I know?" Marion shouted. "He was out when I got here. Pain pills?"

"You find anything?"

"Nothing," Marion said nervously. "I called you soon as I saw him. Then I put some ice on his balls. Nothing. I tried to walk him . . . but he's too fuckin' big to move. What is it?"

Reed ignored the hysterical general manager, walking away from him in mid-sentence. He went into a bathroom which was larger than a small gymnasium and dominated by a sunken tub grander than some people's swimming pools. After throwing open the medicine cabinet, he carefully checked every shelf. There were a disconcerting number of vials with his own name typed neatly on the outside. These he pocketed without thinking twice about it.

"I saw a lot of sleepers," he said, going back into the bedroom. "Would he take a bottle's worth?"

"How the fuck should I know?" Marion shouted. "For God's sake, doc! Give him something. He's gonna die."

"When his time comes," Reed said. "Not before." After opening his bag, he took out a one-milliliter ampoule of Narcan, a general short-acting narcotic antagonist. He filled a syringe, tapped the plunger to free it of air, then administered the substance intra-venously.

In a matter of seconds, the big man's eyes rolled open. He looked around angrily, sat up, and demanded of Reed, "Who the fuck ast you to the party?"

Marion sank on to the bed. "Thank God," he said gratefully, cradling his head in his hands.

"What'd you take?" Reed asked.

"Take when?"

"*Before* you OD'ed."

"Who say?"

"Answer him, Arvin," Marion said sharply. "You were out cold when I got here."

"Not a thing," the big black man said, standing up and doing a quick knee bend to show how well he was feeling. Arvin's injured left knee buckled from the strain and he fell to all fours, a grimace of pain contorting his oversized features.

"Few pills," he said from the floor, "for the pain."

"And before that?" Reed asked. "Last night?"

"Couple sleepers."

"That could do it," Reed said, suddenly feeling very bored, as though all he had to do with his time was save those who could afford to kill themselves with drugs of their own choosing.

"Might as well take him to the Forum right now, Blake," Reed said. "He feels nauseous or dizzy, have the team physician look at him. He'll be all right . . . so long as it wasn't smack."

Marion bobbed his head, swallowed noisily, and said, "I owe you for this one, Reed. Goddamn if you didn't come through for us in the clutch. When I saw him . . . my first thought was . . . oh, Christ . . . with the big one comin' up, this is the last thing we need. . . ."

"Sure," Reed said, "I could see how you'd be scared. These things often look a lot worse than they really are. The only real danger would be if we were dealing with a long-acting narcotic like heroin or methadone. A guy on smack could be up and around and feeling chipper and then go down like a stone a few hours later."

"No need to worry about that, doc," Marion said. "Too many pills is all." He lowered his voice and turned his head so that Arvin couldn't hear him. "He was probably wired. Couldn't sleep. Too much pressure."

"Sure," Reed said. "We're all feeling it. You said so yourself the other day."

"It's over now," Marion said as Reed shut his bag and began to leave. "Thank God for that. I'm gonna keep an eye on him now myself. Personal escort to the game."

"Fine," Reed said. "See you there."

"Right on, baby." Marion beamed. "We ain't got us but one to go."

After Kreiger had left, Blake Marion took out the half-empty vial of pink and orange pills he'd found lying on the floor next to Arvin's inert body. The prescription slip inside the bottle indicated that the pills had come from some downtown clinic. They were made out in someone else's name, which was the reason he hadn't bothered to show them to Kreiger. Whether Arvin had bought them on the street, been given them by a friend, or just stolen them outright, Blake Marion had no idea.

"Do-lo-phine hy-dro-chlor-ide," Marion said softly to himself, sounding out the name of the chemical the pills contained. "Wonder what the hell that is?

"Hell," he sighed. "Leastways it ain't the hard stuff. Hey, *Arvin!*" he called out through the half-open bathroom door. "You okay?"

Arvin mumbled an answer and came back into the bedroom, his towering bulk completely filling the oversized doorway for a moment. "What the hell is this shit?" Marion demanded. "Or do I want to know?"

Arvin mumbled an answer underneath his breath that Marion had no chance of hearing. "What?" he said. "What?"

"S'legal," Arvin mumbled, talking more to himself than to anyone else. "They gives it out on prescription."

"Great," Marion said. "I guess that means it's cool for you to have some made out for someone else, huh? You unbelievable, man. You know?"

Shaking his head from side to side in angry disbelief, Marion went into the football field sized bathroom Arvin had only just vacated. One by one, he shook the remaining pills from the vial into the toilet bowl, making sure that the shredded prescription slip went with them. Whatever the stuff was, no one would be able to identify it now. Then he flushed the john twice, making sure that once the silent, swirling waters had calmed, none of the pills remained floating on the surface.

Despite the awful damage Arvin had almost done to himself, it pleased Blake Marion mightily to know that he had gotten one final piece of work out of Reed Kreiger. Although Kreiger did not yet know it, he had just performed his last official act for the Los Angeles Lakers. After tonight's game, win or lose, Kreiger was going to receive a neatly typed lawyer's letter informing him that his contract with the team had been terminated for "sensitive legal and medical reasons." Within a month, both of Kreiger's "boys," Haymon Jacobs and Hamid Malik, would also be gone. Maybe, just maybe, Malik would be able to catch on somewhere else. Marion sincerely doubted it. Not with his financial situation. Malik was in hock up to his ears. He'd borrowed against his salary and cashed in all his investments and then borrowed some more just to keep his phony spiritual leader living in style. No team in the league wanted a religious fanatic bringing the ball up on the fast break. Jacobs was another story entirely. So far as Marion could tell, he was just nuts.

That they were both stone lunatics was something Blake Marion had known from the beginning. He'd expected nothing less. Still, they had brought the team this far. After tonight's game was over, everyone would have to acknowledge that he was the genius who had put together the deal that had taken the Lakers all the way to the very last game of the championship series. If the club won, the new owners would have to make him president. If they lost, Marion had his story ready. All year long, Dr. Reed Kreiger had undermined his authority, written unauthorized prescriptions, and just generally created disharmony among a cohesive band of eager, winning ballplayers.

Once he cleaned house by letting Kreiger and his two bad apples, Malik and Jacobs, go, no one at all could blame him for not bringing the title to Los Angeles. At the very least, they'd have to offer him more money to stay on as a general manager. Maybe, just maybe, they'd even still see their way clear to make him club president. No matter what happened in tonight's game, Blake Marion knew that his future was assured. He was in a win-win position.

CHAPTER THIRTY-ONE

WITH LESS than three hours to go before the final game of the year began at the Fabulous Forum, the city of Los Angeles lay baking beneath the hot sun of late afternoon like some great urban pizza browning at the edges. No light, sound, or other distraction penetrated into the small bedroom Hamid Malik had converted into his very own private meditation chamber. Within the confines of its four windowless walls, it was always either dawn or dusk, the hour before the sun rose or just after it had set, a time for deep inner reflection and serious self-contemplation.

Hamid had pleaded with Haymon to come sit with him today, insisting that a final meditation would put them both into a perfect frame of mind for tonight's contest. Out of a feeling of gratitude for all Hamid had done for him in the past few months, Haymon had agreed to come. He now thoroughly regretted his decision.

It was all very nice to be sure, the chanting and the praying and the sitting with eyes closed and legs crossed forever and ever. Only it didn't mean a thing. What happened tonight would have nothing to do with how well anyone played. The outcome had already been determined, by a greater power, one who took no notice of such displays of faith.

In the last hour, Haymon's bad left leg had cramped up so painfully that he could no longer tell where it ended and the carpeting began. His thinking mind, which he had promised Hamid he would shut down, buzzed and blinked and flashed like a pinball machine about to tilt. A thousand movies played on the screen inside his brain. Not one of them had anything to do with basketball. Around the edges of his eyes, Haymon could make out a thousand brightly colored spinning spheres, as though all the suns in all the galaxies of the universe were suffused with a rainbow corona. He felt himself leave the room he was sitting in and drift back in time to that green leatherette booth in Hirsch's luncheonette.

"Praying to some foreign *shmuck?*" Liddel demanded of him in that now familiar hoarse whisper.

"Just sitting," Haymon answered, knowing that even though Hamid Malik was just across the room, he could hear nothing of their strange dialogue.

"Sitting ain't gonna get you where you wanna be, kid. You ain't the Buddha." Haymon laughed along with Liddel, his face remaining impassive. "He was a rich man's kid," Liddel said, "who never shot a hoop in his life. Bet you didn't think I knew that, huh?" Haymon shook his head. Liddel knew more than he had ever suspected.

"Do you think the Man cares if you win or lose tonight?"

Haymon shrugged. "Probably not," he admitted.

"Wrong," Liddel sang out, his voice echoing in Haymon's ears. "God loves a winner, man. Just like everyone else. That's why there's so many fuckin' losers in the world. Helps balance the books. Like the ones my old man keeps. Still, He did take the big black stiff out for you, didn't He?"

Haymon had to admit that was true enough. God had struck down Arvin Williams in full view of the multitudes, paying the "Big A" back for a lifetime of arrogant self-indulgence. Haymon himself had nearly fainted when he'd seen it happen, certain that Arvin had been killed so that he could take his place. When he'd seen for sure that Arvin was still alive, a wave of thanksgiving had coursed through his body, one so powerful that it had taken virtually all his self-control to keep from falling on his knees right on the court to offer tribute.

God had sacrificed Arvin Williams on the altar of Haymon Jacobs' devotion. God was hacking out a path for him. Tonight, that path would lead him to the clearing where the light shined all the time.

"Don't tell me," Liddel said cynically. "You wanna know what's gonna happen next, right?"

Haymon could not deny that he was curious. "That's for me to know," Liddel crowed, "and you to find out. But stay tuned, man. We'll keep you posted."

Liddel's voice faded away, leaving Haymon to contend with a body that had grown stiff and sore from being locked into a single position for so very long. Even now, it was his body that was holding him back, as it had all through his life. This physical form, which had bound him so heavily to the earth for so many years, was the final obstacle, the last barrier he would have to surmount in order to break free. The time to shed that weight had come.

For the spirit was willing. Not for a moment did Haymon Jacobs doubt that it was God's will that he lead the Lakers to victory tonight. Although Liddel had not yet told him so, Haymon was positive that God's message could be proclaimed only from the highest platform. Second best just would not do.

"There is a fire," Hamid Malik solemnly intoned, his voice resonating with the same hypnotic rhythm with which he had been chanting all day long.

"Yes," Haymon said, thinking of the fire that had engulfed him so often in the past few months.

"That must burn strong if we are to emerge unscathed. . . ."

So Hamid also knew about the fire. It was no secret that Haymon Jacobs had been selected for a higher destiny. Hamid too was aware that tonight Haymon Jacobs would go forth.

"Let that fire burn. For only when we have become ash and cinder, like that which lies along a railroad bed, can we become pure."

The train. Hamid was speaking of the cold train. Haymon became excited, his heart throbbing so loudly it sounded to him like the booming of a big bass drum.

"With the fire comes the light, the light of healing. The light of a new dawn. Grant us this light."

A silver spot the size and shape of a dime began to glow warmly in the center of Haymon's forehead. Cutting through bone and tissue, it penetrated to the very center of his brain, spreading its glorious warmth all down the length of his body. All that was past no longer mattered. This light alone would bear him toward the future. Experience fell away from him like a coat of old paint being stripped from a wall. He saw himself as an infant once again, perfect, pure, silvered with innocence. He had been plugged back into the universal source from which he had come. Haymon gave himself over to the feeling and drifted away, losing all notion of time.

When he opened his eyes again, he was alone. It was very dark in the apartment, the sun having disappeared, taking the day with it. John Coltrane's music began to throb from Hamid's stereo. The cold train had come to claim its only rider.

Haymon breathed a deep sigh of relief. He knew that this would be his very last game. No more than a mile away, on the playing floor of the Fabulous Forum in Inglewood, California, that single shining moment was waiting for him to make it happen. Once he had, it would all be over at long last.

MAX TRAPP sat perched on the edge of his chair with phone in hand. He had no idea whether or not Arvin Williams would be playing for the Lakers tonight. His man in Vegas, Jerry Pompano, had just told him that the line out there was even money. So far as the boys in Vegas were concerned, the Celtics were still the money team, certain to take the final game of any series, no matter where it was played.

To Max, even money in Vegas meant that there had to be a lot of L.A. action coming in on the Lakers, fives and tens and twenties bet with local bookies, forcing down what would have been a line favoring the Celtics to "pick 'em."

"How far ahead am I?" he asked Pompano, although he already knew. "Gimme a rough estimate."

"A hundred," Pompano said, meaning one hundred thousand dollars.

"And right now it's even money, huh?"

"You got it."

"I'll call back."

Max hung up and began systematically calling his L.A. bookies. No matter how many he asked, he got the same answer. Los Angeles hadn't forsaken its own. Locally, the Lakers were favored to win by half a point, a spread that did nothing for Max either way. Half a point was half a point. Chickenshit.

Pouring himself drinks that he never tasted, Max paced back and forth across his living room, trying to work out his move. He knew he was going to do something wild. Precisely what he couldn't say. Not yet. He needed more information.

Half an hour later, he called Pompano back. "What is it now?" he asked.

"Shit, Max," Pompano said. "You won't believe this . . . all of a sudden, Lakers by one and a half. We got a rumor out here that Arvin Williams is definitely playing."

Max nearly lost his grip on the phone. The word was out in Vegas. Soon enough it would get back to L.A. Knowing that he was racing other men on other phones all over the city, Max hung up on Pompano without saying goodbye. He began calling his local bookies. They were all holding steady for the Lakers minus half a point. Max got down with each of them for whatever they would take on the Lakers, shouting out his bet and listening to it being repeated before slamming down the phone to call another.

With his heart pounding, he called Pompano back an hour later and said, "What is it now?"

"Still one and a half Lakers, but I can't believe it's gonna hold. . . ."

"Get me down for *everything!*" he shouted. "This price only. I want the Celtics. You understand? Boston, plus one and a half. Call me back when you got it."

Ten minutes later, Pompano called back. In Las Vegas, Max Trapp was down for a hundred thousand on the Celtics, just about what he'd spread around Los Angeles on the Lakers. Max slumped back in his chair and started to smile, the smile taking possession of his face like the rising sun turning the morning sky orange. He had just pulled off the equivalent of a three-hundred-and-sixty degree turn on the nose of a surfboard during a tidal wave. The flutter in the Vegas line had been the key. It had taken him only a fraction of a second to decide to shoot the moon and go for it all.

Betting the Celtics in Vegas while putting down just as much the other way in L.A. was not just a hedge. Tonight a hedge would not do. Tonight, Max Trapp was laying odds that he could pull off the high roller's dream, the kind of score that gamblers bullshitted about all their lives.

Max Trapp was going for a middle. Although on paper it made little sense, something in his gut told him there was no other way to play it. If the Lakers won by a single point, more than they were favored to in L.A. but less than the Vegas line said they would, they would have to pay him everywhere. He would be a winner, all across the board.

It was a very tight margin to go in on. A nut bet all the way, something only he would even think of trying. Should it come out some other way, Max knew he would still be all right. The money he would win in one place would cover what he would lose in the other. So far as money was concerned, he was not worried.

For what his impulse bet on the Celtics in Vegas really meant was complete and total immunity. If and when a grand jury ever came sniffing around him for evidence, Max could send them to Jerry Pompano, who would have to testify that Max Trapp had indeed gone heavily against the team he had been backing all season long in the final game of the year. The bookies in L.A. would tell an entirely different story. No one, certainly not some grand jury made up of amateurs, would be able to make heads or tails of it. The smoke screen he had created by going both ways on this game would protect him.

On paper, this bet made Max Trapp look like the sickest plunger of them all, a balding middle-aged man with nothing better to do with his money than throw it away on a game he had once played for a living.

If it came to courts and lawyers once again, Max Trapp would be only too happy to cooperate fully with a grand jury probe. With

Fishback handling his defense, he would have no trouble making a convincing case that the NBA had always depended on the big business of betting on pro games to stay alive. Why else was it possible to get the morning line in nearly every newspaper in the country? Betting made the game go round, as it always had.

If the league chose to bring it all out in the open, Max knew that he was in a position to fan the flames of rumor and innuendo and keep them burning. This time, when the fire died out, the league's good name would be smeared with ashes, just as his own had been so many years ago.

Tonight, the middle was the perfect bet, one that cut both ways like a double-edged sword too dangerous for anyone but the man who had fashioned it to handle. Who else would have had the balls? Only Max Trapp, who had never played any game for anyone but himself.

If he hit this, he'd be a legend. A fucking myth. No one would ever be able to touch him. Draining what remained of his drink, Max got up and went into the bathroom to shower, delighted to know that he was not yet too old or frightened to fuck with the fates. They had not yet made the straitjacket that could hold him. In less than two hours, the Lakers would be out on the court in the Forum, warming up. His money was down, everywhere. It was out of his hands.

AN HOUR before gametime, the streets surrounding the Forum were clogged by a traffic jam of truly Roman proportions. Cars sat enisled in smoking silence, snout to fender to fuming muffler. A special police unit had to be detailed down the wrong side of Manchester Boulevard to extricate the Celtic team bus and escort it to the arena. Reed watched it speed past him as young kids with blond hair spilling out over the collars of their blue nylon baseball warm-up jackets beckoned with red-capped flashlights, urging him to abandon his stalled vehicle right here, a good half mile from the arena.

What for nearly everyone else trapped by it was just another annoying fact of life in Los Angeles made Reed Kreiger furious. His place was inside the Forum. The Lakers needed him there. After what he had done for them today, he was as important as any player. It was Blake Marion's responsibility to have seen to it that he did not have to take his chances in traffic like everyone else.

Seething with anger, Reed could do nothing but watch as Lauren fiddled with the radio in search of the Laker warm-up show. He was the one who had dreamed up Arvin's dramatic pre-game entrance and he was going to miss seeing it happen if he didn't do something about this lousy traffic.

A series of wild and disconnected pictures flashed across Reed's mind, resolving themselves into a vision of himself driving his newly purchased Porsche down the Pacific Coast Highway. The top was down and Callie was sitting by him, her long blond hair streaming out behind her. People were standing by the side of the road watching them flash by, wondering who he was. There was no reason for him to wait. Traffic jams were a state of mind, a situation brought about by people who could not find any way around them. For him, that time had long since passed.

Without looking to see if his way was clear, Reed Kreiger whipped the steering wheel of his rented car one hundred and eighty degrees to the left. Pressing his foot to the floor, he forced the car over the concrete divider running down the center of the boulevard, bouncing it savagely into the opposite lane.

With his hand pressed firmly down on the horn and Lauren shrieking loudly with delight next to him, he sped toward the arena on the wrong side of the road. Pre-game introductions were already under way. He could hear them over the radio. The crowd was going crazy. It was nothing compared to what would happen when they saw Arvin Williams. And he was the one who had planned it all.

Ignoring the sound of sirens behind him and the flash of red police lights approaching in his rearview mirror, Reed drove faster yet. The game could not begin without him. It wasn't possible.

CHAPTER THIRTY-TWO

THEY HAD come from Palm Springs in twin-engine Beechcrafts and Lear Jets with their blue tint wives in tow, wearing matching leisure suits. Television sponsors, fast food franchise kings, condominium developers, investors in the future of America, they held extensive sections of undeveloped real estate that would soon be re-zoned commercially so that new and larger suburban shopping centers could be built.

Without thinking twice about it, they sat themselves down next to men they would have immediately thrown out of their offices, aging lizards fresh from a long winter spent in Miami Beach, their scaly, peeling heads sunburned nearly orange, two-karat diamond rings flashing from their pinkies.

Nodding to business associates of every race while taking careful note of the corporate ties that had brought them all here, they leered at women who were like calling cards, to be presented and accepted without explanation or further introduction.

Above their heads in the cheaper seats, the hardworking citizens of Encino and Reseda were ensconced, clutching large cups of beer and sacks of peanuts in their hands. Season ticket holders for the most part, they counted themselves lucky just to have been allowed inside the building tonight. For this was no ordinary game. They had only to look down at a playing floor strewn with the tentacles of thick black television cables to know this for a fact. All America was watching.

Down at courtside, within the hallowed circle of light cast by a bank of specially installed quartz lamps, every great personality who had ever graced their television screen was in attendance. Stars of television and movies and movies made for television greeted one another in a manner befitting the occasion, daintily slapping five, one beringed hand brushing lightly across the other in mid-air. Cowboy actors well known for their manly bravado embraced each other like long lost sisters, taking care not to mess up each other's hair.

Those at courtside never once gazed back at the cheap seats above and behind them. They recognized only those whose bodily orifices had also long since been sprayed tightly shut with deodorants containing aluminum hydroxide. Looking younger than their years, shorter than their pictures, older than their companions, with every last strand of hair, natural and man-made, woven into place, they smiled at one another constantly, as though toothpaste itself was the material sacrament of their shared religion.

Directly behind them, unnoticed by all, Blake Marion paced rhythmically along the dark tunnel leading from the dressing rooms to the playing floor. It was he who would give Arvin Williams the sign that it was time for him to hobble out on court to begin the game. Reed Kreiger, who had made it possible for Arvin to get to the Forum tonight, was conspicuously absent, both of his precious seats in the Laker box empty.

The Lakers took the floor one by one, trotting out to the foul line to greet one another stoically and stare into space. A landslide of cheers greeted each familiar name. When the introductions ended, it took no great mathematical ability to count only four starters. Still, Blake Marion waited. Only when the referee gestured angrily to the Laker bench for a fifth man to be sent out did Marion drop his hand and step quickly to one side, allowing Arvin Williams to stampede past him like some angry bull being let loose for its pre-dawn run toward the arena where it would die in the afternoon.

For a moment, the crowd sat paralyzed, stunned into silence, unable to comprehend the great drama they had been privileged to witness. Then, as one, they rose to acknowledge this never-to-be-forgotten moment in the history of sport. "A . . . A . . . A . . . A . . . A," they screamed in unison, all the "A"s running together to form a single swooping ski run of sound that tilted down toward the court on which Arvin Williams stood blinking and shuffling at the foul line.

From every seat, the transistorized hum of tiny radios tuned to the special frequency on which the Laker play-by-play could be heard within the Forum gave forth with the news. Val Edwards, primed by the club to make the most of Arvin's dramatic entrance, flailed at the crowd, exhorting them to hysteria. The opening tap was an anti-climax.

Like some nervous playwright pacing back and forth behind the last row of seats on opening night, Blake Marion continued his compulsive prowl along the tunnel behind the Laker bench. With only twenty seconds gone on the game clock and neither team having scored a point, he was at the far end of the culvert when a great blood roar welled up from the crowd. For a moment, Marion stood frozen to the spot. Then he wheeled and set out on a dead run for the court.

Directly in front of the Laker bench, Arvin Williams lay full length on the hardwood, his barrel chest rising and falling in that same eerie pattern Blake had first seen earlier in the day in the privacy of Arvin's bedroom. Over him, with his warm-up jacket already half off, stood Haymon Jacobs, glaring fiercely into space while waving a clenched fist in the air, as though to signal that he himself had felled the great giant who now lay before him.

"WHERE'S KREIGER?" Blake Marion shouted, grabbing hold of the attending team physician. "You gotta give him a shot, doc," he babbled, "like Kreiger did."

The team physician blithely ignored Blake Marion, signaling instead for a stretcher to be brought out. Not until long after Arvin had been loaded onto it like a slab of beef and wheeled to a waiting ambulance, to be rushed to a nearby hospital with sirens screaming, did the team physician realize the wisdom of Blake Marion's impromptu advice.

The young intern on duty in the emergency ward of the hospital had no trouble recognizing the problem, pointing out to the team physician that Arvin Williams was suffering the classic symptoms of a drug overdose. Treating him for a knee injury would do little to bring him around.

On the floor of the Fabulous Forum, Haymon Jacobs had already taken Arvin's place, setting himself up in a position beneath the far basket. All the lights were pointed at him, glaring in his eyes. Currents of adrenaline-fueled electricity coursed through his heart and brain, causing his legs to pump like steam-driven pistons. His hands fluttered at the end of his arms as though they had a life of their own. He literally could not stand still.

"Let him *hear* it," implored Val Edwards, the Lakers' highly paid radio shill, knowing that his plea would run from seat to seat all around the arena. "How about a big one for Haymon Jay, the almighty Hulk?" he begged, flaying the crowd until they began to come around. The businessmen downstairs began a tentative

"HAY-*MUN*, HAY-*MUN*, HAY-*MUN*" while those more familiar with the game upstairs bellowed, "HAYMON *JAY*, HAYMON *JAY*, HAYMON *JAY*," in counterpoint. A dedicated band under the far basket took it upon themselves to improvise, concocting an impromptu chant of "*HULK!, HULK!, HULK!*," each three word cycle punctuated with a grunt of "*UNNNH!*" so that the call took on an urgent Latin rhythm all its own.

The effect of hearing the acclaim he had been waiting for the crowd to give him all his life was not lost upon Haymon Jacobs. As the Forum rocked around to the sound of his name being chanted, Haymon began to smile, his great lips curling back over his teeth in a fixed grin of the most terrible proportions. The smile remained on his face for the rest of the evening, frozen in place.

In his seat in a box down front, Max Trapp clapped a hand to his forehead in pain. "Will you look at that *shmuck?*" he cried out. "*Smilin'!* What the fuck does he have to smile about? Huh? The way he's been playin'?"

Victoria Marrow, sitting next to Max in her best brocaded top, one that stretched and undulated with her every movement, laughed wildly without understanding at all what Max was talking about.

Down at courtside, someone who looked like Warren Beatty was walking to his seat. As she had never done in high school, Victoria suddenly leaped to her feet and began leading cheers, in hopes that Warren would notice her.

With her hair flying madly around her face and her form-fitting top clinging to her heaving, sun brown breasts the way no lover ever would, she made quite a picture, one that was not lost on the tech director sitting in the network mobile truck parked outside.

"Gimme the babe at courtside and get ready to break," he barked into his headset. The cameraman nearest Victoria zoomed in tight and brought her into focus. Another dream realized. For a full five seconds, the attention of the entire nation was on Victoria Marrow. Then the network went to a commercial for cat chow.

On the floor of the Forum itself, unnoticed by either television directors or the faithful viewing at home, the Lakers called time. The final game of the season was about to resolve itself into something more real than the endless slow motion fantasy of its opening minute, which to those who had lived through it already felt like an eternity.

BY THE TIME Reed Kreiger found his seat in the Laker box, the second quarter was nearly over. The large black highway patrolman who had tried to arrest him for driving on the wrong side of a major artery during a critical traffic jam had been difficult to dissuade. After a good half hour spent arguing about it, the cop had bought Reed's story that he was an integral part of the spectacle going on inside the Forum as well as a licensed physician. Turning on his siren, the cop had escorted Reed to a back entrance. So far as Reed knew, there were still cars piled up on the streets outside, many of those who had paid exorbitant prices for tickets forced to listen to the game on their car radios.

With Arvin already out of the building and Blake Marion nowhere to be seen, Reed was forced to watch from a distance like everyone else. Again and again, he got to his feet to shout advice to his old friend, Haymon Jacobs. Curiously, Haymon seemed unaware of all that was breaking loose around him, impervious to advice of any kind.

As a matter of actual fact, Haymon Jacobs had not heard a thing since the sound of his own name being chanted by the crowd had died away. Inside his head it was dead quiet for the first time in longer than he could remember. No whirling pachanga music, no voices urging him on into battle. Not even the sound of the ball smacking against the hardwood penetrated the great and stony silence by which he was now surrounded.

All in that divine quiet, Haymon discovered that he could truly hear for the very first time. There were no voices because there was no sound. There was no sound because there was no game and never had been, save for the one going on inside his mind. This was what God had wanted him to learn. This was what Liddel and Charlie Oceans and Hamid Malik had tried to teach him. The game itself was a very private, silent affair that each man played within the limits of his own experience. The actual scuffling and scrapping and battling that could be seen on court was no better than an illusion, a sideshow for the fans.

As Haymon Jacobs ran up and down the silent, neon streaked playing floor of the Fabulous Forum in Inglewood, California, he understood for the very first time the true nature of this game to which he had given himself so totally. It was a game of life itself he was playing now, one in which desire was the greatest obstacle. All that he had wanted so very badly he had gotten in the end, mangled and twisted and turned upside down by the time it had been delivered to him. Now, there was nothing more left to want. Not even God.

The abuse and encouragement of fans, the names of plays being shouted out by his teammates, the shrill repeated blast of the referee's whistle stopping play were meaningless to him now. For the moment, Haymon Jacobs had gone beyond all that. At long last he was there, at the top of the highest peak a man could scale, the place where emptiness and action were one. All at the same time, this game he was involved in was both totally real and completely without substance. It was going on all around him and solely within his mind. What he wanted to happen once it was over no longer meant a thing. The game was the game. There was nothing else for him to know.

During halftime, he alone made a point of ignoring the intricate diagrams the Laker coach was feverishly chalking on the locker room blackboard. Strategy meant nothing to him, not now. Baskets would fall when they were meant to fall. Rebounds would come to those supposed to gather them in. It was all part of the pattern.

So too was the way the Lakers began the third quarter, playing without a center, utilizing five smaller men to try to run with the Celtics at both ends of the court. From his familiar perch at the end of the Laker bench, Haymon continued to monitor the game just as he had while on the floor itself, watching as the spigot through which all experience ran first opened and then closed, according to the flow of play.

Midway through the fourth quarter, sensing that it was time for him to take his place out there once again, he watched as the man replacing him picked up his sixth foul. Without even bothering to glance at the coach to see if it was what he wanted, Haymon pulled off his warmup jacket and trotted back out into the smoky silence of the contest.

Max Trapp watched him go, unable to believe the way the game had gone. No matter what the Celtics did, they could not put the Lakers away. Cliff Summers had hit shot after shot from impossible distances to keep the two teams within four points of each other all night long.

The floor beneath Max's feet was littered with crushed peanut shells and discarded programs. He had long since taken off his jacket, removed his tie, and sweated through his best shirt. Next to him, Victoria sat in silence, looking pale beneath her burnished copper suntan. Ever since her spontaneous outburst early in the game, she had been subdued, as though aware that there was a larger drama going on before her tonight than the outcome of a mere game.

"Hey," Max said to the guy sitting next to him, "turn it up, huh?" The guy nodded and increased the volume on his radio, as though they were all struggling together to put the Lakers over the top. Max let Val Edwards take over for him. It was easier than trying to make sense of what he was seeing.

"Baby, oh, baby," Val Edwards crooned, mouthing the phrase that had made him famous, "they don't make 'em any better than this even in Hollywood, wherever that is. As the faithful here in the Fabulous Forum remain glued to their seats for the final minutes of a game that's had everything.

"To try and recap. With Arvin Williams out of it, the Lakers have stumbled through. While I can't say it's been an orthodox performance, they're hanging in there somehow. Any comment, Buddy?"

Buddy Jones, the color announcer, picked up the narrative. "Right you are, Val," he said crisply. "Mainly by going with Haymon Jacobs in spots and relying on Mr. Heart, Cliff Summers, the Lakers have managed to keep it close all game long without ever once taking the lead. Time's in. Go ahead, Val."

"Okay, Buddy. Here's how it looks. With a little more than a minute to go, the Lakers are down by five. They've got the ball but what they need is a miracle. Look for Cliffie Summers to take the shot. He has all game long. No need to tell you that one of his patented long distance bombs could mean a mountain right here.

"Hamid inbounds to Cliffie at midcourt. Dribbles to the left side with the right hand. Celtics swarming on defense. Over the time line. Glides to the head of the key. No help there. Swings it over to Hamid. Hamid back to Cliffie. Time ticking on the twenty-four second clock. I've seen him let fly from farther out tonight, I wonder what he's waiting for. Pump fakes . . . lays it on the floor instead. Jukes left, goes right, he's headed for the hoop. Double clutch down the lane, hanging in the air, he's playing please-come-foul-me. . . . Collision underneath, Cliffie goes down, the ball goes up, it rolls, IT'S *GOOD!* AND HE'LL SHOOT ONE AFTERWARDS."

The noise level grew so loud in the Forum Max had to lean closer to the radio to pick up what the announcer was saying. Victoria leaned with him, allowing Max's neighbor a good long look down at her cleavage.

". . . Cliff Summers was lying on his tailbone, staring up at the rafters when that baby rolled in, fans. He must have seen something he liked up there, too, because he's on the line now waiting for the ball, having cut the Celtic lead to three. Cliffie bouncing the ball at the line thirteen times as his habit . . . it's up . . . IT'S *GOOD!* Lakers trail by two.

"Celtics have to inbound now under their own basket with Laker pressure all over the court. Haymon Jay playing the man with the ball, arms outstretched, denying him vision . . . a limited amount of time left in which to inbound . . . AND THE CELTS CALL TIME! Incredible! How would you describe what Haymon was doing out there, Buddy?"

"Just looming, Val. Towering over the end line with those great long arms of his over his head . . . I bet he looked like an office building to that Celtic guard. . . ."

"Hold on, Buddy. Boston Coach Manny Abels is *hot!* I mean, he's all over both refs complaining that Haymon didn't give the Celts the required three feet. They're jawing about that one pretty good down there and if you ask me, Abels has a pretty good case.

"Okay. Nobody asked me. Argument over, the Celts take the ball out once again. Again, Haymon Jay all over the end line. All *over!* They try to inbound over, around, under . . . they can't . . . they run a man into Haymon to try and pick him off . . . he goes down . . . AND AGAIN THE CELTS CALL TIME! Katie, bar the door. Hold on, I don't think they had one left to call. Buddy, did they? I heard a whistle. *I heard a whistle!* Yes, yes! . . . They've called a loose ball foul on the Celts for knocking Haymon halfway to Azusa. And they're already over the limit, which means he'll shoot two. . . .

"Mama mia, are the Celtics hot! Here comes Coach Manny Abels. Here come both assistants. The trainer'll be next . . . jawbone city . . . eye to eye . . . AND THEY *BOUNCE* HIM! It's been coming all game long. . . . Coach Manny Abels has been begging for it and now he's got it. He'll have to watch what's left of the contest like the rest of us. Massive confusion down there . . . but the expulsion means an automatic tech . . . so run this down for us, Buddy."

"Well, Val, as far as I can tell, it'll be a *double* tech. One on the Celts . . . wait . . . yes, one on the Celts for calling a time-out when they didn't have one left to call and one on Abels for telling the ref where he could put his whistle. . . ."

"So it's a double tech. And then?"

"Then they'll shoot the loose ball foul. . . ."

"Meaning. . . ."

"With the Celts over the limit and just thirty seconds left on the game clock, the Lakers will actually have four to make three. I know that sounds a little strange, but Cliff Summers, Mr. Heart, will shoot the techs. Then Haymon Jay will have two to make one on the loose ball foul. And then, incredibly, the Lakers will get to take the ball out afterward."

"Buddy, Buddy, *Buddy* . . . is this *something?* In all my years behind a microphone, I've never seen one come down to the wire like this. And the big guy who brought them this far, the 'Big A,' not even around to see it. This one's for you, big guy, no matter where you are.

"Okay. Back to action. The Forum hushed, silent. You can hear a pin drop. Cliff Summers trots out all alone to take the ball. No one else around and believe you me, he looks very small from up here, a single and solitary figure on the line. What drama. What pressure. All the work, the blood, the sweat, the tears coming down to this, the most amazing three ring circus of an ending any of us up here in the booth can remember.

"Cliffie takes the ball. Stooped over at the line. I may have to whisper. That's how quiet it is in here now. One two three four five six seven eight nine ten eleven twelve thirteen, Cliffie bounces the ball at the line thirteen times as his habit, fires, and IT'S *GOOD!* Lakers trail by one. The Golden Boy comes through again.

"Ball back to Cliffie. Can you imagine how he feels? Tremendous pressure. Incredible pressure. The ball on the floor, one two three four five six seven eight nine ten eleven twelve thirteen fourteen, Cliffie leans, fires, it's on the rim, it's rolling, oh, my God, he bounced it fourteen times and I think he knows it . . . AND IT FALLS *OUT!* Cliffie shaking his head in disgust."

Down on the floor of the neon pit that the Forum had become, Haymon Jacobs stood waiting for his chance at the line. Time had stopped entirely for him, only to begin again by flowing backward with an impossible retrograde motion. The opening minute of the contest was repeating itself with eerie slow motion precision, in reverse.

Now, it was all going away from him, flowing out of his grasp so rapidly that he could barely call to mind all that had only so recently been revealed to him. For the awful truth was that he still wanted it, to win and be famous, a figure loved and respected by all. He wanted it more than he had ever wanted anything in his life. And the wanting stood between him and his goal.

The adrenaline-powered insights that had coursed through his brain at the start of the game had taken their toll, extracting a greater price than he had been able to pay. Now, his arms hung heavy by his side, two sleeves of wet and useless sand. His legs were rubbery and boneless. His vision was blurred, a revolving sea of faces and clicking clocks swimming madly around him. The game had exploded on him, becoming a fevered, sweat-soaked dream too fragmented for his tired mind to control or contain.

For he was not yet ready. He could not yet hold on to the truth that he had experienced and remain above all things, watching. In him, there was still desire and need and anger. His entire life had once again been reduced to a single physical reality. Ball and hoop. Hoop and ball, and the need to make one find the other. This was the end of all action.

As Haymon Jacobs stepped to the foul line in an arena so quiet that the frantic, buzzing sound of Val Edwards' gnat-like voice jumped from seat to seat like some nerve impulse being transmitted across eighteen thousand separate synapses, he could think only one thought over and over, in time to the staccato rhythm of his pounding heart.

This is the end of all action. This is the end. Of all action. This is. This. The end. Of all action.

In his seat not far from the midcourt stripe, Max leaned toward the radio his neighbor was cradling in his arms. What for everyone else in the Forum was only an unforgettable game had become for him a life or death proposition. And all of it depended on what Haymon Jacobs would do in the few next seconds. The hypnotic drone of the radio announcer's shrill voice kept Max from losing complete control of himself. So long as he concentrated on the voice, he would be all right.

"Haymon Jacobs up there now," Edwards crooned, caressing each and every syllable. "Two to make one, so remember that if he misses the first, he'll have another. Lakers down by a single point. One will tie it. At this juncture, I think the Lakers would be happy to go to overtime, *if* they could get there.

"Haymon steps up to the line. For the first time all night, he looks grim, determined. Reaches for the ball, sights, fires, and IT'S AROUND AND *OUT!* The Forum groaning on every miss now. These aren't free throws down there now, fans. Not now. Nothing's free on that floor right now. It's for all the marbles.

"Haymon Jay standing at the line, stock-still, the big grin that was plastered all over his kisser all night gone. Maybe he knows something we don't. Accepts the ball, sights, rears back, fires, and . . . IT'S AN *AIR BALL!* A COMPLETE MISS. DID NOT DRAW IRON. Hard to believe I know . . . but suddenly Laker luck seems to be running cold. Bad. Cold and bad.

"Lakers will inbound. The Celts have no time-outs remaining, neither do the Lakers. They'll go till it's over. Nothing for the Celts to do but play tough defense and try not to foul. No secret Cliffie will be looking to shoot. A Western Union special could put the Lakers on top for the first time all evening.

"Celtics leeching on defense. Pressure all over the floor. Cliffie runs his man into Haymon Jay, accepts the inbounds pass from Hamid, and controls at the head of the key. Haymon sets up underneath the hoop. Cliffie to Malik. Malik to Cliffie, Cliffie dribbling to run down the clock. Looks underneath, no help there. Cliffie see-saws, trying to work closer to the hoop . . . he better be careful . . . they'll double team him if he doesn't hurry. Twelve seconds left on the game clock, six on the timer. He can't wait much longer.

"They're bumping bodies under the hoop. Haymon Jay takes a savage elbow, a right cross to the mid-section, no whistle, he's on the floor. No one moving, no help anywhere . . . Cliffie will have to go it alone. . . .

"Tries to shake his man with a stutter step to the basket. Rocks back and forth, spins, decides to let fly from where he is, off-balance, a long-distance prayer from thirty-five . . . the ball is in the air, off the front rim, bouncing high up over the rim . . . tapped up, no good . . . tapped up, no good . . . tapped up . . . rolling free on the glass . . . AND SUDDENLY FROM OUT OF NOWHERE HAYMON JACOBS COMES OFF THE FLOOR, TAKES THE APPLE WITH BOTH HANDS OVER HIS HEAD AND RAMS IT THROUGH THE HOOP SO HARD THE GLASS TREMBLES, THE RAFTERS SHAKE, AND THE BALL BOUNDS UP AGAIN AS THOUGH IT HAD BEEN FIRED BY A CANNON. CELTS TRY TO INBOUND WITH SIX SECONDS LEFT. HAYMON JAY DOESN'T EVEN *BOTHER* TO FALL BACK ON DEFENSE, HIS MAN'S WIDE OPEN AT THE OTHER END OF THE FLOOR, THEY DON'T SEE HIM, THEY CAN'T SEE HIM, THE BUZZER GOES, THE RED LIGHTS GO, IT'S *OVER*, IT'S *OVER*, IT'S *OVER!* YOUR LOS ANGELES LAKERS CHAMPIONS OF THE WORLD AT LONG LAST, HAYMON JACOBS AND HAMID MALIK WHIRLING IN CIRCLES WITH THEIR EYES CLOSED AND THEIR HANDS OVER THEIR HEADS DOING THE DAMNEDEST APACHE WAR DANCE I'VE EVER SEEN, FANS ALL OVER EVERYTHING, BUDDY . . . TAKE IT, BUDDY . . . I'M JUST ABOUT RUN OUTTA GAS."

"Easy, Val. Take yourself a sip of somethin' cool and expensive. I reckon you can afford it. We all can. That last-second stufferoo just made world champions of us all. Haymon Jay's only basket of the game, and I guess you'd have to say it was the shot heard 'round the world. As old Haymon breaks free from his good friend Hamid Malik and starts to whirl in circles with his eyes closed, all alone in the middle of court, whirling on . . . and on . . . and on. . . ."

CHAPTER THIRTY-THREE

THAT AN impossible last second stuff shot by a stiff like Haymon Jacobs had actually made world champions of the Lakers while putting him over the top in both Los Angeles and Las Vegas was a miracle Max Trapp attributed to more than divine guidance. Simply, his ship had finally come in, bringing with it a cargo of hard green cash that would enable him to live like an emperor for the rest of his life. He was finally the big winner he had always known he was destined to be. They would not be able to talk about gambling in America without mentioning his name.

Having collected a small fortune on the one and only basket Haymon Jacobs had managed to score all night long, Max had celebrated in the proper manner, toasting his good fortune in bars and restaurants all over the city, getting crazy drunk. When the sound of his own dog barking by the side of the house woke him the next day, all he could remember was Victoria propositioning two teenage hookers with a joint in some coffee shop at four A.M.

Despite her efforts, he and Victoria had gone home alone. He had let her do impossible things to him in bed while dreaming about a month in the south of France, trying his luck at baccarat and chemin de fer in the casino at Monte Carlo.

Now he had the kind of buzzing in his brain he associated with an attack by killer bees. The sharp, piercing sound of the dog's menacing growl did nothing to ease the pain. The dog had been trained to bark until he silenced it. He had no choice but to get up.

Forcing himself out from beneath the covers, Max noticed that two of his best ties were looped around the bedposts. A third hung from Victoria's right wrist. He remembered nothing about her having used ties. What a night. After stumbling across the living room, he managed to slide open the plate glass door leading to the pool without waking Victoria.

The brilliant morning sunshine was a further affront to his senses. As best he could, Max shielded his eyes from the light and felt his way across the patio. By the time he reached the dog, he was feeling authentically sick, his gut heaving, a blinding ribbon of pain running around his forehead. Not until after he had quieted the dog with a sharp slap to its muzzle did Max realize why the animal had been going insane.

Halfway up the slope by the side of the house, silhouetted in the streaming morning sunshine, stood a man in a sharkskin suit. Max's first thought was that he was being accosted by some door-to-door Bible salesman.

"Max Trapp?" the man said.

"I know you?" Max asked, squinting up into the impossible sunlight with one hand over his eyes.

"I bring you regards. A good friend says hello."

The first shot caught Max in the chest. The second buried itself deep in his thigh. The third, fourth, and fifth caused him no pain at all. The sixth killed the dog. Max toppled over backward, his legs giving way beneath him as he plowed through the heavy wooden gate leading to the pool.

Landing on his back on red tiles already hot with sun, Max managed to turn slowly on his side and struggle to all fours. A bubble of blood appeared in one corner of his mouth, matching the spreading crimson stain soaking the front of his white silk robe. Somewhere off in the distance, he heard Victoria scream. Then he pitched face forward to the ground.

By the time the LAPD arrived, having been called by a helpful neighbor down the hill who reported hearing shots, the big white house with the picture postcard view of the HOLLYWOOD sign was empty, several stubbed-out joints with lipstick on them in an ashtray in the bedroom the only sign that anyone else had been there recently.

A dead dog, a well-polished Bentley, and the balding corpse of a man soon identified as Max Trapp, former collegiate basketball star, fixer, and producer of pornographic films, completed the tableau. The body lay on hot tiles throughout the morning as police lab technicians took measurements and drew diagrams around a corpse splayed out with one skeletal hand reaching toward the large and well filtered pool its owner would never use again.

The next morning, the L.A. *Times* devoted half a column on an inside page to what it termed an "apparent gangland slaying." Not until six weeks later did the *Times* give the story more prominent play as part of its continuing investigation into the point-shaving scandal that was threatening to destroy professional basketball in America unless some new method of regulating sports gambling could be found. The murder itself was never solved.

EPILOGUE · **A Saturday in March, 1974 · The First Day of Spring**

TAKING CARE not to butt his head on the low and overhanging section of pipe now rusted nearly orange with age, Haymon Jacobs walked slowly through the side entrance into the schoolyard. Although it was early afternoon, the yard was completely empty. He had anticipated this and gone to the trouble of bringing along his own ball. Soon enough, the junior high school kids, many of them black, would appear, telling wild stories about everything that had happened to them the night before.

Not yet fourteen, these kids already knew all there was to know about smoking pot, taking pills, and going to bed with hard mouthed girls they would soon make pregnant and have to marry. The new children of the streets in Brighton were vastly different from the ones he had grown up with. Nothing fazed them. If they had a religion, it was rock music and not basketball. To them all, basketball was just a game, one they were already too old to take very seriously.

Often they talked of getting out, joining the Navy or just moving away. Eagerly, they quizzed him about Los Angeles, never listening or believing when he told them that it was not the promised land they knew it to be. They had seen the pictures and read the magazines. L.A. was heaven, where the sun shined all the time. He did not bother to argue with them. It would have done no good. California was a place he would never see again.

He had come back here more out of desperation than anything else, not really knowing where else to go after being discharged from the clinic. Twice a week now, he rode what had once been the BMT Brighton line into the city to see his psychiatrist. Together, they were making progress. The process was a slow one. He still had a long way to go.

Coming back here to live had been easier than he'd expected it to be. Simply, he no longer knew a soul in the neighborhood. Liddel, Tina, Charlie Oceans, his very own mother and father—they were all gone. Only Liddel was dead, though he found that hard to believe even after having seen the grave. The rest had just abandoned the place as soon as they'd had the chance, running to make new lives for themselves somewhere else. Every now and then, when he went into Hirsch's for the paper, Haymon would see a postcard from Cookie Gross stuck up by the register. Cookie now lived in Florida, where it was warmer.

He was the last one left really. The neighborhood had been handed over to him to protect. As the single curator of this curious museum, he had no display cases filled with arrowheads or shards of pre-Columbian pottery to worry over. Graffiti-covered handball courts and worn green metal backboards were his concern.

Lately, he had been thinking more and more about taking the Parks Department exam. It was good, clean work that would keep him outside in summer and indoors in winter, with plenty of quiet time to himself. He knew he would never have any trouble with the kids. They all still knew who he had once been. Haymon Jay. The almighty Hulk.

From a spot on the cracked concrete where the end lines ran together, Haymon Jacobs threw up a tentative question mark of a jump shot. It hit the rim and went through, rattling the backboard as it fell. His eye was as sharp as ever. He could still shoot with the best of them. Following the ball as it bounced toward the steps where those who had come just to watch had once sat, he managed to save it before it went over the end line. For a big man, he was still quick.

The sun was very warm for a Saturday in March. Haymon could feel it beating down on the back of his neck, warming the tightly corded muscles in his shoulders. That smell was in the air, the sting of salt from the sea mixing with the warm odor of dog shit that had lain cold and frozen on the sidewalks for months. Unseen, the ghost of Abe Reles, Kid Twist, *momzer*, martyr, patron saint of the neighborhood, whistled overhead.

Haymon Jacobs took the ball in his right hand and crossed it over to his left as he dribbled toward the corner. His stiff left leg dragged slightly behind him as he moved. Pretending he had a man on top of him, he faked with his head and shoulders, faked again, and then went up for the shot.

Not yet thirty, with the best moments of his life on a basketball court conclusively behind him, all he wanted now was for this shot to go in. Out of habit, he began counting down the seconds left on an imaginary game clock, timing the count so that the last second would run out just as the ball reached the rim.

At the very top of his leap, Haymon cocked the ball behind his head and snapped his wrists. For a moment, the ball seemed to hang suspended in the air. Then, transcribing a series of backward, pebbled circles in the warm spring sunshine, it began its long and torturous journey to the hoop.

ACKNOWLEDGMENTS

This novel was written in dry California from summer to summer to summer during a period when there was no winter. For taking the time, I would like to thank the professor of library sciences at NYU who opened the old *Herald Tribune* morgue to me, the Kings County Assistant District Attorney in charge of rackets, and the man who for good reason prefers to be known only as the Chicago Fire.

On a more personal level, my undying love and continuing appreciation go out to Ms. Erica Spellman, Mr. Jerry Pompili, Dr. Mel Wichter, and the three wise men disguised as gray deer who watched over me each day as I ran. Finally, I would like to thank Donna, who began as a calm voice in the morning and has since become a clear light all day long.